The Forgotten Daughter

Elsie Mason is the pen name of Paul Magrs.

Paul was born in Jarrow in 1969, and brought up in the North East of England. Since 1995 he has published fiction in many different genres – literary Magical Realism, Gothic Mystery, Science Fiction, Crime and Young Adult. He lectured in Creative Writing for many years at both the University of East Anglia and at Manchester Metropolitan University.

In 2019 he published his book on writing, 'The Novel Inside You'. In 2020 Snow Books republished his Brenda and Effie Mystery series of novels. In 2021 HarperCollins published his book of cartoons, 'The Panda, the Cat and the Dreadful Teddy.' In 2022 he won the Crime Writers' Association prize for best short story of the year.

Whichever genre he has worked in, he has always written about working class women from the north. In many ways Historical and Romantic Saga fiction was the first genre he was aware of, as a child, when he eavesdropped on his female relatives telling tales around the kitchen table in South Shields.

Taking on a female pen name has been wonderfully liberating: he has loved writing as Elsie.

He writes and lives in Manchester with Jeremy and Bernard Socks.

Elsie Mason

The Forgotten Daughter

First published in Great Britain in 2024 by Orion Fiction,
an imprint of The Orion Publishing Group Ltd.,
Carmelite House, 50 Victoria Embankment
London EC4Y 0DZ

An Hachette UK company

1 3 5 7 9 10 8 6 4 2

A CIP catalogue record for this book
is available from the British Library.

ISBN (Mass Market Paperback) 978 1 3987 0 8990
ISBN (eBook) 978 1 3987 0 8983

Typeset by Born Group
Printed and bound in Great Britain by Clays Ltd, Elcograf S.p.A.

www.orionbooks.co.uk

For Olly

Chapter One

Cathy Sturrock was still a beautiful woman. With her flaming red hair and her cat-like green eyes, she was every bit as striking as she'd been thirteen years ago, when she first arrived in the Sixteen Streets.

Back then she had been a penniless kid, turning up almost randomly in that warren of backstreet houses by the docks. She had been running away, with hardly a thought of where she would end up. Some bloke driving a wagon-load of goods up and down the highway between Northumberland and Tyneside had given her a lift and she had ended up here in South Shields.

How had she gone from being a girl with nothing at all to her name to what she was now? Round here they called her the Queen of the Sixteen Streets. Everyone knew Cathy. Everyone could recognise her a mile off. Hers was the beating heart of this community. She was the fiercest, loudest, most compassionate soul in the place and everyone knew it. She had time to help anyone. She had a kind word for all and sundry. She could remember all too well what it felt like when she was nowt and she never forgot it.

The bar at the Robin Hood pub at the top of Frederick Street was where you would find her most nights. Some time ago, the plaque above the front door had been made over into her name and now she was landlady and sole proprietor. How proud she was of that fact! She stood at the bar, all dolled up each and every night and it was like the stage she paraded around on for the sake of her adoring audience. The Robin Hood was all hers and she still found it hard to believe.

To think she had begun here as a bottle washer when she had hardly known which end of a pint was up and which end was down. It wasn't quite fair to say that she had worked her way up the ranks. She had taken the decidedly more unstable – and some would say unsavoury – route of marrying the previous landlord, Noel Sturrock. Now, he was a famous face in these parts, too. He was a horrid, sour-faced old hunchback under whose care this had been a dismal and dangerous establishment. He'd led Cathy a merry dance in their years together but age and illness had seen him withdraw from the heaviest work. He'd become milder and less irascible and difficult. He was content for his wife to run the pub in his stead these days.

Just as well, because the Robin Hood was her whole world. She could hardly remember a time before coming here.

Her early life had been spent in the wilds of Northumbria, somewhere further up the coast, near the old gentle town of Morwick.

A part of Cathy's heart was still lodged in that place, and even in her happiest moments there was a tug of sadness in her chest. She could never forget what she had left behind in that home on the wild coast.

Even while she sat at the bar of the Robin Hood, looking splendid and unvanquishable in one of her signature low-cut velvet gowns, there was always a secret sadness to Cathy Sturrock.

Only her very closest friends had any inkling about that. Friends like Sofia Franchino, who had been Cathy's chief barmaid and best pal for quite a number of years by 1932, when this story opens.

In the spring of that year, Cathy's past was starting to open up again. Things were about to change. At first she assumed it would all be for the better, but it almost turned out to be her undoing. Holding court at the bar of the Robin Hood, Cathy looked like she was the crowned and anointed Queen of the Sixteen Streets and she was going to rule quite happily forever. However, 1932 was the year that things got so bad she almost left South Shields and never came back.

Sofia Franchino was there with her every step of the way. The Italian woman – slightly younger than Cathy's thirty years – had her own problems and dramas that year. The best thing about it all was that the two women had each other to confide in and rely upon. Without that help, they would surely have both been lost.

It was on a Tuesday evening that everything began to change. As far as Cathy remembered, there was no particular reason for the choice of date or day. It was all down to June and what she had decided. She was coming down from Morwick on the train and, though Cathy never travelled very often or very far by train, she understood that timetables and such worked in a particular way and that travellers were at the mercy of their peculiar timings.

June was due in South Shields sometime after seven on Tuesday evening and so Cathy spent days on end in preparation for the arrival. Barmaids Sofia and Minnie were drafted in to work extra hours. The whole place needed sweeping and mopping and dusting and polishing up. All the wooden surfaces had to gleam, as did the horse brasses on the wall, the floorboards, the glasses and the beer pumps themselves. The crown glass windows had to shine, letting multi-coloured daylight beam into the saloon in a way it hadn't for simply years.

Sofia was glad of the extra hours and the few extra bob in her pay packet, but she was confused about the cause of it all.

The two women shared a half of stout at midday, sitting at what had become known as the Women's Table by the open fire. It was a mild spring and chilly out, but the two were warmed through by their morning's busy work. They both had their hair tied up, best pinnies on and they were lathered in dust. 'This place has never been so clean,' Sofia laughed as the rich dark beer slaked her thirst. 'Now, tell me what it's all in aid of, Cathy. You promised me.'

Cathy studied her friend. Cathy was vivacious but Sofia was properly beautiful. She had the dark hair and olive complexion of someone who had grown up right next to the Mediterranean. She had been brought up in Naples, and even after all these years in South Shields her accent hadn't quite been blotted out.

She was looking so earnestly inquisitive that Cathy had to laugh. And she had to tell her the truth. She rummaged about in the pocket of her pinny for a letter, which she unfolded with great ceremony. The paper was dated only one week ago, but it was worn and faded as if it had been opened and refolded and studied like a treasure map and kissed over a thousand times.

'June is coming,' Cathy said.

Sofia rolled her eyes. 'So is Christmas!' she said. 'But who exactly is June? You haven't explained anything to me yet . . .'

The landlady of the Robin Hood bit her lip. Now was the moment. This was when she told her truth. The very thing she had been bottling up so tightly for all these years. Not even her very best, most trusted confidante had an inkling about this secret.

'Oh . . .' Cathy said, and her eyes roved over that worn piece of paper yet again as she flattened it down on the table. She was careful not to dampen it with beer spills. 'Look at her lovely handwriting! Copperplate, don't they call that? I don't know anyone who can write as nicely as this.'

Sofia was losing her patience. 'But who is she? And what does she say?'

Cathy's worried thoughts were already straying. 'Will we have enough food, do you think? I've invited simply everyone. All the regulars. Everyone from Frederick Street. You know what folk are like if there's a free feed on the cards. The place will be swamped. But I don't mind, of course. I want to give June a proper welcome to the Sixteen Streets . . .'

Now Sofia was gritting her teeth and trying to read the precious letter upside down. 'Just tell me who she is! Stop being so secretive.' She had never seen her friend being as nervy and fretful as this. It really wasn't like Cathy at all.

Cathy scanned the letter once more. 'Listen how she writes! "This reunion is one that I anticipate with great joy." How fancy is that? And her only sixteen! She must be so clever. Why, she'll put me to shame!' Then Cathy started glancing around the bar again, looking for any corner that might still need tidying or cleaning or polishing up. She wanted June to see it all and be impressed. She didn't want her to see this place as just a dingy, dirty, backstreet boozer. She wanted her to see it as the palace that it truly was.

'Cathy,' Sofia glared at her. 'You must tell me.'

The landlady nodded. This was the moment for the long-held truth to come out. At last. 'She's my daughter,' Cathy said. 'Junie is the daughter who I had to leave behind.'

Chapter Two

'I've known you for ages and ages, Cathy Carmichael,' Sofia said accusingly. She even used her friend's maiden name, to underline just how many years had gone by. 'How come you've never mentioned this business of having a daughter of your own?'

All at once Cathy looked shamed and uncomfortable. 'I know, I'm sorry. I could never say anything. My heart was broken. I had to pretend that June didn't even exist, just to get by.'

'All these years, though . . .' Sofia said. 'How could you stand it? How could you bear being parted from your own child?' She could hardly imagine what it was like. Sofia was devoted to her own daughter. She complained about her, loudly and insistently. She told her every day that she was the bane of her life. Bella was turning into a properly opinionated madam now that she was almost full-grown. But Sofia couldn't conceive of a version of her life without her.

'There was no choice,' Cathy said, and tipped the dregs of her drink into her mouth, lingering over the sudsy beer foam, as if buying herself more time. She didn't quite know just how much to tell her friend.

'I want to hear the whole story,' Sofia told her. 'Leave nothing out.'

'There's no time today,' Cathy said. 'We've got the sandwiches to make and the spread to lay out.'

Sofia reached over the table to touch her friend's hands. To her astonishment she realised that they were trembling. Cathy, trembling, as she sat in her own pub! Why, nothing ever made her nervous and afraid. After all the things she had overcome! The crooks and the ne'er-do-wells she had seen off the premises. The bar room brawls she had broken up. The very real problems that her drunken hobgoblin husband had provided for her. Over the years Sofia had seen Cathy take many of these things in her stride.

Now though she was trembling. And all because of this mysterious daughter. 'How old is she again?'

'S-sixteen now,' Cathy said softly, looking surprised as she said the word out loud. 'She's grown up. She's a woman now.'

'Like my own Bella,' Sofia smiled. And she thought: imagine if I'd not had Bella with me through all these difficult years! The girl was a handful. Sometimes Sofia felt she was mouthy and she answered back to everything her mother ever said. But Sofia couldn't imagine what it would be like to be deprived of her.

'My Junie's old enough to make her own decisions now, you see,' said Cathy. 'And to travel by herself. It seems that she has decided to find her true mother at last. She wrote out of the blue that she was coming to see me.'

'Out of the blue,' Sofia said. 'That must have been a shock.'

'It was.' Cathy smiled broadly. Her whole face lit up and it was as if she was banishing all her doubts and fears. For Sofia it was just like watching the sun coming out and burning through wisps of rainclouds. 'So that's why we're doing a little party to welcome her. That's all there really is to it.'

'I see . . .' Sofia smiled. She watched as her friend got to her feet and gathered up their empty glasses.

'Shall we get back to work? All that bread won't butter itself.'

Sofia toiled happily through the afternoon on the buffet, making up ham and pease pudding sandwiches and slicing up the sausage rolls. She couldn't help but wonder if Cathy wasn't going overboard though. Was this really the best way to welcome her daughter? By inviting the whole local community into the pub to observe every tender moment? Wasn't this the kind of private event that was best carried out away from the public eye?

When Sofia thought about it all, she realised that maybe Cathy felt safer somehow holding this reunion in full view. This saloon bar was Cathy's little kingdom and here she was queen. The regulars from the Sixteen Streets were her subjects and they were loyal. Perhaps she would feel protected and strong, receiving this young princess from afar, if she were surrounded by her familiar court?

Sofia, chuckling, shook her head at herself as she laid out the best china that Cathy had carried from the Sturrock house over the road. I've read too many silly romantic novels, Sofia told herself. I'm turning this coming party into something much more dramatic than it actually is. Cathy knows what she's doing. I should just let her get on with it. Maybe things won't be as melodramatic as all that.

Famous last words, Sofia would think later, as she remembered these last few hours before Junie arrived in town.

Sofia should have reminded herself of how things always turned out. They never went smoothly and there were always hitches. There was always extra drama and tears and shouting and a dreadful carry on. It was just the way that things tended to be here in the Sixteen Streets.

By the time the Robin Hood's doors opened in the early evening, Cathy had made sure that everything was perfect. Crisp white cloths lay over the buffet tables in the far corner of the Select bar, so that no straying hands could greedily help themselves before the party officially started. Cathy had nipped home for an hour to change into her best new dress – which was a deep forest green and rather modest and slightly matronly, if Sofia had to be honest. Cathy had pinned up her wayward auburn curls and toned down her usual Hollywood starlet make-up. 'How do I look? Like a respectable mother?'

Sofia's heart went out to her. She wanted to tell her friend: I don't think you should change yourself one bit. You can't really change, you know. No one can change their true nature. Oh, but wasn't that the truth! Sofia felt that she had lived her entire life around people who would never, ever be able to alter the least little thing about themselves – for good or bad. People just *were*. They were impossible and you just had to live with it: that's how Sofia felt at the grand old age she was.

'You look like the loveliest mother in the world,' she told Cathy, brushing aside her own misgivings. She thought it would surely be best to go into such a meeting with no pretence. This young girl arriving tonight should simply take Cathy as she was. She would have to get used to this place, these people, this whole world of South Shields, because there was absolutely no way of prettying it up and making it different. Perhaps Sofia should have warned her friend: let the child take you as she finds you. I'm sure she will love you, nevertheless. If her heart is as kind and as steadfast as her mother's, I'm sure that it will all be fine.

It would have been lovely to say something like that to Cathy, but there just wasn't time, and the words wouldn't organise themselves so neatly on her tongue. All Sofia could do was give her best friend a comforting hug and a peck on the cheek. Then all at once the whole pub was filling up with their regulars, all dressed up to the nines and set upon having themselves a good and rowdy do.

The regulars at the Robin Hood liked nothing better than having a party and any excuse would do. Tonight word had gone round that someone very special in the landlady's life was about to arrive for a visit, and Cathy had very generously put on a spread and was offering a free drink to everyone to kick the evening off. She was known for being generous and for living her life in full public view. Whatever went on in the dramatic home life of Cathy Sturrock, her regulars expected to have ringside seats.

Their resident pianist, Martha Blaylock, who everyone called Aunty, took up her position at the battered upright. She sipped at a pint of milk stout, cracked her swollen knuckle joints and launched into a jaunty music hall number. Best to get everyone singing along right from the start was her philosophy. Soon the place was rattling and rolling and the floorboards were shaking as the dancing began. It didn't take long for parties to warm up, not around here.

'It's past seven,' Cathy said nervously, glancing at the old ship's clock above the back of the bar. She was eating peanuts ravenously – she was on her third little packet – and locks of unruly hair were falling out of her 'do'.

Sofia gave her an encouraging smile, but she was in the middle of pouring drinks for the Farleys and their next-door neighbours, the Mintons, who had arrived en masse. She was so busy she couldn't find the breath for one more encouraging word.

Sofia got on with her job of measuring drinks and filling up trays and welcoming the droves of arrivals at the bar. The next time she looked up it was to see Cathy sweeping across the room to where a young woman had just stepped through the pub doors.

June was blonde and curly-haired. She had delicate features and was wearing an expensive-looking long woollen coat. She had two suitcases in her hands and she appeared to be terribly shy and worried.

Hands working automatically at the beer pump, seeing to her customers, Sofia watched Cathy hurry over to her daughter and she found herself offering up a silent prayer.

Oh dear god, let this thing go right for poor Cathy. She could do with some love and some good luck in her life, she really could.

Chapter Three

'Everyone! Everyone listen to me, now!' Cathy was used to shouting above the noise of the pub crowd. She rang the ship's bell above the bar and beamed at them all as they paused their supping and turned to give her their attention. A whole roomful of familiar faces was smiling back at her, and this pleased the landlady no end. What better welcome could there be for young June?

The girl was standing right beside her. She was pretty as a picture in her canary yellow frock and matching shoes. Her tightly curled hair was almost the same shade as her dress and her make-up was perfect even after the rigours of travel in a dirty train carriage. June looked fresh as a daisy and Cathy's heart was swollen with pride.

'I've got someone very special to introduce to you all.'

There were murmurs of interest and already the Robin Hood's regulars had taken careful note of the neat and attractive visitor. She seemed rather high class for around here. Just look at how demure she looked, as well as immaculate and expensive. Her comportment (was that the right word, Cathy wondered vaguely) was very good, too. She stood there, quite unabashed, soaking up all of the attention that was being lavished upon her.

'Who's the bonny lass, then?' someone shouted out and there was a ragged cheer of approval.

'Now, you must be polite and treat her like a lady,' Cathy warned. 'She isn't used to rough sorts like the likes of you!'

Laughter at this, but some of the women bridled at Cathy's words. Who was this young madam who looked like she was putting on airs?

'This . . .' said Cathy, touching June's arm softly and smiling at her. For a second she looked proud and almost as if she was about to cry. Then a new look came into her eyes. Cathy hesitated. She bit her lip. She looked for a second as if she didn't know how to describe the girl. She opened her mouth and said something she hadn't been expecting to say. 'This is a member of my family I haven't seen since she was just a wee bit of a thing. Since she was about three years old, in fact. Now she's a beautiful young lady, look! This is my cousin. This is my Aunt Liz's daughter. This is Junie.'

The girl blushed as the whole room erupted into cheers and hearty greetings. They were even stamping on the wooden floorboards as they welcomed her into the community. 'It's just "June" really,' the young girl said softly, almost under her breath. Only Cathy could really hear her. '"Junie" was what they used to call me when I was a very little bairn. I don't really like it now . . .'

But her words were drowned out by the welcomes and the offers to buy her drinks from the men – young and old – who came up to have a closer look at her. 'She won't be drinking anything alcoholic!' Cathy warned them. 'It'll just be pop! She's still a bairn, really.'

Aunty Martha struck up a few discordant notes on the piano, racking her brains for a suitable song of welcome. After some dithering on the keys she settled on one of her favourites to get everyone singing along, 'The Blaydon Races'. Soon the room was busy and boisterous again and the attention drifted away from the visitor.

'I hope I didn't embarrass you,' Cathy grinned at her. 'I just wanted them all to see how bonny you are.'

June simply smiled at her.

'I'll get Minnie to carry your bags across the road to the house,' Cathy said, eyeing the cases that June had brought in from the street. They were good leather cases. They might get nicked, just sitting there. 'I don't think I've ever seen luggage as fancy as that,' Cathy said. The same was true of the coat that June had arrived in, too. Cathy had never owned anything of such quality in all her life. She shook the thought out of her mind. Of course she wasn't about to become envious.

Then Sofia was there, bringing a tall glass of lemonade for the girl. 'Eeeh, it's good to see you, pet,' the Italian girl said warmly. 'I've heard so much about you. You're very welcome here.'

'Thank you,' said June, accepting the drink. 'It's all a bit surprising. So many people staring at me!'

'We don't do things by halves round here,' Cathy assured her. 'Here in the Sixteen Streets everyone knows everyone else's business. We're quite used to living cheek by jowl. We have a party for every important event – and that includes your visit.' When she looked at June then she seemed almost nervous. She watched the girl delicately sip her lemonade and then set the glass on the bar.

'May I see my room? And splash some water on my face?'

'Of course,' Cathy said, and beckoned Minnie Minton over. 'Show her over to number twenty-one. The door will be open. Get her settled into the spare room and if Noel tries to get in your way, pay the old devil no heed.'

Moon-faced and pale of complexion, the youngest barmaid Minnie looked like she was in a constant state of fear. Today was no exception. She hated being anywhere near Cathy's peculiar husband and what was more, she was nervous of this fancy-looking stranger in the posh yellow dress. 'Righty-oh,

Cathy,' she stammered because, though she was anxious about everything, Minnie also adored Cathy Sturrock and would have gone to the ends of the earth for her.

'Hurry back though, won't you?' Cathy implored the younger girls. 'Because we've put on a little buffet and all these gannets in here will gobble the lot in seconds if you don't get back soon.'

June smiled softly. 'Oh, I'm not terribly hungry, thanks.'

Then she was gone, led out of the bar by Minnie, who was cooing and gasping over her oxblood leather cases.

Now everyone in the bar was singing lustily along with 'My Old Man Said Follow the Van'.

Ada Farley – the fierce and diminutive matriarch from over the road – was suddenly standing at the bar and demanding a fresh glass of Mild. 'Eeeh, yon was a bonny girl, Cathy. You must be so proud of her!'

Cathy said, 'Aye, I am that, Ada.'

The older woman was training her shrewd eye up at the landlady. Cathy was growing warm and discomforted in her matronly dress. She knew that there was no hiding anything from Ada Farley. There could be no subterfuge or secrets where she was involved. 'How long is she down for?'

'She's welcome to stay for as long as she likes,' Cathy said. Now that she thought of it, there had been no mention in Junie's beautifully composed letter about her plans. All she had said was that she'd be arriving on this day and at this time. Cathy had been so keen to agree that she hadn't even thought any further.

'Eeeh, well, it's lovely,' Ma Ada said, accepting her fresh and foaming pint of beer. 'Nice to have some family around you, for once. I don't really think of you as having people, Cathy. In all of these years you've never really talked about them.'

Cathy shrugged carelessly and her expression darkened slightly. 'There's nothing much to say, really. I was brought up in the country by my Aunt Liz, mostly. I don't have a massive tribe like you do, Ada.'

Ada Farley scowled. 'A tribe, yes! That's what I've got. And they've got me on the war path. Have you heard what my oldest lads have been up to?'

Cathy listened good naturedly to her old friend's complaints and mock outrage about the sons she doted on. It was her drunken husband who was the real problem at number thirteen, Cathy knew. The sons were paragons and saints to Ada Farley, but she'd be free of her husband in the blink of an eye if she ever got the chance. There he was, over by the piano, slurring his words to another rendition of 'Cushie Butterfield'.

'My god, I wish Aunt Martha would learn herself some new bloomin' songs.' Ada rolled her eyes. 'It's the same three or four ditties going round and round!'

'She likes to get everyone singing along,' said Sofia, who reappeared suddenly in their midst, bundling up the cloths that had been covering the buffet. 'Look, I've had to let them get at the spread. Everyone's starving, Cathy. There'd have been a riot if I'd said they had to wait any longer.'

Smiling, Cathy nodded absently. 'Let them have it,' she said.

Ma Ada took herself off to the buffet table quick as a flash, wrestling through the mass of bodies lining up with their plates.

'June said she wasn't really all that hungry, after her journey,' Cathy said, feeling oddly deflated as she watched the feeding frenzy in the Select.

Then she realised that Sofia was staring at her with narrowed eyes. She blinked. 'What? What is it?'

Sofia said, 'You know what, pet. "Cousin"? "Aunty"? What is all this? That's not what you told me! You told me earlier today that the lass was your own daughter!'

Chapter Four

Minnie Minton was secretly quite proud of being trusted to show June into her aunt's house. It was an honour, in a way. The girl was dressed so smartly and had such airs about her, it was like a proper lady had come to visit them on Frederick Street.

'This is her house then, is it?' June asked, standing in front of the bow window of number twenty-one.

'Only a hop, skip and a jump from the pub!' Minnie grinned. 'So she doesn't have far to go to work.'

It was hard to read June's expression as she stared up at the reddish orange bricks of the front of the house. Was she disappointed? Perhaps she had been expecting something grander?

'Our house is exactly the same, over the road,' said Minnie. 'They're lovely houses inside. Very cosy.'

June gave her a weak smile and clutched the smaller of her cases more tightly. Minnie – who was carrying the heavier one – suddenly realised: oh, she's nervous, the poor thing. She's just a kid. She's younger than I am, even. And here she is, shoved in amongst all these new people. We must be kind to her. 'Come inside. You'll see. You're very welcome here, June.'

June looked at Minnie's round, pale face and looked pleased to have found herself an ally and a friend.

'Come on,' Minnie urged, and swung open the black front door. The sneck had been left on, just as Cathy had promised.

Inside, the hallway was cool and dim. Just as in the days of Cathy's long-deceased mother-in-law, the place was cluttered with tables and gee-gaws and nick-nacks. The walls were absolutely covered in faded paintings and framed photographs. A colossal Aspidistra ran rampant out of its brass pot and the girls had to veer around its gleaming leaves with the cases.

'Can you believe that Cathy polishes all the leaves with milk? It's supposed to be good for it. I think it makes it pong.'

'Where shall I put my bags?' June asked, peering hesitantly up the staircase.

'I'll show you to the spare room. It used to be the old mother's and it's not been used for years. I'm sure it'll be perfectly nice . . .'

June followed the girl up the wooden staircase, taking note of every detail of the place as they inched along. It was gloomy and cluttered, but someone had clearly dusted recently and tried to straighten things up. June couldn't help herself, letting a demure yawn escape.

'Are you tired?' Minnie asked.

'I might just collapse into bed, actually,' the visitor said. 'If you think that would be all right?'

The barmaid shook her head worriedly, flushing with colour at once. 'Oh no, you mustn't do that. You see, Cathy has put herself to so much trouble for this welcoming. All those people in the pub? They were there for you.'

June gave a watery smile as they reached the first landing and faced each other in the fading light.

'Also,' Minnie babbled on. 'All that buffet food she's put out. She was baking sausage rolls and little pies every night this week, she told me. And she got posh ham from Allen's on Fowler Street, and the nice soft bread with pease pudding.

Oh, she's gone to such trouble. She'd be so upset if you missed it all, pet.'

June pursed her lips until they were a thin, worried line. 'I don't think I could stand being in all that noise this evening. Where I come from, it's out in the countryside. It's like a little farm, really. It's so quiet. Very different from here. When I got off the train I couldn't believe the noise! The hooting and the grinding and the roaring of the traffic, and all the noise from the docks. Even the seagulls are louder than the ones that we have at home!'

Minnie laughed out loud at this little speech of June's. It was the most she'd heard her utter yet. 'I think our seagulls are probably a bit deaf,' she said. 'Because of all the hullaballoo from the docks.'

'Hullaballoo!' June echoed. 'That's exactly the word. Ever since I got off the train and walked up the hill to get here, I've been surrounded by hullaballoo.'

'You'll get used to it,' Minnie told her. 'Don't you worry. Now, shall we get your belongings into this bedroom? How long is it you're planning to stay round here?'

Minnie pushed open the stiff door and led the way into a spacious, old-fashioned but very comfortable bedroom. She lit the lamps and their honeyed glow revealed a room that looked like it had been beautifully frozen in time since the reign of Queen Victoria.

'Oh . . . !' June smiled with genuine pleasure. 'I really don't know. I haven't said what my plans are because I simply don't know.' She sat down heavily on the worn, colourful counterpane. The goose down felt wonderfully soft. 'I'm sort of making it all up as I go along. I left home in Morwick under something of a cloud.'

'Oh, yes?' Minnie was keen to get details. She loved hearing stories – especially scandalous ones.

June looked like she regretted letting her tongue run away with her. 'Well, never mind that. Suffice to say that I just don't know. I'm here and I'll have to see what happens.'

'A new life in a new town!' Minnie said enthusiastically, taking both cases and lining them up beside the washstand. 'How exciting! I can't imagine what that must feel like. I've never been anywhere, of course. I've hardly ever even left South Shields! When I was a bairn and me mam was working at the Biscuit Factory we'd go on the annual day out to the Lake District, but that was ages ago and I can barely remember it. I've been nowhere!'

'I'd be happy never to move anywhere ever again,' said June wearily. She hugged the soft coverlet to her chest and let out a ladylike yawn. 'Must I really go back to that raucous pub and eat pies and sandwiches?'

Barely had Minnie had time to think of a cajoling reply before both girls realised there was a man standing in the doorway. He was only about four feet high and he was glaring at them from under his angry eyebrows.

'What are you two little witches doing in here? This was my mother's room! Up to no good, eh?'

Noel Sturrock was in his shirt sleeves with the tails hanging down over what looked like a set of none-too-clean pyjama bottoms. His haggard face was twisted into a gurning expression that made the visitor gasp and catch her breath. In that instant she felt like she had been caught burglarizing the place.

'Oh, Mr Sturrock,' Minnie said, quickly composing herself. His snide, wheedling voice had disturbed her, too. 'I'm just doing a favour for your missus and getting lovely June here settled into her new place.'

The old man trained his bright blue eyes on the young girl. 'Lovely June, eh? In her new place?'

'That's right,' Minnie said. 'You must know about this already, sir. This is a relation of Cathy's, come down to visit you all the way from Northumberland.'

Sturrock studied June beadily. 'She's nobbut a young lass. What's she doing travelling about by herself? Why's she coming to stay with strangers?'

June sat up straight and stared right back at him. 'I'm not a stranger, Mr Sturrock. Cathy is a close cousin of mine. We're very close family.'

'Oh, aye?' said Noel, his voice dripping with sarcasm. Anyone who knew him would recognise that sneering tone, but he was quite new to June and she felt discomfited by his manner.

'Yes, indeed. And you are, I presume, Cathy's husband?'

'Aye, you presume right,' he said gloweringly. 'Happily married for twelve years or more. Hahaha!' His gurgling laughter came out of him unprompted and it almost made him choke. 'Well, enjoy your visit. Enjoy getting to know your cousin,' he growled, and then stomped away back into the hall. The two girls listened to him treading heavily up a further flight of thinly-carpeted stairs to an attic room. He slammed the door and quiet settled back over the whole house.

Minnie glanced at June. 'Well, that was Noel Sturrock. Don't mind him. He's unfriendly to everyone. He used to run the pub, but he turned it over to Cathy some years ago. She's much better at the job than he ever was and he's gone very bitter about it. He's bitter about everything, come to think of it.'

June's eyes were still wide as she recovered from the shock of the encounter. Even the scent of the man had been bitter and acrid, a mixture of beer and tobacco and unwashed flesh. 'What an absolutely horrible old man!' she gasped.

Her candour made Minnie fall about laughing. 'He is, he really is! I don't know what Cathy sees in him. No one does.'

'Oh dear, Minnie,' June said, sounding defenceless all of a sudden. 'Whatever have I got myself involved in? Where have I landed up?'

Minnie's heart went out to her. This was the first unguarded, genuine thing she had heard the new girl say. She decided in this moment to be her friend and protector. She would guide June through the complications of her new life. 'I'll tell you where you've landed up, lady!' she beamed widely at her new pal. 'You're in the very heart of the Sixteen Streets and, though it may not look it, that's a very special place to be.'

June Carmichael still looked dubious. 'Is it?'

'Oh yes,' Minnie smiled. 'Now, splash your face with water and put more lipstick on. Let's get back over the road to that party! You've got people to meet and sausage rolls to eat.'

June found herself smiling back at the clumsy kindness of Minnie Minton.

Chapter Five

Cathy was exhausted by the end of the party at the Robin Hood that night. She was quite used to dealing with all her regulars and the work that involved, but the presence of her young visitor was putting her under a certain amount of extra strain. All evening she kept a watchful eye on June's progress around the room, as she met various of the locals and made polite chit-chat with them.

What a charmer the girl was! What lovely manners. And she wasn't a tiny bit shy, either. For someone who'd grown up in the wilds of the countryside as an only child, she seemed to have no bother making casual conversation even with the more boisterous party guests that night. Cathy felt a warm glow of pride in her chest – and why not? Why shouldn't she allow herself a little touch of pride, even if she'd had no part in the girl's upbringing?

It seemed that Aunt Liz had done a good job after all. Junie was a credit to her.

Once or twice, as she worked at the bar and scooted busily around the place, clearing away the wreckage of the buffet, Cathy noticed the girl stifle a little yawn. She delicately hid her face with a hand as she did so and again Cathy was pleased to see her so well-mannered. If she'd stood there yawning out loud, the likes of Ma Ada and the others might think her very rude and snobbish. But the girl knew just how to present herself and this was good to see.

'You look worn out. Why don't you leave me to finish up here and lock the doors?' This was Sofia, gently breaking into her flow of thoughts. Both women were standing there with dirty glass tankards in their hands, four in each hand, as they cleared up the messy tables.

'That's really kind of you, Sofia, but no, I can't . . .'

'Course you can,' her friend smiled broadly. 'I know you like to see to every little thing by yourself, but just this once, why don't you let me take over? You can get that visitor of yours home and tucked up in bed. I've seen her yawning. She's had a bloomin' long day, the poor mite.'

It always made Cathy smile to hear Sofia's still-accented voice using very colloquial terms. The Italian girl's face was so earnest and soft with care as she spoke to Cathy. It was really lovely to have someone absolutely on her side and looking out for her welfare. Cathy just knew that Sofia was always going to be on her side and that thought was a very reassuring one.

'All right,' Cathy said. 'I'll do that. But don't go washing everything up and cleaning the tables. We can do all that tomorrow. Just chuck everyone out and lock up.'

'I will,' promised Sofia.

The girl, June, didn't need persuading to leave the party in her own honour. She thanked people for coming along to meet her and received some puzzled stares for her efforts. Some of the attendees would have been there anyway, she realised. They blinked at her and smiled uncertainly as they finished their last drinks of the night. These inarticulate dockers in their rough togs and their factory worker wives. Suddenly June felt rather foolish for thanking people, for behaving as if any of them were really here to welcome her. How conceited of her! How stupid!

'Aye, aye, you're welcome here,' said a horrid old woman with warts on her face. 'It's grand to see the neighbours turn out to welcome you.'

June smiled tightly and thanked the old lady. As if anyone was really bothered that she was here! They were just pretending, weren't they? They were just being polite and nice. Oh, why had she gone round talking in that hoity-toity voice to them all, like she was visiting royalty? She could hear the echo of her own squeaky, silly voice in her head and she felt foolish because of it.

'Eeeh, doesn't she talk so nice?' said the dreadful bony woman who'd played the piano so thunkingly and tunelessly all evening.

June had a headache because of the horrible music and all the smiling that she'd had to do.

And all at once there was that girl who had been so kind to her earlier. The girl with the smudgy eyes and the puddingy face. What had she been called? Minnie. Yes, she'd felt almost like someone who might become a friend. Well, maybe. She was clearly kind-hearted and she'd been there when June had come face to face with that appalling hunchback person who was supposed to be her uncle.

This really was a nasty place she had fetched up in. I'm in some kind of Charles Dickens story, she thought, panicking slightly as the saloon bar started to clear and people went noisily home. I'm living in the slums with a cast of unwashed grotesques!

'Did you have a lovely time?' the moon-faced Minnie asked her. She seemed so simple and straightforward, this girl. There were no hidden thoughts or mixed feelings to her. June almost envied her simplicity.

'Oh, it was fine,' June said. 'Though now I'm ready for my bed.'

'Wasn't the food smashing?' Minnie asked. 'I've not had a blow-out like that for ages. I love your aunt's baking. She doesn't do it all that often nowadays, but she's a dab hand when she does.'

'Yes, very nice,' June said, though she hadn't thought the offerings all that special. She'd nibbled on one end of a soggy sausage roll and taken a couple of bites from a sandwich that was spread with some kind of fish paste.

'Here's your aunt coming over to collect you now,' Minnie said.

Collect me? June bridled at her words. Like I'm some kind of child still? It's a bit late to start treating me as if I need caring for like a child! Just let her try . . . The spark of anger she felt just then surprised her. She tried to quench it as Cathy swept over, bringing her new coat.

'Ha'way then, bonny lass. Time to get home. I hope you enjoyed our little do in your honour.'

June took her coat and slipped it on. 'Oh yes indeed, Aunt Catherine.' She simpered a little as she looked at Cathy.

None of the tension in the air was apparent to Minnie Minton. 'I'll be off home then,' she grinned. 'If that's all right? Eeeh, it's been smashing meeting you tonight, June. I feel like I've made meself a brand new friend!'

June kissed her doughy cheek with a pert, dry little peck. 'You certainly have. Friends for life.'

'Eeeh!' beamed Minnie, then turned and hastened off home.

Minnie knew she was going to catch hell from her da for staying out so late this evening, but as she stumbled out of the bar and onto the cobbled lane, she decided that it was all worth it. Junie Carmichael really seemed to her like she was going to be her friend for life, and Minnie couldn't have been happier.

June was rather quiet as Cathy led her across the road to number twenty-one. Ah, she must be worn out, the landlady thought to herself.

'Soon have you settled,' she promised the girl. 'Will you want a cuppa before bedtime? Or some Ovaltine, perhaps?'

'Not for me, thank you,' June said.

The interior of the house was just the same as before. It was gloomy and cluttered. It felt even more oppressive than it had a few hours ago. This is where I live now, June thought. This dark place with brown walls in the middle of a slum . . .

What on earth have I done? She felt panic rising up in her chest. And what did I really expect it to be like? Did I expect Cathy to be living a grander life than this?

June didn't really know anymore. All she knew was that she couldn't stay at home in Morwick. Her boats were burned and she had no choice.

This dreadful place had to be her home now.

She stood in the back parlour in her red coat and felt the walls closing in around her.

Cathy was bustling about with the kettle on the range, lighting the gas. 'Are you sure? Maybe cocoa? You must have something. Come on, take off your lovely coat. At least look as if you're staying.'

She was becoming rather bossy as she cajoled the young girl. June felt herself growing annoyed at this flurry of words directed at her. Glumly she shrugged off her coat.

'You're overtired, that's what it is,' Cathy smiled. 'Here, I'll hang your coat up in the lobby.'

June seated herself at the dining table and idly traced patterns in the toast crumbs left on the cloth.

'What can I get you?' Cathy asked, sitting down opposite her.

'I'm fine,' the girl assured her.

'You'll be ready for your bed.'

'In a moment,' June said. Then she fixed the older woman with a piercing stare. She was pleased to see Cathy flinch in surprise. 'I just want to ask you something first.'

'Oh . . . ?' said Cathy. 'What's that then?'

The girl's voice hardened. 'Why didn't you tell all those people the truth? Why did you say you were my aunt? Why didn't you tell them all that I'm really your daughter?'

Chapter Six

It was the next day and Cathy was having frothy coffee with Sofia at Franchino's ice cream parlour. They were sitting in a secluded booth at the back of the white and mint green Art Deco parlour which was owned by Sofia's family. Cathy was warming her hands on her cup and blowing on the rich roasted coffee to cool it as her friend stared at her in amazement.

'So, what did you say to her?' The Italian girl's eyes widened. 'Did she really sound annoyed with you?'

'She sounded annoyed and upset,' Cathy said miserably. 'And maybe she had a point?'

Sofia was flabbergasted. She didn't know what to say to her friend at all. Yes, she too had been surprised to hear Cathy introduce her daughter to everyone as her cousin, but she hadn't known that June herself had known the truth. Imagine how that young girl must have felt. She had been disavowed by her own mother! Why, she must have felt as if she had been disowned in public. What a horrible feeling that would be.

'Well, I don't know . . .' Sofia said awkwardly, though the look on her face told Cathy that she had grave misgivings.

'Oh god.' Cathy sipped her coffee and it was still so hot that it stung her lips. 'I thought I was doing everything right, didn't I? Putting the flags out and welcoming her into my world. But

I've done it all wrong, haven't I? I've upset her and turned her against me already.'

'I'm sure it's not too late to sort things out,' Sofia consoled her. 'Look, she's only just got here.'

'But we've started off on the wrong foot already.'

Sofia sighed. 'Have you seen her this morning yet?'

'Uh, no,' Cathy said. 'I knocked and stood on the landing calling her name, but she was dead to the world still. Or she was ignoring me. She never came down before I left the house. I think she's avoiding me and she hasn't even been here a full day!'

Sofia had rarely seen her best friend so cast down. 'I'm sure things will sort themselves out. She will see that you were doing what you thought was the right thing.'

Cathy said, 'I didn't know she knew, you see.' She looked at Sofia imploringly. 'How do I explain that to the lass? I didn't know that my bloody Aunt Liz had told her the truth.'

Sofia shook her head. 'But why was your aunt even lying to her in the first place?'

A cloud passed over Cathy's face. Sofia would have sworn that the daylight in the ice cream parlour had actually dimmed for a moment. 'That's a long story,' she said at last. 'It all happened years ago. I . . . I didn't choose . . . I never chose for it to be this way.' Her expression curdled and to Sofia's dismay, Cathy seemed about to cry. 'This is all Aunt Liz's fault. All of it.'

'Drink your coffee, it's cooled down a bit,' Sofia said. 'Do you want something to eat? Some ice cream? Would that help?' At the first sign of upset, Sofia's instincts told her to feed the person up with treats. 'Cannoli?'

Cathy shook her head. 'No, thanks. Look, I better have this coffee and get back to Frederick Street. Otherwise she'll be up and about and be all by herself. Or worse, she'll have Noel talking to her. He'll make things worse. I just had to get out for half an hour and escape.'

'I'm glad you came to see me,' Sofia said. 'You can always turn to me when you need help.'

'Thank you,' Cathy said, and dutifully drank her coffee. Its sweetness and delicious strength surprised her. It almost made her feel stronger. 'I'll tell you the story, I promise. I'll tell you about Junie and how I had to leave her with my aunt.'

'You don't have to tell me if you don't want.'

'No, I'd like to. I'd like to get it off my chest. I've bottled all of this up for years and years. No one at all has heard the story since I arrived in South Shields.'

Sofia looked amazed. 'So long? How do you manage to bear such secrets?'

By now Cathy was on her feet, pulling her coat back on. She had her basket for fetching bread back to the house. 'Come to the pub this evening, if you can, after supper,' Cathy said. 'And we'll talk. But first, I must try to sort out this whole situation. And make some peace with my daughter.'

After Cathy left, Sofia picked up the emptied cups and couldn't help thinking how odd and unaccustomed those words sounded out of Cathy's mouth.

Cathy found her husband sitting at a littered dining table, dipping a burnt crust of stale toast into his tea. He sucked his teeth and crowed at her. 'You've missed that young lass of yours! She's gone! Yes, ha! She's gone!'

Cathy set down her basket and went pale. 'What? She's left?'

Noel shrugged his shoulders. 'How should I know? What do I know about all these comings and goings? This place is like a flamin' doss house these days with young lasses coming and going . . .'

Cathy felt the usual anger rising up and making her throat feel like it was constricting. For all these years this man had known just how to wind her up. Why had she tolerated him for all this time? How many years had she felt trapped here with him? Why had she flung her whole life away, dedicating herself to this place, this marriage, this home and the pub? I've been an idiot all my life, Cathy thought miserably. And now I've upset my daughter and driven her away already.

'What's wrong with you, anyway?' Noel snapped, noticing the desolation in her face. 'Why, yesterday you were skipping around having a lovely time. Planning a party. Making the place look nice. Baking sausage rolls even! What's happened to you?'

Noel wasn't all bad, of course. This was something Cathy understood deep down. Something that hardly anyone else ever realised. There was a note of concern in that peevish voice of his that only she would ever hear. Underneath his caustic tone and his habitual sneer, she could tell that he was genuinely concerned to see his wife looking so perturbed this morning. He could see that she was on the verge of tears and that something had gone awfully wrong.

'Aw, hey now, lass,' he said. 'Look, don't look so worried. Yon girl hasn't run away. Don't fret about that. She never took her bags with her. She's coming back.'

Cathy had her face in her hands, trying not to cry. She looked up sharply. 'Really?'

'Aye, aye, it's true. She went out about half an hour since, all dolled up and bonny. That daft lass came and called on her. They seem to have made fast friends already. What's she called? One of the Mintons from down the road.'

'Minnie,' said Cathy. 'Minnie came calling on her?'

'That's right. Took her out. They barely said a word to me, but they said that Minnie was going to show her round the town. So she could get her bearings. See the sights. That daft Minnie was taking the lead and taking over everything, chattering away. I said, don't you want to wait till your Aunty Cathy gets back and you can see her? And that young lass Junie gave me such a look. Like you were the last person she'd ever want to see. So, what's gone on, Cathy? Have you two had words already?'

She didn't know what to say to him. She felt like she was caving in. The fact that he was suddenly sounding caring was enough to do her in. 'Oh, Noel. I've made so many mistakes. I thought I was old enough now to stop making mistakes. I thought I could put everything right for once. I thought I was doing right by saying that she could come here . . .'

The grumpy old devil was staring at her levelly. Those bright blue eyes of his! They could always see right into her. He could always tell what her heart was feeling, damn him. 'That's not your cousin or your niece, is it? That girl's related a lot more closer to you, ain't she?'

His wife nodded helplessly, letting the tears come up at last. 'You know. You always knew. You were the only one who knew my secret.'

'Aye, lass, I've known for years you had a secret daughter. I never knew much more than that, but I knew she was your secret shame.'

'You once threatened to tell the whole town!' she threw back at him.

'Ah, that was years ago. Before we were married and settled. We all say and do crazy things when we're young.'

In Cathy's memory it hadn't quite been like that. He had manipulated her, and emotionally blackmailed her. He had taunted her with knowing her terrible secret. Then she had married him, submitting herself to him for all these years. The matter of her daughter, hidden away in the far north, had never been mentioned between them again.

Until now.

Noel licked his thin, purplish lips. 'Well, you invited her here. This is your problem to sort out. I wouldn't dream of sticking my nose in. I suggest you make your peace with the lass. I'm not about to live in a house with a family at war with itself.'

Chapter Seven

Minnie kept casting sidelong glances as the two girls bustled along, hoping that her new friend was at last cheering up and starting to enjoy herself.

Not yet she wasn't, Minnie realised, as they wandered through the leafy avenues of South Marine Park. June was in a proper gloomy mood and hadn't said a single word for about ten minutes. Look at the way she was frowning! She wasn't just gloomy, Minnie thought. She was furious!

But look at how she was dressed. So pretty, so smart. Minnie would have given anything for a chic outfit like the one June wore today. She hardly knew how to describe it. She was like someone off the films. Like one of the dummies from the big store in town in the ladieswear department where Minnie liked to wander sometimes, perusing the styles and pretending she had money to spend. Well, most of Minnie's outfits were cast-offs and hand-me-downs. Luckily she was a marvel on the Singer sewing machine, just like her mam was, and she could make anything fit her perfectly. But that didn't stop all her outfits being second-hand.

Just look at June! In that tailored jacket. Cerise with a cherry-coloured trim. And a perky little hat! She looked like she was going to a wedding rather than taking a stroll around the front at South Shields.

The sun was out and it was a beautiful sparklingly blue day. They had glimpsed the sea as they walked down Ocean Road and Minnie had started shouting out excitedly. 'Look! There it is, Junie! It's our sea! Isn't it lovely?'

But June had rolled her eyes. 'I grew up right beside the sea. It's the same sea as this, Minnie. It's nothing new to me.'

Her withering tone didn't put her new friend off. 'But look how beautiful it is, Junie. All glimmering with silver and deep blue stretching out for miles . . . all the way to Norway, I suppose! Look at the trawlers and the ferries, look how small they seem!'

Had June tutted at her? There was a small clicking sound that made it sound like she had. But Minnie tried hard not to mind. The new girl was disappointed and angry. She had to take her mood out on someone.

Now they were walking by the well-tended flowerbeds of the park and June refused to take notice of all the flowers as Minnie called out their names. 'Oh, aren't they gorgeous, Junie? I wish we could have a little garden but all we've got is a backyard with a privy, same as your Aunty Cathy. I tried growing petunias and pansies in a window box at the back of ours but it's too shaded. Our side of the alley's right in the shadows most of the day and everything withered and died. It was so sad.'

All at once June spoke up. It gave Minnie a turn to hear her joining in the conversation after so long stewing in her silence. 'Back at home I had my own little patch of garden. Ever since I was a little girl. Mummy . . . she gave me a little square of garden near the back door and I had a wooden spade and a tin kind of hoe thing. She bought me packets of seeds to start me off and I loved it. I grew carrots and sweet peas and potatoes. I couldn't believe it when the green shoots came up. I made these, I thought. It was something I had done with my own hands.'

'Oh, lovely,' Minnie grinned, delighted that Junie was speaking up. 'And did you grow flowers, too?'

'Sometimes, but Mummy said they were weeds, really. They were just wildflowers that were coming up on my patch. I thought they were lovely. Purple vetch and dandelions and wild, blood red poppies. Mummy showed me that you had to pull them up. You had to get rid of them to let the other things grow. The things you really wanted.'

'I'd have liked the poppies,' said Minnie. 'Better than mouldy old potatoes.'

'That's what I thought, too,' said June. 'But Mummy knew best. She could be quite fierce. She knew what was right and I had to learn . . .' June shrugged and smiled bitterly. 'Still, I don't have to worry about that anymore, do I? I don't have to worry about her. She's not my mummy anymore. Aunt Liz, I suppose I should call her. That's all she is to me. She's just my aunty and I doubt I'll ever see her again, now.'

Minnie hesitated before asking a personal question, wary of June flaring up with her bad mood again. Surely Junie was wanting to be asked questions, though? With the way she was letting things out. It was as if she had decided she wanted to talk.

'This is the lady who brought you up? Who you thought was your natural mammy?' Minnie felt clumsy with the words, trying to say just what she meant. She was very worried about upsetting her new friend and confidante.

'Yes,' said June. 'She was all my world. We lived in a farmhouse on the Morwick Estate, right by the sea. It's very beautiful. I grew up right near the beach and sometimes I'd run down there by myself, first thing in the morning.'

'Oh! It sounds lovely,' said Minnie, just imagining this life of having your own garden of wildflowers and whole beaches to yourself.

'I feel like it's all been taken away from me, all of it,' June said, her face darkening again. For one horrible moment Minnie thought she was going to cry.

'What happened?' she asked.

'Maybe it was my own fault, I don't know,' June said. 'I mean, I admit that I'm argumentative and headstrong. Mummy – Aunt Liz – said that I'm a bit of a handful. We were arguing about something, something to do with boys, and she flew into a rage like I'd never seen before.'

'About boys!' Minnie said.

'I'd been playing out with some of the lads who worked up at the big house. Stable boys. I hadn't come back till late. Mummy was livid with me. "I know what you're doing! I know, you don't have to lie to me, missy!" Well, I'd never heard her so nasty. She was going hysterical.'

'Huh, my mam gets hysterical with me sometimes, too,' Minnie said, and sat down wearily on a brightly-painted park bench, inviting June to sit with her. 'Especially when it comes to boys. God, she went crackers just the other week when I was out, down on the beach with the other lads and lasses from Frederick Street. The Farley boys and all that lot. She was saying, "Eeeh, what if the tide came in and swept you all away? What if your campfire got out of control and you all got burned up?" And I said, Mam, we were only cooking sausages. And then she went, "What if you got yourself up the duff messing about with boys like that?"' Minnie hooted with laughter. 'I said, "Mam! Who's gonna look at me? I'm not getting up the duff with no one! Don't say rude things!" Eeeh, it was such an awful row!' Yet Minnie found herself laughing now as she recalled it.

June was nodding very seriously. 'Yes, my mother had the same worries about me. Me and the stable lads. They were trying to show me how to ride the horses. It was thrilling, Minnie.

Really wonderful beasts. But my mummy was convinced we were doing bad things instead.'

'Eeeh . . . !' June sighed. 'What are old people like, eh?'

June shrugged. 'Well, as it happened there was a bit of rude stuff going on. I got them lads to show me their winkies in the barn, of course.'

'What?' Minnie covered her mouth with her hands.

'Oh yes, I had them all lined up in the barn. Even the oldest one and he's nearly twenty. I made them show me what they all had, since they were so proud of them!'

Minnie squealed. 'Junie! No wonder your mam was mad with you!'

June shrugged. 'She wasn't to know what I was really up to. It was all just in her fevered imagination. But she knew I was up to no good and, when I got home late, she went wild. She screamed and yammered at me and I weathered it all, until she said the worst thing. The very worst thing she'd ever said to me in all my life.'

'And what was that?'

'She screamed it in my face: "Aye, bad blood will come out, won't it? You're no better than *her*, are you? You're no better than your bloody mother, are you?"'

'Oh!' Minnie gasped.

'And I stared up into her twisted face. This woman I'd always assumed was my mummy and I couldn't believe what I was hearing. "But you're my mother!" I said, and she looked even angrier then. Angry with herself, I should think. She was furious for letting the secret out. And now it was out – after all those years, all my life – there was no way of hiding it away again.'

It was less than a week ago but already it felt like a lifetime to June. A whole lifetime of hurt feelings and anguish had widened the gap between the bitter and rejected person she was today and the happy, carefree girl who had once known exactly who she was and where she belonged.

June told Minnie: 'I got the whole story out of her. About who my mother really is. My true mother. And where she lives. The whole story came out, bit by bit, all that terrible night. And the woman who I'd thought was my mother was crying and sobbing. By the end of it all she was begging me. She was beseeching me to put it all behind us. She regretted telling me any of it. I was still her daughter. I would always be her true and only daughter . . .'

'Of course,' said Minnie. 'Your real mam is the one who brought you up.'

'But I was angry too, by then,' June admitted. 'I told her, "You lied to me. And now I don't know who I am anymore." And my mummy told me that she had lied in order to give me a better life. My first mother had gone to live in the city, with the bright lights and all the people. She had gone off to live a more exciting life and she had left me behind.'

'The bright lights of South Shields!' Minnie chuckled. 'Well, I suppose we do have nice lights on Fowler Street at Christmas.'

June was hardly listening to her. 'I was determined all of a sudden. I can't tell you how I knew I had to do this thing, I just did. I knew I had to come here and find the woman who was really my mother. And I have to ask her outright. I need to know why she gave me away.'

Chapter Eight

Cathy missed Sofia living just nearby. For years her best friend had lived in the next street. When anything came up or there was an emergency, the two women only had to dash round a few steps to fetch each other.

However, as time moved on, the Franchino clan felt they needed more space than their two-up two-down afforded them. Tonio Franchino was ambitious and for years he had had his eyes on the large houses with spacious gardens by the seafront. He had his sights set on Seaburn for a long time.

Because of the success they were having with their ice cream parlour, Sofia had pulled back on her hours at the Robin Hood, too. She barely worked there at all now, merely helping out during special events, such as Junie's welcoming party. Mostly Cathy was left alone with young Minnie, who was keen to help with everything and a good little worker really, but she was a bit gormless. She wasn't the same as having Sofia by your side.

Right now, Cathy could do with some support from her oldest friend here in the Sixteen Streets. This morning's chat in the ice cream parlour wasn't enough. Sofia always kept a level head and made the best plans. Together the two of them had faced some rotten disasters and come through mostly unscathed – such as the time that their barmaid friend Ellie was murdered by her horrible fancy man and her body was found in the cemetery at the top of the hill. Or when Sofia's youngest child, Marco, had the croup and they maintained a vigil throughout the night thinking he was going to die, or when her elderly mother went missing that time and they'd all thought she'd gone gaga and thrown herself from the top of Marsden cliffs.

Together, they had been through an awful lot.

Sofia had been there to help Cathy through the more challenging moments of her marriage to the irascible Noel. She had been there to talk sense into her when no one else could. She had helped her figure out just what it was she was trying to do with her life when the whole thing seemed opaque and crazy even to herself.

Sometimes Cathy wished she'd made a whole different set of choices in her life. It was all so arbitrary, really. She had pitched up in South Shields when she was only slightly older than Junie was now. She had bumped into Noel's kindly, nosy, strange old mother and been taken immediately under her wing. She had come here and within a year they had faced love and disaster and war and even a worldwide plague. Cathy had found herself falling in love – not with Noel, not exactly – but with the life that she could make for herself here. She could see herself as the landlady of the little pub at the top of the street. Had she really talked herself into seeing Noel as something more human than he was, simply to achieve that goal?

Ah, but he had manipulated her, hadn't he? He had twisted things round to his own advantage. He had just about blackmailed her, the wily old devil. And somehow she had wound up falling into his grasp.

His old mother had died and had broken both their hearts. He used the grief they felt as another means of softening up her feelings towards him.

The old hobgoblin was a drunk and a crook and he was involved in all kinds of unsavoury business, but he had made her promises. She could take his pub. She could do all the work. She could make this place her very own. She would never be uncertain about her place in the world ever again.

Yes, it was all so random. Why, she had only arrived on this street because her weary feet had led her this way. She had only wound up in the Sixteen Streets because she had managed to get a lift with a randy old bugger driving a cart from her hometown down to the Biscuit Factory in South Shields. She had escaped his clutches and pelted into the slums by the docks and here she was! Here she still was . . . how long? Thirteen years later.

Was this how June was feeling now, she wondered?

It must be, surely. She must be thinking, why here? Who *am* I here? What must I become? How do I live? Who do I belong to?

No wonder Junie was confused and angry. She thought she knew who she belonged to and Cathy had flung it all back in her face. In public, in front of all the friends and neighbours. Cathy was shocked by herself. I was so busy putting on a good do, she thought. I was showing off. I was bragging about myself and my importance here. What do they call me? The Queen of the Sixteen Streets. And look how proud and ridiculously puffed up I am as a result of all that respect! I'm in love with myself and my own importance. I wanted to show off to my own poor bairn, who was feeling lost and alone and all at sea. Yes, she might be bonny and well dressed and brittle in her manner. She was nervous and scared though, and then I went and rejected her.

Oh, Junie! Cathy thought, pulling her woollen shawl about her as she traipsed the streets. This was her habit when she had to think something through. She wandered up and down the length of the Sixteen Streets, through the back alleys and up the broad cobbled lanes heading up the hill. It cleared her mind, inhaling both the stiff salty breeze from the sea and the smoky, delicious fumes of the Biscuit Factory. Her hair twisted free of her headscarf and hung around her face, much more messily than she'd usually allow anyone to see in public. She felt distraught, consumed with these thoughts that she had done absolutely everything wrong. I'm a fool. I'm a stupid, show-off fool. I've started turning into someone just like that rotten husband of mine! Now, there was a thought that chilled her to the bone.

Eeeh, what am I like, she thought. But then, really, she had had no idea, had she, that Junie had learned the truth? As far as Cathy had known the bairn still believed that Cathy was just an aunt, just a cousin.

Aunt Liz had changed everything. She had broken the confidence and told Junie the truth. But why? Why on earth would she single-handedly destroy the web of fiction that she herself had created all those years ago?

Cathy hadn't wanted to lie. She hadn't wanted any part of the lies her own aunty had told. She had wanted nothing more than her own child back.

But it had been made impossible, and Cathy's heart had been broken.

It had taken her years to get past all of the grief. She had had to build a whole new life, keeping her true feelings and all the upset hidden deep inside her heart.

Damn her Aunt Liz! She was the cause of all of this.

Every last bit of it was down to her. That horrible woman – who Cathy had once loved with all her heart – had ruined everything.

Oh, Junie, where are you? Cathy implored silently. She looked up the hill and down the hill, her shawl and her auburn hair whipping about as the wind grew stronger. She wanted the chance to explain. She wanted to tell her daughter the whole truth. Surely she could understand that? She'd understand the choices that Cathy had been forced to make?

But what if the girl had run off? What if she had already left the Sixteen Streets? And what if there was no further chance for Cathy to put things right?

Chapter Nine

The two girls stayed out for the remainder of the day and into the evening, exploring the streets and the sights of June's new town. Minnie was a willing and enthusiastic tour guide, regaling her new friend with local legends as well as whatever scraps of her own experience came to mind.

June smiled and listened, while inside she was all turmoil. She couldn't put aside her thoughts about her two mothers and what they had both put her through. She hardly knew who she was supposed to be anymore.

Minnie insisted they buy fish and chips at the kiosk by the shore and their hot deliciousness distracted June briefly from her woes. After turning up her nose at Cathy's banquet the previous evening, she found that she was starving today. The fried food went down a treat, and Minnie took note of her relish.

'See? They're smashing, aren't they?'

June smiled and this gave Minnie hope that she might just buck up yet. 'Let's go down Marsden rock and see if there are any lads around,' Minnie suggested. And so they caught a trolley bus that took them part way along the seafront, until they came to a spot where there was a huge rock sticking out of the foaming sea. Its top was home to what looked like a hundred thousand perching seabirds. The sands below were a soft, inviting gold and in the early evening sun, there could surely be nothing nicer than to go and explore those shaded hollows and nooks of the caves under the rock and the wonderful-looking sands.

The pair of them hastened down the staircase cutting a zigzag pattern down the steep face of the cliff. Minnie held in her usual wooziness at the height of it and she held tightly to the rope banisters as she made her way down, determined not to show her fear to June.

Down on the beach June's spirits seemed to lift.

There were indeed boys down here, and girls, too. It was as if all the young people of South Shields had agreed to meet and fill up this beach together, like a small utopia of their own. 'They're just like the gulls and the gannets on top of the rock,' Junie laughed. 'Squawking and vying for each other's attention.'

'There's the Farley boys, look,' said Minnie, partly whispering as she pointed out two lean and lanky young men. They were in their twenties, slightly older than most of the others round here. They were stripped to some kind of shorts and had turned lobster red in the sun. Their hair was brylcreemed down and to Minnie's eyes they looked just like film stars. 'Tony and Tom,' she told June. 'They're my next-door neighbours. There's two others, but they're just little lads still. These two . . . they're like gods, aren't they?'

June shrugged, studying the fellas. It was true, they did stand out amongst the others on the crowded sands. 'They're not bad. Especially the tallest one.'

'That's Tony, he's the most handsome,' Minnie sighed happily. 'I know them all really well. The Farleys are like the most famous family in our part of town. Everyone knows them.'

'Famous, eh?' asked June.

Minnie nodded firmly. 'Oh, yes. Remember, I introduced you to their mother, Ada, at the party last night.'

'I hardly remember anyone from last night. It was all a bit of a blur.'

Minnie was barely listening, however. She was making her way determinedly over to the tartan blanket where the two oldest Farley boys were sunbathing. 'Yoo hoo!' she called. 'Hello, you two!'

June noticed how the two grown men looked up to see Minnie stomping towards them and both tried to hide their wincing irritation at her. Have I made friends with the town's most foolish and embarrassing girl, June wondered? Perhaps I'll have to throw her off.

The two Farley boys shaded their eyes against the sun to see the girls. 'Now then, Minnie,' said the younger one, Tom. He was the friendliest and the one that Minnie had a real soft spot for, despite her thinking Tony the better looking. 'What are you up to today?'

Minnie looked proud with herself. 'This is my new friend, Junie, and I'm showing her round the town.'

They stared at June carefully, taking in her fancy cherry-trimmed jacket and her general demeanour of superiority. Tom grinned at her, 'Oh, you're the one who belongs to Cathy, aren't you? Who the do was for last night?'

June nodded stiffly. 'That's right.'

'My mam was telling me all about it,' Tom went on. 'She was saying just how excited Cathy's been about you coming down to visit. She's been on tenterhooks all week, making plans and everything. I was there when she was sitting in the parlour, and she must have got that letter from you out of her bag a dozen times, smoothing it out and reading it again. "Listen how she writes things, Ada!" she kept saying. "Eeeh, how clever does she sound?"' Tom laughed, but not in a nasty way.

Minnie glanced at June. 'See?' she said. 'See how she was looking forward to seeing you?'

Tony, the oldest of the Farley boys, was the shrewdest. 'Is there something the matter?' He fixed June with a bright blue stare. 'Are you not happy to be here, pet?'

'It's nothing.' June wafted a hand in front of her face, as if she could dispel all of her problems. 'All I want to do is enjoy myself now. That's allowed, isn't it?' Her voice had gone sharp and her face looked slightly less pretty, Minnie thought, when she acted peevish. June unbuttoned her jacket and knelt down on a corner of their thick blanket. 'May we join you for a while? What are you drinking?'

Tom laughed. 'The best Newcastle Brown Ale! Have you ever tried it? It's new, really. Here, have a sip and try.'

'How old are you two?' Tony suddenly asked. 'Should you really be accepting sips of beer on the beach from grown men?'

'We're both over sixteen,' Minnie laughed. 'I'm seventeen, as it happens. But you've never asked me before, have you? You've never been interested in plying *me* with beer before!' She laughed as she too plumped down on the rug and the soft powdery sand.

June took a glug of warm beer and it tasted wonderful and bitter as it went straight to her head.

Following the party the previous evening, the Robin Hood was especially quiet tonight. This was just as well because Cathy was running the place single-handedly and couldn't have coped with any kind of sudden rush. Minnie had the day off and Sofia had cut right back on her hours since she had moved house and lived further away.

It was fair to say that Cathy felt somewhat deflated and lonely as she worked at the bar that evening. Not that any of her regulars would have picked up on her mood. Most of them were too pie-eyed to notice anyone else's feelings anyway.

She drifted through her tasks in a doleful state, keyed up with anxiety but without anything she could do about it. She kept glancing at the clock and wondering when Sofia would come by. She had promised, hadn't she? After supper, when she'd fed her whole family at the new house overlooking the sea. She'd hop on the tram and come here to see Cathy so they could carry on talking. That had been the arrangement, hadn't it?

There was so much that Cathy wanted and needed to get off her chest. It was as if the long-suppressed past was welling up inside of her.

'Smashing do that, last night,' said Mr Chesney, who lived at the bottom of the street and had something to do with the bakehouse at the Biscuit Factory. 'That niece of yours looked overwhelmed by all the attention.'

'Aye, she was,' Cathy nodded at the florid, tubby man. He looked like he spent his time at work eating all the misshapen biscuits that emerged from the oven. Now that she looked closer, he even seemed to have golden crumbs in his tash and side whiskers.

'You take good care of that lass,' Mr Chesney said. 'A pretty girl like that in a place like this, there's all sorts of trouble she could get into.' He wasn't being salacious or suggestive, he was just offering pointed advice, as the father of his own three boisterous girls. Still, Cathy felt a shiver go through her. Yes, now she was responsible for Junie. Now she had to be a parent at last. She had missed all the childhood stages and leapfrogged straight into this part. The part in which a girl could get herself into trouble – a fact that Cathy knew far better than most.

And tonight – just her second night in South Shields – her daughter was out there somewhere in the town, getting up to goodness knows what. And maybe she'd be doing it just to worry and spite the woman who had turned out to be her mother.

Chapter Ten

Just as she had promised, Sofia turned up at the pub some time before closing to share a drink with the landlady. She found Cathy all of a pother.

'Do you think she's staying out late just to worry me? Just to spite me?'

Sofia sipped the small glass of cherry liqueur she had been offered on the house. 'Perhaps she is. Or perhaps she's just enjoying herself and seeing the town. She hasn't seen much of town life, you say? She grew up in the countryside, just like you did?'

Cathy nodded. 'Aye, and she'll be a lot less worldly and sophisticated than she appears to be, as well.'

'I don't think it's time to go combing the streets just yet,' Sofia told her. 'It's only just after ten.'

'Perhaps you're right . . .' Cathy sighed and leaned against the bar, studying the reflections of the firelight in her ruby-coloured glass. Thank goodness the pub was extremely quiet tonight. It wasn't much good for her profits, but she was glad of the quiet, it had to be said.

'I've never seen you so ill at ease about anything,' Sofia told her. 'Well, not for years, anyway.'

'She's my flesh and blood, that's why. For years I've tried to put that fact out of my mind, but seeing her here, now, it's all become so clear. She's mine, Sofia, and I'm responsible for her.'

'You told me you were going to explain it all to me. Why you lost her. You were going to tell me about it all.'

'Aye, I will. If I talk about it, if I make even one person understand, maybe I'll feel better about it.' She smiled at Sofia. 'I know all these bloody people round here. I know everyone! But there's only really you I can talk to, Sofia.'

So, for the rest of that evening at the Robin Hood, Cathy rolled out some of her story for her friend. Like a precious bolt of rich fabric that had been laid away at the back of a cupboard, her past had been hidden from the light and the dust where nothing could touch it. Now, as she started to reveal it all, she found that the colours were still rich and vivid and the intricate patterns were very much intact.

'I always talked so glibly about coming from a big house in Northumberland, didn't I? If anyone ever asked I'd say that I came from grand folk and that I grew up by the sea. And I'd never say very much more. It wasn't quite true, but it wasn't wrong, either. I did grow up in those kinds of surroundings, but I was just a maid of all work. I worked in the big house belonging to the Logan family. I was in service there from the age of eleven, when my Aunt Liz told me I had to start earning my keep.'

'The age of eleven!' Sofia gasped, thinking of her own carefree childhood in the backstreets of Naples. Her family hadn't been rich, but they hadn't been so poor that a mere bairn had had to be sent out to skivvy!

'It was quite normal, really.' Cathy shrugged. 'Maids of all work were started off very young. There was a lot to learn, so we had to get on with it. I had to be there before dawn each day and I was lighting fires and dusting and going round cleaning and polishing everything in sight. I was good at it all, really.

I was a good little worker, I was praised by the other staff. I was promoted to taking breakfast in bed to the mistress and serving it in the dining room to the men. It wasn't a large staff, but it was a big house and they had us working like mad.'

Sofia tried to picture her friend at such a young age, scurrying around in some kind of drab maid's outfit and wearing her fingers to the bone for the sake of some grand family.

'It's cruelty, all that,' Sofia frowned. 'It's like living in the last century.'

'I didn't know any better. I didn't know anything else. I was an only child, my parents were both dead and gone. My Aunt Liz had taken me in and I lived on her small farm at the very edge of the Logan estate, and she had taught me from the very start what hard work meant.'

'Aunt Liz is also the one who brought up June?' Sofia asked, putting it together in her head.

'I'll get to that. Aunt Liz was harsh and gruff, and she worked me like a dog, but at least she took me in. I had nowhere to go and even though she wasn't the softest or kindest of souls, I did grow to be grateful to her. She wasn't that old, looking back, and maybe she resented having this orphan dropped on her. She taught me to tend to the chickens, fetch their eggs, wring their necks. She had me out in the fields doing all the work that I could manage at that age.'

Sofia didn't much like the sound of this Aunt Liz.

'Anyway, I grew up in the Logan household. I worked hard and felt almost like one of the family. Mrs Logan was kindly, really, at first. Mildred. And though there was a gulf between their place in the world and my own, they weren't cruel or horrible to me. And I was only a handful of years younger than their only son and the heir to the Logan fortunes, Christopher.'

'Ah,' said Sofia, catching a glimmer in Cathy's eye as she mentioned his name.

'Oh, he was a bonny lad, Sofia. My god, you should have seen him. He had everything! The world at his feet and this whole estate was going to be his one day. But he wasn't obnoxious or snooty. When he noticed me, scooting in and out of his room with jugs and basins, and lighting his fire for him, he was kind. He spoke to me almost like an equal. He loved to ask me about my aunt's small farm and the animals. He even loved to hear about the pigs! I had a pet pig I hand-reared one year. The runt of the litter. She was born in June, so that's what I called her. Christopher loved to hear my stories about how she was getting fatter and inquisitive and one day he even rode his pony up the hill to the farm to see her for himself.'

Sofia said eagerly, 'Go on then, you and this handsome lad fell in love . . .'

'I don't know whether we did or not. I think we were just young and excited and daft. We loved each other's company. We ran wild, really, in the grounds of that estate. It went on for miles! And there were woods and beaches and even caves in the cliffs. I never got much time off from my duties but when I did, I'd go off with Christopher. One minute we were children, running around being silly and just pleasing ourselves and then, all of a sudden it seemed, we weren't children anymore. And when we met it was in secret.'

'I see,' Sofia smiled.

'Well, it was wrong, really. I see it now. I wasn't really a grown-up. I just felt that way. And he was older. He was wrong to do what he did with me.'

'Are you saying he took advantage of your innocence?'

'I've thought about that a lot over the years and I don't think so,' Cathy said. 'I hardly know what I think. But suddenly there was the war starting and he was signing up to go straight off to be an officer. He was in love with the uniform and the training courses he had to go off and do. He strutted around showing off, delighting his father, old man Logan. I saw his mam's face, though. She was so upset and frantic with worry even though she tried to hide her feelings from the men. I felt the same, too, when he went marching off to war. No one – none of us – knew what he and all the others were marching off to.'

'D-did he die?' asked Sofia.

'Of course he did,' Cathy said bitterly, and reached for the ruby liqueur bottle and poured them another tot. 'He came back only once, on leave. Briefly. He was different. He had seen things he couldn't even explain to his parents. He told me a little more than he told them. There was this look in his eye I didn't like. It was as if he'd come back with something missing. His limbs were all still intact. He hadn't been injured. He seemed unscathed, really. But I knew there was something missing . . . inside.'

'Anyway, it was that brief leave he had when we went out on his old pony. We went all over the estate, through the fields and along the seafront. All the places where we had played as bairns. He built a fire in the mouth of the cave we had once made our den and we didn't even discuss what we were going to do. But we both knew deep down what was going to happen next. I drew him into that cave and I undressed us both in the firelight. What was I playing at, Sofia? I must have been mad.'

'How old were you? Fourteen still? Fifteen?'

'About that. It was wrong, I know. But I felt at the time like we had to do it. And it bloody hurt. He was clumsy and not very careful. It wasn't what I thought it was going to be like. And then he cried! I was under him and he was like a deadweight on top of me. We were wet and sticky and then his tears were plopping down on my face. None of it was how I had imagined and when he got up and started dressing again, his manner was brisk. He couldn't even look me in the eye. And all at once I felt I had made a mistake.

'And I also knew – it was strange but it was true – that something was stirring inside of me. We had made life spring up inside of me that afternoon. I knew already that I was going to have a bairn. It's crazy, but I knew straight away, before we even left that hidden corner of the beach . . .'

Chapter Eleven

Sofia watched as her friend went about her closing time chores. She rang the ship's bell and cried out, good-naturedly, waking up the drunken regulars from their mumbling stupors. 'Off ye gan! Get yersels home! Yer wives'll be waiting for yers!'

They murmured complaint but they took heed of her, as they always did, and went shambling to the exit. Bantering by the saloon door, both hands on her hips, Cathy looked like she hadn't a care in the world. She guffawed, throwing back her head to laugh at something some drunken old get had said. You would never know how, just moments before, she'd been spilling her darkest, most tender secrets to Sofia.

Ah, what a story she'd been unfolding! It spoke so much about the lack of love in Cathy's life. Going right back to the start she had been merely tolerated rather than cherished. She had been used and exploited rather than raised carefully to feel herself worthy of love. Sofia had always intuitively known this about her friend, but now some of the gaps in her story were filled and she understood her even better.

As the ragged old men were sent stumbling out into the badly-lit street, Cathy watched over them with a careful eye. She had so much to give. Her gruff, joshing manner hid the softest and most bruised heart Sofia had ever known.

'You're back! You're here!' The shrill cry broke the Italian girl's reverie. She realised that it was Cathy who was shouting out, her composure broken, her relief hopelessly evident.

Her daughter Junie had returned to the Robin Hood at closing time, bringing young Minnie with her. Minnie looking bedraggled and worn out after a day spent with the girl. Junie still looked more or less immaculate in her cerise and scarlet suit. Her hair was slightly awry, perhaps, and was her bright lipstick somewhat smudged? Her expression was petulant and almost peevish as she glared about the untidy and smoky saloon bar.

Cathy shooed out the last of her late-night drinkers and hurried over to tell her daughter: 'I was that worried about you!'

For a second Sofia thought she might reach out to hug Junie. The girl's basilisk stare stopped her in her tracks. 'I was just out seeing the town. Minnie here offered to show me all the sights. It just took rather a while, that's all.'

Minnie was beaming, glad to be credited like this. 'Ah, it's been a smashing day, hasn't it, June? I think we've both caught a touch of the sun.'

It was true that Minnie looked rather red, but it might just have been high spirits. Cathy frowned slightly and said, 'I think you should tell me if you're going to be out so late, Junie. I've been very worried about you.'

'Have you?' the girl raised her eyebrows. 'I'd have trouble believing that. You've got through all these years without worrying about me, haven't you? You've gone through all my life without hardly thinking about me at all!'

Minnie gasped at this and Sofia winced. She saw Cathy's face fall as she took in Junie's words. 'That's not fair and it's not right. You don't know what I've thought about and worried about all these years.'

'Well, I wouldn't, would I? You were never in touch, never a word from you.'

'I sent cards! I sent what I could! I wrote letters.'

June shook her head firmly. 'No, you didn't. I never had a letter or a card from you in all my life.'

All the air seemed to rush out of Cathy's lungs. The colour vanished from her face. 'What? But I did! I wrote loads of them. On your birthday, each Christmas, without fail!'

June was still shaking her head. 'They never came to me. Believe me, I'd have remembered. Nothing ever came for me. It was just me and Aunt Liz. She was the only one in my life.'

'She . . . she . . . must have . . .' Cathy seemed to have trouble getting her words out. 'She didn't give them to you. She never read my words to you. That . . . she . . . Aunt Liz . . . she kept me out of your life. Not even my letters.'

The girl's mouth hardened. 'They must have gone up the chimney. Everything you ever sent.' There was a tinge to her voice that was almost mocking and cruel, as if she still didn't quite believe that Cathy had actually sent her letters and cards over all those years. It was as if she thought Cathy should still suffer regardless, just in case she was lying.

'I swear to you, Junie, I sent word. I wrote. I sent money. Small gifts.'

'June,' her daughter said. 'My name is June.'

Sofia noticed that Minnie was hanging on every word. Why, she'd be storing up everything she heard here tonight. Every shameful morsel of gossip. She was kind-hearted, was Minnie, but she was a chatty thing. She'd spread this story far and wide. 'Minnie, I reckon your mother will be frantic. You'd best get home.'

'Ah, she won't worry about me, Mrs Franchino,' Minnie grinned at her.

'Still, I think you should go home now,' Sofia told her. 'We have to lock up. June will be tired.'

Reluctantly Minnie turned to go. 'Eeeh, June. It was a lovely day, wasn't it?'

June just nodded her head briefly, dismissing the simple-hearted girl.

'I'll be off then. I'm working here on the 'morra, ain't I, Cathy?'

Cathy simply nodded vaguely. 'Aye, hinny. See you the 'morra.'

She and June were staring at each other like they were locked in combat. They were like a mongoose and a snake, Sofia thought. If one moved too fast the other would make their deadly strike.

'And I better go as well,' Sofia told them. 'I forget, I've a long way back home these days. I'm not just in the next street anymore.'

Both mother and daughter ignored her.

'Aunt Liz wasn't as kind as she seemed,' June said at last. 'All my life she's been my whole world. She gave me everything she could. She dressed me up like a little doll. I owe her everything. But in the past few weeks I'm learning more and more. Her love that she showed me wasn't kind and it wasn't even loving. It was about owning me. It was about possession. She didn't really love me at all.'

Cathy's eyes were bright with tears as she heard June talk like this. The girl's voice didn't falter. She showed hardly any emotion. She said these terrible things almost in a monotone. 'Oh, hey now, lass,' Cathy said. 'I'm sure she did her best.' Even as she said this, she thought: What am I doing? I'm defending the woman who ruined my life!

'Do you know what she said to me?' June asked. 'When the truth came out? Just last week. She said, "You need to learn the truth. You're old enough now, June. You need to understand that I'm not your mother and never was. Your real mother didn't care enough to bring you up herself. She never had enough love in her heart to bring you up and she ran away from here. She left you with me and I've done what I could but you're grown now, and my job is done." That's what that dry old stick told me. Just out of the blue like that.'

Cathy cried out at the cruelty of it. 'Nay, lass? Really? That's what she did?'

Sofia was watching all of this very carefully from the sidelines, ignored by the two of them. As she watched June's face crumple and the tears come spilling down her face, she couldn't help thinking: it's too polished a performance, this. June's a girl who knows just how to put on an act. She's someone who knows how to twist people around her finger. And just look at Cathy, now! She was compelled – she couldn't help herself – she was flinging herself forward to embrace the girl as she sobbed.

June allowed herself to be gathered up by her mother. She seemed to shrink and become weightless and devoid of all strength in a flash. Her tears flowed freely and Cathy was crying too. 'You're here now. You're with me. You're with your mammy again . . .'

Sofia was frozen, watching all of this. Her heart should have been warmed. She should have felt touched at the sight of this reconciliation. It was what her best friend had been longing for.

Yet she couldn't feel any of those things. Sofia thought: this girl is a wicked liar. Cathy has fallen for every word of this. She's at the girl's mercy now and there's nothing I can say or do to help her.

Chapter Twelve

They settled into a kind of peace, then. Cathy led her girl out of the pub to her home at number twenty-one. She made them hot milk on the stove and watched her daughter drink it wordlessly at the table.

Noel came shuffling down in his ragged dressing gown and glared at them both appraisingly. 'All reet, honey?' he asked his wife and she nodded.

'Everything is just fine,' she told him. 'Our June was just out seeing the town today. She was getting to know the place.'

They both watched the girl finish her warm milk and she seemed much younger than she actually was. She yawned and something in the way she did it reminded Cathy of one of the cats that old Teresa used to have traipsing into the house. Now only a couple of those cats were left. There was Thomas, of course, who Cathy adored. But there hadn't been a new cat brought into their house for ages. Now Junie was here. Yes, she's my own stray little cat, thought Cathy tiredly.

'Can I go up to bed now?' the girl asked earnestly.

'You must come and go as you want,' her mother told her. 'This is your home now. You belong with us.'

Noel looked for a second as if he was about to mutter a complaint of some kind, but he resisted. Instead he carried the lit lamp into the hallway to guide June up the stairs. When she was away in her room, Cathy turned to her husband, trembling with tears. 'I've got her back under my wing, Noel. I never thought I'd see the day.'

'Well,' he murmured grudgingly. 'You've never told me the whole story of what went on, but I'm glad you're happy, lass.'

He sounded almost kindly, she thought. Like the child had brought out some tenderness even in his cankered heart.

The last trolley bus out to Seaham groaned and clanked as if every yard along the seafront was a huge effort. Sofia sat hugging her bag to her stomach and was glad there were hardly any other passengers and no one she knew. She was so used to people sitting down and talking, filling her head with idle chitchat. It was a friendly town where people chattered away without having to know you. As it happened, working at the counter of Franchino's, Sofia knew a vast number of people to pass the time of day with.

Tonight she was glad to be left in peace as the tram rumbled its way home, with the wires fizzing and buzzing overhead. In the gliding darkness she picked out the shapes of the dark cliffs and the softly silver horizon, far away in the North Sea. She felt peaceful and tired, her mind filled up with Cathy's worries and excitements.

She hardly had any time to think about her own life, and maybe that was just as well.

Coming all this way to Seaham, just to go home. She didn't feel settled yet in the bigger house Tonio had insisted they buy. He'd been saving for years and then gambling their deposit in card game after card game. Again and again he'd raised their hopes and blown them and left them with nothing all over again. Sofia had resigned herself to never having anything: to the idea that his terrible habit could land them with nothing at all one day. She had resigned herself to living forever in their cosy home in the Sixteen Streets. Why, in the end, she'd been happiest there, hadn't she? In the smoky confines of those streets, where she was just a few doors away from all her best friends.

But it was never enough for her Tonio. For years he had kept on staking everything they had – even the business which sustained them and kept them fed – on the hope of living somewhere much grander. The fool had made himself ill with all those anxious hopes.

Speaking of feeling ill, Sofia's stomach was churning as the tram came to a squealing stop. It was time for her to hurry off, but she felt queasy all of a sudden, just as she had earlier in the day.

As she dismounted she frowned, wondering what she'd eaten. That fish at lunchtime, had it been a bit off?

She walked stiffly and the sea breeze cooled her face and calmed her breathing. She headed home through the darkened streets wondering, what did that wave of nausea feel like? It was just like . . . it felt just like . . .

And all at once certainty gripped her.

Oh, not again. Surely I can't be?

But she knew it. She knew just when she had felt like this before.

Home again and she still wasn't used to setting foot through their doorway. The house was so big, and so grand. It was almost embarrassing. So much fancier than where they had come from, than anywhere she had ever lived.

'We only deserve it,' her old mother would say, quite gruffly. Nonna accepted the grandness of their new place as her due. Why, of course the Franchino clan – Sofia, Tonio, Bella, young Marco and their Nonna – should be living in what felt like a mansion overlooking the sea. They were a grand family and they had lived in the obscurity of the old back streets for way too long.

Sofia smiled to think of her ancient, indomitable mother hobbling along with the aid of her ebony cane. These days she went round acting like the queen of the manor and Sofia was happy to indulge her. The poor old devil had had a tough life.

We've all had a tough life, Sofia mused, as she headed through the quiet house to her messy kitchen at the back. Was everyone in bed already? She was used to there being more noise and more life in the place.

'Where's Dad? Is Marco in his bed? Where's Nonna?' she asked her daughter when she found her in the kitchen.

Bella was contentedly eating home-made ice cream at the kitchen table. She had a Ngaio Marsh mystery open on top of a heap of dirty plates and dishes and she was completely absorbed in her book. She looked up blearily at her mother. 'Oh! Hello!'

Sofia smiled indulgently at her daughter. Bella was a young lady now. She drifted in and out of the house like a restless spirit, usually dressed up like she was going to an elegant soiree. She favoured dresses and heels and taking hours to pile up her jet-black hair into a style she'd studied in some film magazine. She was so glamorous that Sofia's heart ached with pride for her. She seemed to live half inside a kind of dream world and the temptation was always there to warn her; to suggest that life could never live up to the way she imagined it. Bella had her own share of her father's crazy dreams. She took all of that from his side. She really needed to become more practical and down to earth. She could do with listening to her mother. Life wasn't all elegant dresses and impractical shoes and exciting novels. Sofia knew that for a plain fact.

'Everyone's in bed,' Bella told her. 'Marco was very good, for once. I thought I'd wait up for you.'

'That's very kind of you,' Sofia smiled. 'Good book?' She went to make black coffee. She was lucky: she could drink coffee as late as she liked and never miss a moment of sleep. As soon as her head hit the pillow she was away, every time. Tonight though, her stomach curdled at the prospect of strong coffee. Maybe weak milky tea would be best.

'I've not been able to stop reading all day,' Bella smiled. 'I was down on the beach and I barely stopped reading.'

'Were you with all those lads?' Sofia frowned. What could she do, though? All the lads and lasses here hung around together, down on the beach. The days were long and sunny. The beach was where they loved to congregate. But she knew her Bella was sensible. Look at her! She dressed like a duchess and she always took a book with her. How much trouble could she get herself into? She was a sensible girl, and her mother was glad.

'The whole gang was out. The Farleys. Everyone from Frederick Street. And that Minnie, whose parents own the fish shop, who works at the Robin Hood. She came down with that new girl. The one who Cathy threw the party for.'

'Oh, you've met June, then?' Sofia asked. 'What did you make of her?'

Bella pulled a face. 'I'm not sure. She wasn't very friendly. She was flirting with the boys . . . but there's something hard about her. Something tough and almost resentful.'

Sofia nodded, pouring steaming hot water into the teapot. 'Yes, I think poor Cathy's going to have her hands full, taking that one on . . .'

'Oh!' Bella gasped as if remembering something all of a sudden. 'There was a visitor earlier on. Someone knocking at the door at suppertime. Pa wasn't in yet and Nonna sent me to answer it while she was cooking.'

'Who was it?' Sofia asked. She felt a strange coldness in her chest, just for a moment. A sense of foreboding and she wasn't sure why. There was nothing about Bella's bright manner to make her feel worried. It was just someone calling at the door. What was so odd about that? 'Was it a bill of some kind?' Money was tight, of course. This place had over-extended them. Each month she had to be careful with cash when it came to paying the bills.

'He didn't even leave his name or a card or anything,' Bella shrugged. 'He said he was looking for you. He had come to call to pay his respects. He was a proper handsome looking fella. He had an accent.'

Sofia set down the kettle and she felt that coldness run right through her. That sensitive stomach ache she had felt earlier flared up suddenly much worse. 'An accent?'

'Italian,' Bella smiled. 'I wondered if it was someone you knew from home. From the old country.'

Sofia opened her mouth to speak and nothing came out. Her thoughts were racing as she watched her guileless daughter return to her murder book. 'This man,' she said, and her voice sounded strange and distant to her own ears. 'Was he wearing a fedora? Bella, listen to me. Tell me. Was this man at our door, was he wearing a black hat?'

Chapter Thirteen

In the days that followed, Sofia behaved as if she was being hunted. She kept going over and over the scene with Bella in the kitchen that night. Maybe there had been a mistake?

'Yes,' her daughter said, shrugging lightly. 'The man at the door was wearing a big hat with a large brim. Black and a bit dusty. So what? Lots of fellas wear hats.'

Sofia felt the world tilt on its axis. She rocked back on her heels and had to grasp the corner of the kitchen cabinet.

The man with the black hat was here! After all this time.

He was a folk legend. A figure of terror from a fairy tale. He was a vengeful spirit and that black hat could be a disguise for anyone who wanted to exact revenge. For many years Sofia had been expecting him to step out of the shadows of their past. Someone wearing that shaded hat was eventually bound to catch up with her and Tonio.

Oh, there'd been mistakes in the past. False sightings. Figures she'd glimpsed out of the corner of her eye and then had been so relieved to realise her mistake. And then there was that time – more than ten or more years ago – when she had been absolutely convinced that she had fallen into the deadly grasp of the man in the black fedora. But then he had just turned out to be some thug from Newcastle, and not Italian at all.

It hadn't been the Franchino family's past catching up with them after all.

Not that time, anyway.

But this . . .

Somehow Sofia knew that this was really him. Some dreadful instinct was kicking in and warning her. This man had caught up with them and found them at last. At long last, just when they had thought life was getting better. When they were living as if they were a bit more prosperous. Just when Sofia was thinking she might be pregnant again.

Oh god, she kept thinking in the days that followed, rediscovering a devoutness she hadn't felt since her childhood in Naples, please let it not be him. Please god, let him leave us alone.

She kept quizzing her daughter about the brief visit. 'What did he say before he went? Did he say he'd come back?'

Bella was perplexed by this whole carry on. She'd never seen her mother act so strangely. 'I don't remember exactly. He turned on his heel – he was wearing beautiful shoes. Hand-made, you could tell. I think he said he'd come calling again . . . he particularly wanted to see you and Papa again.'

Sofia swore softly under her breath. For the next week or so she flinched every time she heard the front door slam or the doorbell chime. At one point, when Tonio came breezing noisily indoors while she was cooking, she got such a shock she dropped a bottle of white wine vinegar on the kitchen tiles. The sharp scent stung her nostrils and she shouted at her husband in irritation.

At night she couldn't sleep. She had terrible dreams of murder and pursuit. Fed up with her unaccustomed tossing and turning, Tonio snapped on his lamp and stared at her questioningly. 'What's the matter with you?'

She bit her lip and couldn't tell him. She knew that he was prone to fretting and worrying even worse than she was.

When he was anxious his gambling habit got worse, in a nasty spiral that she was all too familiar with. Sofia had decided that Tonio didn't have to know about this visitation until it was absolutely necessary.

She could, however, tell her mother. Yes, Nonna might know what to do. Perhaps she might even throw back her head and laugh. 'Why, you daft young fool. It is just a legend! It's just a silly thing we say. There's no real danger from this man in the hat!'

She found Nonna in the long back garden, proudly tending her new little patch of flowers and vegetables. She sat in the sun shelling peas into a colander. The old lady shaded her eyes as her daughter approached and Sofia saw that her mother's skin was like faded, crumpled vellum. She had become so old, so quickly. Sofia had hardly even noticed, she had been so busy in recent years worrying out herself, about her husband, about this new house.

She sat down with her mother in the vegetable patch and asked her straight out: 'Do you still believe that one day the man in the black hat will come for us?'

Immediately the old woman stiffened. Instinctively her claw-like hand reached for the bulky crucifix that hung about her neck. When she looked at Sofia her milky eyes were wild. 'What? Is he here? Has he come at last?' There was a terrible note of fear in her voice. Sofia was used to her mother sounding indomitable. Why, she was the woman who took her silver-topped cane to those Johnston boys and broke the wickedest one's head wide open! She didn't fear anything at all, but now her yellowish skin had turned very pale. 'Tell me it's not true, Sofia.'

'I-I'm sure it's nothing,' Sofia stammered. 'But Bella told me she answered the door just the other night and . . . and he was standing there. In his hat, asking after me. With an accent as thick as nougat.'

The old woman crossed herself and swore in her native tongue. A curse so old and awful that Sofia could only half-understand what she was saying. Then all at once Nonna was struggling to stand. Colander and peas were left scattered on the ground as she reached for her cane. 'He's found us . . . He's caught up with us . . .' Then she started hurrying towards the house as fast as she could, hobbling along with her arthritic hips.

'Mama,' Sofia called after her, striding to catch up. 'I never meant to scare you. I'm sure it's nothing. I should never have said anything. It's nothing really, is it? It's just a silly story . . .'

But her mother swung round on her heel and her face was a rictus of fear. 'A silly story nothing! Are you crazy? He's come for us and I tell you, Sofia, we're dead! The whole lot of us! All the Franchinos are dead!'

'She blames us. She says it's all Tonio's fault, and mine.' Sofia shook her head miserably over her espresso. She was sitting in a booth at the back of Franchino's with Cathy.

'I'm sure it's all old people's superstitious nonsense,' Cathy tried to reassure her. Yet she remembered the last time that Sofia had thought she was being pursued by the legendary man in the black hat – all those years ago – and the immense relief she felt when it turned out to be a horrible mistake.

Sofia was almost on the verge of tears. 'This is all bloody Tonio's fault, you know. Just like everything! And just as ever, I try to shield him from the truth, and from the consequences of his stupid, stupid actions . . .'

'But . . . what did he do?' Cathy asked. 'What did Tonio actually do to cause all this fear of reprisals, all these years later?'

Her friend sighed. 'It was when we left Italy. Years ago. We had to sneak out. We had to run away. It was all down to Tonio and his gambling debts. He gambled with the wrong people, didn't he? The kind who never forget.'

Cathy tried to be logical about it. 'But you told me that when you absconded and left the country, you or he threw a dart at a map on the wall. Your coming to South Shields all those years ago, it was random! It was purely by chance. No one could ever link you to this part of the world. How would your enemies ever find you?'

Sofia looked bleak. She looked like she would never be reassured or consoled again. 'Yes, but what's this ice cream parlour called, Cathy? What name is emblazoned in pink and green at the front of this place? What do we call our successful business?' She put her face in her hands. 'What were we even thinking of? We were idiots! We have given ourselves away! We have drawn our deadly enemy straight to us!'

'I'm sure this can't be true,' Cathy frowned. 'I mean, the world isn't really like that, is it? Deadly vendettas and gangsters and suchlike? I mean, it just can't be true, can it?'

Sofia stared at her friend in amazement. 'Of course it is! Especially where we come from. Naples is even rougher and more frightening than South Shields, Cathy. And that's it! Our lives are over now. We are doomed!'

Chapter Fourteen

Unbelievable!

Cathy Sturrock could hardly credit it. If she wasn't seeing it with her own eyes she wouldn't have believed any of it.

But her husband – that bad-tempered crookback – was being kind to her daughter, Junie.

'I've never had a bairn of my own,' he shrugged lightly when she pointed this out to him. 'And this is the closest I'll ever get, isn't it? When I make her breakfast or take her a cup of tea in bed, I almost feel like her Da. It's a very strange feeling, and one I wasn't expecting so late in my life.' There was a dreamy note in his voice and Cathy felt exasperated. Was he doing this on purpose just to rile her up? Was he being sardonic, somehow, and putting on an act? But no, it all seemed genuine enough. Her Noel was actually fond of Junie! He couldn't do enough for her.

'Hell's Bells,' Cathy muttered. 'I wish you'd bring *me* tea in bed. And buying kippers off the van! I've never had that treatment! Fancy getting *her* special little treats!'

He gaped at her in astonishment. 'Surely you aren't envious of your own darling daughter, Cathy, love?' This was late one night as they sat with nightcaps and the radiogram playing, after Cathy had locked up the pub for the night. She was dead on her feet and in no mood for Noel's shenanigans.

'Of course not. I only want the best for her. And I should be glad that you've taken to her, Noel. I'm grateful, of course, that you don't mind that she's here in our home.'

Noel sucked on his woodbine and picked shreds of tobacco off his purple tongue. 'That lass can stay here just as long as she likes. She completes us, I think. She makes us a complete family at last.'

She raised both eyebrows at her husband, realising that he was in earnest. A tenderness she hadn't felt in some time crept over her as she remembered that loss he had suffered, just before they had married. His elderly, formidable mother had been carried off in the second wave of the Spanish Flu, not long after the end of the war. It seemed like such a long time ago, that gentle ending she had, but it was still so very fresh for her devoted son. In many ways Noel was a selfish beast, an impossible man, but there was a strange sweetness to him, way deep down, when it came to his affections. He would do anything to hide those feelings most days, but on occasion he would let people see how he felt.

The fact was, Cathy knew – or rather hoped, deep down – that the old devil loved her just as much as he'd loved his mam. Now it seemed that he was adding young Junie to the pantheon of females in his heart.

'I'm glad,' she told him, sipping her hot black tea. She'd added a splash of whisky, as she always did this time of night. 'That lass can't have had much love in her life. Aunt Liz brought her up and I thought she could be trusted to give her the love she never really offered me, but I don't think she did.'

'Poor June grew up with little love and now she feels like she never really belonged to anyone,' Noel observed. 'That's what she told me when we went down the lane the other night.'

His wife gave an audible gasp. The two of them had been out walking the lane together and she'd been confiding in him! Cathy couldn't help it, but she experienced a little stab of jealousy as she pictured them ambling along: the straight-limbed, slim young girl and her galoot of a husband. Why, they were closer even than she thought!

'I'm getting up to bed,' she told him, feeling woozy with exhaustion as she got up.

'Hey, you get your sleep,' he told her. His face was a picture of concern. 'And don't fret. June will come to see that you're OK in the end. She'll come to love her mother at last, I'm sure of it.'

Cathy felt herself clenching her teeth as she went up the stairs to her room.

On her way past Junie's door she gave a light tap. 'Is there anything you need, hinny? Are you settled?'

But there was no reply. The girl was most likely asleep already.

The next day, when Cathy saw her in the town centre, Sofia was in a right state.

'You're usually so calm and unflappable! You're the one I look to when there's some kind of crisis. You always keep your cool!' Cathy was shocked to see that Sofia had barely combed out her long, beautiful hair. She'd pulled a shapeless hat over her head. She didn't even have a scrap of make-up on.

'Sssh,' Sofia said as they rounded the marketplace, hurrying along in a shower that fell coldly on the market stalls. They took shelter under an awning as the rain briefly intensified, bouncing off the cobbled pavement. 'I'm trying to keep a low profile. I'm just getting some chores done . . . Eeeh, but really, I don't know whether I'm coming or going.'

Cathy stared at her. 'You'll make yerself ill! Is this all this business of the man in the hat still? Cathy man, that's daft. You know it is!'

Her friend looked very bleak. 'I talked to Mama about it and she's as worried as I am. She says that people at home never drop their grudges. They always find their victims in the end.' She grasped Cathy's arm and squeezed her in desperation. 'What am I gonna do? I've got bairns'. What if he hurts Bella and Marco? And . . . and the new one . . .'

'What?' Cathy couldn't follow her. 'What new one?'

Her friend bit her lip, realising she had let a secret out too early. 'I . . . I think I'm expecting again.'

'But that's wonderful news!' Cathy burst out, just as another spatter of cold rain fell against them. 'Are you sure?'

'Not yet, but I know. I know deep down. But it's not good news, Cathy. It's terrible news right now. Not just because we can't really afford it, but because of this man with the black hat coming after us. We're all in danger, I just know it.'

Some plain speaking was required, Cathy thought. Sofia was just getting hysterical. It was ridiculous! She was letting this damned superstitious nonsense spoil her life. 'You should be happy right now. You need to forget all this daft stuff.'

There was a strange, dark look in Sofia's eyes. 'It's not as easy as that. You'll see. You'll see that I'm right.'

'Rubbish!' Cathy tried to laugh it all off. 'I think we put these obstacles in our own way sometimes. Just to stop ourselves being too happy and too optimistic. It's a way of guarding against disappointment in life.'

Sofia gawped at her. 'Really? Do you really think people do that? On purpose?'

She nodded. 'Oh yes. We can spoil things with worrying. I've done it myself. I think we can poison our own chances of happiness. And we mustn't, Sofia! We must never do that!'

The rain was petering out and they prepared to dash through the puddles towards Ocean Road and Franchino's, where Tonio would greet them with piping hot coffee from his beloved machine.

We have to remember to be happy, Cathy kept telling herself. We must embrace all the lucky things that happen to us. It's all too easy to poison everything with resentment and regret.

It was something to live up to. Could she keep hopeful and block out her own anger and bitterness?

She could only try.

'Ladies! Ladies!' Tonio greeted them expansively as they stepped into the family café. 'How wonderful to see your beautiful faces! See? Your usual booth is empty and ready waiting for you.'

Sofia reached over the counter to kiss her husband.

'Oh!' he said. 'What's this for?'

'I'm counting my blessings,' she smiled. 'Cathy reminded me to.'

'Clever Cathy!' Tonio grinned and urged them to sit while he brewed them a perfect coffee.

Chapter Fifteen

He came to the house again when the old woman was by herself.

For several days he had been watching and waiting. He'd been wondering how to approach this problem.

He actually quite liked this town, the more he came to see of it. Parts of it even felt familiar to him. A port. A coastal resort. He longed to try the coffee and the ice cream at Franchino's, but he was wary of revealing his presence in the wrong way. It had to be just right. He had to make himself known in just the right way.

The old Nonna. That was the way to go about this whole thing. He would go and see her first.

He remembered her. Back at home. Years ago she had been formidable and gruff, living in the house by the church, right at the top of the hill. He could remember seeing her sitting on her front doorstep with a polishing rag, cleaning all her silver as she sat in the sun. Spitting and glowering at passers-by. She had known everyone in town.

Maybe, when he knocked on the door of this house again, she would remember him? That would make things much easier.

He was nervous. He actually felt nervous! A great big man like him, who prided himself on fearing nothing and no one.

Ah, but he had to get this just right, didn't he?

So he dressed himself up smart. His dark suit, his pressed cream shirt. He put a flower in the buttonhole like he was heading to a funeral to pay his respects. The landlady of the guest house on Ocean Road flapped around him. 'Oh, you do look smart, oh you do!' It had been his home for two weeks, this poky, dingy, cheap little rooming house, and he was sick of the sight of it. He despised her chirpy voice as she fussed around him. He barely answered as she went on about how he looked this afternoon. He felt like he was sick with nerves.

He walked all the way along the clifftop road to Seaham, pulling in deep breaths of sea air to calm him. The gulls whirled and screamed above his head and the surf boomed far below on the beach. The noise of the seaside actually calmed him and allowed him to focus on his visit.

This simply had to work. He had gambled everything on this. Everything he had.

He followed the winding street of the estate to the door he had visited just a few days ago, when that beautiful young girl had answered. Sofia's child! Fully grown and just as lovely as her mother had been. The sight of her had given Mario quite a turn, transporting him back through the years in an instant.

He'd almost been tongue-tied talking to her. Ridiculous!

Today, after watching them, after spying on them all, he knew that he was likely to find just the old Nonna at home, and that was exactly the way he wanted it.

He adjusted his hat brim against the glaring sun, took a deep breath, and marched smartly up the front garden path.

He rapped on the door and it took some moments for her to answer. He could hear her mumbling complaints as she took the chain off the hook and unlocked the door.

Then she looked up at the giant silhouette on the doorstep and in an instant her face was filled with fear.

He gasped. She was having a seizure, or something. Her ancient, wrinkled face was twisted up and her mouth had fallen open. She stepped back quickly and held onto the doorframe to keep upright. As he lurched forward to help, she squawked in fear.

'Get away from me!' she screeched when she could get her words out. 'Go away! Please!'

Mario was just as startled as she was. 'What? But . . .'

Her eyes blazed like a lioness whose cubs were under attack. 'Leave us alone! You have no right to be here!'

Well, she wasn't having a stroke and expiring on the spot. That was something, at least. She was leaning heavily on her cane and she was breathing hard, clutching her side and looking at him with utter loathing. She looked so skinny, tiny and helpless. Mario felt like he could crush the life out of her with both hands.

'You don't understand,' he said, trying to sound reasonable. He stepped into the shaded hallway, over the threshold. 'Please, let me explain . . .'

At this invasion of her home the old woman began screaming blue murder. In the old house, in the Sixteen Streets, such hullaballoo would have brought help running in an instant. But here the front doors were much further apart. All the fancy houses were detached from each other. Here in the new house there was no one to hear Nonna Franchino screaming for help.

Mario became flustered, slamming the front door behind him, which only made the woman scream more wildly. Now she was shut in with the brute! She knew that she had only seconds left to live.

'Why are you doing this to us? This persecution! It is wrong, wicked.'

His eyes widened with surprise, advancing on her as she shambled backwards down the hall. 'What?' She was talking Italian, he realised. Their shared Neopolitan dialect, though it sounded old-fashioned on her lips. She sounded like she was unaccustomed to speaking these words. It had been so long, he supposed. 'Please, calm down.' he counselled her.

'But you're him! The one we've been expecting! All these years!' Now she was getting hysterical again. She stumbled and gripped tightly onto her walking stick. 'The Man in the Black Hat!'

'What?' he said and snatched off his ancient fedora. 'This?'

She didn't look any less terrified of him now that she could see him properly. Thick, dark wavy hair. Deep, expressive eyes. Compassionate eyes. Though to her they just seemed terrifying. The fathomless eyes of the man who had come to murder her!

'We always knew this day would come,' she said, slumping as if the life was already rushing out of her.

He took one step closer. 'I don't know what you're talking about, old Nonna.'

It was one fatal step too close.

In an instant she raised her silver topped cane and brought it down, with every iota of her strength, upon the top of his bare head.

He woke up with the worst headache of his whole life.

Somehow the feeble old woman had dragged him into a kind of dining area and he was slumped on an upright chair. His hands and feet were bound with dampened strips of cloth and he felt like a hostage as he sat there getting his bearings.

He could taste blood. It had run down from his matted hair into his eyes and his mouth. She had dabbed some of it away and the bleeding had mostly stopped.

She had knocked him out cold, the old devil! She had clonked him on the head and knocked him out. And somehow she had managed to drag him into another room. She was clearly stronger than she looked.

He tried calling out to her but his voice was just a croak. Even trying made his head pound horrendously. What if she had done him some fatal kind of damage with that blow? The horrible irony of it almost made him want to laugh. To have come all this way and to be felled in such an ignominious manner!

'O-old Nonna . . . ?' he wheezed and croaked. He looked down to see dark red blood, almost dried and crusty now, all down his best cream shirt. Oh, he had dressed up so nicely to come here. His best clothes, carried so carefully from Naples, just for this day.

She was back all of a sudden, still gripping her ebony walking cane like she was about to clout him again. 'You'd better start talking,' she told him grimly. 'You'd better start explaining yourself, Man in the Black Hat. What is it you really want with my family?'

Chapter Sixteen

That night, Sofia had offered to lend a hand behind the bar at the Robin Hood because young Minnie had to work at her parents' fish shop. 'Betty's' had always done a roaring trade as the Sixteen Streets very own fish and chip shop.

'I'm worried that they're going to insist that Minnie works there full-time,' Cathy fretted out loud to her best friend. 'She may be a bit daft, but she's a good little worker.'

Sofia barely had pause for breath between pulling pints all evening. 'You could ask your June to step in. Train her up. Why, she could pay for her keep maybe!' Sofia nodded across to where Cathy's daughter was standing slap bang in the middle of the saloon bar, wearing one of her fancy outfits from the big store in Marwood, showing herself off for everyone to see. Sofia was quietly unimpressed by the way that girl acted like she was better than everyone else in the place. She had a right snooty nose on her, even if Cathy couldn't see it. All Sofia could see was her friend being taken for a ride.

Cathy shook her head firmly at Sofia's suggestion. 'Oh, I don't think working behind a tatty bar like this is for my Junie. I think she's made for other things.'

Sofia stared at the landlady, astonished by her words. Was she being sarcastic, or trying to be funny? 'tatty little bar? Cathy, you'd deck anyone who called this place tatty!'

She shrugged her bare shoulders and hoiked up her low-cut dress. 'You know what I mean. We mothers always want better for our children than what we have, don't we? I don't want Junie to have a life of drudgery like mine. She's made for better things.'

'Hmm,' said Sofia, not trusting herself to give a proper reply. She was thinking that Junie was already carrying herself about like a proper little madam and that a spot of drudgery might just do her some good. Why, the Cathy that she had known and loved for years would surely agree with that? It was ridiculous that she was indulging this shrill, over-dressed brat, just because she was her daughter!

Ah, Sofia realised with a flash of insight. But Cathy was new to parenting. She thought indulging her daughter was the best way forward. She thought she could keep her by seeing no wrong in her. It might endear the girl to her if she let her get away with murder.

Sofia thought: I'll have to warn her. This isn't the way to carry on.

But tonight at the bar of the Robin Hood wasn't the time for that heart-to-heart talk. The orders kept coming and coming, money changing hands and beer getting slopped on the tables and floor. The air was thick with fumes and smoke and ragged singsong.

The other astonishing thing about the bar tonight was the joy in the face of Noel Sturrock. It was almost as sinister as it was surprising. Sofia had never seen such a grin on his gnarled old face! What on earth was tickling that old devil's fancy, she wondered? He was even singing along with Aunt Martha as she plonked away on the yellowing ivories of the upright piano.

But it was the girl June who was behind that, too, wasn't it? She was right beside him, grinning and fluttering her eyelashes. What was the girl playing at with her bizarre behaviour? It was almost as if she was flattering the old landlord, which was perverse for more than one reason. Sofia shuddered to see her carrying on and laughing and joking with that old crookback.

She noticed that Cathy, as she worked, was keeping a watchful eye on the pair of them, too. They were capering and dancing about to the music now, making the other punters laugh. Junie was playing the hoity-toity young madam, consenting to dance a silly tango with the grotesque old goblin. They looked like a scene from a fairy tale, a pantomime, and Noel played his part to the hilt as the other drinkers clapped and chortled.

'What do they think they're doing?' Sofia said at last.

'Ah, they're just playing on.' Cathy smiled rather tightly. 'Isn't it marvellous though? Who'd have thought that Noel would get along so well with my . . . my daughter? I always thought he'd reject her out of hand. He was scandalised by her very existence, you know, and the fact that she was born out of wedlock. I thought it would have been a nightmare, the two of them coming into contact. They were like the two sides of my life that must never, never meet.'

Sofia poured them both a swift half of stout to fortify them both during a lull in the orders. 'Oh, yes?' she said, sounding quite sceptical. She had learned over the years never to accept anything that Noel Sturrock did at face value. There was always a subtext, always something shifty and nasty underneath. Cathy was daft and had forgiven him for all sorts of dreadful behaviour over the years. She loved her life here in the pub and these streets and so she forgave him for leading her a merry dance.

And what a merry dance he was doing now, Sofia thought. He was kicking up his skinny legs and lugging the weight of his hump around, whirling about the room, sweating like a demon out of hell. And here was Junie, skipping and twirling like Esmeralda the gypsy girl with her Quasimodo. Oh, what a terrible thought! Sofia almost laughed out loud at them.

She heard Cathy say, 'Yes, it's wonderful that he's taken to her. And she seems so fond of him, too. It's a kind of miracle. It's peaceful at home. No ructions, no tension. I have a happy home at last! My daughter is with us and Noel . . . why I think Noel might actually be content as a father at last! Who'd have thought it, Sofia? Isn't it incredible?'

All Sofia could do was smile and nod. But it was a sickly smile and a dubious nod. She didn't trust that old goblin or that young flibbertigibbet as far as she could chuck them. 'I hope you're all very happy,' was what she said to Cathy, and she felt like the words were glib and insincere as she heard them come out of her own mouth. 'I only want the best for you, Cathy,' she added. 'You deserve it.' She longed to add, 'And you deserve better than those two,' but she didn't, in the interest of keeping the peace.

As the last hour of opening whirled blearily by, Sofia felt like she was dead on her feet. What a bloomin' long day it had been, after a full shift at Franchino's with Tonio and now an evening behind the bar. The money was welcome of course, but she found herself becoming short-tempered, almost snappish with tiredness. She was hardly in the right mood to listen to Cathy opening her heart once more. But what could she say? She could hardly tell her to stop, to clam back up.

'My Aunt Liz hoodwinked me,' Cathy admitted as they stood behind the bar that night. 'That's how she got to keep my daughter. She stole her from me. That's why I'm quite so glad to have her back. That's why I'll indulge the girl. I'm just so grateful that she's here, after everything.'

'Stole her?' Sofia frowned. 'How can that be? What do you mean?'

Cathy's face was hard, and to Sofia's surprise she had to blink away sudden tears. 'It's true. She played a nasty trick on me. When I was weak and vulnerable. Just when I needed her most.'

'I don't understand,' Sofia told her.

'Her and that Doctor Marter. They tricked me. He was her fancy man. Well, I knew that already. He was a funny old stick. They would laugh and carry on every time he came out to the farmhouse. Why, even when I was a bairn and I had childhood illnesses, when I had my arm set in plaster once when I fell out of a tree, he came out to our house, which was unusual, really. We weren't grand and couldn't pay his rates. But there was slap and tickle going on, wasn't there? Him and my aunt.'

'Oh, really?' Sofia smiled. 'Was that so bad?'

Cathy's face darkened. 'When I was caught, when I was found pregnant, he was of course the one who came to ours to confirm it. Those were dark days. Christopher . . . well, Christopher was dead. They had just had the telegram. The whole of the estate was in mourning . . . Oh, it was awful, Sofia. I didn't know what to feel. Really, I think I was numb. All I could feel was this twisting in my guts. It was new life, twisting away in there already. New life that really had no right to be there . . .'

They watched Junie link arms and dance on the bare boards with that ridiculous fool Noel Sturrock. All the while, Sofia was listening carefully to the tale of how June's birth was handled and how Cathy was hoodwinked by her nearest close relation and her fancy man, Doctor Marter.

Chapter Seventeen

It was a drizzly night by the time Sofia made her way back home, all the way to Seaham. Her head was buzzing with the story that her best friend had told her. She was tired and almost too worn out to feel anything much, but still her heart went out to Cathy and what she had suffered because of her aunt.

Sofia couldn't imagine being deprived of her own child, Bella, or her son, Marco. If anyone had ever come to separate her from them, she would have fought tooth and nail. She would have died trying to cling onto the bairns. Both had barely been out of her sight for more than a day at a time.

She would feel the same about the new baby, too. The life that had ignited inside of her just recently, like a tiny pilot light flickering away . . . it was something she was carrying very carefully. She would defend it to the death, she just knew it. This was the way she had been brought up.

Having to relinquish her child . . . She couldn't even imagine what that must have felt like. It made her admire Cathy and her strength even more. But at the same time, it made Cathy seem almost like a stranger to her. She could not imagine how it felt to be Cathy. Not at all.

'I was up in the pudding club and Christopher was dead,' Cathy told her. 'The telegram had come and his mother had read it out to all the staff of the big house. We had never seen her like that before, white and trembling with rage. Her life was over then, the old woman. I call her old woman, but I suppose she was about the age I am now?' Cathy had blinked and frowned, working out the sum, looking back through the years. 'She blamed him, you know, her husband. Old Henry. She never spoke to him again, as far as I knew. She told him – I heard the argument myself – that he'd sent Christopher off to his death. He'd driven him away with all his talk of obligation and glory and doing his duty. Like so many Christopher had marched off to the front . . . and he never came back.

'All this while I knew I had to do something about the fact that I was carrying the dead man's child. I was nothing but a child myself . . . how could I know what to do? So I told Aunt Liz everything. She got the story out of me and she was brisk and practical. She knew just what to do.

'I would work until I started to show. I would leave service before anyone could guess what the matter was. We'd have to scrape by, with less money coming in, but Doctor Marter – her accomplice in this matter – could help out there. She was always vague and bashful when she mentioned the doctor. When he was in the house, she blushed almost like a girl. He came to examine me and confirmed my state and my due date. Together the two of them stood there and they told me what they had decided. They told me my fate . . . And the big idea? Well, their plan was that I would hide at home in the farmhouse and Doctor Marter would deliver my child there when the time came. But it would be very hush-hush and they would pretend that it was my Aunt who had borne the child.'

'What?!' Sofia had gasped at this point in the telling. 'How could they get away with that?'

Cathy shrugged. 'It's remote. Everyone minds their own business. My aunt was unmarried and yes, there'd be a scandal, but what did she care? There was a baby involved and suddenly I could see in her eyes: this was something she was longing for. Ah, I should have seen the danger signs right then, but I didn't want to. I just wanted a way out of my difficulties. I wanted someone to sort it all out for me.'

'My god though, the subterfuge!' Sofia said. 'It must have been so hard, being confined all those months.'

'It was better than still being up at Morwick Hall,' Cathy frowned. 'That was, by all accounts, a terrible and gloomy place after Christopher's death. The life and heart went out of it. Like I say, his mother ceased talking to his father and Old Henry stalked about like a shadow of his former self. Then, one night, only weeks after they had the news about Christopher, his father took out his service revolver and blew out his own brains. Apparently you could hear the shot ring out all through that massive house in the early hours of the morning. It woke everyone up and they all knew at once what had happened. No, I look back and I'm glad I was hiding away indoors on my aunt's small farm . . .'

Sofia went round collecting dirty glasses after they had chucked out the evening's drinkers. She had watched Noel Sturrock escort his fresh-faced step-daughter home, the two of them promising to make a fresh pot of tea for Cathy. It was hard to think of anything other than the dark tale that Cathy was unfolding.

'What happened then?' Sofia asked her. With bones aching tiredly, she longed to go home, but at the same time she wanted to hear the rest of the tale.

'Well, with the old man dead now, we knew it was even more imperative that we keep the secret of my baby from the old Missus up at the hall. Why, she had no one left in her family. Wouldn't she come to take my child away as soon as she knew all about her? There was no heir, there was no one there apart from that bereaved old woman. She became a grasping, acquisitive old bitch, too. I knew that she would take anything that she considered her own, and that would include Christopher's child.

'As the months went on, my aunt and the doctor married. He was free and so was she and it was a quick and easy thing for them to do. They seemed happy in their union and in the lies we were all telling.

'Then, after what seemed a lifetime, I gave birth. I had been in that house, locked away indoors through the summer months, hiding away my huge belly . . . and it was worse than I could have imagined. I really bloody suffered. The Doctor was there, ready at hand . . . ready to lance that baby like a gigantic bloody boil. I remember how excited my aunt was. She was kind, mopping my forehead cool, doing everything her new husband told her . . . I felt like I was drifting out of my own body as they fussed round me. Then the pain would rock through me and I'd be back again . . . screaming and cursing the whole lot of them. Cursing at poor, dead Christopher for putting me in this position in the first place. I used language that I didn't even know I knew!

'Then at last, the baby was born in the first light of dawn and it was so peaceful all of a sudden. I know every mother says that their baby was perfect and looked like an angel, but it was true. She was so calm and lovely. She wasn't even red and screaming. My Junie was just perfect and my heart was hers from those first seconds, and I held onto her and I held on hard. My Aunt came and told me I was a brave and clever girl, but I mustn't be stupid. I mustn't be selfish. I must let her take the baby from my grasp. She had to be cleaned up, she had to be checked . . .'

'Oh . . .' Sofia heard herself moan, frightened for the girl in the story. Knowing what was going to happen next.

Cathy nodded. 'Yes, they cleaned her up, my Junie. They wrapped her in a beautiful soft blanket that Aunt Liz had crocheted through the long, quiet evenings of my confinement. They let me take another look at her. Doctor Marter had washed himself up after stitching me. He was drying his hands and rolling down his sleeves. He told me, 'You've done very well, Catherine. You have done your aunt proud.'

'And then . . . then they told me that it was best if I never held her ever again. I must make the break with my daughter, right then and there. No bond must be allowed to form between us. Junie belonged to my aunt now. It was all for the best. Couldn't I see? The ruse that had begun as something to hide my shame, it must become a permanent state of affairs. Junie was the child of my aunt and her new husband. That was simply how things must be. And I must go away and relinquish my rights to belong to her or to love her. Once I had recovered and could stand again, I had to go away. At once. That's what they told me then. Before my Junie was even two hours old . . .'

Chapter Eighteen

When Sofia arrived home much later than planned that evening, her whole family was waiting up for her.

She knew it as soon as she put her key in the lock and swung the door open. Stepping into her spacious hallway she was aware of the whole place somehow holding its breath in anticipation. She knew: something was going on.

'T-Tonio . . . ?' she breathed.

Oh, please don't let it be anything terrible, she thought. I cannot cope with anything like that tonight. Nothing more! Even just listening to Cathy's horrible story had taken it out of her tonight.

'We're in the kitchen,' he called back. His warm, reassuring tones. 'It's all right.' How reassuring was he, really, though? It seemed awful, but he had led them to the brink of financial ruin again and again. Sofia had long ago found herself ceasing to rely on him for reassurance.

Tonight there was such a curiously suspended feeling in the house she was glad to hear his familiar tones.

She took a deep breath and went into the kitchen.

There they all were. The faces of her beloved family. Young Bella and Marco, her mother, Tonio. They looked watchful, sharp, slightly worried.

'What's going on?' Sofia demanded.

'We've got a visitor,' Bella told her. She was glad that her daughter was quick to give her a straight answer. 'He came back again.'

'Who did?' Sofia asked, just as she realised the truth. 'The Man in the Black . . . !'

Before the words were out, she clapped eyes on him. There he was. At the far end of her fancy new kitchen. He was sitting on a high stool and his famed black hat sat crumpled on the breakfast bar beside him.

He looked utterly defeated. His tangled dark curls were dampened with . . . hold on – was that blood? Yes! There was a thick trickle of dried blood down his handsome face. Someone had tried to dab it off.

He still looked handsome, though. Some distant part of Sofia's mind was noting the fact that her long-dreaded nemesis was a very attractive man.

'What's been going on?' she asked tightly as she locked eyes with the person whose coming she had feared for so many years.

And in that instant, as she stared at him and he stared back, the penny finally dropped.

'*Mario?*' she said. 'Mario Grapelli . . . ?!' She almost choked with surprise. 'It's you? You're the Man in the Black Hat?' This question she chased almost immediately with, 'Why are you bleeding? And who tied you up . . . ?'

It took some minutes for all the truth to come out.

Sofia's ancient mother ruefully admitted to being the young man's vicious assailant. But all she'd done was defend herself and their home. As far as she had known, he could have been a rapacious attacker, come to murder them all. That was what they had all been expecting of the Man in the Black Hat, wasn't it?

'But that was all superstition!' Tonio cried, breaking out the grappa as Bella struggled with the knots that bound their visitor. 'Wasn't that just a mixture of nightmares and that silly Winnie reading the tea leaves?'

The women had to admit that yes, that was true enough. They had built this imaginary figure into a terrible spectre over the years. It had hardly any basis in truth. 'Yet there he was! Haunting our front porch in a black fedora. Naturally I attacked him.'

'You could have smashed his skull in,' Tonio worried, passing a strong drink to the injured man.

'His wounds are superficial.' The Nonna tossed her head and reached for her own glass. 'Come on, he deserved it. Terrifying an old woman like me!'

So far the young man hadn't said a word. His dark eyes moved warily from one member of the Franchino clan to another. Who knows what these crazy people would try next? At last his gaze settled on Sofia as she examined the gash on his forehead.

'Mario Grapelli,' she sighed in wonder. 'Is it really you?'

He nodded and winced as the movement gave him a stab of pain. He swallowed down his drink and said, 'It's taken me years to find you all. But here I am.'

Tonio was looking shifty. 'Look, if you're here for revenge . . . if you're here to take back your money . . . everything I won from you . . . it was all quite legitimate. I won those games, I won everything.'

The younger man laughed. 'And you swept the table clear of all our money and ran off into the night with it all wrapped up in our mother's tablecloth!' He shook his head, chuckling. 'Yes, my brothers and I . . . we still all laugh about that night. You were so shifty! So pathetic! So terrified of us all! Off you went haring into the dawn and as far as you were concerned, you had cleaned us all out.'

Tonio looked utterly shamefaced as all his family turned to look at him. 'I know. I was so much younger then. And I regretted it almost immediately. All of Naples was buzzing with the story that your lot wanted revenge. That my life wasn't worth living if I stayed in town . . . !'

Mario shrugged. 'We had to save face somehow. Of course they put stories around. A bit of fear to spoil your fun.'

Sofia's mother looked like she wanted to batter him again, for all the worry and distress his family had caused. 'We fled the country because of you! Tonio here was so convinced that you'd have us murdered in our beds!'

'An over-reaction,' Mario said carelessly. 'You have to take these things with a pinch of salt. However, our mother was more furious and murderous than all the rest of us. Apparently you had also won the hand-written recipe for her mother's fior di latte? The best ice cream recipe in the world? She said her sons had no right to give that away . . . with it went all our family's good luck. She was very superstitious, bless her heart!'

Bella cried out, 'The fior di latte! So that's where the recipe comes from!'

Tonio nodded unhappily. 'To be honest, it was your mother and what she said about that recipe that made me think our lives were forfeit. It was about more than money. We had stolen your family's honour and birthright.'

'Quite,' smiled Mario. 'The older families take those kinds of things very seriously. But quite honestly, did you really think we would pursue you for all this time? And try to kill you, even now? Over the winnings in a game of cards and an ice cream recipe?'

Tonio shook his head vigorously. 'No, of course not! Not all these years! But . . . these women, you know. Someone said they had seen you and your hat in the wet dregs of tea leaves at the bottom of a cup . . . or someone had a terrible dream . . . and you must admit, Mario, you cut a formidable figure in that hat and coat.'

He smiled. 'I'm not here to hurt anyone. I'm not here to cause trouble. I came merely to find old family friends, that's all.' He smiled warmly at them all, still wincing with the pain in his head. Then he turned to look at Sofia in particular. 'And most of all I wanted to see you again, Sofia. My first sweetheart. Do you remember all that time ago? When we were kids? I had to come and find you, to see how life is treating you.'

Sofia found that her throat was parched and that the grappa Tonio had poured her wasn't helping at all. All she could do was stare at the rumpled, bleeding, handsome Mario Grapelli and nod hopelessly.

Yes, I do remember. I remember all too well, she thought. He was my very first sweetheart. The first boyfriend I ever had. And this night, all these years later, she realised with a shock that she still felt exactly the same way about him that she always had.

Tonight The Man in the Black Hat was bringing her a feeling of a different kind of dread.

Chapter Nineteen

She knew that Tonio was lying wide awake beside her.

It was so late by the time that they all got to bed in that big house with the sea view, but even so Tonio was still tossing and turning. She knew that her husband had all kinds of terrible thoughts racing round in his head.

Eventually he clicked on the shaded lamp on his bedside table and stared at her.

'What?' she said, sounding peevish and tired.

His worn, familiar features were softly lit a gentle shade of apricot. How worried he looked! His combed-over strands of black hair were hanging loose like errant threads. She would have liked to snip them off.

'You still are in love with me, aren't you?' he asked, in a parched kind of voice.

'What?' Sofia couldn't believe they were going into this in the middle of the night. 'Look, Tonio, we're both worn out. We've had late nights, talking and talking downstairs and you've been drinking that terrible grappa with Mario . . .' She could hear her voice growing fainter as she spoke into her pillow.

It had been three late nights in a row with their Italian visitor. Mario had become one of the fixtures and fittings at the Franchino home. Both Nonna and Tonio were longing to hear all about the people and the goings-on in their native town. Who'd have thought it? Sofia wondered, as she brought out dishes and trays of food for them. Years had gone by without anyone even mentioning Naples. All this time, it turned out, they had been craving to know all the local gossip. Mario was only too happy to supply all their needs.

Now that the drama was off and the danger had dissipated, he had become an easy and affable guest in the Franchino home.

Their young daughter Bella even seemed to have something of a crush on him. And no wonder, really. He was as handsome now as when he had been her age, back when Sofia had known him. Sofia shook her head smiling at the sight of her daughter just about sitting at his feet. She was drinking in stories about the families and the customs of Naples – all the old legends that Sofia had thought she herself had forgotten. Bella had never shown any such interest in her roots before.

Mario had held them all spellbound for several nights, returning for dinner and sitting up late. Even Nonna was charmed and had the grace to look shame-faced whenever the fellow's head wound was mentioned.

Now Tonio was out of the bed and pacing around on the fitted carpets of their new bedroom. His wife propped herself up on one elbow to watch him. He looked tubby and rumpled in his striped shorts and vest. There were stains of spaghetti sauce on that vest, she noticed. 'Tonio . . . ?'

When did he start looking so middle-aged, she wondered? When did her husband become this barrel-shaped short-arse with hardly any hair? Sofia frowned at her own horrible, treacherous thoughts and hoped fiercely that she hadn't let her own self slip quite as far. She kept trim and smart, didn't she? Surely people looked at them and said, 'Why, look at that beautiful girl with that tubby old guy! He's done well for himself, hasn't he?'

Oh, she hated the superficial part of herself that thought like this. It was a horrible burden, really. What did looks matter at all? Since her earliest recollections, Sofia had been told she was beautiful. It had blighted her life and she had become hopelessly vain in every way. She tried to suppress it and be a nicer person, but these values had been instilled in her from birth by her mother. 'And I was a great beauty too,' the old woman always added. 'All the women in our family have been beauties and we always, always marry beneath us.'

'Tonio,' she told her husband. 'Come back to bed. What are you doing?'

'He's so handsome and charming,' Tonio was muttering. 'I hate him!'

'I thought you liked him!'

He glowered at her. He was deadly serious, she saw. 'I do! I did! But then I keep thinking. He was your first love. He deserves you. He should have taken you from the start. Of course you'd prefer him to me. I only stole you away! I don't even deserve you . . .'

'You're raving!' she told him. 'You're talking rubbish.'

'It's true,' Tonio sat down heavily on the bed. 'I made you run away with me. I took you away from all the competition.'

'What?' She felt confused and longed just to return to her dreams. In fact, now that she thought about it, she had been dreaming of the hot, beautiful, soft golden light of Naples. She had drifted back there in her sleep and it had been incredibly vivid. 'Look, Tonio, you took us away from home and we came here because we were in danger. They would have murdered us all – even Bella – if we had stayed.'

He looked at her very glumly indeed. He looks as if he is making a confession, she realised. 'I thought . . . I thought that might be true. The danger. There were mutterings and there were whispered threats in the street. There were notes put through our door, remember?'

'Yes,' she said. 'You were really frightened for us.'

His shoulders sagged. 'I was more frightened for myself. Of losing you. I knew . . . I knew any day that someone . . . perhaps Mario Grapelli himself . . . would snap his fingers and you'd go running back to him. They were my enemies in more ways than one.'

Sofia shook her head. 'I would never have gone off with him. Not before we were married and certainly not afterwards!'

Tonio shook his head. 'I saw you look at him tonight. I see there's still a glimmer there. There is still a spark there.'

'A spark!' she cried. 'Don't be ridiculous!'

'I know spark when I see one.' He lay down gently, turning away from her. He stretched out like one used to chronic back pain. After a pause he said, 'You would tell me, wouldn't you? If you really felt a spark?'

She groaned. 'I don't feel a spark! I feel nothing for him, Tonio. I promise you. I feel absolutely nothing like that for Mario. He's just someone who's never grown up. I would never be interested in him again. I promise!'

Tonio seemed gratified by that. Her outburst sounded just impassioned enough. He grunted and became more pacified. Then he wished her sweet dreams, as he had done every night of their marriage, and then he started snoring.

Now it was Sofia's turn to lie awake while her thoughts went churning around.

Next day saw her sitting with Cathy for one of their regular coffee meet-ups in their booth at Franchino's.

The ice cream parlour was busy and for a second Sofia felt guilty that they were taking up space that could be given to regular customers. However, she had a lot to talk to Cathy about, so her heels remained dug into the worn lino.

'I think I didn't tell him the truth, Cathy,' she said, peering through the aromatic coffee steam at the zinc bar, where her husband worked tirelessly, chortling happily with his customers. 'By the time the conversation was over, I realised that there was more than a shred of truth to his fears.'

Cathy was surprised. 'This Mario person? So you're still carrying a torch for him?'

'Oh, I don't know . . .' She twisted her face and even then she looked bonny, Cathy thought enviously. 'I really don't know. Maybe Tonio has put the seed of doubt into my mind? Maybe he's done that himself? But I was dreaming about Naples all night. That's three nights on the trot. I'm remembering things about home that I had assumed I had long forgotten. It's like a part of me is coming awake again . . .'

Cathy sipped her coffee. 'This sounds dangerous to me. I'd be very careful, if I were you.'

Sofia nodded. 'I really don't want to rock the boat. Why would I? I thought my life was perfect and settled . . . and . . . and why would I want to bring myself any trouble?'

'Exactly,' Sofia smiled. 'So anyway, when do I get to meet this famous Man in the Black Hat?'

'Tonio has promised him fish and chips and a pint of beer in a proper English pub,' Sofia smiled. 'What better place to take him than to Frederick Street? We'll be there tonight and you'll get to cast your eye over him then.'

'Oh good,' Cathy grinned. 'It's been too long since we had a handsome man call by . . . I'm looking forward to meeting Mario Grapelli!'

Chapter Twenty

With all the recent carry ons, Minnie was feeling a bit left out.

Her sunny nature was dimmer than usual as she chopped up tatties in the back of her family's chip shop.

'It's all going on for everyone else,' she complained to her mother. 'Everyone else's life is so exciting! And look at mine. It's just the same as ever. It's all grafting!'

Her mother, Betty, had better things to think of than her daughter's many dissatisfactions. She was running her own business and had things like deliveries to deal with, not to mention all the paperwork and the totting up that she had to do almost every day. The whole thing was a headache and some days she even wished she'd never opened her own fish bar. Over ten years of this! Sometimes she felt that her skin was turning into crispy golden batter.

'At least you haven't got rats,' Minnie shrugged. 'That's the rumour about the Franchino's ice cream parlour.'

'Rats!' squawked her mother.

'Aye, they're having to lay down poison, apparently.' Minnie shuddered.

'Don't talk to me about vermin!' her mother warned her. 'I've enough to bloody well think about!'

Today she was quietly fuming about the fact that someone had vandalised the newly-painted sign above the shop front. After years of putting up with the same old sign in which the beautifully scrolling letters of 'Betty's' had been rudely supplemented with the prefix, 'Swetty', a new sign had been paid for. But almost as soon as it was up, some little bugger had repainted 'Swetty' on the flaming thing. Somehow the insult felt even worse for *still* being misspelled. Some ill-educated ruffian really had it in for her! They had defaced her premises and her sign that she'd been so proud of. Yes, maybe it was vainglorious of her to name her fish and chip shop after herself, but why shouldn't she? Betty had scrimped and saved and worked and slaved for years for this triumph.

Did people really think she was sweaty? The thought mortified her. Yes, maybe she went a bit bright and red when she was behind the hot bar and working over the bubbling vats of beef fat. But she was clean, wasn't she? She had a bath regularly on a Sunday. How dare they go casting horrible aspersions like that!

People didn't like to see others getting above their stations. Not round here. That's what it was. You had to know your place and stick to it.

Personally, her money was on one of the Farley boys as the perpetrator. It was just the kind of thing those larksome lads would do. She could imagine one sitting on the other's shoulders in the middle of the night, scrawling on her pristine new sign. Those buggers! They thought they could get away with anything!

These were the thoughts whirling around Betty's head as she dipped and floured all the fish fillets ready for the evening fry. Her ham hock arms wobbled as she worked and she paused to give her pits a furtive sniff. Fresh as a daisy! No fear! How dare those cheeky buggers call her 'swetty'!

'Are you even listening, Mammy?' Minnie was staring at her.

'Eeh, Minnie love, think about someone else's problems, won't you, lass? Ha'way. Get them bloody tatties cut. Look at the ones you've done! There's not two the same size and shape!'

It was true that Minnie's mind wasn't on her job. She was too busy thinking about her friends and the fun she imagined they were having. Her new friend June had bragged about getting dolled up for the evening, and how old Noel Sturrock was letting her play at being a barmaid at the Robin Hood for the evening. Well, Minnie would love to see how that worked out! June was so fussy and smart – just how was she going to cope with a job that Minnie herself found tiring?

I hope they're not thinking of replacing me with June! She worried that the Sturrocks were about to make their pub an exclusively family affair.

And then there was Bella Franchino. Another friend who Minnie saw at the beach and the park, hanging around with all the lads these summer nights. Well, right now she was full of talk about their visitor from Naples. Apparently he was a right bonny bloke. Middle-aged apparently, but he was a real looker, like someone off the talkies. Apparently he was gonna be down the pub tonight as well. Sofia and Tonio were planning to take him on a typical night out in the Sixteen Streets to see how he liked it.

Eeeh, I'd love to get a look at him! Minnie thought, chopping away at the potatoes. She was getting all her frustrations out by hacking away at the spuds. But isn't it awful? When life's going on all around you yet you can't be part of it?

It always seemed that way for Minnie Minton. She never really felt like part of the pack. Something always set her apart. Was it the way she looked? Or the daft things she said? She could never be sure why she was never really in the swing of things. Mind, but June was! Why, June was brand new to

South Shields and already she was one of the most popular lasses on the town!

It was a talent, Minnie thought. Popularity was something invisible. It was something you either had or you hadn't. Some people just glided through life and everything went marvellously for them – people who were sparky and confident like June, others who were beautiful like Bella and her mam, Sofia. But if you were a bit lumpy and slightly boss-eyed like Minnie then you had no chance. (Oh, yes, she had seen herself on a photograph and had been horrified to see that she was cross-eyed. 'Why didn't you tell me, Mammy?') What you ended up with was a lifetime of running after everyone else. You ended up never quite catching up with the others.

And no one ever came running after you.

However, after opening up time that evening, when the fat fryers were bubbling away and the room filling up with steamy heat, Minnie got a nice little surprise.

As usual there was a queue straight away. Right from its first weeks of being open, over ten years ago, Betty's fish bar had been an immediate hit on Frederick Street and there was a queue forming each evening before the door was flung open. Her mammy was raking it in, but the way she fretted over the paperwork, you'd never think the place was a success. For herself, Minnie was proud of what they had achieved here at the top of the street, in the premises that used to be the tripe shop.

She stood ready at her usual station, ready to hoik out shovelfuls of golden chips from the dripping. Betty stood at the till with her pad of paper, taking orders. They had served only about three lots of customers before a small group appeared at the counter, all dressed up and beaming at Minnie. This was her nice surprise! She gasped in sheer pleasure as she realised that the Franchinos had popped in – the whole family! Bringing with them this exotic Italian visitor.

'Mario,' he introduced himself, leaning over the metal counter and shaking hands with both Minnie and her mother. 'Am I having the honour of meeting Swetty Betty herself?'

Betty flushed an even darker red at his mistake. 'Someone defaced my sign!' she shouted at him. 'I'm Betty Minton. There's no "swetty" about it, thank you very much!'

Mario's face fell, seeing he'd upset her. 'I'm sorry.'

Sofia swiftly repaired the damage. 'And this is Minnie, who works with me sometimes at the Robin Hood and is a friend of Bella's.'

Minnie's face lit up as Mario gave her his full attention. 'Oooh!' she managed to say as he kissed her hot, greasy hand.

'*Che Bella*,' he told her, which she took to be a lovely compliment.

All the Franchino's were dressed in their Sunday best on a Friday night. The little lad of twelve was in his Sunday best with a tie, and he was looking at the visiting cousin with hero worship in his eyes. The whole family was clearly making a night of it and starting off with a fish supper from Betty's. Even the old Nonna was there, got up in her finery – which made her look like she was off to a funeral.

'We haven't seen you lot round here since you moved off to your fancy new place in Seaham,' said Betty accusingly. 'We all thought you'd got too grand for us!'

The old lady snorted, inspecting the battered fish fillets on display. 'Hmm, we are very grand! Yes, we're slumming it, coming back here. But Cousin Mario wanted to see where we used to live. This is it, Mario! This is the awful dump where we had to scrape by for years. It's rougher than home, isn't it? It's shabbier than Naples!'

But Mario Grapelli simply smiled and his whole rugged face lit up, Minnie noticed. 'I love it here,' he said, fanning himself against the heat of the fish bar. 'It feels just like home.'

Tonio Franchino bellowed with laughter. 'It's a warm, sunny night. We can sit at the top of the hill by the graveyard to eat our suppers. You get a smashing view of the docks from there, Mario! We'll polish off this lot and then we'll get to the Robin Hood. Cathy and all of them will be keen to get a look at our famous Man in the Black Hat!'

Minnie helped her mother serve the Italian family and, as they paid up and left clutching their hot paper parcels, she felt her excitement ebbing away. That was the highlight of her night, just as usual. Watching other people having fun!

'Stir your stumps, lass,' her mother growled at her. 'There's the rest of the queue to serve, y'knaa.'

Minnie turned away, scowling. She contented herself with thinking a single rude and rebellious thought. Her mother *was* bloomin' sweaty, no matter how much she protested that she wasn't.

Chapter Twenty-One

'What? The sea? The sea here, in South Shields?' Mario was laughing as he stood cradling his pint of warm beer. 'It's very nice, yes. Is so cold! I put my feet into the waves and I was frozen! And it's grey . . . is brown! Is all the wrong colour for the real sea.'

Standing behind the bar, Noel Sturrock was bridling with temper. This foreign fellow had been bragging all night and he longed to take him down a peg or two. 'All right, Mr Smarty Pants. What colour is the sea in your precious Naples then?'

'Aaah.' Mario's eyes took on a distant look. 'Is the bluest blue. Is green and blue. Is deepest and lovely. Is like jewels. All the colours there are beautiful. Is like being in another world.'

'And I suppose everything here is dull and gloomy?' Noel growled.

Mario looked around to see that he had all the late-night drinkers at the Robin Hood hanging on his every word. He smiled broadly. 'Why, this place has its very own charms. Is lovely in own way. My friends have shown me around. I see everywhere and I like it.'

'Aye, well,' Sturrock said, looking surly. 'You should mind out for putting down the place you're visiting. The locals can take against foreigners, you know.'

Tonio Franchino had heard enough of the old landlord hectoring their guest. The hunchback was bellicose and bitter. He hardly ever had a good word to say to anyone. 'Cousin Mario is hardly a foreigner now. Just a short while here and he feels quite at home. Just like we did, all those years ago. South Shields is so welcoming to its visitors!'

Noel was scowling as Aunty Martha struck up another tune from her strictly limited repertoire on the old upright.

'More drinks!' Tonio cried, shelling out for another round.

He was spending a lot of money tonight, his wife thought to herself. It was as if Tonio wanted to show off his largesse to Mario. He wanted to seem like a hale and hearty type of guy: the kind who knew everyone and who everyone liked. Usually that persona was the one he adopted in his own ice cream parlour. Everywhere else, Tonio was a good deal more shy and diffident. Tonight, though, he was drifting to the piano to join Mario in song.

What . . . ? Sofia blinked and saw that Mario had gently displaced Aunty Martha at the piano stool. She was blushing as he flattered her out of the way and pressed his broad, strong fingers down on the ancient keys. Now he was playing something familiar. Tonio was at his side and they both clearly knew the tune well because they began singing at the same moment. Their deep, loud voices rang out clear as bells in the smoky room.

Tonio singing out loud like that! Fancy that! Accompanying Mario, their voices blending rather tunefully. If only Sofia could put her finger on the tune. She smiled as she watched them draw the attention of everyone at the Robin Hood. Even her Nonna was enjoying herself, muttering tunelessly along with the aria.

It was an old operatic piece. Something that Sofia would never be able to name, but it stirred an odd, nostalgic feeling in her . . .

Then Cathy was standing beside her, smiling broadly. 'Yer handsome visitor's proving to be quite the hit!'

'Oh, Cathy!' Sofia shook her head. 'It's been the strangest thing. I've never seen him for years and years. I'd pushed the very thought of him out of my mind, if truth be told. Along with all the faces of all the people I ever knew in Naples. And now here he is! Just look at him, singing with Tonio . . .'

'I am! I can't help but look!' Cathy laughed. She couldn't help staring at the broad column of his throat, revealed by the open neck of his shirt. He looked like he'd been carved out of marble. To Cathy's eyes he was like one of those statues out of the old art books come to miraculous life in her saloon bar.

'It's been a lovely visit,' Sofia admitted. 'It's brought back all kinds of feelings and memories. Even Bella is interested in hearing about home. And then, when we took him to Franchino's . . . you should have seen his face! He looked around like he was in wonderland. Tonio gave him a frosted glass dish of our best handmade ice cream. He even put a sprig of mint on top of the melting cream and that great big strong man looked like he was going to weep . . . '

Cathy rolled her eyes. 'You lot are all so sentimental!'

'Mario said he hadn't tasted the like since his old grandma had died, and his mother. The Grapellis are much fewer in number than when we left and they've lost a lot of what they had. It's all rather sad. My heart goes out to him.' She was staring as he sang, slowing the song right down as he reached the final mournful bars.

Cathy was studying her friend very carefully. 'He's reminding you of how you used to feel about him . . .'

The Italian girl waved this suggestion away. 'I was a bairn, then. I didn't know what feelings were. Not compared with what I know now, about love and ties and family. But he does remind me . . . of how it felt to be young.' Her eyes were brimming with bright tears as she confided in her best friend. 'And it hurts, Cathy. Did you know that? It hurts to be young. We forget that. Is all pain and heartache and growing pains. And then it hurts again to remember all of that. It hurts when you remember and you miss those growing pains . . .'

Cathy stared at her friend. 'Being all philosophical! Sofia – I think you've had one too many of those fancy liqueurs tonight.'

'Maybe I have,' Sofia laughed. 'But maybe it does me good to be reminded of things like this. I've been feeling bloody old and tired lately, with all the changes and all the work. Why am I working so hard?'

'Because . . .' Cathy pulled a wry face. 'Because you people are ambitious. And your husband is a hopeless gambler, too, of course. You have to keep on working as hard as you do in order to provide for your family . . .' Cathy was never less than honest with her friend.

'I'm tired,' Sofia said firmly. 'And I need to start feeling like myself again . . .'

Her train of thought was interrupted by a kerfuffle going on at the piano. Noel Sturrock had interrupted the Italians' song. One moment he was carrying a trayful of drinks to one of the tables, next thing he was bellowing at Mario to stop playing. 'We've had enough of that awful dirge! Ha'way, fellas, give it a rest! That's not the kind of tune that we want in here! You're spoiling the bloody mood!'

The rest of the drinkers in the saloon would have disagreed with him. Noel knew only too well that they'd been lapping up Mario's impromptu show, but he wasn't having some foreign fella coming in and taking over. What a bloody show-off!

'Is all right.' Mario got up and smiled good-naturedly at the landlord. 'Was very rude of me to push my way in.'

'No, no, no,' cried Aunty Martha, flapping her long, sensitive fingers in protest. 'Oh, you sing so beautifully! And you played so much better than I do . . .'

'Shut up, Martha, and play,' Noel snapped at her. 'Give us "My Old Man Says Follow the Van". Something cheerier, at any rate! This isn't the place for bloody opera!'

Aunty Martha humbly did as she was told and soon the bar room was merrily singing along. Mario returned to the Franchinos and quietly finished his pint, smiling ruefully.

Cathy Sturrock had a few choice words for her husband.

'Who does he think he is?' Noel growled. 'Bloody Eyetie! Showing off in my pub like that!'

Cathy glared at him. 'I think you'll find it's *my* pub, Noel. These days the Robin Hood is all mine. You signed the tenancy over to me, if you remember, because you couldn't be bothered with all the work anymore. And you've got no right to berate anyone under my roof, no matter how much opera they sing!'

Noel was mutinous and cross as he turned to leave. He'd leave his wife to clear up the place herself. 'Are you coming back home, Junie?' he asked the young girl, who had watched enthralled from the sidelines all evening.

'I did think you were right to tell that Italian fella off, Uncle Noel,' she told him as they returned to number twenty-one Frederick Street. 'I can't bear boastful types like that. What was he like? Saying the sea here was brown and horrible! Saying there was no colour here, not like his precious Naples!'

Noel was gratified that Junie was taking his side. 'I know! Horrible man!'

'If he's so keen on bloody Italy, he should have stayed there,' June said firmly. 'There's nothing wrong with South Shields. I think it's lovely here.'

'Aah, you're a good lass,' Noel told her, leading the way into the dark hallway of their home. 'Look, why don't you stop calling me Uncle, eh? It sounds so strange. If you like . . . you know . . . you could even start calling me . . . *Da*? What would you think of that, young Junie . . . ?'

Chapter Twenty-Two

The next morning Minnie Minton couldn't wait to get up and out, in order to find out everything that had gone on at the Robin Hood. She had missed it all – as usual – working at the fish bar till closing time.

She banged on the door at number twenty-one and a yawning June answered her. Her friend was in casual clothes but she still looked immaculate. She wrinkled her nose as Minnie bustled into the house. 'Phew . . . what do you smell of?'

'I can't get the reek of beef fat and batter out of my hair,' Minnie admitted cheerfully. 'I have to wait till bath night tomorrow.'

June pulled a face. 'I think we should get to the public baths this morning, don't you? I'm not going about with you reeking like a fried supper.'

'I'm not much of a swimmer . . .'

'Ha! You don't have to be. The whole point of the baths is to wear a revealing cossie and swan about for the lads to stare at.'

'I don't have any kind of cossie, let alone a revealing one!'

In the parlour they sat down with Cathy and Noel and a vast shiny pot of tea. 'Morning, Minnie, lass,' Cathy, smiled. She was glad that June seemingly had a loyal and devoted follower in Minnie.

'Do you have a swimming costume Minnie could borrow, Cathy?' June asked her mother.

'Swimming?' Cathy smiled. 'That's a good idea on a warm day like this. Yes, I'm sure I can dig something out . . .'

Noel was leafing slowly through the huge newspaper, glaring at the girls as he laboriously turned the pages. 'Just you's be careful,' he counselled. 'I don't agree with young girls running about in public with hardly anything on.'

'Noel . . .' Cathy said, with a roll of her eyes. 'They'll be perfectly safe.'

'There are some funny buggers out there,' Noel snapped. 'It's best not to put temptation in their path.'

'Thanks, *Da*,' June said, picking up her teacup and smiling at him primly. 'We'll be sure to be careful.'

'Aye, well, see that you do,' he said, with a slow and gratified smile. At least someone was talking respectfully to him. And there! She had called him *Da*. Quietly, diffidently – but she had definitely called him 'Da' for the very first time.

The fact wasn't lost on Cathy. 'W-what did you just call him?'

June smiled very sweetly. 'I called him "Da". Is that not right? It's just that he asked me to, last night after the pub closed and . . . well, it just seems natural for me to do so.'

All at once Cathy looked confused. She looked from June to Noel, who was acting as though butter wouldn't melt in his mouth. 'You asked her to call you "Da"?'

He nodded. 'Aye, she feels like the daughter I never knew I was missing for all these years. It's like . . . like suddenly we're a little family. That's what it's like, isn't it?'

Cathy took a sharp breath. Then she asked June, 'Well, wouldn't you feel better calling me "Mam"? Would you like to call me "Mam", then?'

Her daughter looked at her with slightly widened eyes, as if this was an entirely novel idea. She seemed to consider the matter carefully. 'No, if you don't mind . . . I'll carry on calling you "Cathy". At least for now. Is that all right?'

Cathy gulped down her disappointment. 'O-of course. You must do what you feel like, Junie . . .'

'*June*, remember,' her daughter smiled. 'Junie was a baby's name. Now, would you mind looking out that bathing suit for Minnie? I'm sure she won't mind if it's rather old-fashioned. Everyone's eyes will be on me, not her!'

The old baths on Derby Street looked like a palace or an old castle to June's eyes. There were towers and gables and a tall front entrance. Once you were through the turnstiles after paying your coin at the little wooden counter, the place became a bit more lively and less formal. The echoing spaces within rang with shouts and delighted cries and whooping. The thunderous noise of the churning water sounded like the North Sea itself was being held captive inside the grand building.

Minnie was looking worried and so June linked arms with her, finding their way to the ladies' changing area. There they had to put their clothes on a hook and hope that no one made off with them while they were swimming.

'Aren't you looking forward to a bathe?' June asked. 'And getting all of that grease out of your hair?' She was yanking off her own blouse and skirt, carefree and laughing in the small cubicle she had chosen for them. 'You'll soon see – the whole world doesn't have to smell like fish and chips!'

Minnie unrolled the towel and the costume she had borrowed from Cathy Sturrock. The costume was like something from the early twenties, with ruffled legs and fabric flowers sewn onto the chest. It smelled strongly of mothballs. 'I think this must have belonged to old Ma Sturrock,' she frowned, holding it up.

'Ah, never mind that!' June urged. She was unhooking her bra and revealing her breasts to the room. Minnie's eyes went out on stalks. The girl had no shame! She didn't care that there was no door on their cubicle and just anyone could see her if they cared to look. Minnie's face was scalding as June shed the last vestiges of her clothes and stood entirely naked on the green tiles before her. 'What?' she asked, seemingly perplexed by Minnie's stare. 'Have I got something you haven't got?' She laughed at Minnie's prudishness. 'Come on! We're all lasses together here!'

Minnie couldn't help staring at the perfect shape of the girl, though. June was, in her eyes, absolute perfection. She was like a pint-sized goddess in the changing cubicle, dragging on her skin-tight costume and snapping the shoulder straps neatly into place. Her breasts were perky and pointed, her bottom was round and full. There was absolutely nothing to pick fault with. She was the luckiest girl alive.

Minnie, on the other hand, knew she looked dreadful in the saggy, slightly wrinkled vintage outfit borrowed from Cathy. Even without the benefit of a mirror anywhere in the changing room she knew she looked a sight.

'Ah, never mind!' June grinned, yanking on her rubber bathing cap. 'Just jump in and keep underwater and then no one will ever see what you look like!'

June scooted through the disinfectant foot bath, sloshing through the brownish yellow slop, and Minnie reflected that her new friend perhaps wasn't as kind as she might be . . .

'Ooh! It's absolutely heaving with fellas in here!' June cried as they emerged into the cavernous hollow of the pool itself.

'It's Saturday,' Minnie mumbled. 'We've come on the busiest day.'

'Oh, lovely!' June sighed, taking in the spectacle of all that tossing, sparkling, bright blue water teeming with sun-burned male limbs and torsos. Legs kicking spasmodically and powerfully, arms thrashing water into white spume. Boys and men of all ages were dive-bombing and surging, dashing along the wet tiles at the sides. They were dunking each other and larking about and having themselves a high old time.

June looked thrilled at the sight of all this boisterous chaos. She looked like she couldn't wait to dive right in. Minnie, on the other hand, was filled with dread.

'Oh, there's those Farley boys,' June said as they scurried along the slippery tiles to the shallow end. 'See? They've brought their younger brother and they must be teaching him how to swim. The fat one, look. Is he daft, do you know? He looks a bit simple. Oh, but aren't the other two lovely looking! Look at the little shorts Tony's wearing! That's daring, eh, Minnie?'

Minnie hardly knew where to look.

Soon they were joined by Bella, who was wearing an equally daring continental-style two-piece swimsuit. Her hair was up in a cap like June's and she looked just as bonny as ever. 'Hello, you two!' she grinned, hurrying over to the pair of them. 'I thought it would be cooler in here today, out of the sun, but no luck! With all these people in here it's like being in a big pan of boiling potatoes, bubbling away together!'

June laughed at this. 'A few of these fellas seem to have potatoes stuffed down the front of their bathing trunks!'

Minnie was shocked at her coarseness, but Bella just laughed. 'Have you seen the Farley boys yet?' she smiled.

'Let's go over and talk to them!' June suggested.

Suddenly Bella was remembering the scene in the pub last night. 'Hey, your old uncle Noel was pretty rude to our visitor Mario last night. And to my dad, too! Stopping them singing and shouting his mouth off . . .'

June gave a carefree shrug of her pretty, bare shoulders. 'He's not my uncle, actually, Bella. He's my da'. I've accepted him as my very own daddy now. What do you think of that, eh?'

Minnie took note of Bella's surprised reaction, before dashing over to the ladder and lowering herself into the murky green shallow water. If she crouched down here maybe no one would notice what a fright she looked. But by the heck! Wasn't the chlorine in the water strong? Her eyes were smarting and running with tears already.

Chapter Twenty-Three

After the baths, the usual thing was to get a mug of hot Bovril. June turned up her nose at the very thought as Minnie explained the ritual. 'It's just the thing, when your hair's still wet and it's chilly out. You see everyone standing round, sipping their drinks, milling about with their breath puffing out, and it's delicious.'

June shook her head and swished her smooth cap of damp hair back and forth imperiously. 'Well, it's hardly chilly outside today and I can't bear that awful drink. What do you think about going for a frothy coffee?'

They latched onto Bella, who was leaving the baths at the same time they were. She was a bonny girl, but there was no side to her. She had a truly sweet, unspoiled nature. So much so that, when Junie cheekily said, 'If we tag along with you, will we get a coffee on the house?' she simply laughed and agreed that yes, they ought. As her guest at Franchino's they'd surely get free drinks. June nudged Minnie at this, as if she'd somehow tricked or outwitted the girl.

As they wandered through the sunlit streets from Derby Street to Ocean Road, Minnie allowed herself to consider the misgivings that she was having about her new best friend Junie.

Was it possible that the girl from the north country was less nice than she had originally supposed?

Minnie's own ardent need of a best friend, and her complete and utter trust in anyone who started to behave like one, might perhaps have blinded her. But as the days and weeks of their friendship went by, even Minnie was starting to detect slight flaws in young June's character.

Wasn't she a little bit brittle, snappish and touchy? Didn't she always like to have her own way? Wasn't there just a touch of cruelty in her laughter, and hadn't she said some dreadful things to Minnie herself, all under the guise of making silly jokes? Sometimes the immaculate and ladylike June could be downright nasty.

Oh, but it felt both good and daringly disloyal to be thinking such thoughts! Perhaps it was the lingering sting of chlorine in her eyes and throat that was making Minnie think awful things about her friend. She had had such an unpleasant time at the baths. There had been nothing enjoyable at all about the experience. Except perhaps – and here she allowed herself a small, secret jolt of pleasure – those brief moments of seeing June standing there in the buff. Unashamed and perfect and laughing and joking like she hadn't a care in the world. That little moment had made the whole thing worthwhile for Minnie, in ways that she would hardly dare articulate.

Then, all of a sudden, the three girls were at Franchinos and Bella was pushing open the heavy glass doors, babbling away about the pistachio ice cream that her father had made the week before. They were greeted with the usual fragrant, steamy atmosphere and a chorus of hellos from a bunch of familiar faces, including Tonio's, behind the counter. Bella's father was in his usual monogrammed pinny and he absolutely glowed with pride when he clapped eyes on his daughter.

'Look how beautiful you look! Shining from the bath! Just like when I used to put you in the sink to wash you at the old house. Remember that? Being bathed in the scullery? Ah, not so long ago!' Tonio was almost weepy at the thought of his baby girl being all grown up.

'Hush, Papa!' she laughed. 'I've brought my friends and I've promised them coffee on the house. Is that all right?'

Only Minnie noticed the slight wince he gave at this. 'Of course! Nothing but the best for my daughter's lovely young friends. And they mustn't pay a penny!'

'Maybe we could try some of this pistachio ice cream that Bella's been telling us all about?' June put in. 'It sounds out of this world.'

'Of course! Of course!' Tonio laughed, and started busying about at the coffee machine.

The girls occupied a corner booth, eating ice cream and chattering away for an hour or more. Bella stayed long enough only to eat pistachio ice cream with them – it was a delicate, subtle flavour that made June wrinkle her nose, undecided whether she liked it or not. Minnie exaggerated her own pleasure to make up for June's lack of enthusiasm. Bella shrugged and smilingly gathered up their used dishes and tiny spoons. 'I must go and help my da',' she said. 'He looks run off his feet. See you later, girls!'

Once she was gone, Minnie gently upbraided June. 'You were getting it for free . . . you could have been a bit nicer.'

June looked scornful. 'Did it taste nicer for being free? No! I had to be honest, Minnie. In fact, it was rather nastier than I told her. There were funny bits in it and they made it taste bitter to me. We'd have been better off with plain vanilla, I think.'

'Still,' Minnie said. 'It was given to us kindly.' She was glancing around as she spoke, keeping an eye out for any of the rumoured rats. Probably they'd all been killed by now. Or maybe it had just been malicious gossip?

'So what if it was given kindly?' June scoffed. 'You are too used to blindly accepting second best. That's what's wrong with you, lady. You don't believe that you deserve anything at all and so you're just glad of any scraps that come along . . .'

Minnie was nodding thoughtfully at this, thinking: She's not wrong, is she? And the same is true of friendship, too . . . But then she shook her head, pretending that she still had ears clogged with swimming bath water.

'They must be worth a bob or two, the Franchinos,' said June musingly, more to herself than Minnie. She gazed around at the silver mirrors and the art deco fashionings of the parlour. 'It's rather sophisticated in here. More like somewhere you'd expect to see in the big city.'

'Like the big city near where you grew up?' Minnie asked.

'Morwick?' June had built the little market town up into a wonderful fantasy version of itself whenever she described it to the gullible Minnie. 'Well, that isn't a city exactly, but it has very sophisticated, swishy places. I'm used to going to very fancy places, you see.'

'I bet you are,' Minnie smiled, secretly thinking: And that's what's made you so downright snooty. Again she tried to stamp out these little cinders of rebellion that kept glowing in her thoughts.

'I wonder if it's all their money that this cousin of theirs, this Mario, is after . . .' June frowned. 'It's a long way to come just to say hello. Just to have a holiday. He must be after something, mustn't he?'

Minnie said, 'Bella thought it was revenge! The whole family thought he was a gangster at first, out to do them all in.'

June's face lit up. 'How thrilling! Did they really think that?'

'Apparently it's the kind of thing that goes on in families like theirs, where they come from. Vendettas!'

At that very moment – as if magically summoned by being talked about – Mario Grapelli arrived through the door, with Sofia Franchino dressed in her best fur-trimmed red coat. The two of them looked a picture, standing by the counter as Tonio fussed round them. Both tall and good-looking and happily laughing at some story Tonio had begun telling them.

June was watching them carefully, her eyes narrowed. 'I wonder why he's here. It's all a bit fishy, I think. Don't you, Minnie? Don't you think there's more to this than meets the eye?'

Minnie was slurping molten sugar dregs off her coffee spoon. 'Hmm? Oh, I shouldn't think so, June. He's just here to see people he used to know. What's so suspicious about that?'

'Don't you know anything?' June rolled her eyes at her friend. God, but she was a dimwit. June was almost at the end of her tether with Minnie. Just look at how lumpish and hopeless she'd been at the baths! It was an advantage to have a less-than-attractive friend at your side, to make yourself look better and to make her feel glad and grateful that you'd chosen her as your pal. But really, there were limits!

June sighed and continued watching as Sofia and Mario went to take a table in the middle of the room. 'When someone comes out of the past like that there's usually a good reason for it. And that's usually something to do with money or violence or . . . *sex*. That's what I reckon.'

Minnie stared at her friend as if she was talking a foreign language. 'How did you get to be so clever?'

'I read a lot,' June said. 'And I listened to the woman who brought me up. The woman who I thought was my mother. She knew all about human nature. She knew *just* what people were like, and she warned me. I grew up not trusting anyone. There's always another story under the one you think you know. That's always true, Minnie Minton.'

Minnie gave her friend a sickly smile. 'To be honest, I prefer a simpler view of the world. I prefer to see the best in people.'

'Then you are a fool,' June told her.

Chapter Twenty-Four

Mario kept asking Sofia, 'do you remember this?' and 'do you remember that?' At first the questions amused her, especially when they brought back funny little details about life in the old country. The smells of the streets after rainstorms, say, or the gory and grotesque forms of the produce on the fish stalls in the streets. She found that she could remember all these things only too well! Even the sound of Mario's accent had her recalling sharp little moments and pictures that she had stored away many years ago.

These small promptings of his could irritate her, too. As the days of his visit went on and on, she began to feel somewhat badgered by his attentions.

This lanky, loping man in the open-necked shirts. He swaggered through the streets of her town like he owned the place. He wore his fedora again, atop his tangle of dark hair, and she wondered now at how she had ever found him intimidating, even terrifying. He was just Mario: the first man she had ever looked at and felt true, grown-up desire.

She felt like his little questions were directing her attentions back to those times, insistently, day after day. It was starting to irk her. She felt that she wanted to drop the act of being polite hostess and yell at him: 'Just leave me alone, Mario! My life is here now! Can't you understand?'

That Saturday she kept him moving. From a visit to Tonio at the ice cream parlour, to the heights of the town from where they could get a view of the sea and Wallsend. She kept her visitor moving and kept distracting him with views and titbits of stories she knew about her adopted town. When they were looking at the spread-out tumbled rooftops of town, she found herself explaining that South Shields had been a port ever since the Romans had lived here. She warmed to her theme because she loved this story. It was the tale of how Italians had always lived here, first among the many races and cultures that thronged here in this outward facing harbour. 'The whole world was welcomed here,' she smiled at him, a warm breeze ruffling her fur collar about her face.

Mario looked at her and thought how lovely she looked. He was only half-listening to her quaint lecture. 'Huh, Romans,' he shrugged. 'How typical of them. Boastful, show-off Romans. They get everywhere.'

She laughed at him. 'But don't you see? It was such a great comfort to me when we first came here. Knowing it was a place that our people had been coming to for so, so long.'

He shook his head, smiling. 'When you came running here. Running away from me . . .'

'We thought we were in danger,' she said archly. 'Tonio feared for our lives. My mother was convinced we'd all end up with a knife in our backs.'

Mario pulled a strange face. 'Your husband feared he'd lose you, yes. He took you away from me. He whirled you away. He told me this again, just the other night, when he was drinking. We were playing cards and he said: "I took her so I could be sure of keeping her."'

Sofia's smile curdled in the warm salty breeze coming up from the harbour. 'You played cards with him?' She turned and led the way back down the hill, crossing the tramlines and the cobbled streets. 'Oh god. Why did you play cards with him? You know he's hopeless . . .'

'I don't have much money for him to win from me,' Mario laughed. 'We played for pennies only. It was just the fun of it, and he wanted to get things off his chest.'

'I knew I shouldn't have let you sit up alone so late, the two of you . . .' She shook her head like they were errant boys.

'Mostly he was showing off . . . about winning you. Taking you away from me. He was so proud of himself. "I may not be handsome and strong like you, Mario. But I won her, didn't I? And I kept her."'

She was scandalised by this. 'That's what he said to you? In that very tone? Like he was crowing? Like I was his . . . possession?'

Mario looked her in the eye and nodded firmly.

'Damn him, the fool,' Sofia muttered. She kept quiet as they wandered through the sunlit lanes. Her plan was to reach the Sixteen Streets and to show him the little house that they had lived in for so many years. Somehow it had seemed important that he see it. She felt the need to make him appreciate how well they had done for themselves. She wanted Mario to see the improvement in their lives, from the tiny two-up two-down near the Robin Hood to the sprawling house with a view of the sea where they lived today.

Somehow it felt a little like hollow boasting now, as they reached her old street and she pointed out which door had been theirs for so many years. There was a new family in there now, who she only knew to say hello to. Both the mam and dad worked down the docks at the Biscuit Factory. The Dodds, they were called. A nice family, by all accounts.

'This was your home,' Mario smiled, gazing up at the white net curtains. 'Where you spent those years with Tonio and bringing up lovely Bella and Marco. It makes me sad, really.'

He rubbed his eyes with his palms and she thought: oh come on, now. Surely he isn't wiping away a tear?

She tried to distract him. 'Can you smell the Biscuit Factory?'

He closed his eyes and breathed in deeply. 'Oh yes . . .'

The aroma was intoxicating. Sweet, molten, buttery biscuits. To Sofia it was the very scent of home. The gentle, syrupy pollution came rolling up the hill on a daily basis. 'Is lovely,' Mario said. 'Do you know what it reminds me of?'

She looked at him questioningly.

'Confetti,' he said. 'That sweetness. Do you remember?'

All at once she did: sugar-coated almonds in pastel shades of pink, lilac and blue. They had called them confetti. They were given out in little bags at weddings as favours. Yes, the sweetness of the biscuits on the air was rather like that old, nostalgic scent of the confetti.

She looked at him. 'You never married, then, did you? You never found someone of your own.'

He turned away, almost shyly. 'I never married, no. And now it's too late. Life is over.'

She followed him as he walked down the sloping street. 'Don't be ridiculous! You're no kind of age. You're about the same age as me! We're not decrepit yet!'

He shook his head and whipped off his dusty black fedora. He whirled it around his head in a theatrical gesture, as if he could encompass the whole of the Sixteen Streets, all of South Shields and the vast world beyond. 'I have almost given up,' he admitted. 'I have so much to give. So much love. But I am ready to give up all hope, Sofia.'

She didn't know what to say to that.

'I'm going now,' he told her.

'What? Where?' She was startled. He was marching away, back in the direction of Westoe Road. 'Where are you going?'

'Back to my guest house. I want a quiet time tonight. I am rather thick-headed after last night and the pub. Thank you, thank you, for showing me round the town. And remembering with me. Thank you, Sofia.'

Without a peck on the cheek or another word he was off then, hastening down the way.

She felt oddly bereft for a moment and then told herself: snap out of it, woman. You're being ridiculous.

Early that evening she found herself alone in the kitchen with her mother.

The old Nonna was shrewd as a harpie.

She reached up and grasped Sofia's chin in one claw-like hand. She gazed so deeply into her beautiful eyes that her daughter flinched. She knew that her mother could always read the plain truth there. She had always been able to look straight into Sofia's soul.

'You're pregnant!' her mother gasped. Her face lit up with delight. Then a flicker of darkness crossed her face. 'And you're falling in love!'

Sofia turned away in fright. 'What? What are you saying? You're crazy!'

Her mother wouldn't let her go. She was like a terrier with a stolen bone. 'You're expecting – don't lie to me! And you're also falling in love. But the man who gave you the baby . . . he isn't the one you're in love with, is he? That's true, isn't it? I'm right, aren't I?' Her mother's voice rang out in triumph and Sofia was glad it was just the two of them at home to hear this.

'No! Hush! You're being crazy!'

'We'll see! Ha!' crowed the old woman. 'What are you doing, girl? It's you who are crazy! What age are you, carrying on like this? What's got into you, Sofia?'

'Oh, leave me alone, Mama,' Sofia shouted at her, and dashed out into the garden, where she could sit by herself and look at the sea. And there she could wonder: what really *has* got into me? Am I really going crazy? My mother's not always right, even though she thinks she is. She isn't right about this . . . *is* she?

Chapter Twenty-Five

They were doing it just to get on Cathy's nerves.

Look at them carrying on! Her calling him 'da' and even 'papa' and 'daddy' now. And him! That crazy old idiot was calling her 'darling daughter' and 'dearest one'. Funny how they always managed to do it within Cathy's hearing, all this simpering and cooing over each other.

Perhaps it was like a game to them? They wanted to rile her up with their effusions of love and affection. They wanted to make her feel left out completely.

But why? To what end? What kind of satisfaction could her daughter and her husband possibly get out of making her feel like this?

Well, Noel had spent years picking at her and irritating her and twisting her arm, just for the fun of it. Oh, not physically. He had never been the kind to physically abuse his spouse. She was twice the size of him these days and she could fetch him such a clattering if he even so much as pinched her skin or poked a bony elbow into her side. Physical violence wasn't as bad as the constant war of nerves and niggling and whiny palaver that Noel generally put her through.

Back in the day, he had begged her to marry him. She completed his life, he had said. She was more than he ever thought he deserved. She gave true meaning to every aspect of his existence. Oh, why was I ever such a fool to fall for his emotional blackmail? She had fallen for his enticements, his promises of security. Yes, that was how he had snared her. He had offered her security.

She had also consented to marry him in order to appease the spectre of his dying mother, Theresa, who had been the person who had taken Cathy in when she first arrived here in the Sixteen Streets. Theresa's kindness was something she would never forget, and she felt like she was still paying it back each and every day she woke up in the same gloomy house as horrible bloody Noel Sturrock.

And now this! Insult heaped upon injury! She had recovered her long lost daughter from the past and the forgotten wilds of Northumbria. But what manner of person was this who had come to stay? Snooty and snotty. Way above herself and looking down on Cathy. Conniving and sly, Cathy thought. Her young heart is brimming with bitterness. What a terrible thing!

She knew that her daughter was intending to make her suffer for being left behind at the farmhouse with Aunt Liz. Cathy saw that now, she had only come here to get her revenge. And she was taking it in just the small, sly, nasty, pricking and poking ways that Noel preferred. In some ways – yes! Junie was much more like Noel's daughter than Cathy's. Impossibly, she somehow shared his cankered and calculating nature.

Oh, why couldn't she be happier? Why couldn't she find some peace and contentment in being safe and settled now, like Cathy had? Why be bitter? Surely if Cathy could learn to forget about her Aunt Liz and the misery she had wrought, then surely Junie could, too?

'Oh, wait till you see us tonight!' Noel was telling her. His scratchy voice made her pause in her reverie and she looked at him. They were having scrambled eggs for their midday meal and he had a buttery smear on his chin because he ate so messily. She passed him an ironed napkin, the fabric soft with decades of use.

'What's tonight?' she asked.

He rolled his bulging eyes. 'I've been telling you, woman! Eeeh, can you never listen properly? Your thoughts are always elsewhere these days. Ha! And I'd have thought that these would be the happiest days of your life, what with your daughter back, and your family complete . . .' He jutted his chin at her and crammed another forkful of egg and toast into his mouth, chomping with great relish. 'You should be happier, Cathy Sturrock!'

She hated being told just how happy and cheery she should be. Much of her life was spent at that bar in the Robin Hood, smiling and being welcoming, even if that was the last thing she felt like being. A fake, broad smile was her stock-in-trade, but she was buggered if she was going to be forced to wear one at home as well. 'Just tell me what you're planning,' she told Noel, with a hint of warning in her voice.

'You'll have to wait and see tonight!' he promised. 'But there's been loads of practising going on. Loads of training! You'll be so glad when you see the surprise! Why, it'll be a load off your shoulders, hinny!'

By the time the evening rolled around Cathy had more or less guessed what the surprise was going to be.

Noel told her to doll herself up for coming to the pub, but he added that she wouldn't be working tonight. She wouldn't have to work her fingers to the bone tonight, oh no! She could sit at the Women's Table with her rotten old cronies and drink herself sick, if she really wanted to. Tonight all the responsibility was to be taken off her and she could let the new bar staff take over.

'The new what?' she asked, though she had worked out already what he had planned.

Sure enough, come half past seven when she left the house and crossed the road, it was to a Robin Hood where the bar staff was comprised of a much younger set. There was Minnie, who had been promoted to chief barmaid, and who looked very proud of the fact. The beaming, moon-faced girl was wearing a rather low-cut, old-fashioned frock hastily borrowed from her Aunty Maureen on Westoe Road.

Minnie's presence behind the bar was no surprise. The slightly more surprising thing was the fact that June was now in charge of the bar. She had her hair up in a chignon like Cathy often did and – blow me! Cathy thought – she had somehow managed to get into Cathy's wardrobe and pilfer one of her trademark velvet gowns. As she came sashaying out from behind the bar, June demonstrated that she could wear Cathy's clothes very nicely indeed. She was less buxom, but she had an innate elegance that became her very prettily. Cathy found that she was staring at her with very mixed feelings: outrage and pride vying to be uppermost.

'What are you doing?' she gasped.

'Why, I've learned to do your job, Mother dear!' Junie laughed. 'It only took a couple of afternoons to master everything there is to know!' There was something coarse and braying in her voice, Cathy thought. She had changed her whole manner, even the way she stood and swaggered about in full view of all the drinkers in the tavern. She was putting on a turn, Cathy realised, just like an actress or some Music Hall act. But still . . . she called me 'Mother dear'! Even though her tone was mocking, she had still called Cathy 'mother'.

'But you needn't . . .' Cathy said, dazedly. 'I never suggested . . . you needn't have to work here.' She wanted to say: I want better for you. I want you to do something better than I do.

June tossed her head and laughed in Cathy's face. 'But I already love it! I'm a natural! Daddy Noel says he's never seen someone pull a beer pump with a more natural air! I'm a marvel, he says.'

Cathy turned to glare at Noel. Yes – he was interfering. It was all his doing, this. He was doing it just to get under Cathy's skin.

And the girl . . . what had she done to her accent? It was broader, more twangy and exaggerated.

'What'll you have to drink, Cathy? You can just sit yerself down and enjoy the evening!' June pushed her mother towards the table by the fire, where Ada Farley, her psychic friend Winnie and a couple of others were making space for her. 'You can just let me take your usual place,' added her daughter with a wink.

As she sat and accepted the drink that was plunked down before her – a half of milk stout – Cathy suddenly realised what Junie was doing with her voice and her whole manner.

And she really took in for the first time that her daughter had more make-up on than usual. All that lipstick, all that bright rouge! She had made herself into something of a clown.

Cathy took a swig of her drink, watching her daughter carefully and she realised: Junie is parodying me. She's sending me up. She's doing a comic turn as me, knowing it'll make everyone chuckle.

June also knew that it would cut her mother to the quick.

All night Cathy sat there making small talk with her friends, sipping beer and watching her daughter cruelly parading around. She felt so passive and horrible in the face of this performance, for she knew it was meant nastily. It was a parody of Cathy, but it was more. It was some kind of cock-eyed attempt at supplanting her, here in the heart of her own hard-won world. Surely . . . surely Junie knew just how much it was hurting her mother?

Chapter Twenty-Six

Sofia's mother watched Mario very carefully. She narrowed her eyes and stood by the brand-new stove that she secretly loved to use herself, even though she complained about everything to do with the new house and all its fittings. 'Is all too new! Too spick and span! An old peasant woman like me – what use do I have for these indoor plumbings?' For some reason the indoor toilet being in the same room as the lovely new bath had scandalised her. 'Is not clean.'

By now – during the summer of 1932 – she was much more at ease with the comforts of her new home. She knew, deep down, that she was indebted to her daughter and Sofia's not-so feckless gambling husband for the life she was leading. What would I be without them? Where would I be now? Back at home with the drapes drawn on the belting sunlight all day, beetling about between the washtub and endlessly scrubbing the tiled floors of the dust that came blowing in through the shutters.

Naples was a dusty and dirty place, she remembered that. She had been reminded of so much with Cousin Mario's visit. His stories had reminded her of the kind of life she would have led if Tonio hadn't suddenly demanded one day that they all run away to a destination he had chosen at random, with just the throw of a dart.

Life would have been quite different and she was grateful.

'Ah, so much sugar!' she complained. 'It will be so sweet! It more like a dessert you're making.'

Mario wasn't put off for one second by her tongue-clickings and head-shakings. 'You listen to the way I do it, old lady. This is Mario's special pasta sauce. And yes, it is sweet. But life is sweet, as I see it, and sauce is an expression of life, is it not?'

He was such a talker! 'You could charm hind legs off donkeys,' Nonna had accused him more than once during his visits. Secretly, she loved to hear him talk, to tell tales of the old town and the people she had once known. Why, she even loved to have him assert his own recipe for spaghetti sauce as being superior to hers! What was life without tussle and disagreements? None of her younger family – Sofia, Tonio, Bella, Marco – would ever dare to quibble with the way she cooked their food. In more ways than one, Mario was a nice change for her.

'Half a lemon? Are you crazy? It will be too sharp, too tart.'

Mario shrugged, squeezing the bright yellow hull of the lemon until it was dry. He tossed it along the bench, along with the other detritus. A messy cooker! Nonna thought, with happy disapproval. What will Sofia say when she sees the mess she has to clear up?

For this special meal, Mario was really going to town. There was a fish of some kind in the oven, baking with cream and fennel. He had made something complicated with meat from pigs' trotters that he had bought from the butcher on Fowler Street. He tied up the parcels of meat with string, layering sage leaves inside and nuggets of garlic. Such a fuss he was making! How many courses were they getting? It seemed a lot of effort to go to . . .

'My way of saying thank you to all of you for your hospitality while I've been here. You Franchinos have been like a second family to me. I didn't expect to be welcomed, but I hoped for it.' He stirred his sauce contemplatively. It was bright red. Almost impossibly red. He let the old woman taste a smidgen and she licked the spoon with a grudging nod of approval. 'Nice.'

Then she thought about just how she had welcomed Mario, the first time she had met him. 'Has the wound on your head healed properly now?'

He ruefully touched the spot and laughed. 'You'd never know it had ever happened. Is nothing.'

Still, she was ashamed of herself. A little proud too, but mostly ashamed. 'I was defending my family, that was all.'

He glanced at her as he worked at the stove. 'I wouldn't expect anything else.'

'They are all very precious to me. Even Tonio. He's an idiot, as you know, but he is precious to me, too.'

'I know,' said Mario, and went to fetch a large pan for cooking pasta in. 'What are you trying to tell me, Nonna?'

She narrowed her eyes at him. 'I don't know what you're planning. I would call in Winnie, who can see the future. But her predictions have been very inaccurate lately. I could do better than Winnie!'

Mario told her, 'I have no plans, Nonna. I'm going home soon, that is all. I'm returning to Naples because it's time that I did, and because it's my home. This is just an English sojourn for me. I don't belong here, like you all do.'

Her heart squeezed tight inside her chest, like it was being shut inside the pages of a book. His mention of home and belonging brought a sweetness to the back of her throat that was even sharper than the sauce she had just tasted. 'I see.'

'This meal, you see, is my thank you and farewell to your family. That's why I go to this effort.'

Stiffly she said, 'I'm sure it will be lovely.'

He studied her briefly. She smiled at his scrutiny. My god, she thought, but he's handsome. He's like the men she remembered from back when she was a girl. Those forearms, exposed by his rolled sleeves. The delicate profile of his nose and chin. He was like a saint on the plaster wall of a cool, dark chapel on a bright hot afternoon. She could imagine – forty years younger and in a different life to this one – falling head over heels for him herself.

She shook her head, took off her thick glasses and spat on the lenses. 'Foolish woman!' She rubbed the glass with a corner of her pinny. 'I . . . I think we will all miss you, Mario.'

Now he grinned at her and before she had a moment to squeak in protest, he had gathered her up in both strong arms. She felt herself being lifted off the tiled floor. 'Set me down, you cretin!' she howled, going dizzy as he whirled her round. How long since she'd been taken in a man's arms and danced round like this? It was impossible to say. 'Stop it, Mario! Enough! You'll have the dishes over, and then where would we be?'

The best dinner service was out, cleaned of cupboard dust and waiting for the products of Mario's culinary labours.

It really would be a splendid meal. It would be a night to remember.

'You're a good lad, really,' she told him as he set her down at last.

He grinned at her and she thought: how red his lips are, and his teeth are so white. He's had a healthier life than ours these past couple of decades. He's eaten better and lived in the sun. We are pale and faded and sickly, living in this damp land.

'After the dinner I want to ask you all to come back there with me,' he suddenly burst out.

'What? Where?'

'To Napoli! Back home, of course! I want you to travel home with me. Is not dangerous now. The Grapellis don't want to murder you all!' He laughed out loud at this. 'Don't you think it's time you saw home again?'

The old woman's heart was going crazy, rattling like dried seeds inside a pod. 'No! I've put it all behind me. I know I'll never see home again. I'm used to that idea. I've made myself not care anymore . . .'

'But think of it!' he said. 'The heat. The sun. Seeing that sea again. And hearing the noise of the streets. Our language, spoken everywhere, so loudly. All that gabble!'

She smiled and inhaled the cooking scents he had filled their kitchen with. Surely the man was a sorcerer, brewing up potions to snag the heart and dazzle the senses. 'No, is too late. My heart would pack up on the journey. The boat! The trains! Is too far for me now. Is much too much.'

'Only a holiday,' he said. 'That's all I'm suggesting. Come for a month, stay with me. The Grapelli house is so quiet now . . .'

All at once there was a note of pleading in his voice. She didn't like it. She decided she would have to be firm. 'No, Mario. I'm not coming home, not for a month, not for forever, not for anytime at all. This place is my home now – and the same is true for my family. That choice was made many years ago and here we stay.'

He returned to stirring his pasta sauce, with a mutinous, sulky look on his face. How beautifully those bright and shapely lips could pout, she thought. But no, she would not let this lad change her mind.

What a seducer he was!

'What about Sofia . . . and Tonio? Bella and Marco?' he asked. 'Do you think they will come? How do you think they will respond to my question?'

Then a chill of fear went through the old woman. 'Th-that you must ask them yourself,' she stammered.

'I will,' he said.

Suddenly she was fearful. She remembered the lovelight she had seen kindling in her daughter's face. *This man is dangerous. He's a danger to our little family. Why, I believe he means to break it up.*

Chapter Twenty-Seven

Everything Mario cooked for them that night went down extremely well with the Franchino family.

'I haven't tasted food like that for years and years,' Tonio toasted the visiting chef. He looked bleary-eyed with nostalgia as he raised his glass of red wine. They were the best glasses out: the ones with the bubble of sea-green glass in their stems.

'Oh! Better than my cooking, I suppose!' said the old Nonna caustically.

'Better than anyone's!' Tonio laughed at her. 'I think Mario has true talent. Those pigs' feet . . . !'

Bella delicately covered her mouth. 'Those *what* . . . ?'

They all laughed at her. 'But wasn't it delicious, Bella?' her father said. 'You must learn this. It is important to forget what something really is, or where on the pig it came from. You must appreciate things without prejudice.'

Sofia chuckled at her husband's clumsy philosophising. 'I think you need to slow down with the Chianti.'

'No, tonight it's a celebration. Tonight we salute our friend from our home town. The man whose coming we superstitiously dreaded for all that time. Remember how we shivered at the very sight of a black brimmed hat? How crazy we were! But I now think that our superstitious dread was that we would be reminded . . . we would be forced to look back at where we came from and that would make us unhappy. Do you see?'

Sofia wished her garrulous husband would sit down. 'Not really. Come, shut up now and let us eat our dessert . . .'

'Like Lot's wife!' Tonio cried expansively. He sloshed a little of his wine onto the tablecloth and Nonna let out a squawk of dismay. 'Or . . . Orpheus!' he went on, undeterred. 'See? The lesson is that you must never look back where you came from. Otherwise terrible, awful things will happen.'

The old woman had beetled off to the kitchen for a cloth and baking soda, muttering under her breath about clumsy oafs slopping red wine.

'You're showing off,' Sofia told her husband. 'Now, sit again and enjoy the final course that Cousin Mario has made for us.'

Bella was already tucking into the creamy confection. 'It's really lovely.'

Mario was sitting in pride of place at the table, looking very pleased and not a little tipsy himself. Was he even slightly misty-eyed, Sofia wondered? Oh, really, what was Tonio spouting off about now? Her husband was still going on!

'So, we were never going to look back to our home in Napoli,' Tonio said. 'We were content to try to forget it. But in recent weeks we have been reminded by Mario where it is we come from and who we are. This food tonight, it brings us the very *savour* of the place we ran away from and I'm not ashamed to say it brings tears to my eyes. Thank you, thank you, Mario – for making me see that our home is nothing to be scared of.'

At this, Tonio sat down heavily in his rickety wooden chair at the head of the table and smiled owlishly at the messy plates and leftovers. Nonna tutted and scrubbed at the wine stain he'd made.

Everyone looked at Mario as he got to his feet. It was all proper speech-making tonight, Sofia thought. These men! They could get so pompous and proper!

Mario kept his speech short and to the point. 'All I want to say is – come home with me. Come back to Napoli with me. All of you.'

There was a stunned silence. None of the Franchinos were quite sure at first what they had heard him say. Young Marco's eyes widened till they were as big as the dinner plates. All looked amazed, apart from Nonna, who had been expecting exactly this nonsense. Her heart felt heavy as she abandoned the purple blotch of wine and eased herself back into her seat.

'Mario, you're not serious . . .'

He shrugged. 'I am. I have told you what you all mean to me, and I think I know how you all feel about me. Like I say before, the Grapellis are depleted in numbers. So many have died and our house – the dark-shuttered house by the church at the top of the street – it's empty, almost. I have the grandchildren of my mother's cats but not my mother herself. There's only six of us human beings still living in that family house now.'

'But we can't just up sticks and leave . . .' said Sofia. 'We've only just moved into our new house . . . and there's the business!'

He waved her objections aside. 'No, I mean, come for a holiday. In this first instance. Come and see the place again. Breathe in that different sea air and see what you've been missing. What you've been secretly longing for . . .'

'A holiday?' Tonio was frowning, turning the word over in his mouth. It was like he had never heard the word before. 'No, no, I can't close the business. We'd go bust! We'd lose the lot! We can't afford it! Shipping us all over there – and for what? Just to have fun?' He shook his head heavily. 'No, I'm sorry, Mario. It's impossible.'

The old grandmother had folded her arms and was glowering at the man who had thrown their evening meal into chaos. 'He tried the idea out on me this afternoon and I told him it was ridiculous. I said I would never go back. Yes! I would be like Lot's wife! I'd turn into a pillow of salt.'

'A pillar of salt, Nonna,' Bella corrected her.

'What?' Nonna shouted. 'Who cares? I'm not going anyway!'

Tonio added, 'And Bella. She is in school. So is the boy. And I need Bella here to help me at the ice cream parlour . . . is too far for a young girl to go waltzing off . . .'

Mario listened to them making their excuses. His face was changing. Growing harder, perhaps? Closing itself off from them, protecting himself from disappointment. He turned to Sofia. 'How about you, Sofia? Will you come home to Napoli and see home again?'

She realised she was holding her breath. When she saw that everyone was looking at her, she let it out with a slight hitch. Her heart was pounding in her breast as she realised what she was going to say . . .

'Of course she can't go with you alone!' Tonio laughed. 'It's indecent! A married woman going off with a man like that. Of course she doesn't want to! It's unheard of!'

But Sofia shook her head and all of a sudden it was all very clear. 'I would like very much to travel with you, Cousin Mario,' she said in a clear voice. 'Yes, I want a trip. Yes, I want to see Naples again.'

There was uproar at the table. All at once Tonio was back on his feet, shouting and beseeching her. 'Are you mad? What will people say about this?' And her mother was shouting too, 'There will be no good coming from this! Is terrible idea!' Her daughter Bella was simply staring at her with an amazed expression. Perhaps there was also a dancing light of . . .

encouragement? Admiration? There was some glimmer of mischief in her daughter's eyes.

In the midst of all of this, Mario was smiling at her. He looked like a man who had staked what little he had on a game of cards and come up trumps. God knows, Sofia had seen enough gambling men and their fierce, hopeful faces in her time, especially sitting here at her own kitchen table. She had served them wine and sandwiches and pasta often enough. The fervent, intent faces of gamblers. And the almost beatific gleam of triumph on those faces when they won. That was exactly how Mario looked right now.

He thinks he has won me, Sofia thought to herself.

She cut through the babble of voices around the table: 'Look, it's a holiday. I deserve a holiday, don't I? I haven't had a holiday in years . . . I deserve some rest, don't I?'

They were all looking at her. All of her wonderful family. They were looking at her with such love and concern. She was the heart of their little family. She knew they were all thinking: how are we to manage, even for a few weeks, without her at the hearth with us?

Her mind was made up. She had to go away.

'Mario will look after me. It will all be fine. I will be back before you know it . . .'

She was also thinking about the child growing inside of her. It was no bigger than a prawn at this stage, she supposed. No one need know about it yet. Her mother would tell no one, until Sofia wanted her news to be known. A trip right now might be Sofia's last chance to relax and enjoy herself before the whole business of bringing up another, late, unexpected child started happening all over again.

It was a small window of freedom in her life. A window through which the scents of lemons and honeysuckle and lavender and thyme came wafting.

'It will be a scandal!' her mother warned her. 'And how terrible . . . to leave your own children at home!'

'But . . . I don't understand . . .' Tonio was saying, opening his mouth like a fish dying on a slab of marble.

'I mean no harm, nor anything improper,' Mario assured the Franchinos. 'You know that. I will protect Sofia with every iota of my being. How about . . . how about we take with us a chaperone? Eh? Just to make everything look more decent and proper?'

'A chaperone?' Tonio frowned.

'What are we living in?' Sofia laughed. 'The nineteenth century? Do I really need a chaperone?'

Mario grinned at her. 'What about asking your friend Cathy? Ask her to come with us. She looks to me like a woman who needs a holiday. Just as much as you do, Sofia! Why not ask her?'

Sofia stared at him, open-mouthed. Why, it wasn't such a crazy idea, was it?

Chapter Twenty-Eight

On the day that the two friends arranged to meet, they had both had rows with family members.

'Families!' Sofia burst out. 'I'm sick of the whole lot of them!'

The two women kissed each other's cheeks as they met up on Fowler Street in the middle of town. Both looked mithered and cross.

'What's happened now?' Cathy asked her.

'It's my mother, she's said some awful things to me in her time. You know she never minces her words.'

Their plan had been to spend their morning off together, wandering idly around town and catching up with each other's news. They both loved to stare in shop windows and pretend they were rich. The large new department store was their favourite destination and they had a favourite table in a corner of the sophisticated coffee bar on the second floor.

Sofia waited until they were secluded there before she told Cathy what her mother had said. 'I wash my hands of you!'

Cathy was shocked. 'She never did! I couldn't imagine her saying that to you in a million years. She's devoted to you.'

An almost shifty look came over Sofia's face. 'Well, there's a reason for it. She's furious with me right now, but she won't say so in front of all the others. It's all this hissing, like she's a snake I've trodden on.'

'Oh, Sofia!' Cathy couldn't help laughing.

'She said that she's babysat me and mollycoddled me all my life! And now she must stop.'

'What? But haven't you prayed for her to stop interfering in your life? Haven't you begged her all these years to stop? And anyway, aren't *you* the one who's spent all these years looking after *her* . . . ?'

'Not how she sees it.' Sofia sighed and stirred her coffee. No way was it as nice as the coffee at Franchino's, but it was good to sit in a place where no other members of her family were lurking. 'She says, "Now you must take care of your own destiny."'

'What does she mean by that?' Cathy frowned. 'Do you think she might be losing her marbles? Seriously, Sofia. Why's she talking about destiny?'

Sofia sipped her tea and took out a packet of cigarettes. It was rare that she smoked. Her hand was trembling, Cathy saw, as she lit one for both of them.

'Well, I've been having an awful time with our Junie,' Cathy said, covering up Sofia's upset with her own tale. 'She's being a proper little madam. This morning I told her that I felt hurt by the way she was carrying on at the bar. I told you, didn't I, that she was doing a kind of impersonation of me?'

'No, you never did!' gasped Sofia. 'An impersonation?'

'Wearing one of my cast-off frocks and putting on this daft, common voice. Flirting with all the men and standing there with one hand on her hip. She's watched me closely, I'll give her that much. But she means it to be hurtful, Sofia. They present it as this nice thing – oh look, now June's working behind the bar and pulling her weight. But there's something nasty and sarcastic about the way she does it . . .'

Sofia frowned as she inhaled delicious smoke. 'Are you sure? I'd be pleased if someone took some work off my hands, even if they did it sarcastically.'

'Well, I asked her this morning, when Noel was out of the house. He was off out, up to no good, I should imagine. I took her aside in the scullery and told her she'd hurt my feelings. That was a big mistake. She actually looked pleased. Her eyes went all bright. "Good!" she snapped. "Because your feelings will never be as hurt as mine were. You'll never feel like I did when you abandoned me and never came back."'

Sofia gasped. 'That really is a little madam talking. Was she really as snappy as that? How dare she!' And all the while she was wondering: what makes Cathy so passive in this? Why does she put up with the little monster?

'Maybe she had a point . . .' Cathy sighed. 'I tried to explain that I had no choice, but she won't listen to any of it. How I went back again and again to Aunt Liz's house. In those months I lived in Morwick, I was scraping a living working in a shop rather like this one. I was trying to save up money so I could get somewhere proper to live and look after my daughter. It was all that I could think about. But when I went back each time I was 'Aunty Cathy' to my baby daughter. I was allowed to hold her only briefly each visit, less and less each time . . .'

'Oh, Cathy . . .'

'And eventually, when I was at my weakest and my most homesick and missing my baby the most, my wicked Aunt Liz turned on me. She had been planning this all along. "Me and my husband have decided that it's for the best if we simply adopt the child. You have nothing to offer her. We can give her security, a roof over her head and a proper life. We have decided that we should make the ruse we have all created into a living reality and you, Cathy, ought to disappear from the scene. Otherwise your daughter will grow up confused and upset by it all. Now you should give her the best chance in life that you can and *go*."'

Sofia was really appalled. 'But this was your Aunt Liz who had brought you up since you yourself were a girl . . . !'

'Quite. But now she saw her chance of having her own little family. She had manoeuvred me into this, her and her fancy man doctor. They had engineered all of this and I could see them poisoning my little girl against me. I refused to be sent away, you see. I kept turning up at their door and demanding to see Junie, just like any mother would. But the baby cried. As she became a toddler she howled and bellowed at the very sight of me. Like she was scared of me! And I knew that they had poisoned her young mind against me. Well, what was I to do? I had to turn away. It was all just too upsetting for both of us. Aunt Liz sat there gloating as she made my baby cry. It was like Junie was going to throw a fit whenever she saw me. God knows what they had said about me. So, I just came away and I thought . . . one day. She'll know the truth. One day she'll come to find me. Or she'll find out that I was forced to go away . . .'

Cathy sipped her cooling coffee and took a firm hold of her emotions.

'And that's what happened in the end, isn't it?' Sofia said. 'She came to find you when she was of an age to. She came to find out the truth.'

'Yes, and she hates my bloody guts!' Cathy moaned. 'She really does, Sofia. You should have seen her looking at me. That look in her eyes – just like my Aunt Liz! Now she belongs to Liz more than she ever did to me.'

'I don't think either of our families are making us very happy at the moment,' Sofia said.

'You can say that again.'

'You should tell her. The whole story. You should explain it all to her. And about her father . . . tell her about Christopher.'

Cathy looked tearful for a moment. 'I should present her with a father she can never have? I'd be taking something else away from her. How much would she hate me for that?'

Sofia thought about this. 'You can't really win with her, can you?'

'The decisions were all made in the past,' said Cathy. 'Maybe it's too late to sort everything out.'

'It will all come right, I'm sure it will,' Sofia smiled at her friend.

'Right now that seems unlikely.' Cathy sighed and Sofia took her hand in a sudden, determined grip.

'Look, lady,' she began. Here Sofia took a deep breath. 'What do you say to a holiday then?'

Cathy blinked with surprise. 'A holiday? Where?'

'Somewhere far away. How much money do you have saved? Can you get your hands on it?'

'I've been salting away money for years,' Cathy smiled sadly. 'All for June. What do I ever spend money on? I keep the same few dresses, we never go anywhere. That pub is like a little goldmine. In my head I was creating a nest egg for my daughter when she came back to me.'

'She doesn't deserve it!' Sofia cried. 'You should spend it on yourself!'

'Sofia!' Cathy found herself laughing. 'What are you saying, that we should just go? Could you really leave them all? What about Bella and your little Marco?'

'They have Tonio, they have their Nonna . . . why, they barely need me at all!'

'But where are you saying we should go?'

'Napoli!' the Italian girl burst out. 'By rail and sea and rail again! Come with me and Cousin Mario to Napoli!'

'What? I can't go that far, it's impossible! Why, I've never even been abroad before!'

'Let's *go*,' Sofia said urgently. 'We can sort out all the details. We can make this happen for us. Why don't we, eh? Let this lot here at home stew in their own juices. Why don't we two just . . .*escape*?'

Chapter Twenty-Nine

Cathy loved the moment that she told her nearest and dearest about her plans to have a holiday.

'I mean, I've never had one, have I? All I've done all my life is work work work every day. Don't you think it's about time that I had a little time to myself?'

They were having a fish supper early on Friday evening before the pub opened. Junie and Noel had forkfuls of chips halfway up to their faces. Their eyes were wide. Their mouths were hanging open. If only they could have seen the gormless, surprised looks on their faces!

'What did you say just then, pet?' Noel frowned at her, his great shaggy brows knotting together.

'She says she's leaving us!' Junie burst out. She was scandalised. 'She just told us, didn't you hear? She's going away!'

Aye, Cathy thought with private satisfaction. And the smug pair of you deserve it, an' all! Oh, she was gratified to see the shock on their faces. The pair of them looked like she'd just upped and slapped them.

'It won't be forever. It won't even be for very long . . .'

'How long?' asked her daughter, in a cold, wounded-sounding voice.

'We don't know yet. But it's a long way to Italy and

Naples is quite far south. Sofia reckons the trains are very slow, and . . .'

'Italy! Naples!' gasped her husband. 'What's all this? Gallivanting! The continent! What about the expense? Eh, have you thought of that? Yon Sofia has got a fortune, we know, cos her husband won a mint at the gambling table. They have that business and the big house in Seaham. Maybe that one can afford to go gadding about abroad, but we can't!'

Cathy pursed her lips determinedly. She could weather any objection Noel threw at her. She had rehearsed this in her head. 'I have money saved up.'

'Oh, you do, do you?' he sneered. 'You've been siphoning it off the profits from the pub, have you? You've been stashing away the housekeeping and hoarding it in your knicker drawer, have you?'

This made her angry. 'How dare you? The only reason the books for the Robin Hood balance each month is because of me! The only reason that place is still going at all is because I took over the running of it! Under you . . . why, under your care that place was sinking fast! It was complete chaos! Don't you dare talk to me about underhand dealings and siphoning off cash! My god – you old devil! You bloody hypocrite!'

Noel was out of his chair and just about capering around the room in fury. It was fury mixed with delight. This was just the kind of thing he adored. Any kind of fractious argy-bargy and the elderly goblin was in his element! It had taken years of rows before Cathy clocked that he actually relished this kind of confrontation. He thrived on the sparks that flew between them when they clashed like this. Right now he was building this up into a real humdinger of a fight. 'Hypocrite! Hypocrite, am I?'

Deliberately Cathy calmed herself down. Determined not to give him the satisfaction of a full-blown battle, she breathed evenly and stared at him levelly. 'There's nothing you can say or do to stop me or to put a spoke in my wheel. I deserve this opportunity to enjoy myself and you can just hadaway to hell, Noel Sturrock!'

'All this time, you've had enough money for a foreign bloody holiday stashed away in your room in cash, have you? Even when we were struggling to make ends meet? All through the General Strike? You secretly had all that cash hidden away?'

'That's nothing to do with you,' she said.

He actually yanked at his own thinning, greasy hair. 'My god, you'd have thought I'd have sensed it! I should have smelled the money under my own roof! How could I not?'

The truth was, Cathy hadn't been keen on hiding her savings in the house for that very reason. The bundled notes were stashed in her ancient carpet bag, deep underneath her bed. There was always a risk that Noel would one day hunt them out and make off with them, spending the whole lot on his usual drunken floozies and whatever else took his fancy. But women were not allowed to open bank accounts in their own names, at least not without permission from their husbands. It was a pernicious situation that meant that she slept each night on top of her savings, hoping and praying that Noel would never sniff them out.

Now he knew all about the money. Now he knew that she had enough to blow on a trip to Italy with her best friend. A feeling of excitement rose in her chest as she took a mouthful of battered cod and chewed. It was going to be the holiday of a lifetime!

Across the table from her, Junie's eyes were welling up with bright tears. 'I don't understand. I've only just come back to you. I'm only just getting to know my . . . my real . . . my real mother. And now you . . . you're leaving me *again*!'

Ah, this one was like a knife twisting in her guts. Junie really knew how to make the pain count. Her eyes were moist but her mouth was hard as she said these things. This was one who had saved up her pain for so long getting ready for revenge. She really knew how to inflict hurt on someone and she really enjoyed it. This, more than anything else, was painful to Cathy. Her daughter had grown up to be a spiteful person. What an awful thing.

Cathy forced herself to be resolute, reminding herself just how June had been acting these past few weeks. The girl didn't really love her mother. She wouldn't really feel deprived of her company. All she was was jealous. She was furious, as was Noel, at being outfoxed. Cathy had pulled a blinder. She was telling them, in so many words: you two are going to treat me like I'm soft as clarts, eh? Well, I'll show you. Ta-ra! I'm off on holiday!

Cathy told her daughter: 'You and your lovely adoptive daddy will be fine all on your own here. You love each other's company so much. Why, I don't suppose you'll even notice that I've gone!'

Her two opponents glared at her over their cooling fish suppers. Both their appetites had vanished.

'Plus,' Cathy went on with a fond smile. 'Look how brilliantly you managed to pick up my skills at work, Junie. You'd mastered everything in a mere two days! Why, I'd say that you were absolutely ready to step into my shoes. Now, you must look after the Robin Hood well, though. I'm trusting you two with the whole place while I'm gone. You must both do a very good job!'

'I . . . I . . .' Junie stammered.

Hoisted by her own petard! Cathy thought. She got such a kick out of mocking me and impersonating me. Now the little minx could do it full-time. See how she likes that!

Noel was staring at her with something approaching respect. 'I still don't see how you've saved up enough money to go to Italy!'

'I'm a good saver,' she said. 'And I've been stuck here for what feels like a lifetime. Oh, and I'll tell you something else, too, Noel Sturrock.'

He stared at her miserably, wondering what on Earth was coming next.

'Remember when your poor old mother was on her deathbed? And she accomplished the miracle of persuading me to look at you in a different light and actually think about marrying you? Remember how Old Theresa talked me into giving your life some actual meaning and saving you from being a lonely old monster?'

He grunted at her. 'Aye, lass. I do.'

'Well,' Cathy grinned. Here came her trump card. Oh, how she had longed to bring out this secret before, but never had. 'You see, Noel. What she did was *bribe* me. Aye, she did. She paid me in notes. Two hundred pounds in hard cash. That's how your dying mammy sealed the deal. I can see her now, counting them out on her eiderdown and telling me to hide them out of sight. "Now you'll look after my Noel, hinny, won't you? If I give you everything I've been salting away . . . "'

'*No* . . .' said Noel, quivering on the spot like he was going to take a fit.

'It's all true!' Cathy cried. 'That's what she said. "One day, Cathy, one day when it suits you, maybe you can use this money to have yourself a fine old time! But first look after my son. No one else will ever love him. He'll be alone forever unless you take pity. Here, take everything I've got, love. Then one day, one day . . . perhaps you can use it to run away."'

Somehow she got an echo of Theresa's lost, almost forgotten voice in the way she spoke her words. That wheedling, cajoling note the old woman had. Noel listened like he was at a séance and when Cathy fell quiet he howled like a dog.

'Off you go, then!' he barked at her. 'What do I care? You bloody selfish bitch! You've been planning this for years, I see that now! Well, bugger off abroad with your foreign pal. Junie and I will be fine here alone, won't we? Eh? Eh? Won't we, Junie love? We'll be happy here all by ourselves!'

Junie stared at Noel and then back at her mother. Junie didn't look quite so sure anymore.

Chapter Thirty

It was evening on the sands at Marsden Bay a week later. The Farley boys had built a small campfire to fend off the cold as the skies darkened to aquamarine. It was a beautiful summer's night. A small crowd of young people was gathering. There was excited chatter and laughter. A couple of lads were lugging a crate of Brown Ale down the narrow steps to the beach, clinking all the way.

Jackie from the butcher's shop on Fowler Street had brought a bundle of fat sausages and was cooking them on an improvised griddle. They smelled delicious as they sizzled and popped.

Up on the clifftop, June and Minnie had watched the young people gathering for a little while. Minnie felt very left out of all the fun. Her best friend was in a stinking mood tonight and she couldn't understand why.

'What's the matter though, June love? What's got you like this?'

June scowled at her. 'Don't *love* me, Minnie. No one *loves* me.'

Minnie's insides froze at this. Her friend's tone was so nasty and poisonous. She had never seen her as bad as this, although she knew that June was prone to some awful moods. She tried to distract her, 'Hey, look at the Farley lads, stripping down to their shorts and running into the surf! The tide's coming in! Maybe they'll get swept off to sea!'

June shrugged. 'I don't care what happens to anyone, frankly.'

'Eeeh! Look at them running about in their pants! Remember when they took off every stitch that day when they didn't think anyone was looking? Do you remember? But we saw everything when they were jumping in and out of the water?'

'Yes, I do,' said June wearily.

'Eeeh! They'd die if they knew we'd seen their tiddlers!' Minnie laughed, desperate to get a smile out of June.

But June wasn't going to comply. 'Let's go down there,' she said, standing up suddenly. She had bits of grass all down her smart dress and didn't even mind. 'I can see that Bella Franchino down there, and I've got a bone to pick with her.'

Minnie got up to follow her to the steps, mystified.

As they approached the campfire, the whiff of scorching sausages and baked potatoes made Minnie's stomach rumble. She realised she'd had nothing to eat all day. Maybe she could convince the lads to give her something?

'How, Minnie! Now then, lass!' Tom Farley called out, and she blushed to see him standing there in his trunks. His skin was covered in brilliant droplets of seawater, glinting in the last of the sun. His brother was rubbing himself down with a thin, faded towel and grinning at the new arrivals.

'Bella Franchino,' June called out, and the tall Italian girl whirled round at the sound of her name. Her jet black hair was tied up in a knot and she was wearing her two piece bikini again, which was very becoming on her. It showed off her impressive bust to great advantage. 'Oh!' she said, smiling. 'June! Minnie!'

She was so welcoming and sweet, Minnie thought. She didn't deserve the furious glare that June was giving her. 'Hey, you, lady,' June snapped. 'I blame your lot! I blame your mother!'

'What?' Bella looked confused. 'Whatever do you mean?'

All the lads and lasses gathered round the fire were paying close attention. There was the hint of a barney in the air. Having fun was all very well, but a fight was something else!

'You know what I mean,' June sneered. 'Your bloody mother! She took my mother away! She enticed her away, her and that Eyetie fancy man of hers.'

Bella looked shocked. 'What?'

'You heard what I said, lass. Your dirty mother and her Eyetie fella – that slimy Mario bloke – they've run off and they've taken my mother with them!'

Bella took a step forward, her expression darkening. 'Don't go throwing words like that around. That's very insulting.'

'I will not!' June burst out. 'I say things as I see them! And that fella is indeed an Eyetie. Just like you all are! Not to be trusted, none of you.'

Bella kept her voice level, 'I think you'd better go home, June.'

'Will I hell! I want to know what you knew about all of this. Did you know that they were planning to run off? Did you know they were plotting with my bloody mother so she could escape as well?'

The dark-haired girl looked mystified. 'There was no plotting that I was aware of. And no one has escaped from anywhere. They've just gone off on a holiday for a while.'

'A holiday!' June laughed mirthlessly. 'We'll never see any of them buggers again! They've run off!'

'No, no, don't be daft,' said Bella, shaking her head and trying to reassure the upset girl, though by now she sounded less sure of herself. Could June even be right? The circumstances of this whole Neopolitan holiday, and the abrupt way Mario had vanished with Sofia and Cathy . . . maybe it had all been a bit strange after all? 'It's a holiday, that's all,' she said, trying to convince herself that's all it was. 'Your mam and my mam, they both work so hard, don't they? They've not had any kind of holiday before. They really deserve this. You shouldn't begrudge them, June.'

Their voices had been getting louder. More young folk had gathered round the cooking fire to see what all the palaver was. Tony Farley tried to calm them down: 'It's all something and nothing, lasses. Come on, make your peace, we're trying to have a nice night, here . . .'

But June wasn't in a mood to be pacified. Minnie knew the folly of trying to interfere with her pal's dark moods. 'Begrudge them! Begrudge them nothing!' June snarled. 'Do you realise how lucky you are, Bella Franchino? Your mother has doted on you all your life. You've had her with you every day since you were born. She thinks the bloody sun shines out of your arse!'

Bella flushed at this and some of the lads were laughing. 'I know that,' she said. 'And like I say, she deserves some time of her own. We can all look after ourselves without her for a while . . .'

But June wasn't done with her protest. 'What about *me*, though, eh? I've never had a proper mammy. Just an old aunty pretending I belonged to her. Then eventually . . . eventually I find my real mother. And what is she? Some rotten old bitch who couldn't really give a fig about me. And she's married to some awful crookback who she can't even stand! And then – at the first opportunity – she goes waltzing off to the continent! She has left me alone all over again!'

June succumbed to loud, jagged sobs then. She balled up her fists and squashed them into her eye sockets, as if she could send the treacherous tears back where they were coming from. Her whole body shook with emotion.

Bella couldn't help the tender part of herself responding to the bitter girl's distress. She hurried forward and put an arm around her shoulders. 'There, there, love. I'm sure you've got this wrong. I'm sure you're overreacting . . .'

'*No . . . !*' June cried and reacted to Bella's touch as if she was scalded. She shrugged her off and then turned on her. She thrust her away with the flat of both hands and Bella staggered backwards on the sand, astonished by the girl's reaction.

'Hey, hey, hey!' Tom Farley waded in, through the deep sand, trying to interpose himself between the girls. Minnie, too, dashed forward to stop the scuffle. The crowd around them was less helpful, immediately striking up a chorus of: 'Fight! Fight! Fight!'

June was like a girl possessed. She didn't give Bella a moment to think. In a second she was upon her, stretching out her arms to grab handfuls of her black hair in both fists.

'Get her off me!' Bella yelled. 'She's bloody mad!'

'You're a scabby whore!' June was yelling, shaking Bella and trying to scratch at her face. 'You and your mother are both bloody whores!'

Then both girls were down on the sand. Bella was flattened under the slight but determined weight of the Sturrock girl. It took three of the lads to prise her off and drag her away. Still spitting and kicking, June continued to scream abuse at her enemy.

'W-what's wrong with her?' Bella gasped, realising with a painful wince that June had yanked a handful of hair out of her scalp. 'What have I ever done to her?'

Minnie shook her head wordlessly, appalled by the actions of her friend.

'I suppose,' Tom Farley said, 'she's upset about her mother running off to Naples with your mother. Maybe she's envious? Or maybe she misses her?'

'I think she's bloody crackers,' his older brother frowned, still holding his towel around him.

They all stood by the fire and watched June gather her wits together. She turned and stomped off, back across the sand, towards the cliff steps. 'Are you coming, Minnie?' she yelled back, over her shoulder.

Minnie shrugged apologetically at the others. 'I'll just see if she's all right,' she said, and hurried after her friend.

'Eeeh,' Tom Farley shook his head. 'What are lasses like, eh? There's always a bloody carry on.'

Then the lad from the butcher's was shouting out that the sausages were cooked and it was time to eat, and everyone pushed the unfortunate scene out of their minds. Even Bella, who had lost a clump of hair in the fracas.

Truth be told, Bella was pretty upset that her own mother had, as June put it, 'waltzed off to the continent'. But it did no good to complain about it, did it? Sofia and Cathy had made up their minds in a flash. They had gone off together – with Cousin Mario – on this great jaunt. There was nothing that anyone at home could say that would put them off.

But it was only a holiday, wasn't it? That's all it was, no matter what that loopy June had said. It was just a holiday and soon they'd be back and everything would be normal again.

Bella joined in with the feast on the beach with the rest of her friends, convincing herself that this was so.

As the stars came out and her scalp stung, she couldn't help torturing herself with the thought: but what if Mama and Cathy fall in love with Naples and what if they *never* come home again . . . ?

Chapter Thirty-One

After a few days of being there, Cathy bought a postcard and wrote to Noel.

'You really wouldn't like it. The heat would be even worse for you than it is for us. I bet you wouldn't go out at all! The toilet arrangements here alone would send you into a blue fit.'

Just going out to buy a card and a stamp and finding the post box seemed like an arduous day's work. She ended up with a fussy card with lacy edges and four tiny photographs of the teeming streets of Naples.

The photos looked exactly how it was here: dark, busy streets. Shadows hot and dark as hell. Then the brightest sunlight she had ever seen, slicing down through the canyons of the alleys.

She also wrote a few sentences about the journey they had taken to get here. How the ship had made her sick for a whole day. How the trains were huge, like great metal dragons pumping out steam. And how they had travelled through deep, twisting valleys through the guts of the countryside. She had loved the slight breeze when the train picked up enough speed, but mostly they had ambled and clanked along at a walking pace.

She told him that the skies were impossibly blue. The very air was hot, but it wasn't the kind of heat that dragged you down. Rather, it seemed to lift Cathy up. At least, that's how it had been before they had arrived in the city. The heat here had been like walking into a steam bath occupied by thousands of other people. When she and Sofia and Mario had emerged onto the marble platform of the terminus at Napoli, it had been hard to catch her breath. The way everyone was dashing about in the heat almost had her panicking.

Of course, she didn't go into any such detail in her postcard to Noel and June, nor did she say anything too negative about her adventures. She didn't want them thinking she was having an awful time or had made some kind of mistake by coming here.

She made jokes about the horrid toilet arrangements and the horribly overpopulous streets. She stated how Noel would absolutely hate it all. She was very careful to tell him that she and Sofia were in love with everything they saw. Everything that happened, every new sensation she experienced – sweet, flat white peaches, eating pizza in the street, seeing donkeys ambling past their own front door – all of these things were novel and wonderful.

In her card Cathy pretended that she didn't feel nervous and silly and jumpy and utterly alien.

It took her almost a week to settle into the place.

It didn't help that she had brought all the wrong clothes.

'But what else could I have brung?' she protested. 'I don't have many clothes. These are just my best ones. I have clothes that suit living in South Shields . . .' South Shields – where everything is breezy and cool and prone to showers, even in the summertime. Here she felt like she was about to faint when she stepped out into the lane wearing her best woollen coat. She ended up carrying it over her arm, and then her cardigan as well. Even her feet felt clumpy and too hot.

Sofia fared rather better, remembering what it was like and had packed accordingly. Still, the summer heat came as something of a surprise to her, too. 'I had forgotten exactly what it is like,' she confided in her friend. 'It's been so many years. My blood has chilled and become northern. I'm finding it as hard as you to acclimatise . . . !'

In fact, Sofia was finding a number of factors quite difficult to deal with.

'I've lost my language!' she wailed, at the end of their first few days in Naples. 'I thought I could remember. I didn't even have to practise. I assumed it would all come flooding back to me.' She shook her head sadly, smiling ruefully at her own foolishness. 'But then today, in the shops and in the street, I found myself flummoxed and all confused. The words all around me were like . . . like babbling. Like the noise of a busy stream flowing all around me and all I could do was paddle to keep afloat. I couldn't follow half of it.'

They were sitting at the kitchen table having a scratched together meal of fruit and pasta and bread and cheese. The kitchen was in the courtyard at the heart of the old Grapelli household, and half of it was open to the skies. It turned out that Mario's family home was a number of houses connected into one. It was a kind of shabby, run-down palace, patrolled by exhausted-looking cats and one or two elderly relations and friends that he neglected to introduce his visitors to.

Mario fed them and listened to their complaints and the stories of their adventures. 'You'll soon be talking properly again,' he reassured Sofia. 'You have to remember, you're hearing all the dialects here, all running at once. As well as the many languages of everyone coming into the port. It's confusing, I know.'

Sofia looked worried as she ate. She seemed edgy and nervous, and Cathy was surprised. She had expected her friend to settle straight back into life here. She thought the heat and the noise would be her natural element and she would welcome it. But as they ate she confessed: 'I don't feel at home here at all. Too much time has gone past. It's not my own place anymore.'

Cathy tried to buck her up. 'Mario's right. It'll all make sense to you in a day or two. Your language will come back. You'll get used to it all. Look at me! Look at how I'm learning to cope!' That evening, Cathy was in a cream satin slip at the dining room table. Her arms were bare and cool and she couldn't help thinking what people at home would think of her. Fancy sitting at the kitchen table in her underwear! Somehow it didn't really matter here.

The sky above the open courtyard was turning a deeper shade of pinkish blue. Stars were appearing as it darkened. She breathed in the nighttime scents of the flowering plants and the fruit and the cat pee and the drains and the strong coffee Mario brewed on the hob for them. Even though some of the aromas were horrid, it was all starting to seem wonderful to Cathy. It was the scent of somewhere she had never been before, and she was ready to drink it all in.

'I must write a card to Tonio,' Sofia said. 'Though I don't know what to say. I am experiencing this on his behalf, too. I must see the place through his eyes. What would he want to hear?'

Mario told her, 'He'll want to hear that you're having a good time. You are enjoying yourself.'

Sofia watched him light a lemon-scented candle to keep the insects off them. 'Perhaps I've forgotten how to enjoy my life? It's been work work work for so long, I don't know how to relax.'

Cathy thought that sounded like a terrible thing. She knew it wasn't true of herself. Yes, their arrival with all their luggage and the shock of all the crowds and the heat had been very disconcerting at first. But already, after a handful of days, she could feel herself unwinding inside. It really felt as if all the tightly coiled springs of her internal mechanisms were warming up and expanding and unwinding. She could feel herself growing lighter and somehow brighter. The sunlight was getting into her soul.

She grinned across the table at Sofia and Mario. 'Thank you – the pair of you – for letting me come along with you. I'm very grateful. This feels like a once-in-a-lifetime kind of trip. I'm happy that I came.'

Sofia took hold of her hand. 'I'm glad you're here. Otherwise I'd be completely lost! I'd forget who it was I've become.'

Mario was beaming at them both. 'Well, I'm so proud to have you both here. I feel like I have a wonderful harem!'

Cathy burst out laughing. 'A harem! Eeh, you cheeky devil!'

But didn't he look handsome? He was even more untucked and casual than he had been in South Shields. Tonight he was in a bright white vest with his shirt hanging open all the way down. His face was ruddy and bright. He had caught the sun as soon as he had arrived back home; it was like his skin just greedily drank it in. He looked handsome and so pleased with himself.

'This house must be very lonely,' Cathy said. They had glimpsed the other occupants, but Mario had explained they were all elderly, distant cousins. Mostly they kept themselves to themselves, shuffling about like shadows.

'The heart and soul has gone out of our home,' he admitted. 'You should have seen it years ago. Do you remember, Sofia? Our house was always crammed with people.'

She nodded, remembering coming here once or twice when she was quite small. Holidays and festivals. She even remembered the very young Mario himself back then, doted on by his mother and his aunts. 'I came here with my mother, before she fell out with yours.'

He laughed. 'Oh, those old women! They were all terrible! Much fiercer than all the men!'

They finished their meal and took a nightcap, staring up at the brightening stars. It was cooler then and Sofia suggested that an early night might be just the thing. Take advantage of the cool to catch up with their rest. They finished their drinks and said goodnight to Mario.

'Let's be wicked,' he said. 'We'll leave all the mess and the washing up till tomorrow.'

It did indeed feel like a wicked thing to do, but Cathy relished the new sensation of not tidying up before bedtime. It was just one more exotic thing.

She and Sofia took the staircase up to their adjoining rooms and, once they knew they were out of Mario's earshot, Sofia sat down and made her confession.

'What confession?' Cathy asked, helping her comb out her tangled hair.

'It's hard to say,' Sofia said, biting her lip.

'Come on, you can tell me.'

'Can I? You will be appalled.'

Cathy caught her eye in the fly-blown mirror. Oh dear, it's serious then. I thought she was just messing on. 'What is it, Sofia? What's going on?'

'My bloody old mother was right,' Sofia admitted. 'I think I'm falling for him. For Mario.'

'Ah, no, hinny . . . you're not, are you?'

'I thought if I came here with him, I could work it all out. I would know how I felt.'

Cathy stopped tugging on the tats in her jet black hair. 'Eeeh, lass. And how do you feel now then?'

'I think . . . I really might be very confused. I am hating this place, I really am. It's stinky and dark and dirty and much worse than I remember. Maybe I'm just confused and mixed up, coming back to this place. Yet I feel like I really am falling in love with Mario. I really don't want to, but I am.'

'Oh, Sofia man,' Cathy groaned. 'Hell's bells! What the devil are you going to do?'

Chapter Thirty-Two

Following Sofia's admission, Cathy started to take her role as old-fashioned chaperone much more seriously. Her job was to save Sofia from herself. If her primitive urges were leading her in a direction she might later regret, Cathy would be there to make sure nothing untoward went on. She felt like an old maiden aunt, going everywhere with the couple.

Mario was seemingly oblivious to all this carry on, even Sofia's slightly altered attitude towards him. He was keen to show off his hometown, and led the two women around all the main thoroughfares and the twisting backstreets, equally proud of the vast monuments and the fountains and statues as he was the surging crowds in the stall-lined streets of the Spanish Quarter, where he lived. Here the apartment blocks rose six storeys high and blotted out much of the daylight.

Mario was recognised here, and people called out to him. He was given respect as one of the last of the Grapellis. He introduced Sofia to people: 'Remember the Franchinos? They ran away with all our money! They even took Nonna's ice cream recipe!' He explained this to bent old men sitting on rickety wooden chairs, airing themselves in the sun, or to vast old ladies beating dusty rugs in the alleyway. All these people would look Sofia up and down and chuckle 'Ah, the Franchinos!'

It was as if Sofia's family were an old joke here: the family that got up and ran away in fright. Sofia blushed to think about it.

'What would our lives have been like,' she wondered aloud to Cathy. 'If we'd stayed here, as we were meant to? What do you think, Cathy?'

But how was Cathy to know? She herself had made a move at a crucial point in her life, ensuring that everything about her future turned out differently than she'd once anticipated. She'd had no choice about the matter. Life, as far as she could tell, was about making the best of things when all you really were was a hostage to fortune.

Limply, as they ambled through the cobbled lanes, all she could offer Sofia by way of wisdom was: 'Who knows? Your life might have been richer, but you would have been poorer in some ways. You think you work hard now, but I think here you would have been worse off.'

'Do you?' Sofia said, with an enigmatic smile. She hurried after Mario, who was striding ahead with that daft black hat still perched on his head, despite the rising heat of the morning. He seemed determined to show them every corner of the city, and Sofia was content to dash after him.

What about your baby, growing inside of you now? Cathy wanted to ask her. She wanted to stop her, take her aside and earnestly quiz her. You're flirting with Mario, telling me you're actually falling for him, but that's Tonio's child you've got growing inside of you. Mario doesn't know about that, does he?

But there was no chance to talk to Sofia all day, as they wandered through the alleyways and under shaded passageways. They took a clanking funicular up the steep hill to the top of the town. There was a certain vantage point from which Mario said they would get a spectacular view of the bay and the volcano.

'The volcano!' Cathy laughed, thinking he was just being daft.

'Oh no, Cathy, he's right,' said Sofia. 'Have you never heard of Vesuvius? And Pompeii and Herculaneum?'

Cathy blushed, ashamed of her ignorance. 'I never had much education . . .'

Mario was happy to explain, sweeping his arms about dramatically as he told the story of the eruption in ancient times. As they came to the viewpoint and saw the whole of Naples spread out before them, he was acting out being the clouds of ash that filled the air, turning night into day. He showed how the molten lava was flung up into the sky and rolled down the mountainside to engulf a whole town and wipe everyone out.

'But that's horrible!' Cathy gasped.

'It was a very long time ago, but we never forget it,' Sofia told her.

'Just imagine it!' Mario said proudly, leading them to the railing. Everything about the view was sparklingly precise and clear in the sun. The distant volcano was the colour of a deep, fresh bruise. 'It could blow again at any time. The whole thing could happen at any moment with no warning.'

Cathy was appalled. 'What? Any moment? Are you sure?'

'So they say,' he shrugged. 'Here, we live on a knife's edge.'

'I'm not sure I'd enjoy that,' Cathy said, shooting a significant glance at Sofia. Yes, you're living on a knife's edge too, lady! Then she looked down over the railing at the deep drop below and went dizzy. 'Oh, it's quite steep, isn't it?' She gazed down at the panoply of jumbled rooftops. 'At least we don't have volcanos in South Shields,' she muttered, and the other two laughed.

When they made their way back down the hilly streets towards home, dodging through the crowds, Sofia looked disconcerted. 'I think I keep seeing my mother!' she laughed. 'It's ridiculous! She's not even dead but it's like she's haunting me. Keeping her beady eye on me.'

Mario didn't seem at all surprised. 'Napoli is full of tiny old women in black dresses and shawls. They're all as fierce and crazy as your mama.'

'She's not crazy!' Sofia protested.

'Hmmm,' Mario smiled, not so sure. 'I wish she had come with us. So many people here remember that old woman fondly.'

Sofia had been introduced to half a dozen different decrepit old souls almost every day they had been here. Her terrible ear for the local dialect let her pick up the fact that she was being fussed over as 'the long-lost beautiful daughter of that terrible Franchino woman'. Oh, wouldn't Nonna be delighted to hear that her name was almost legendary here, in the place where she belonged! She would glow with pride when Sofia told her.

'There's a lot of soldiers about,' Cathy frowned. She didn't like the look of them. On almost every wide thoroughfare they were clustered in groups of two and three. Sometimes they could be seen strutting about alone, parading proudly in their crisp, elaborate uniforms and their black shiny boots. It was very disconcerting to see the heavy guns they lugged with them. When they stood in groups smoking nonchalantly, their guns hung down and it was quite intimidating to walk by and catch their appraising eyes. Cathy made sure she looked away each time.

'The Carabinieri,' Mario shrugged. 'It's just a way of life these days. I hardly even notice them.'

'I don't like it,' said Cathy. 'They're very threatening.'

'Are they not the most handsome soldiers you've ever seen?' laughed Mario. 'I thought you'd appreciate them, Cathy.'

But Cathy wasn't stupid or as ill-informed as people thought her. She read her newspapers and she listened to the wireless. She knew fascists when she saw them.

'It's all so much cleaner than I remember it,' Sofia kept saying. 'All the streets I grew up in, they used to be filthy, once upon a time. I'm not misremembering, am I, Mario? The steep streets would be running with stinking water and sewage. There were rats and bags of stinking garbage. Fish heads and tentacles and guts in the gutter and blood running over the cobbles from the slaughterhouse.'

Mario nodded. 'You remember it well. And it stank, didn't it? Rotting fish and fermenting horse shit! This time of year your head would be swimming with the stench. But is clean now. All is much cleaner.'

'See?' Sofia smiled at Cathy. 'Things are nicer here now. People are out sitting in the street eating their supper! They could never do that in the old days. It's much better now. I guess it's all down to Il Duce and the changes he's brought . . .'

Cathy tightened her lips. She didn't want to get into a row about politics here and now. She watched Sofia becoming enthralled by all the improvements that had been made. She watched her becoming more and more entranced by their wily host.

Yes, he was wily, Cathy thought. There he went, swaggering along in his shirt sleeves and hat. Buying them a bag of oranges and ripping into the bright skin with his perfect teeth. The juice covered his chin and he wiped it off with his sleeve, passing fat, bursting segments of fruit to both Sofia and Cathy. 'Tell me these aren't the very best you've ever tasted . . .'

Despite the heat of the late afternoon, Cathy felt a chill go through her. She remembered something Sofia had told her, just a few days ago, about the hot, dry winds that came rippling through the city. Legend had it that these dusty siroccos were of evil intent. What a terrible and savage place this is, Cathy thought. With mountains that explode and winds that are evil!

'The dry sirocco, it is said, can steal your spirit away,' Sofia had told her.

Yes, that was just how Cathy felt. Our very spirits are being slowly stolen away from us. This place and this man are taking us over.

Chapter Thirty-Three

Cathy sat at the kitchen table in the courtyard during the hottest part of the day, writing yet another postcard home. In her imagination, Noel and Junie were hanging on her every word about her first trip abroad; the pair of them really cared about how she was getting on. In her mind's eye they were much more devoted to her than they were in real life. But real life was different, she knew that. In real life the pair of them could be getting up to all sorts of bad behaviour. She dreaded to think what they might be doing while she was away.

Cathy was missing the smoky and noisy confines of the Robin Hood in the evenings. How ridiculous was that? Here she was free to do just whatever she wanted. There were no pressures on her to get on with work, perhaps for the first time in her life. The lack of those pressures was disconcerting, though.

Their tickets home were open-ended. It wasn't quite clear when their holiday would be coming to an end. This worried Cathy somewhat, since she felt beholden to Sofia and her changing moods. What if she suddenly decided that she was going to stay here forever? Only a couple of days ago that would have seemed like an absurd thought. Not so much now. Cathy had been watching her friend closely and was aware of the turmoil inside her.

It wasn't so much the thought of travelling back home by herself that alarmed Cathy. That didn't really hold many terrors for her. What she dreaded was the idea of was reaching South Shields and having to explain to Tonio and the rest of her family that Sofia was staying in Naples with Mario.

The card lay half-written on the table and Cathy sat there in the sun, lost in her thoughts. She jumped when Mario sat down opposite her.

'Lovely lady,' he smiled at her and she rolled her eyes. She was quite used to all this kind of flannel from Mario. 'You should be resting in the hottest part of the day, don't you know that?'

She shrugged. 'I try, but I can't get used to it. Sofia can. She's having a nap.'

He nodded. 'She fits right in with life here. It took her a few days to see it, but she belongs here, with us.'

Cathy watched him as he got up and started messing around with his complicated coffee pot, which he filled and set upon the hob to boil. 'You're wanting her to stay with you, aren't you?' she asked him outright. 'That's what all this is about. It's not just some nostalgic trip home. You've really set out to win her back.'

He raised an eyebrow at her and a slight smile touched his lovely lips. Damn him, Cathy thought. She still found him attractive, even though she knew he was a selfish sod.

'You see through me, Cathy,' he smiled. 'And I have to thank you for coming along as this chaperone. You are my . . . what's the word? Alibi.'

'I am?'

'Yes, your being here means that we were allowed to do this. No one would think anything funny was going on.'

'Nothing *is* going on . . . is it?' she frowned.

'Not yet.'

She gasped. 'What are you up to?'

'You said it yourself. I intend to win her back. She is mine.'

'You're deluded. You're crackers!' She didn't mince her words as she watched him take out his mother's best tiny cups and saucers. Steam was already starting to issue from the coffee pot's spout. 'Sofia's a happily married woman. She's not going to chuck away everything just for you. She never was yours.'

He shook his head vehemently. 'When we were twenty, we were everything to each other. She sat here with my mother and she told her how she was going to marry me and live here. She said it, Cathy! My mother could never understand afterwards, why she changed her mind. Why she disappeared.'

'It was Tonio,' Cathy sighed. 'You know that. She fell in love with Tonio.'

Mario's expression curdled like milk left out on the table. 'Him!' he cried scornfully. 'What woman would prefer that little . . . *blimp*! That fat little blimp, to me!' He shook his head and savagely straightened up the cups.

'You made out you were so fond of him when you came to Shields,' Cathy said. 'You went on like he was your friend.'

He shrugged. 'That was so I could get close to Cathy. Why would I want to be friends with that old fool? He's greedy and stupid and old before his years. All he cares about is hiding his gambling problem and that business of his. Has he paid enough attention to his wife? Has he given her a life that she deserves? I think not.'

The coffee was ready and Cathy watched him pour out a richly smoking stream into the thimble-sized cups. She hardly dared respond to his questions. She was almost afraid of agreeing with him. Over the years, Sofia had told her enough about her marriage and how neglected she felt. It was neglect at the root of this, Cathy thought. Sofia is vulnerable because Tonio has neglected her. She has laid herself open to Mario and Mario is ready to take advantage. Cathy felt like she must stand up for her friend against this dangerous man. Who knew what he might do next. He was capricious and powerful and they were in his power.

'Sofia has made her own choices,' Cathy said in a level voice. 'You can't go making choices for her or trying to kidnap her out of her life. Who do you think you are?'

He grinned. 'I'm the man she really loves. The man she always really loved.'

'The Man in the Black Hat,' Cathy said, with a hint of mockery, as she accepted his coffee.

'That's just a joke. A figure from a folk tale. A character to dread. I turned up in that hat to let her know – to let them all know – that the past was catching up with them. That was why she dreaded seeing me again. She knew it meant her old life was dead. She would have to come with me.'

'But what about her children? Bella and Marco are grown now and they belong to that place. And the old mother . . . do you really think Sofia would leave her there?'

None of these objections seemed insurmountable to Mario. 'We can send for them. They will come here. You have seen this house now. It has many rooms to fill. It is waiting for a family. Her family.'

Cathy stared at this difficult, selfish, dangerous man and she thought: you're just lonely. That's all this is. You want a family around you. Somebody else's will do. Sofia's family. You're determined to take them away from Tonio and bring them here.

'And Tonio . . . ?' Cathy sipped her coffee. 'He would just be left there, sitting on his own forever?'

'He deserves it,' Mario said. 'Do you know what Sofia tells me? She tells me personal things I cannot bear to hear. For years that man comes nowhere near her. He doesn't even touch that lovely woman. Can you believe that?'

Cathy shook her head. 'It's no one's business how a couple behaves . . .' But she too had heard the same thing from Sofia's lips. It was a bitter complaint she had repeated over the years and Cathy was shocked to hear that her friend had confided in Mario as well. It seemed like a foolhardy thing to do.

'He does not make love to her,' Mario said, sitting down heavily again. He sounded affronted, almost angry. 'I tell her: she should not waste her life on this man who has given up on life. How can she be happy? If he does not take her in his arms? If he does not make love to her with all the joy and the strength that he has in his heart? Tell me, Cathy, does that seem right to you?'

She gulped her coffee and shook her head. No, of course it didn't seem right. Cathy knew all about compromises, however. She knew all about marriages that didn't work in the orthodox way. How to explain all of that to a man like Mario, who saw everything in such stark and simple terms?

'Cathy needs a man like me,' he said. 'She has always needed me.'

A stab of irritation went like heartburn through Cathy's chest. 'You're thinking like the lad of twenty that you used to be! You're just thinking about love and desire and how thwarted and frustrated you feel. You're not thinking about real life at all, Mario.'

'Oh, I am, Cathy. This place, this house . . . is it not real life? The streets outside, are they not real? The realest place you ever saw?'

'Maybe they are,' she said. 'And I even think Sofia is liking it here more than she did at first. She's fitting back in here, even enjoying it. But she can't move back here with you, Mario.'

'I think she can,' he said, splitting open a packet of cigarettes and offering her one. 'I think she should.'

Cathy was caught off guard then. She let something slip that she shouldn't have. She let Mario light her cigarette and she said, without thinking: 'But what about her baby?'

Mario's eyes widened. 'Her what . . . ?'

And all at once Cathy felt sick.

Then he was smiling, as if Sofia pregnant was even better. Even if it was another man's child. Even Tonio's, who he seemed to despise. Bringing Sofia and her unborn baby here was even more of a theft. Even more of a triumph. And his home would be even more full of family. Cathy could see, all of a sudden, how Mario was thinking.

Chapter Thirty-Four

Cathy felt sick and furious with herself for letting out Sofia's secret. It felt like a ticking timebomb in that mostly empty house at the top of the hill. Sooner or later, Mario was going to use the knowledge to his own advantage.

But how? How could any of this work out to his advantage now? Cathy had let slip that Sofia was pregnant with Tonio's child. She was expecting her own husband's child. Surely that made it harder – if anything – for Mario to steal her away now?

Mario was tricky, though. He was calculating and determined, Cathy could see that. She had seen that all along.

'What's the matter with you?' Sofia smiled at her that evening as she dressed to go out in the town. 'Help me with the back of this dress, would you? It's all hooks and eyes . . .'

'It's beautiful,' said Cathy.

'It's an antique. It belonged to his mother . . . you don't think it looks too old-fashioned, do you? It's not weird, is it? Going out in town in a dead woman's frock?'

Cathy smiled. 'His mother was obviously a very stylish woman. This is really lovely. It fits you perfectly. I've never seen you wear a gown like this.'

'Maybe it's too showy,' Sofia frowned. Then she looked Cathy in the eye. 'So, what is the matter with you today? You seem jumpy . . . almost guilty.'

'Do I?' Cathy fiddled with the hooks and eyes, glad of the distraction. 'Oh, it's nothing really. I . . . I was just writing a postcard and started missing home and everyone. Daft, isn't it? No one there really gives a hoot about me . . .'

'Cathy, that's not true and you know it.'

'Maybe.' She tried to smile. 'But it's funny, when you get away from your normal life, and get a fresh view on it, it makes you wonder, doesn't it?'

'Makes you wonder what?' Thoughtfully Sofia was smoothing the ruched material down her arms and touching her stomach, where the baby was yet to start showing.

'Nothing, nothing.' Cathy tried to wave her own seriousness away. 'I suppose I'm looking forward to going home more than I expected I would.' She finished the last fastening. 'Aren't you?'

Sofia sighed deeply. 'To be honest, Cathy, I just don't know anymore.'

The plan for that night excluded Cathy. It was Mario's idea.

'Do you mind though?' Sofia fretted. 'It's not to do with me. It was Mario's suggestion.'

Cathy made light of it, though she was boiling with annoyance inside. She sat smoking at the kitchen table and said, 'No, of course not. You two don't want me tagging along for every single trip out, do you? For god's sake, I'm not an actual chaperone, am I? You two have loads to catch up on. Loads of old sights to see. And I'm not really hungry this evening, to be honest. There's some bread and cheese from the market. I'll just peck at that . . .'

Sofia stood worrying in her borrowed finery. She looked absolutely gorgeous, with her hair piled up and a silk shawl draped over her shoulders. 'If you're sure you'll be all right . . .'

Mario was beside her suddenly, in a dark suit with a loosely-knotted scarf hanging down the front of his shirt. His unruly tangles of hair had been tamed and combed down with water. As soon as they stepped out into the warmth of the evening street they would dry and spring up again, Cathy knew it. No matter how buttoned up and combed down he might be right now, there was something irrepressible about Mario. He would not stay on best behaviour for very long.

'Enjoy your quiet evening,' he told Cathy, with an inscrutable smile.

'I will,' she promised him, with a narrowed glance which she hoped he would take as a warning. But really! A warning – *him*! He'd do as he pleased, whatever the outcome and she just knew it.

Oh, he was lovely looking, though. As she watched them sally forth into the Neopolitan night, Cathy could have kicked herself for melting once more over his looks. But it was just looks, that was all. There was nothing wrong with just looking.

From her place at the table in the courtyard, Cathy could hear the tall front doors slam.

There was no way she was sitting here all night. No way.

It was a snap decision. She was up on her feet in a flash. She pulled on her heaviest, most disguising woollen and found a floppy-brimmed hat on the wooden stand in the dark hall.

She was going to follow them, incognito, through the city streets.

Cathy didn't stop for a moment to consider whether she was being rash or foolish. She simply knew that this was the right thing to do.

Off went her battered slippers and she laced up her walking shoes, quickly, quickly, before she could lose track of her quarry.

She slipped out into the night, pulling the heavy doors of the Grapelli home closed behind her. Outside in the busy street the night air felt soupy and uncomfortable. How much nicer it would have been just to sit in the courtyard reading her book all evening. Out here she was getting jostled and buffeted about as soon as she entered into the swiftly-flowing crowd.

But there they were! Only a few hundred yards ahead. They were unhurried, ambling along in the unruly melee as if it was their natural element. They stood out at mile, those two; Sofia in her borrowed midnight blue frock. Cathy had never seen her wear something low-cut and daring like that! All her bosoms were on show, and Cathy had been too polite to mention it. Probably it had always been the style, here in this louche country! Heads were turning in the street as Sofia was led along by Mario. It turned out it was very easy to pick her out in a crowd.

And to follow her. That's what Cathy did. Feeling guilty and lumpy in her cardigan and stout shoes. Oh, what am I playing at? She wondered at herself. Somehow she always ended up in the midst of drama and palaver. Surely all this would go wrong and she would end up hopelessly lost in the dark and wild streets of Naples! She would wind up getting murdered . . . or worse! Perhaps she should have popped a knife into her bag, just in case she needed to defend herself against thieves and killers? But that cheese paring knife would have been no good anyway.

Her thoughts were rambling and idiotic as she fought through the evening crowd, desperate to keep her friends within her sight. It was a jolly, laughing, boisterous crowd. Really, it should have been fun being out here in all this good-humoured humanity, but instead Cathy was feeling mithered.

You fancy him too, don't you? She allowed herself to think the terrible thought. Yes, it was there, that feeling, and there was no denying it. The rebellious suggestion bubbled up to the surface of her mind. Yes, I love the look of him too and he sends me somewhere in my imagination that I never thought I'd go. That was another reason she was so dead against letting

Mario and Sofia get up to any kind of clandestine wickedness. Cathy's own jealousy was spurring her on to follow them through the winding cobbled streets.

No, no, she told herself. It was all concern for Sofia, that was why she followed them. This man was capricious and dangerous. She felt he could do absolutely anything, and that Sofia was entirely within his power.

Her pursuit of them went on for hours that night.

They couldn't sit still! They perched at bars and at low tables outside rough cafes. They were toasted everywhere by people who seemed to know Mario and treated him as if he was showing the love of his life the best night of hers. Sofia was laughing and gabbling away in what sounded to Cathy like very natural, fluent Neopolitan. Had her native speech come back to her, unbidden, magically, all in a rush? She was carrying on like she didn't have a care in the world.

Cathy kept a careful distance, feeling like a strange kind of spy. She stood in doorways and slimy alleyways, a few doors down from every place that her friends paused to eat and drink. Her stomach was rumbling and her head was throbbing. She felt like crying. She felt more left out than she had ever felt in all her life as she watched them crouch at a table by the roadside, sharing sloppy slices of pizza.

She doggedly kept on their heels as they finished their meal and went in search of dessert. The streets became steeper. The crowds were more raucous. Soon they were walking in a more lonely, shadier part of town. Cathy had to be very careful to hang back and muffle the clip-clop sound of her footsteps.

They came at last to a vantage point high above the town. It was even more steep than the one from which they had looked at the volcano the other day. A low railing at the very edge didn't look too substantial. A kind of shiver of warning went through Cathy as she watched Mario draw Sofia on.

'Come, come see the view,' he said. At least, that's what it sounded like to Cathy. The two of them were both speaking their local dialect now and that was another thing that made Cathy feel shut out.

They stood together and all at once he clasped hold of her.

Sofia looked ready to receive his kiss.

There was something hard and almost angry-looking in the way he held himself, Cathy thought. She clung to the shadows and she seethed with frustration and . . . *fear*.

Yes, fear. Because he didn't look like a man who was set upon passionately kissing his lover.

All at once, in Cathy's eyes, he looked instead like a man who was about to do something terrible. A man who knew he might not get his heart's desire. A man who was fearing he might lose out again. For just a second, he looked like a man who might be set upon violence.

Chapter Thirty-Five

It was a scene that would come to haunt Cathy for a long time. The very recollection of that moment at the top of the town, overlooking all of Naples, would embarrass her for years. It was just mortifying.

She saw the tension and the intent look on Mario's face as his strong hands grasped hold of Sofia, and she didn't pause for a second. She leapt forward, out of the shadows, and yelled at the pair of them.

'Sofia, man! Watch out, you damned fool! He's going to shove you over the edge!'

She shouted this at the top of her voice, startling both of the lovebirds.

'What . . . ?' Mario gasped as he realised who this was, lurching towards him in a floppy hat.

'C-Cathy . . . ?' gasped Sofia, looking horrified.

Cathy seized hold of her friend. 'If he can't have you, he's going to kill you, Sofia. Look at that crazy light in his eyes!'

Sofia struggled to free herself from her friend. 'You're the bloody crazy one. What are you talking about?'

'I saw him tense up as he took hold of you.' Cathy was looking wildly from one to the other. 'He was getting ready to shove you over the railing to your death! You were right in the first place about him, Sofia. He's going to kill you out of revenge and spite . . .' As she tried to explain herself, Cathy found she was running out of steam. Both Sofia and Mario were looking at her in amazement. Mario had stepped away and was leaning nonchalantly against the low railing and he even looked amused by all of Cathy's melodrama.

'So, tell me, Cathy . . .' he chuckled. 'What are you doing here? How do you come to be here, jumping out at us in a private moment?'

Cathy defiantly tossed her head. 'I followed you! Aye, I'm not ashamed to admit it. I went through the whole town, dogging your footsteps tonight – and I'm glad I did an' all. He's just been buttering you up, Sofia. He's been winning you over and then he got you up here and he was going to do you in!'

Sofia's mouth was agape as she tried to take in what her hysterical friend was saying. One moment the two of them had been here alone, high above the hot, sultry stew of the city, enjoying the view and the cooling night breeze. He had stepped towards her and there had been love in his eyes. She saw it properly there in his face and knew that, when he took hold of her, he was going to kiss her, hard. Long and deep and sweetly. She knew that this was the moment it was going to happen and Sofia had known that she was happy to submit to it, and to him. The moment – long in coming – had arrived.

But then Cathy had come barrelling out of the shadowy alley behind them, screeching like a banshee.

Sofia's lips almost stung with the feeling of not getting that kiss. Her heart pounded with frustration and fear and also, anger.

'Cathy, you don't know anything. Why would Mario want to harm me?'

'Because . . . if he can't have you, then he wants no one to have you.'

Mario laughed out loud. 'What is this? Some kind of opera? Or a cheap Hollywood movie?'

'I saw the way he was with you just then,' Cathy said. 'It was frightening.'

Mario shrugged. 'It was just passion. Maybe you've never seen such a thing?' He looked mockingly at Cathy and she felt like slapping him.

'He would never hurt me,' Sofia said.

'I'm more likely to hurt myself,' Mario said, jumping up and taking hold of the iron railing. Next thing he was up on top of it, balancing precariously. His whole weight was on the not-too-steady-looking barrier. 'Yes, look at me!' he shouted, wobbling slightly as the two women stared at him in appalled horror. 'If you do not take me, Sofia – I will jump! If you tell me you do not want me, I will go to my death!'

Cathy caught a quick glimpse of just how high up they were and how dangerous this silly stunt of Mario's was. Typical man! Suddenly – by showing off and doing something utterly stupid – he had made this whole thing all about him.

Sofia was looking up at him and Cathy was amazed to see there was admiration and even laughter in her face. 'Oh, get down, you fool!' she babbled at him. 'You absolute *citrullo* . . . !'

He carried on standing there, framed against the darkening skies, looking like some bizarre piece of classical statuary. 'I mean it, Sofia.'

'What, that you are going to jump? Don't be ridiculous.'

'I mean . . . that I love you, and I should never have let you go.'

Cathy shouted, 'See? I knew he was up to no good!'

Sofia gritted her teeth. 'Cathy, keep out of this. You've caused enough fuss here tonight.'

'I was trying to save you from yourself!' Cathy felt rather hurt by her friend's attitude.

'By following us around all over the city? We're adults, Cathy! We can take care of ourselves and make our own decisions.'

Cathy frowned. 'I didn't trust him . . . I still don't.'

Mario coughed loudly. 'Look, I'm still up here. Am I jumping or not? I don't think I can keep my balance for much longer.'

As they looked at him there was a nasty scraping noise. Old metal rubbing against crumbling brick. There was another sinister screech and the two women realised at the same time what it was. 'The railing's giving way!' Cathy yelled.

'Get down from there!' Sofia cried and leapt forward to grasp hold of his shirt.

Everything seemed to happen all at once. Mario flung himself forward, back to safety, landing squarely on top of Sofia and Cathy. The railing he'd been balancing on with foolish bravado came loose as he kicked free and it tumbled off the viewpoint heavily down through the skies. Then there came a very noisy crash as it caused a lot of damage to somebody's rooftop far below.

'You might have killed someone!' Cathy gasped.

'We'd best get away from here, then,' Mario said ruefully, jumping up. With exaggerated gallantry he helped Sofia to her feet. She looked winded and pale and a whole lot less amused by their escapade than she had earlier.

'That could have been you, falling all that way,' she said, going to peer over at where the railing had dropped like a stone.

'But would you have cared, Sofia?' he asked.

'How can you even ask that?' she threw back at him.

Cathy was squinting into the gloom far below. 'I don't think it actually went through anyone's roof, but it knocked a load of tiles loose and damaged a chimney.'

'Let's get away from here,' Sofia said, shivering and pulling her shawl tighter round her shoulders. 'I've had enough of this evening now. I want to go back.'

Cathy looked at her thinking, how is it she could look only slightly ruffled, after being knocked to the floor like that? Sofia looked more beautiful than ever. As she turned to walk back to the steep cobbled alleyway, she was acting rather aloof with both Mario and her best friend.

'Look, I'm sorry if I've mucked things up and made everything worse,' Cathy tried to tell her as they all walked home, exhausted. 'I was only trying to help.'

Sofia didn't say anything. She just gave her a tight little smile and Cathy couldn't work out how she felt at all.

Mario was loping along behind them, thoroughly pleased with himself. 'I quite enjoyed all of that! Did you see me, balancing on that railing? It could have broken at any moment! I could have fallen and had my brains dashed out, couldn't I?'

Cathy pulled a face at him. 'That might have been for the best.'

Nothing she could say could make him angry. 'Oh, Cathy Sturrock, I love you!' he cried.

'Don't you *love* me,' she muttered. 'There's been far too much of that carry on as there is.'

The three of them walked on in silence, rejoining the late-night crowds of the city. The two women were quiet but nothing, Mario found, could spoil his ebullient mood. Yes, his moment of seizing a kiss with Sofia had been broken. Absurdly, it had been interrupted by that foolish friend of hers. Mario had been thwarted at the very moment of his triumph. But it was all right. It would keep, that moment of seduction. He had seen the look in Sofia's eyes. Now he knew for sure how she felt about him.

Mario was pleased with himself as they walked home that night because he now knew for sure just how Sofia felt.

He knew that she belonged to him.

Chapter Thirty-Six

The following day and the day after that it was all rather stilted and awkward at the house on Via Toledo.

Mario kept out of the women's way. He was up with the larks, when the first street vendors were setting up their stalls outside. The heavy front door slammed and he was off. Neither Sofia nor Cathy asked him where he was dashing off to.

'I suppose he's embarrassed,' Cathy mused as she tried to brew coffee in his battered, blackened silver pot. It was trickier than Mario had made it look, but she was determined.

'Embarrassed . . . !' Sofia echoed, amazed. She was in her nightie at the kitchen table and this derisive response was the first thing she'd said to her friend since the night before last.

'Well, yes,' Cathy went on. 'Declarations of love and all that. Jumping up on that railing . . .'

'I don't see why he'd be embarrassed,' Sofia said. Then she looked her friend up and down as if to say, 'You, on the other hand . . .'

Cathy ignored her and went back to coaxing coffee out of the foreign pot. She scalded her fingers and scattered soggy grounds everywhere but eventually she produced a thick, oily liquid that wasn't a million miles from coffee. 'Want some?'

Sofia shrugged and grimaced.

Cathy sat down opposite her. 'Listen, lady . . .'

Sofia put up her hands. 'Don't start. I feel bloody awful this morning. Sick as a dog.'

'I was just about to ask you . . .'

'I can't answer questions now. I don't know anything anymore.'

Cathy sipped her boiling coffee. Actually, it wasn't half bad. She felt her stomach gurgle and realised they had no provisions for breakfast. All at once she felt like they were prisoners here in Mario's big house.

There was a fat bluebottle buzzing around the kitchen and she felt it preying on her nerves.

'What are we going to do, then?' Cathy asked. 'What happens now?'

Sofia was frank with her. 'I honestly don't know.'

'But do you love him back? Do you really feel the same? Are you ever going back home?'

'Oh, Cathy, stop going on.' Sofia put her hands to her ears, as if she could block her out. I'm the bluebottle! Cathy thought. Buzzing around her head and making her feel sick with irritation.

'Am I to travel back to England and explain it all myself?' Cathy asked. 'Do I have to be the one who goes to see your poor family? Am I to tell them, she's staying where she is . . . with Cousin Mario?'

'He isn't really my cousin,' Sofia muttered.

'You know what I mean,' Cathy said.

'I . . . don't . . . know . . .' Sofia gasped and looked more upset than Cathy had ever seen her.

Mario bought bread and oranges and peaches at the market. He knew they would be sitting at that table with nothing to eat. He'd surprise them. He'd spoil them. He'd cut through this sulky, soggy, very English silence that had been hanging over them since that night on the town.

Why couldn't they laugh about things together? That whole scene with the falling railing had been funny. At least he'd thought so. And wasn't he the one who'd almost perished? If he could laugh about it now, he didn't see why those women couldn't.

Everything was such heavy weather to them! That was the essence of being English, he thought. In her years in South Shields, Sofia had made herself so thoroughly English that she could no longer live properly. She couldn't live through her feelings and passions. She was all bound up in her thoughts and obligations, just like they all were. Cathy was a terrible influence on her! She was a lovely looking woman, but she was puritanical and narrow, Mario thought. It would take a lot to make a woman like Cathy bend to his will.

But she liked the look of him, didn't she? He'd seen the way she looked at him when she didn't think he noticed. Why, both these English ladies were in thrall to him. They followed his every move like wary cats, sitting poised, ready to flee or pounce.

Despite all the complications (and who really cared about complications?) Mario found this tangled web of desire and indecision rather exciting. Let them argue and worry and fight over him!

He was going to claim Sofia sooner or later, he just knew it. He was going to take her back and make her his, just as she always should have been. He was going to make that thief and gambler Tonio Franchino suffer horribly at last, just as he'd promised his mother he would. Tonio deserved it! Revenge had been a long time coming.

Bearing bagfuls of fruit and other supplies, Mario went bursting back into the house and surprised both women. They were on their second cups of coffee, smoking and sitting in their dressing gowns. They looked like slatterns perching there and this delighted Mario as he unpacked his shopping.

'We'll eat something,' he told them both sternly. 'And then you'll both dress yourselves up and we'll go out and have a nice day.'

Cathy squinched her nose at him. 'I don't think either of us are in the mood for sightseeing.'

He wasn't having that. 'Yes, you are. Look at you two! Wasting your lives sitting at a table! You must eat and get ready. We are going out to the beach.'

Sofia stared at him. 'But I don't want to go to the beach. I want to stay here.'

'Hard cheese,' he grinned, showing off one of the English phrases he had picked up during his visit there. 'You are in my house and you will do as I say.'

In the end, the lure of sunshine actually drew them out of the house. As Cathy dressed in her bathing suit and then pulled a loose wrap about her shoulders, she felt somewhat better and more relaxed than she had done for days. The sunlight through the narrow French windows in her room was lovely and soft. There was a tiny balcony overlooking the private courtyard two storeys below. There was the scent of lemon and verbena drifting up from the trees down there.

It was beautiful here. She ought to be enjoying her time. As she'd said once before, it was the holiday of a lifetime. She had never been anywhere like this before, and who knew when she would get to come somewhere as nice as this again. Really, who cared what daft Sofia got up to? Let her take all the lovers in the world! Let her behave just how she wanted to behave. Why was it up to Cathy to keep a watch on her?

Let them all go to hell! Cathy shocked herself with her irreligious thoughts, sparing a glance for the elaborate crucifix over her bed and the portrait of the Madonna and Child above the washstand. What she really meant was: I'll keep out of their business. They can look after themselves.

Then, when she glanced down into the courtyard, she saw them. They were standing by the kitchen table, which was still littered with the scraps of their breakfast. They were standing close together. They were canoodling. That was the only word for it.

Oh, Sofia, her friend thought. Are you really going to throw everything away just for the sake of this man?

As she watched Sofia making a show of herself downstairs, Cathy also thought: I would, as well. I'd chuck away everything for him. I really would.

She took a deep sigh and pretended she hadn't watched him kissing Sofia like that, and Sofia responding so urgently. She would pretend that everything was normal and quite above board. She'd do her best to enjoy a day at the seaside – on the most softly golden sands that she had ever seen, Mario was promising.

Yes, just have some fun and relax, Cathy thought. Forget about all the complicated business of love. What do you know or care about love?

Chapter Thirty-Seven

That afternoon, he deliberately altered the mood of their little group. It was a palpable, caring thing that Mario did. Somehow he took them back into their holiday mood and provided a convivial atmosphere.

The beach he took them to was as golden and secluded as he promised. It was just a short, noisy bus ride away. They arrived with their ears clanging with the noise of crowds and engines and their heads stuffed with gasoline fumes, but after just a few minutes on the soft, sandy beach they felt calmer and happier.

Mario showed them the nicest spot to lie in under the sun. Then he hurried away to a kiosk and brought them ices. Everything about him proved his willingness to please and divert them. He wanted to scrub away the tensions and palaver of the preceding days.

The flavoured ice in cones of paper was delicious. The two girls shed the outer layers of their outfits and lay down under the beating sun. They licked their hunks of ice like cats would, and almost as wordlessly.

Mario left them in peace, hurrying to the water's edge. Within seconds he had chucked off his shoes and socks. The tide came shushing in, foaming lacily round his brown, dirty bare feet. Then, with barely a thought, he had flung off his soft cotton trousers and his crumpled shirt. He ran out into the water in his slightly baggy, ancient-looking underwear.

'That man has absolutely no bloomin' shame.' Cathy shook her head at him. His broad dark back and shining hair had disappeared beneath the waves now. He kept reappearing as he swam, popping up here and there at different points in the churning water, swimming with great energy and confidence.

Sofia was watching, too, her eyes fixed on the horizon, and her thoughts clearly elsewhere. 'I suppose men feel they have to do things, to show off. To win us over. I don't know. I don't really understand them . . .'

'Ha! You're right, they're impossible, aren't they?' Cathy said and thought about her own experience of men. Well, she'd hardly known her young beau Christopher at all before he went off to war and got himself blown to bits. They had belonged to very different worlds and knew that they would never be allowed to be together. The times they spent were clandestine and innocent. Apart from that last time, when he was so set and hard and determined on taking what he wanted from her.

And Noel! Well, he hardly even counted as a man, did he? He was a supernatural kind of being, like a goblin or a demon. He was old womanish, peevish and nasty in his moods. He was hardly a good example of his own sex.

Then there had been Matty Johnston of course, who Cathy had found herself drawn to so powerfully. She blushed to remember what she had got up to with him all those years ago. One of the dangerous Johnston clan. She hadn't been able to resist him. And how they had been disturbed and discovered by Noel as they made love in the saloon bar of the Robin Hood that night! But Matty had been passionate and wonderful with her. She had lost him years ago, but the anguish she had felt back then, more than ten years ago, was still fresh in her soul.

Cathy could feel it once again right now as she lay on the sand and thought about how little she knew about men.

Next to her, Sofia closed her eyes and lay on her back, letting the insides of her eyelids glow scarlet. She felt like she was drinking in the goodness of the sun's rays. Mario had warned them not to stay too long under the direct sun. 'What with you both being delicate flowers,' he said, before running off to swim. 'You must seek shelter under cliff edge.' He was right. It would be sensible to move before long, before they burned or turned themselves sick with the sun fever, but right now it was just lovely. Cathy was delighted to see her troubled friend calming down.

'Women don't have to prove anything,' Cathy murmured. 'They are just women. There are so many things we have to go through that silly men don't. We change, our bodies change, we do the most extraordinary things with our bodies . . .'

Sofia opened her eyes and looked up at her. 'Yes, men are just men. They grow up and they're the same all their lives. Just a bit fatter and balder, like Tonio. But it's like they have to prove all the time what they are. They have to keep showing off that they are really men.'

Cathy shrugged. 'I suppose they're always fighting and competing with each other for a reason. They're very primitive, compared with women.'

The two of them laughed at this and watched as Mario finished his swim and came wading back through the shallows to the sand. His baggy underpants were clinging to him in a way that made Cathy blush. Did he seem bothered? Not at all. He came swaggering up to them with his clothes bundled up under his arms and no sense at all that his immodesty was showing so obviously.

'Was your swim nice?' Sofia asked him, and the spark of desire between them was unmistakable.

'Bellissima,' he grinned, and shook his wet curls like a dog would, showering them both in tiny droplets.

Cathy rolled her eyes. 'We were just talking about men . . .'

'Ha! Oh, yes?' he said.

'About how men always seem to have to prove their manliness. To show off that they're men.'

He sat down on the sand to dry off in the sun's rays, frowning with interest at what she was saying. 'Go on . . .'

'It seems to involve knowing things,' Cathy went on. 'Knowing how to do things, knowing things about the world, knowing how to carry yourself, to be. Who teaches you these things? Who teaches you to be a man?'

He frowned heavily and looked out to the sea he had been splashing around in so happily, moments before. 'My papa,' he said. 'My old da, as I think you people of the north call fathers? Alphonse. He died a long time ago.'

Sofia reached up to touch his arm: a consoling gesture he smiled at, before taking a deep breath and continuing. Mario laughed suddenly. 'He didn't teach me all that much, for there wasn't really time before he was taken from us . . . but there were some things I do recall.'

Cathy felt herself becoming tender towards him as he confided these things. She felt less challenging and abrasive towards this brash Italian man.

He said, 'Very simple things, my father taught me. He said them out of nowhere, just as we were going to the football or walking in the streets together. He would say them as they occurred to his mind, you understand? He said – keep your keys in one pocket and your wallet in the other and never change where they are. So that you know where they are always. You never have panic.'

Cathy smiled at him. 'What else?'

'Two other things I remember. Never hold in . . . what is the word when your wind is broken?'

Both women started laughing. They couldn't help themselves.

'My father say, never hold in the broken wind in your bottom. You hurt your insides, like Uncle Sal did. He went to hospital for that. You must let out that bad air, even if it stink.'

Sophia burst out, 'Pumping! You're talking about pumping!'

Cathy could hardly believe what she was hearing. 'And this was the great advice your da passed down to you?'

Mario put on a phoney hurt look. 'Is good advice, I think.' Then he smiled warmly at them both. 'Then the third thing he tell me he said was the most important of all. He said, a man needs to find a woman – the exact right woman – to make his life with. She will give him his kids, his family, his whole life. He must recognise her when he first see her, and he must never let her get away from him. He has to treasure her, whatever happens.'

Strangely, there was no frisson of tension at this. Cathy didn't feel like he was putting pressure on Sofia again. It wasn't yet another salvo in his assault on her wedding vows and the status quo. He was simply stating the paternal wisdom which had been passed down to him.

Then Mario added, 'There was one more thing that my lovely, gentle father taught me. Showed me, really, for it was a practical thing. It was maybe a week before he died. He took me to the mirror in the bathroom and he stood there with me. He used the soap brush with the big bristles and covered my cheeks and chin with suds, staring into my face as he did it. I could smell his breath: tobacco and dark coffee and grappa . . . and something acrid that was just him. And he took out this blade – this bare, cut-throat blade. I didn't fear it or him, I just held so still, like he told me to.'

'That's so lovely,' Sofia said. 'He taught you how to shave.'

'We had almost the same face, so he knew the bits that would get nicked and cut if you weren't careful. He showed me how to swerve around these mistakes he had made on his own face, all those years. Mama came to the doorway to watch a little worriedly as he used that blade on me. There were a few dribbles of blood as he worked and let me take a go. But it was soon done. My face was perfect and gleaming. We congratulated each other and opened beer. Then a week later he was dead.'

Cathy felt the last bit of the story like a punch to the gut. 'What . . . ? How . . . how did he die?'

Mario looked bitter. 'A foolish end. A street brawl. We don't know if he caused it or was an innocent. He was hot-tempered, though. He was in a crowd on the Via del Vecchio Pozzo and he wound up getting stabbed in the belly. They ran off and left him dying there in the dust. First we knew of it, a crowd of our neighbours came carrying him up to our door. Mama went hysterical of course. That night she told me: "You must be man in our house now."'

Sofia remembered it all. She had been perhaps eleven or twelve at the time. 'You were only thirteen,' she said.

He nodded and looked up at the glaring sun. 'I think we should move to the shade now.'

As they gathered up their things and looked for somewhere cooler to spend the balance of the afternoon, Mario became noisy and silly again. 'What I would love above all is at least two wives. Maybe three! I have enough love and joy to give all.'

'Mucky bugger,' Cathy laughed. 'You're just greedy and selfish.'

'I never said I wasn't,' he protested. 'But could you imagine? What if the three of us were like a family? Living like we do now? Just us three forever – how happy would we be, do you think?'

Sofia punched him lightly on the bare shoulder and called him an idiot. Both women were scandalised by what he was saying.

'Just think of it,' he said. 'Who says we ought to live just like everyone else?'

Cathy knew that the world worked very differently, though. You couldn't just love who you wanted. You couldn't move everything around and destroy everyone's family in order to live the way you wanted to. You simply couldn't be selfish like that, could you?

The three of them found the most alluring patch of shade on the silky sand and fell quiet then, sated by memories and Mario's foolish philosophising. They dozed away the afternoon till it was time to return home and eat.

It was a peaceful day, all told. A healing day. That was until, as they tiredly returned to the streets, Mario encountered the Carabinieri.

Chapter Thirty-Eight

The three of them wandered back into the city feeling more light-hearted than they had for days. They were even laughing as they strolled along and Mario was larking about, linking arms with one woman and then the other. Cathy pushed him away, not too roughly, and he staggered into the street much to Sofia's amusement.

'Hey . . . !' he yelled, and dashed after Cathy, as she dodged other passers-by. Next thing, they were tussling playfully in public.

'Get off me, you fool!' Cathy laughed.

That was when the policeman arrived. Without any preamble, he raised the butt of his heavy weapon and clubbed Mario on the head.

Before anyone could react in shock, Mario dropped to the pavement.

'Leave these women alone,' the Carabinieri shouted at the prone Mario.

Sofia was horrified, surging forward and falling to her knees to check he was all right. The crowd of passers-by drew back and swerved around the scene of violence. They flowed around them like a river around an island, knowing the wisdom of avoiding the police.

'What did you do that for?' Cathy demanded of the young, hard-faced official. 'He didn't mean any harm!'

'We were just horsing around,' Sofia told him crossly, and then realised that he didn't understand a word she was saying. She stumbled with the Italian, '*Stavamo solo facendo gli stupidi!*'

But the policeman wasn't impressed. He brandished his gun at them. To Cathy's shock it looked very like a machine gun. Was he threatening to spray them all with bullets if they didn't start behaving? 'What's wrong with you?' she cried. 'You can't just go clubbing people to the ground for no reason.'

Sofia was reviving a groggy Mario, who was bleeding from his temple. A great stripe of sticky, dark blood covered half his face. He spat and a tooth accompanied the pink spray onto the pavement. 'You bastard,' he muttered, earning himself a kick in the stomach as he tried to stand. He fell again and the women screamed at the policeman, whose fellows were taking an interest by now, and were swaggering over to see what the fuss was about.

'Leave him alone!' Cathy was beside herself with fury, wanting to grab the gun out of his hands. He only looked about seventeen, standing there in his stupid feathery hat.

'Go home at once,' the policeman said. 'You are drunk and disorderly.'

'*Non puo dirci!*' Sofia told him. 'You can't tell us what to do.'

Cathy shook her head at her. 'Yes, he can. He's a *fascist*. That's exactly what he does. Come on, let's get Mario home. We can sort of brace him between ourselves.'

'Where do you *miscredenti* live?' the policeman barked, and Sofia told him. 'Ah, the quarteri di bassifondi.' He sneered as he described the place Mario and Sofia hailed from as the 'slum district'.

'Ignore him,' Sofia said, picking up the gist of what he'd said. Together they helped the dazed Mario to his feet and hurried away, under the watchful and contemptuous eyes of the young Carabinieri.

'He's lucky I didn't punch his lights out,' Mario said later. He was sitting on a kitchen chair under the stark bare bulb so that Sofia could get a good look at the cut underneath all his blood-soaked hair.

'Well, if you'd done that he'd have shot you in the street like a mad dog,' Cathy said. 'And all his bullyboy mates would have come running and taken me and Sofia away god knows where. So then where would we be, eh?'

Sofia dabbed at his head wounds with a cloth dampened with alcohol. 'You can't retaliate against people like that, Mario. You have to watch that temper of yours.'

Mario carried on swearing colourfully, cursing the whole brood of fascisti who were running his country. 'The place is gone to the dogs since they took over.'

'I thought you were glad that the streets were cleaner and all that malarkey,' Cathy teased him. 'I thought you liked the fascists?'

'I never said that,' he muttered darkly.

'It'll all end badly, you mark my words,' said Cathy. 'Having bairns strutting about the place with weapons like that. It's ridiculous.'

They sat quietly for a while, listening to Mario hiss and gasp at the alcohol's sting. 'You might need stitching,' Sofia fretted.

He swore about that, too. 'No way. It'll heal by itself.'

A dismal mood descended on the courtyard kitchen as the sky began to darken. 'Let's have a drink,' Cathy suggested. 'Will that cheer us up?'

Mario shrugged and suggested, 'Under that cupboard there, right at the back. There's a bottle of the limoncello that mama always made.'

The final bottle of the thick, sugary liqueur was retrieved from its dark storage corner. Cathy jolted at the tartness of it as she took her first sip from an ancient crystal tumbler. 'Jesus, that's gorgeous,' she whispered as it burned all the way down her throat.

'Mama used big fat lemons growing in her courtyard here. She made bottles every year. This is the very last one left.'

There were tears in Sofia's eyes as she sipped. 'I remember this! From being little. I was allowed to have the tiniest little bit. Wicked, really, giving a child strong drink like this! But the taste of it . . . this transports me back.'

Mario held up his glass in a toast. 'To better times.'

'*A tempi miglori*,' Sofia smiled at him.

Cathy tried to rouse them out of the torpor that the violent scene in the street had brought them to. 'The day had been so lovely until then!'

'Oh, it was beautiful,' Sofia enthused. 'Going to the beach was just the right thing to do. I felt like all the tension of weeks and weeks was flowing out of me. Thank you, Mario.'

He shrugged. 'Was nothing. Is just the beach. You live here, you take all that for granted. I thought you'd want to see it, the pair of you . . . you'd want at least one day by the sea.' He swallowed thickly and suddenly looked rather sulky. 'That is, before you go home again. To your South Shields.'

This mention of home brought another shift in atmosphere to the room. For some reason, Mario had mentioned the unmentionable: he had broached the subject of the two of them leaving.

All kinds of unspoken questions were hanging in the air. They muddled the already cloying atmosphere of mixed feelings.

The three of them drained their elegant glasses of limoncello and Cathy filled them up again, responding with a long-rehearsed landlady's instincts. 'It will be hard to leave here,' she said, smiling at Mario.

He grunted, staring at Sofia, who avoided his eye. She wouldn't be drawn on this. Not tonight. It really wasn't the time to talk about the future.

'What was that toast you said, Mario?' Cathy broke into their mute tension. 'Just before . . . teach me it, would you?'

'I'll tell you what it was,' said Sofia. *'A tempi miglori.'*

'And it means "to better times?"' Cathy asked. 'I'll drink to that. I'll remember that.'

Mario drank and looked up at them both. His kitchen had women in it again, talking loudly, chattering and being busy. He had loved having these visitors here. 'I thought these were the better times. I thought they were already here. I really think this time together . . . has been wonderful.'

Chapter Thirty-Nine

He kept on drinking through the next day, growing gloomier as he anticipated their leaving. The weather changed too, as if in response to his mood. There were thunderstorms over the wide bay and it turned an unpromising brownish grey colour. The narrow streets became dingy and the rain that sluiced down the gutters and into the courtyard was chilly. It was also apparent that Mario's house was quite leaky. He watched crossly as the women set out vast pans and buckets to collect the drips.

'Who would ever want to stay here? And live here? I can see why you would both want to abandon me. Is no good here.'

For some reason, as he drank the remainder of the limoncello, he was wearing his battered black fedora once more.

'You should let the cuts and abrasions on your head have the air on them,' Sofia told him.

'Huh, what do I care.'

'You might go septic.'

'What is *septic*?'

She tried to explain, but it was all lost on him. He was determined to be as miserable as possible. 'See how life is? One minute happy, top of the world. Next minute, you are flat on arse in gutter.'

'It was that bullyboy did that,' Cathy told him. 'It's because your people have let these awful fascists get in charge.'

'I never let them!' he shouted. 'I never wanted them.'

'Well, I wouldn't live in a place with police like that charging about with machine guns,' Cathy said flatly. 'Bugger that. They put me right off the place.'

'What of you, Sofia?' Mario said glumly, staring at her across the puddly kitchen table. 'Are you put off the place, too? Or will you stay and make me a happy man again?'

Sofia smiled sadly and managed to look annoyed with him at the same time. She shook her head at his selfishness, his crassness, his simple-mindedness. 'You think you can just demand that people do what you want. That's what you do, Mario. You express your desires loudly and plainly and expect people to be just as straightforward.'

'What is wrong with that? World would be a better place if more people were like this.'

Sofia laughed. 'Maybe.'

'And anyway, I have learned that being clear and plain about what you want is best. I let you go all those years ago because I didn't make it obvious how I love you. Then you run off with that fat rat Tonio. And him taking my grandmother's recipe for the best ice cream in the world! He is a rat. A thieving rat.'

Sofia flushed. 'He isn't a rat!'

'But he's fat. And he's bald. And he's not looking after you.'

'Mario . . .' she got up and went to him. Cathy had to look away for a moment, embarrassed by the intimacy of the gesture as Sofia took Mario's head in her hands. She stood beside him and hugged him to her, so his face was buried in her small, very slightly rounded belly. His fedora fell unnoticed onto the floor and he let out a muffled moan of frustration and misery.

Cathy turned to leave the kitchen, feeling like an intruder on their scene. She backed away, holding her heavy coffee cup in both hands. She loved the lumpy smoothness of the hand-thrown cup. Like everything here, it had a home-grown, authentic feeling to it. Everything had its place in this home because it had been here for many years. Things here had a sense of belonging to them.

Cathy looked at her friend cradling the tousled, injured head of the man who professed to have loved her for years. Did Sofia feel like she belonged here? Is that what she was experiencing now? Cathy imagined it would feel like a dull, dragging ache in the belly, like the monthly pains she knew all too well. It was the feeling of belonging and needing but knowing you can't stay.

The landlady of the Robin Hood paused by the tangled boughs of the lemon tree, staying to watch in fascination as Sofia hugged Mario. Or rather, submitted to his clinging hug and simply stood there, gently stroking his beautiful hair.

There was no doubt about it, he was a bonny man. Why, he'd managed to turn Cathy's head, too, she had to admit the fact. There was something powerfully charismatic and animalistic about the sheer force of him. He made you want to submit to that plain and simple forceful nature of his. It would feel like lying out in stormy weather and letting the rain soak you through and the thunder ring out loudly in your ears.

But Cathy knew that this was just her own long-subdued passionate nature responding to the summer storm that was Mario. Why, he was less *her* man than he was Sofia's. All they'd had was a mute flirtation, hardly even that.

Cathy stared, trembling, as Mario pushed his face into Sofia's belly. There was something almost unnerving about the sight, as if he longed to be inside her womb like her growing baby was. Is that what he saw in Sofia, perhaps? A kind of mother figure?

Sofia softly ruffled his hair and made him cry out sharply as she accidentally touched the swollen flesh wound. He pulled away and looked up at her ruefully. 'You're going to hurt me, one way or another, aren't you?'

'I still think you should have got your head stitched,' Sofia told him.

For some reason, Cathy was thinking about vinegar and brown paper. Jack and Jill, she thought. How absurd, to remember an old nursery rhyme just now. Mario had fallen and broken his crown and now he sat nursing his thumping head in his damp and dripping kitchen.

'Are you really going home to England tomorrow?' he asked her.

'Yes, of course I am,' Sofia said very bluntly, so he would have no doubt about it. 'You know I am, and why I have to. I have a life and a whole family there. I cannot and will not leave them.'

His face became harder, expressionless. But even from across the courtyard, Cathy could see that his eyes were filled with tears now. She wished she had left when she got up to leave. Why was she standing here with rainwater dripping down her neck, holding a bowl of cooling coffee, watching this poor man have his heart broken? Yet Cathy found that she couldn't turn away.

'I really love you, Sofia,' Mario told her.

'And I think . . .' she sighed. 'I think I love you, too. But as a cousin. As a family friend of my youth. *Uno amico della mia giovinezza.*'

'No . . .' he said. 'Not just that . . .'

'It's true,' she told him firmly. 'And the loves of our youth are important. They are fierce and true and maybe they never go away. Maybe they make us who we are today. But they are not our only lives, Mario. They are in our pasts. They are long gone. We must live the lives that belong to *us*, not to our younger selves. Not to the people we might have been.'

This was a long speech from Sofia, as she spoke her tumbling, churning thoughts out loud and tried to keep a firm grip on them. Yes, Cathy thought. She's right. We can't pretend to be who we used to be, not any of us. We must fully inhabit the people we are today and live the lives that truly belong to us. The force of those words went deeply into Cathy's heart and she even allowed herself to dwell for a second on her own problems.

Cathy wasn't even sure Mario was listening to her properly. He just kept a grip on Sofia's waist. His strong arms were wrapped tightly around her hips and he held on grimly as he sobbed. There was fresh blood in his hair from the ruptured wound and Sofia was helpless, standing there as the man robbed of hope cried himself out.

Chapter Forty

He saw them off at the terminale and he barely said a word. A day or two had passed since the worst of his tears. He threw no more accusations and recriminations at them. He had stopped begging Sofia to stay. There were no attempts at blackmail and not even the slightest hint of violence, apart from the crockery he smashed in the courtyard.

'Oh, Mario! Your mother's things. She looked after everything so carefully . . .'

The many cats scattered to the four winds, disturbed by the noises of destruction. When all the pottery was lying in shards, he stomped out of the house and returned with a paper sack of fresh bread, fruit and cheese. 'For the journey,' he said gruffly. 'So you don't starve to death. That train never stops for days and there is no car for dinner.'

They lugged their holiday bags and their sack of provisions to the station in the middle of the city, with Mario helping them every step of the way. There was none of his light-hearted banter or flirting. His eyes were dark and hooded and his lips were sealed.

On the concourse, the three of them stood clustered together in the midst of the crowd dashing hither and thither. They ignored everyone else. They even ignored the stern watchfulness of the Carabinieri, much in evidence on the platforms. The cool, dusty marble of the station echoed with the noise of a thousand other journeys.

The journey that the women were embarking on was towards a place they already knew inside out. A place that was almost too familiar. It felt like everyone around them was setting off into the exciting and the unknown and here they were, heading back in defeat, like people who were happiest in the world that they already knew.

Whistles were shrieking. Engines were growling. Soot and smoke went billowing up the hot, muggy platform. People were stirring, jolted into departure. Heavy doors were slamming and suddenly Mario had his arms around them, one at a time.

Cathy's heart was thumping loudly in her throat. My god, the feel of those arms around her! They were so thick and strong. His flesh was the colour of burned custard and he smelled so wonderful to her as he pecked both her cheeks and gazed into her eyes. 'You and your family are welcome here, forever, Cathy. So long as there are Grapellis here in Naples. You will come back one day, I know it.'

'Yes . . .' she said. 'I will,' feeling as if she was under a spell. But did she really mean it? Was this somewhere she could see herself coming back to? There was a strange stirring in her knotted, travel-wary stomach and then as far down as her loins. Oh yes, she would return. She'd return next week if she could. Three weeks wasn't enough at all. Three weeks? Was that really all it had been? The dates muddled up in her head. It was like Mario had bewitched her, messed up her senses and destroyed her sense of time.

Now he had his face buried in Sofia's jet-black hair. She had let the heavy blue-black mass of it hang down, and Cathy had wondered whether she'd be better off tying it up for travelling. But now she could see how Mario was losing himself in her flowing tresses. His arms were around her waist and, now that Cathy looked closer, she saw that he was trembling hard as he muttered into his love's ear.

'Now you must go,' he told them both abruptly, breaking away and taking up the bags again. 'Look! Everyone else is aboard! You must dash! Come!'

Then he seemed to scoop them, plus all their belongings, into his arms and bundled them aboard the massive, antiquated train.

They had covered miles before they said much to each other. The city's criss-crossing railway lines were a complicated blur that was soon left far behind them. Before long, the azure bay and the distant mountain were barely a memory.

Cathy fished around in the sack of provisions Mario had thrust at them as his parting gift. She found some of those strangely flat, pale fruits that they called Saturn peaches. She inhaled their sweetness and found her mouth filling with saliva, like she was suddenly ravenous and craving the taste of the place they had just left.

'Have one,' she told Sofia. 'You didn't have any breakfast.'

She found flatbread and soft sheep's cheese in the bag, too. He'd popped a bottle of wine in there, but Cathy thought that might be a bad idea. They didn't want to be travelling with sore heads.

'Give me the wine,' Sofia told her.

Right at the bottom of the paper sack there was a tiny black box. The velvet that covered it had lost its nap, and its hinge opened with a tiny creak. 'Oh my bloody god, Sofia,' Cathy gasped. 'You'll never guess what's he put in here with the packed lunch.' She snapped the box closed again quickly.

Sofia put down the corkscrew she was fiddling with. 'What is it?' she blinked, almost irritably.

'Here.' Cathy handed her the box and watched her carefully.

Sofia paled as soon as she saw what kind of box it was. 'Why, the bloody fool,' she muttered as if to herself. 'Didn't I keep telling him? Wasn't I firm enough with him? What's bloomin' Tonio going to say?'

Cathy said, 'You just have to hide it from him. Maybe you can find a way to send it back to Mario . . .'

'No, no . . .' Sofia said. 'Can you imagine? I've already broken the poor fella's heart once, twice, three times! Imagine if he got this back in the post . . .'

Cathy had to admit that her friend had a point. But really, what had possessed Mario to put this most precious of all objects in a sack of peaches, cheese and bread? What if they'd missed it? What if they'd scoffed the provisions and overlooked the tiny black box? What if that repository of hope and history had been simply tossed away with the sticky peach stones and the rinds of cheese and crusts of bread? It didn't bear thinking about.

'It must have been his mother's,' Sofia said, holding the wedding ring up to her face. She didn't remove it from the box, almost as if she feared it as a magical, talismanic object that would take over her mind. She didn't want to actually touch the tiny, glittering, exquisite thing.

'My god, I think it's diamonds, Sofia,' Cathy said, coming to sit closer. 'What must that be worth?'

'I've no idea . . .' Sofia whispered. 'Look at it in the light! It's like it's been hidden in the dark for years and now it's drinking in all the light of the sun . . .'

As if on cue, the train rounded the forested curve of a deep valley and the midday sun came flooding into their shabby carriage. The diamond ring that had been passed down through generations of Mario's family was ablaze with myriad colours.

'Is there no note with it?' Cathy asked.

Sofia frowned. 'Nothing. What could he say? What more did he need to say? What do you think this means? It's obvious.'

'I suppose so,' Cathy said softly. 'He's offered you everything. Now he's given you this. It's so . . .' She shook her head, seeing the panicked, stricken look on Sofia's face. 'What are you going to do? Hide it away?'

There was a moment of clouds passing in front of Sofia's expression. They churned as she thought this over. 'No, no . . . I can't! Look at who I live with. My mother! Why, there's no keeping secrets from her. She's like an old bloodhound in widow's weeds. I know she goes through all my things when I'm out of the house.'

Cathy was shocked. 'She never does!'

'There are no secrets from her. And also Tonio . . .' She clicked her tongue sorrowfully and shook her head. 'I hate saying this. It feels shameful. But you know what a gambler he is. He's a good man, but he is . . . incorrigible. And nothing is safe. He goes looking for cash, valuables, everything. He goes hunting through the house for things to gamble away.'

'Nay, lass!' Cathy swore. 'That's even worse than I thought!' She also thought: Sofia has no secrets at home, nor privacy. What a life to go back to! What a life she's spurning the devoted Mario for!

'If I take this . . . precious thing, this priceless ring back to my house . . . it will be found. And there will be uproar. There will be trouble. What am I doing with another man's ring?'

Tears were springing into Sofia's eyes and Cathy mutely cursed Mario. Even at a distance Mario was causing them bother!

Sofia leapt to her feet and in one swift motion thrust down the carriage's window. 'I'll throw it out! That'll be an end to it!'

She almost managed it, too. Cathy responded with alacrity and grabbed at her arm just as she was about to fling the wedding band into the deep green valley. 'No, no! You can't, Sofia! That's history. That's someone's whole family history of love. You can't, you just can't!'

The carriage was much noisier with the clanking and the shunting of the wheels coming in. The baking heat was breaking over them, too, with a glorious scent of pine trees. 'Then what do I do, Cathy? You tell me! You're always so bloody clever. You tell me what to do with it?'

It was like a curse. This twinkling expensive ring sat on Sofia's palm like a curse that her beloved had placed on them.

Then suddenly Cathy had an idea. 'Give it to *me*. I'll look after it. It will be safe with me, buried deeply in all the junk and clutter of the Sturrock household.'

Sofia saw at once that this was the best option that they had. 'Here, take it.' She snapped the lid shut and urged Cathy to hide it deep inside her travelling bag.

'It'll be safe with me,' Cathy promised her.

It was a foolish and rather rash promise. The two women thought that the ring and Mario could cause them no more trouble. But as they carried on their journey north, with each mile taking them closer to their faraway home, neither of them knew that their troubles were really only starting.

Chapter Forty-One

Minnie Minton never really expected to have much attention. She was the kind of girl who was always just there. She was on the fringes of things, on the very edge of everyone else's notice, but she was always present nonetheless. She had lived on Frederick Street for the whole of her life and was unremarkable to most people. She was one of the youngest of the Mintons and not a very bonny lass. Most people thought her a bit slow.

But Minnie wasn't at all slow. Her mind ticked and whirred all day long, brewing up thoughts and ideas she would never dare to divulge to anyone. If she gave utterance to half the things that passed through her brain they would surely lock her up! She'd be in the madhouse and they'd chuck away the key! She was sure of that. Sometimes her own wild ideas shocked even herself.

It was all too easy to pretend to be a bit dull and rather plodding. Especially in a family with lots of brothers and sisters and cousins dashing in and out. Her parents had taken in waifs and strays from other families and so their little house had always been teeming with other bodies, and there was always a million jobs to do. Minnie was a good worker and could be relied upon to help out her poor, exhausted mother.

This summer, she had more to do than ever before in her life. She had to help out most days at her mother Betty's fish bar, but she also had responsibilities at the Robin Hood. With Cathy Sturrock off gallivanting on the continent, she had to be there most evenings to help. There were still pints to pull and pots to wash. Noel had trained up Junie to work behind the bar. At first it had been a kind of joke, but then it had turned serious. Minnie thought that Junie was probably cursing the day she ever arrived here in the Sixteen Streets. It couldn't be denied though, for a girl who had been so prim and tidy in the first place, Junie was a natural as a barmaid. She had become confident, strident and loud, holding forth from her place at the bar and making herself popular with all the regulars.

Minnie pulled pints and took coins and watched amazed as Junie grew to fill the space vacated by her mother. Even Junie herself seemed surprised by her new role. 'I thought I would hate it,' she confided one evening. 'But I'm actually quite enjoying myself.'

The evenings were long. Under Cathy's guidance and care, evenings at the Robin Hood finished promptly at the legally licensed hour. She rang the ship's bell loudly and gave them all time to sup up and clear out. Cathy would stand by the doors and eject the last lingering boozers into the street. Everything was done correctly under Cathy's watch. However, with her gone, Noel Sturrock had instituted a few new rules and his rules, it turned out, meant that there weren't very many rules at all. Late in the evening there would be lock-ins. An air of complicity and unruliness would be the order of the day. The doors would be locked and bolted and the place would still be full. The curtains would be drawn and the lights turned down, so as not to draw attention. One or two of the local police were invited in for free, clandestine drinks, just to keep them sweet.

Minnie's opinion about the matter wasn't asked for. No one cared what Minnie thought. She was the kind of person no one paid much attention to. She was expected simply to work at the bar till the very early hours. She was meant to do just what she was told and keep working and keep pouring the drinks until she was dead on her feet.

June never complained, either. She loved the late boozing hours. She said it was like being in a dream, as the clock inched along past one a.m., two a.m., and they were still there. She would crack open a bottle of brandy and keep helping herself to potent swigs of the stuff. She offered some to Minnie, who was thrilled to be getting drunk like this with her best friend. Minnie's head spun until she could barely count out the right change when she served customers even more pie-eyed than she was.

She was half aware that the money flowing over the counter during these late after hour stints was going straight into Noel's capacious pockets. He was shifty and triumphant. 'I'm getting one over on that faithless hussy!' he cackled, and handed over a pocketful of sovereigns to his adopted daughter for her help. Minnie was rewarded with a single coin, bestowed upon her as if it were great riches. She accepted it humbly, knowing that she would work for nothing if she was asked to. She would have stood here working her fingers to the bone for free if it meant that she could be close to June every hour of each night.

Ah, that was the thing. That was one of the difficult, tricky, secret ideas that went whirling about in her mind. Minnie Minton's brain was whizzing with thoughts that no one could ever know about. Every now and then, she would stop and allow herself the luxury of thinking her thoughts at the proper speed and revelling in them. Now, a little bit moony and drunk on that stolen brandy, she stood by the dirty sink of slops, washing glasses, and she indulged herself in her secret thoughts: I love her. I love that Junie Carmichael. It's daft and it's not the kind of thing that's possible or proper. I'm her friend and I'd do anything for her. She knows, I hope, how much I love her. She must be able to see it in my face, every day. I see her every day and every night. And still that's not enough. I love Junie Carmichael. I love that girl to bits . . .

'Hey, dreamer!' June shouted down her lughole, making Minnie jump out of her skin. The object of her love was standing right beside her, looking tipsier than even Minnie was. She was breathing hotly into her ear. 'Are you asleep standing up, or what?'

Minnie blinked her eyes and Junie laughed at her puddled, dopey expression. 'What? I was just . . . I was . . .'

'It's almost three o'clock in the morning,' June sighed. 'Have you heard that lot through there? They've been singing non-stop since midnight. Aunty Martha's just about passing out at the piano. Her face is wet with sweat and tears. It's a brilliant night, isn't it? Every night just gets better and better.'

They were all being too loud, Minnie thought with a distant part of her mind. A last little rational nightlight was burning somewhere deep inside and it was telling her: the noise was rocking the whole pub to its very foundations. The street would be waking up. They'd be looking out of their bedroom windows, all the decent denizens of the Sixteen Streets. They'd be peering out through their bedroom curtains and swearing: 'What the divil's all that bloody noise about?'

Yet they wouldn't wonder for long. They'd see the light and the noise emanating from the Robin Hood. The whole place was radiating a reckless kind of lawlessness these days. Everyone knew that Cathy was away on holiday and that Noel had set about having himself some fun.

'He's going to run this place into the ground,' Minnie suddenly said aloud to Junie. 'It can't go on like this, even if he's bribing all the bobbies. He's going to ruin this pub for Cathy . . .'

'I think that's the very idea.' Junie shrugged. 'And do you know what? That bitch bloody well deserves it.'

Chapter Forty-Two

'All the young 'uns are spending the warm nights on the beach,' Minnie told her mother. 'It's so warm and lovely that they're taking blankets down there and sleeping all night by the fire.'

Betty Minton looked scandalised as she shovelled chips from the deep-fat fryer. 'Whatever for? What's the point when they've got perfectly good beds at home, most of them?'

'Oh, I can see the point,' Minnie smiled dreamily. 'I think it would be smashing waking up and hearing the sea right beside you.'

'Knowing you, you'd be in the wrong place and getting swept out to sea,' her mother scoffed. 'We'd never see you again.'

'I think it's probably safe,' Minnie said.

'It's all an excuse to run around all night and be rude,' Betty said severely. 'I'm not as green as those potatoes. I know what goes on. I was young once, an' all, you know.'

Minnie felt uncomfortable under her mother's gaze. 'Did they sleep out all night when you were a lass, Ma?'

'They certainly did,' Betty said. 'And we knew exactly what they were gettin' up to. I would have nothing to do with that carry on, and neither will you, my lass. I've brought you up to be a decent, sensible girl.' She lowered her voice a fraction so the people in the fish queue wouldn't hear her next words.

'Not like that pal of yours. I thought she was a respectable sort when she first pitched up here, but from what I hear, she's no better than she ought to be.'

'Who, Junie . . . ?' Minnie even liked saying her name out loud.

'Aye, that one. They say that she dresses like a trollop, standing behind that bar. And your da' says the language off her is something awful! She goes on like she owns that whole pub. I'm not sure I'm happy about you working there, our Minnie.'

A jolt of fear went through her. 'Oh, I have to be there. I have to help them, especially with Mrs Sturrock away abroad.'

'There's another one!' Betty crowed. 'What sort of example is that to give your long-lost daughter? Haring off abroad? Where did she go to, Spain?'

Minnie shook her head. 'Italy. And from what Bella tells me, she's on her way back. Her and Bella's mam sent a cable last night, apparently . . .'

But 'Swetty' Betty Minton wasn't listening properly. She was squinching up her face as she took the supper order from the next customer, a tiny old woman with a speech impediment. 'What's that, Katy Mars? No, we don't have skate. Or cod roe.'

Dealing with orders took their attention for a few moments and then Betty picked up the thread of the conversation once more. 'Now, that Bella Franchino, she's a much better friend for you, our Minnie. She's a respectable kind of girl, so sensible – and smart! I'm glad you're knocking about with her a bit more.'

'She's very nice,' Minnie conceded. She had known Bella since they were at school together. Bella had kept an eye out for the clumsy, scruffy girl from Frederick Street. Over the years they had drifted apart, especially with Bella's family moving to their grand house by the sea, but in recent days they had been palling up together again.

Minnie was toying with trusting Bella with her secret. She knew she could rely on the Italian girl. This secret of hers felt like a real burden and just quietly telling one person about it might help. A discreet and kind person like Bella – surely she would listen as Minnie unpacked her soul? She wanted to tell her things that even she didn't fully understand. Maybe Bella would say, 'What? Feelings like that? Oh, don't worry about them, Minnie pet. Everyone gets feelings like that from time to time! You mustn't worry about that. It's not strange. It's not wrong . . .'

Perhaps they'd be sitting in one of the private booths at the back of her father's ice cream parlour and the pretty Bella would pat her hand or something. They'd be eating ice creams out of those delicate bowls. It would be so consoling and comforting to hear Bella say words like these to her.

'You really don't think it's all that . . . strange?'

'Why, of course not!' Bella would laugh. Not a nasty laugh, or a mocking one. It would be light and carefree. She would be amazed to hear that Minnie had spent fretful nights lying awake. 'What a waste of energy worrying is! Why would you even think that you were made wrong? Why would you think you were so different to everyone else?'

Here Minnie would take a deep breath and become candid: 'But it is different, isn't it? For a lass to love another lass like this? To have feelings like this about another young girl? Doesn't that make me wrong? Isn't it bad?'

Bella would shake her head quite vehemently. 'No, Minnie, no!' she would insist. 'They are your feelings. There is nothing wrong with them. It's all natural. There is nothing at all wrong with you.'

How Minnie's heart would leap with joy and hope at this point! 'And . . . and . . . do you think I should tell her, eh? Should I tell Junie about these feelings I have?'

At this point the daydream took a swift nosedive. Her idealised vision of Bella looked horrified. 'Oh god, no. Don't say a word to her! Never tell her anything about any of this. You mustn't, Minnie. It would be a bloody disaster.'

Then her reverie burst like bubbles of hot oil on the surface of the deep-fat fryer. Her mother was digging her in the ribs. 'Hoy you, lady! Get your head out of the clouds! We need three battered haddock . . .'

Then she was back at work and thinking that in the dream, Bella was probably completely right. It would be dangerous indeed simply to hand over your heart and all your secrets to Junie. She adored the girl, but she didn't trust her.

She looked up then and saw, startled, that the real Bella Franchino was standing there, asking for a paper cone of chips. She beamed at Minnie and her ma.

'Ooh, we were just discussin' you!' Betty told her. 'I was saying how you're a better influence on my daft daughter here than that piece from Northumberland.'

Bella laughed at this. 'I should hope so!'

'Mind, it's funny how your mam and her mam are best of buddies,' Betty went on. 'Is there any word on how their holiday's been? I bet they've had a row and fallen out. That always happens on holiday, in my experience. Folk get right on each other's tit-ends when they go away together.'

Minnie rolled her eyes at her mother's coarseness, but Bella just laughed. 'We had a cable saying they're en route. I suppose we'll hear all about their adventures soon enough.'

'You'll be glad to see your ma again.' Minnie smiled at her.

'Oh, yes,' Bella sighed ruefully. 'Our house has become a tip since she's been gone. It's me da, he's terrible. And Nonna! Well, she's taken to her bed for the whole time. She's gone into a massive sulk about it all. I've had to carry her meals up to her, but she's barely touched a thing. She just mutters about Naples and how she wishes she'd gone with mam. She keeps saying she'll never see her homeland again. Last night I took her some broth and she said she might as well die and then she won't be a burden on us anymore.'

Betty sniffed disapprovingly. 'Aren't old people awful, eh? Miserable buggers. Minnie, when I get old and complaining, you've got permission to toss me in the fat fryer and feed the street with my battered corpse.'

Minnie's eyes went wide with dismay. 'Oh, Mammy! That's a terrible thing to say!'

Her mother cracked up laughing, holding her sides. 'Eeeh, Minnie. You're soft-hearted and you're daft, do you know that? Whatever are we gonna do with you, lass? You're too bloody daft, you are.'

Chapter Forty-Three

For the weeks and days of her daughter's absence, it was true that the old woman had taken to her bed in an almighty sulk. Her mood was so dark and dense that it could be felt all over the house by her son-in-law and granddaughter. They tiptoed carefully past her door and when they took her food and drink, they got used to the wordless scowl she trained on them.

'I understand, Nonna,' said Bella softly. 'You wish you had gone with Mam and Cathy. Now you'll never have another chance to see your homeland.'

The old woman looked at her with blazing eyes. They dissolved into tears as Bella held her gaze. 'I am an old fool. And your mother needed me there. Why didn't I listen? I let her go with that man . . .' She started shovelling up the risotto Bella had brought her. 'What if she never comes back to us, Bella? What then? I will blame myself for the rest of my life . . .'

This sent a chill through Bella's heart and downstairs she asked her father: 'You do think she'll come back to us, don't you?'

He looked at her, appalled. 'What makes you doubt your mama? What makes you say this terrible thing?'

Papa looked so untucked and dishevelled, sitting in his usual chair, drinking strong spirits in the early evening. His sparse hair was wayward and his shirt was unfastened down to his navel. Looking around, Bella realised that the whole room around him was in a similar state. The kitchen was even worse, with peelings and leftovers strewn on the surfaces, emptied cans, eggshells, dirty dishes and forks. 'Will you help me clean?' she asked Tonio, but suddenly he was struggling woozily to his feet.

'I have to go out,' he muttered. 'I have . . . a game.'

He was gambling again. Without Sofia there to focus on him, he was going out six nights a week and not returning till the early hours. Bella never heard him shouting and crowing about his winnings. Not once did he empty his shabby jacket pockets of notes on the kitchen table, as she'd seen him do before. The only conclusion to come to was that he was losing, each and every time he went out of that door into the night. There was a defeated air about him, she realised, like a punch-drunk man staggering back into the ring.

Oh, Daddy, she thought. Don't you see? You could just stay at home tonight. Nothing is dragging you out there to do this thing. I wish you would stay at home with us tonight.

But out he went, fussily trying to seem cheerful and in control. For Bella's benefit he was pretending to enjoy these evenings out.

So the nights of Sofia's absence went by, with Tonio stealing out into town to the pubs by the docks where he could gamble, and the old woman banging her ebony cane on the floor beside her bed whenever she wanted anything.

'I think I'll die before Sofia comes back,' she announced one night. Her face was shining with spiteful thoughts. 'What do you say, hey? She'd feel sorry then, wouldn't she?'

Bella tutted and picked up her supper tray. 'You mustn't say such wicked things.'

Nonna collapsed back onto her lacy pillows. 'Wickedness is all I have left.'

Then one day out of the blue came the cable announcing that Sofia and Cathy were returning from Naples.

Nonna clutched the envelope and her face was bright with tears. 'They're coming back! They're coming back at last!'

Downstairs Tonio was blurry with last night's drink. Unshaven and reeking of smoky pubs he sat at the kitchen table. 'When? When? How soon will she be back?'

Bella read out the few precious words once more: staccato and wonderful words that Mama must have dictated to a person sitting at a counter in Naples. She read out the date to her father and realised: it's sooner than it will take to make this place shipshape.

She pulled on her pinny and told him: 'I can't work at Franchino's today. I have to clean this place. Look at it!'

Tonio glanced around like he hardly knew which room he was in, let alone how dirty it was. 'My Sofia! How many months has she been gone?'

It wasn't even a single month since he had left them on her trip, but Bella thought: we've all fallen to bits without her.

She asked that sweet, daft lass Minnie Minton to come and help her clean and tidy. Minnie came gadding round without a moment's hesitation.

'Eeeh, this is a bonny house,' she gabbled. 'It's like visiting a palace!'

'A very mucky palace,' Bella said ruefully.

'We'll soon sort that out,' Minnie smiled, and set to work with the kind of grit and elbow grease habitual to someone used to scrubbing down the counters and the fryers at a fish and chip shop.

They worked all day, beginning with the worst of the detritus and ending by polishing the wooden furniture and the china ornaments Sofia had carefully collected. 'Your mammy has such beautiful things,' Minnie told her. 'This house is lovely because she can have them all out on show. In the old house, everything was tucked away in cupboards and on top of wardrobes, wasn't it? It was the same as our place. Mind, everything gets broken round our place, with everyone dashing about and so many of them . . .'

The pair of them were fussing around for hours, making the house livable again. As a treat, Bella cooked a special supper for Minnie, making a creamy pasta sauce from her sulking Nonna's recipe book. Minnie glowed with all the attention. 'Thank you, Bella. You're so nice to me.'

Then she was up on her feet: 'My shift at the Robin Hood! I'll have to dash for the tram! Mr Sturrock and Junie will have my guts for garters!'

With sauce down her blouse and a whole day's worth of house grime in her hair, Minnie hurried off to catch her trolley bus. Before she left, Bella told her: 'You're a good friend.'

Minnie's eyes widened. 'No one's ever said that to me before!'

Bella bit her lip. 'Listen, don't let that Junie hurt your feelings. I can see you think a lot of her . . .'

Instantly Minnie went on the defensive. 'I don't know what you mean. She's all right. She's just a bit sharp because she's unhappy, that's all.'

Then Minnie was hurrying away, down the street to the tram stop on the cliff road. 'Just be careful of her!' Bella shouted after the plump girl, but Minnie was already gone.

The house was rather quiet when Bella stepped back indoors. Oh, but it was tidy and clean in a way that it hadn't been for weeks. Bella couldn't wait for her mother to see how her home had been cared for in her absence.

After the day's busy work, she went to bed early and fell straight to sleep. She didn't even wake when her papa came clattering noisily indoors at three in the morning. His pockets were empty and his eyes were hollow. He collapsed onto his bed in his clothes.

It was some time after eight o'clock that Nonna came thumping out onto the landing. She was up and dressed for the first time in three weeks. She rapped with her cane on Tonio's and then Bella's doors.

'What are we waiting for? Get up, the pair of you! We have to be out! We have to be at the railway station! Today's the day! Come on! Get up!'

Chapter Forty-Four

They arrived in Newcastle much too early, of course. Nonna had got all her timings wrong and seemed to be under the impression that they had to hare across Tyneside in order to be there when Sofia arrived. In fact, they were up and out so early they found themselves having to sit on the draughty platform for hours, whiling away the time till the London train showed up. Young Marco looked barely half awake, with his hair all tousled up.

Bella was sent running back and forth to the cafeteria to bring pots and cups of tea to where Nonna was sitting. Tonio looked tired and nervous beside her, anxiously waiting for the return of his wife.

'It is good we are here,' Nonna observed, genteelly sipping her tea. 'But this is like drinking dishwater.' Despite the rising heat of the summer morning, she was wearing her best black lambswool coat and, from a pocket in its depths, she produced a hipflask. She emptied some of the contents into her unsatisfactory tea.

Bella mused aloud, 'I wonder if Mama will be changed by her travels.'

Tonio was disturbed by the thought. 'I truly hope not.' Deep down he was dreading the thought that Mario might be with

Sofia when she arrived at the station. He could picture him still clinging onto her, laying claim to her, refusing to let her go. Tonio had been dreaming of such things for weeks; it had made him clammy and fretful all summer.

The small family sipped tea and sat on the breezy concourse, watching other families and travellers come and go.

'We should have gone with her,' Nonna told Tonio at one point. Her voice was low and terse.

'I know,' he said. But they left it at that. It didn't do to dwell on things and dig too much into regrets.

Then, around midday, with no herald whatsoever, the tall black train from London rounded the distant curve in the tracks as its vast length surged over Tyne Bridge and entered the station. It gave an urgent hoot, filling up the concourse with hissing steam. The brakes screeched and at once the heavy compartment doors were crashing open, one after the next.

It was hard to pick out their quarry in the flurry of faces and cases and hurrying feet. Then Tonio gave a cry and started running and waving his arms.

No sooner had Sofia stepped down from the train she was startled by him. She dropped her bags on the platform as he seized her. 'What . . . ? What are you doing here . . . ?'

'It was Nonna's idea to surprise you.' Tonio found himself more emotional than he had expected to be at the sight of his wife. She looked so golden and glowing with sunlight. Why, in just a few weeks she had changed from the pale, exhausted person he had grown used to seeing into this goddess! Yes, she was a goddess descending from the train with her best friend in tow and coming to mix amongst them all in the earthly realms of Tyneside. 'You look so beautiful . . .' he blubbed and buried his face in her breast.

'Tonio!' she gasped, moved and embarrassed by his display. 'You'll have people looking at us! Look, you're drawing attention!' She extricated herself and then her gaze fell upon the solemn Marco. Sofia grasped her young son to her. Marco was wordless with emotion at the sight of his mother again.

The rushing crowds were moving round them like water round rocks in the river, but Tonio paid them no heed. Now he was wailing and shuddering, clinging onto his wife with both trembling arms. 'I thought you were gone forever. I don't know why, but I have nightmares . . . I thought I had lost you.'

Cathy was standing beside them and she caught Sofia's eye at that moment. It was all too plain what she was thinking: he doesn't realise how close his dreams had been to reality. Cathy sighed and shook her head to see another man clinging onto Sofia for dear life. What was it about her that inspired such crazy devotion? Cathy could have done with some of that kind of love. Perhaps not here, though, in front of everyone in Newcastle station.

'Hello, there,' Bella said to her, and squeezed past to join in with Sofia's hug. The old woman was stiffly on her feet, hovering at the edges, waiting to greet her daughter.

Clutching their bags and cases, Cathy felt a wave of sadness go through her. Wouldn't it be lovely, she thought. To be greeted like this. To have your whole family sweep you up as soon as you set foot on English soil, showing how much they loved you and how much they had missed you while you were away. She tried to picture Noel Sturrock loping about on the platform, sobbing and wringing his hands. She imagined her daughter Junie looking relieved that her mammy was back. Neither of these images was easy to summon up. Cathy gave a deep-felt sigh and realised how much she was envying Sofia.

'Can I get some help with all these bags?' she asked the others as they broke off from their emotional scene. She shivered: it was cold here. The breeze came through the station, straight from the North Sea. For one bleak little moment Cathy felt like she would never feel warm again.

*

It took them much of the afternoon to get coordinated, catching trains back across Tyneside to Shields and carrying all the holiday luggage with them. They were chattering the whole time, with Bella flinging questions at her mother, and even the old Nonna looking animated as Sofia described the places she had been and the things she had done.

Cathy and Sofia – after so many weeks in each other's constant company – said a hurried goodbye at South Shields station. The Franchinos were hurrying for a trolley car to take them out to the coast, of course, and Cathy was heading alone to the Sixteen Streets. Bonded in complicity by the dramatic experiences of their travels, the two women embraced each other quickly and exchanged a significant look. It was as if they were promising each other to keep most of what was said and done in Naples a secret from everyone else.

Let's not even try to explain to people, the difficult parts of it all, they were saying. Nobody else would really understand.

Then they parted and the Franchino family carried Sofia off, babbling and laughing and happy to be together again.

With two heavy and battered cases, Cathy was left alone. She struggled down the stone steps and found herself in the middle of the town that had been her home for so long.

Eeh, but it looked so drab today! Fish wrappers and strewn newspapers swirled down the dusty main street. The day was warm but the sunlight was pearly under the low-hanging clouds. Cathy paused to pull a cardigan on and was determined not to feel sad and disappointed at arriving back home.

Come on, Cathy Sturrock, she told herself. You're coming back to your whole life. Your pub, your people – and what's more – your very own daughter. Really, your life is better now than it has been for many years. That's true, isn't it?

Then she toiled along the road and into the tangle of streets where she belonged. In many ways she felt like she was arriving for the first time, just as she had all those years ago. Back before the end of the war, when the Spanish flu was starting to run rampant through the warren of the Sixteen Streets. Back then she hadn't known where she was going. She had her whole life ahead of her. The same quiver of anticipatory fear she felt then accompanied her now all the way up the hill of terraced houses.

But why should I be fearful? She wondered why she was feeling so strangely about getting nearer to home. I know where I'm going, don't I? I know who awaits me and what my life consists of. There are no surprises or nasty shocks waiting for me here, are there?

She hefted the heavy bags in her hands and the leather handles slipped in her sweaty fingers. Her heart was pounding with exertion and nerves.

Oh hell, thought Cathy Sturrock. What am I coming home to? I've got the most awful feeling about what I'll find at the top of this hill.

Chapter Forty-Five

There was dried egg on the lace of the tablecloth. It hung in clotted strings of dirty white and yellow, gumming up the flowery pattern. The worst thing about it, in Cathy's eyes, was that the spilled egg was completely dried out. This meant that someone had made the mess and then they'd simply left it.

In the same way that they had left the empty plates and cups and greasy knives and forks on the table. They were in the kitchen, too, piled on the sides and in the sink. The stone sink was elbow deep in mucky grey water. There were sodden crusts of bread and god knew what else floating about in the scum.

Cathy had her teeth clenched together as she moved through the dingy downstairs rooms of her house. She didn't dare unclench them in case she started to scream.

Oh, how could they do this? How could they live like this and let their home get into this state? And how dare they not think about her arriving home to find the whole place wrecked like this? It was the home she had inherited and which she had tried so hard to keep nice, just like Theresa, Noel's mother, would have wanted. Mind, old Theresa had been a bit of a slattern when it came to housekeeping and cleaning, now that Cathy thought back. The place had been full of dust and grime back in the long-ago days of Theresa Sturrock.

In fact, it felt like the whole of number twenty-one Frederick Street had slid backwards in time to those shabbier days. Unmoored without Cathy there to keep it decent, the house had floated backwards into grimy neglect.

She took a deep breath and bellowed: 'Where the hell are you?' Her voice was shockingly loud in the confines of the scullery. 'Noel . . . ? Junie . . . ?'

She listened to the echoes, ears cocked for signs of life.

'Are you there, you buggers? Are you home . . . ?' She was fuming. She felt the colour rising up her throat and up her cheeks, making her whole face blaze. How dare they let their precious home get into this state? How dare they make her come home to face this diabolical welcome?

There was worse to come in the backyard.

'Oh my piggin' god . . .' she muttered sacrilegiously as she stepped out into the yard. There had clearly been some hideous kind of blockage in the outside lavatory. The stench was indescribable and there was evidence of some dreadful kind of overflow on the concrete. Cathy started gagging and retreated to the scullery.

'Noel!' she shrieked. 'Noel Bloody Sturrock! Where the hell are you?'

But no answer came. Was he hiding under his bed, the shiftless old crookback? He'd be terrified of her wrath, quivering in all the dust and muck beneath his undoubtedly filthy pigsty of a bed.

Right, Cathy, she told herself. You've had a holiday and now you've got your work cut out for you. Time to roll your sleeves up, lady.

First things first, however. Before she started tackling the unholy detritus left by her so-called family, Cathy had to find a hiding place. There was something that she had to look after.

She left all her cumbersome bags in the cluttered hall and took only her handbag upstairs with her to her bedroom.

There was a stale, unaired smell about the place, as if that lazy pair hadn't even opened the windows in the summer warmth to let the clean sea air blow through the rooms.

She put all her resentful, furious thoughts aside for a moment and hurried to her bedroom, shutting herself inside. Mercifully, here was a bright and tidy oasis in the fetid nightmare of her home.

Where to hide the ring?

She realised her heart was beating almost like a thief's. This was absurd because she had been entrusted by Sofia to look after the heirloom. Yet she felt like someone who had made off with it, her eyes raking greedily over the cluster of jewels. She turned it round in the sunlight, thinking: I don't think I've ever held anything so precious and expensive before in my whole life. This ring is probably worth more than this mucky sodding house and the Robin Hood put together.

She held it for several long moments. She tried to figure out what the jewels even were. Was it fanciful to think they were diamonds? Who knew how rare and precious this ring truly was. Perhaps it was all the treasure that the Grapelli family still owned? This was the only thing of true worth they still possessed? And look how easily and blithely Mario had passed it to his Sofia. His beloved Sofia. Cathy felt her breath hitch in her throat. She had never heard of a more romantic gesture. Mario had lost her, but he had still wanted to give her this tiny piece of treasure.

Cathy turned it round and round and tried to imagine being the woman to whom something like this was given. Just imagine being that girl. Being that important to someone as wonderful as Mario.

She swore ripely under her breath and sighed.

Her dressing table had jewellery drawers that were almost completely empty. Some cheap junky earrings she had bought from Shields market. A silver chain she had treated herself to years ago. Nothing of any real value. Not even sentimental value. She wrapped the Italian ring in a faded handkerchief and stowed it away in the cedar-scented dark. She had complete faith that it would be quite safe there.

Then she took a moment to compose herself and went back downstairs.

All the rooms had been used and made uninhabitable. Even the best room, at the front of the house. There were emptied bottles and sticky glasses left out for her to clear up. She frowned as she noticed bright red lipstick on some of the glasses. Now, either Noel was encouraging her daughter to take strong drink, or he'd been having those harlots of his inside the house.

Cathy felt her blood begin to boil again.

It was just as she was turning to leave the best room that she happened to glance down at the same moment that her nose detected an unfamiliar, rank odour.

'Oh, no . . .' she whispered, recoiling with horror.

It was Thomas, the oldest of the cats descended from old Ma Sturrock's feline army. He was a skinny old tabby that Cathy had known the longest, almost from the beginning of her life here in Frederick Street.

Poor Thomas was lying forgotten, partly hidden by the settle. His head was resting on his dirty paws, his eyes closed and his face gentle with sleep. Cathy knew even before she touched him that he was dead. The rough fur felt just like an old stole, chucked casually on the carpet. The lifeless feel of him was horrifying to her.

He'd been left to die unnoticed by the people who lived in this house. Thomas, who had lived there for all those years. They hadn't fed him and they had accidentally shut him up inside this room. For how long? Just how long had this poor old cat suffered alone in the best front room?

Cathy felt raging anger coursing through her whole body. Then a tidal wave of sorrow and hopeless pity swept through her. Poor, poor old cat. She sank to her knees beside him and wept for him and wept for herself. She wept for her ruined home and her awful, dingy, inescapable life.

Chapter Forty-Six

The pub was even worse.

When Cathy hurried over the cobbles to the Robin Hood she had a sick feeling in her gut. She knew what she was going to find there.

He had let the place go to rack and ruin. The whole place had gone to hell. When she swung open the saloon door and staggered into the main bar the floor felt sticky underfoot. She was greeted with an almighty stale, beery, foul stench. She gagged and covered up her mouth as she stared, wide-eyed at the disgracefully messy and dirty public bar.

It looked as if no one had done any cleaning for three weeks.

Her mind raced. Why, Noel? Why would you let such a terrible thing happen? Even in his most slapdash days in the past, when he ran the place by himself, it had never got into this shabby state. This was unsanitary. If anyone from the brewery or the council happened by, Cathy was sure that they would be shut down on the spot.

How could you, Noel? she raged inside her head. This was the worst thing he had ever done. What was it all for? Was it to show her? Was it to exact some petty kind of revenge for her going off and leaving him for these few weeks? But how petty was that? How spiteful could he get? What kind of a man resented his wife so much that he tried to destroy their shared business?

Because that's what this was: wilful destruction. There were shards of smashed glass tankards on the filthy floor. Behind the bar she found the floor swimming with cigarette butts and spilled drinks. The mirror on the wall – beautifully painted by an old friend – was hanging in smithereens. What on earth had been going on here in her absence?

At first the whole bar was eerily quiet, which somehow made the scene of devastation seem even worse. Then she became aware of a small splashing noise. It was a discreet noise, as if someone was busy doing something and trying to keep quiet about it.

'Who's there?' called Cathy defiantly.

There was a pause, and then a tremulous answer: 'It's only me, Mrs Sturrock.'

In the slop room behind the bar, Cathy found a frightened-looking Minnie Minton hard at work. She was presiding over a sinkful of dirty-looking water and about a thousand smeared pint pots. Her hair was tied up and her moon-shaped face was bright pink with exertion. 'Oh, Mrs Sturrock! You're back! We knew you were coming back . . . I . . . I thought . . . I'd make a start on all the . . . the . . .'

Cathy was just staring at her. The poor girl looked as if she was about to faint with fright.

'Where's my husband?' Cathy asked. 'Where's June?'

Minnie shook her head. 'I don't know where they've gone, Mrs Sturrock.'

Cathy felt like grabbing her and giving her a good shake. 'You can't protect them.'

'I mean it! I-I don't know where they are . . .'

'Have they been here in the evening, when the place is open?'

'Yes . . . yes, mostly.' Minnie blinked her huge, cow-like eyes at Cathy. 'Oh, but it's been horrible here, Mrs Sturrock. There's been all these strangers here. I think they're folk from the pubs by the water. Rough types. There's been gambling and stuff going on that I know you would never allow on your premises.'

'I see,' said Cathy stiffly. 'Go on, Minnie. What else?'

'I'm not telling tales, or trying to dob Junie or Mr Sturrock in it, but they haven't been looking after this place.'

'Yes, I can see that.'

'I tried to tell them. I told them that you'd be unhappy. I said, just think how upset she'll be when she gets back and sees it like this. And they . . . they just laughed.'

Cathy was grinding her teeth together. 'Both of them? Both of them laughed at you?'

'Y-yes . . . they thought it was a great big joke. "Serves her right for leaving us here! Leaving us to do all the work while she's off enjoying herself."' Minnie clamped her mouth shut then, as she watched Cathy's furious reaction to her words. Perhaps she had gone into too much detail.

'The buggers,' Cathy muttered. 'The bloody buggers. I'll string them up when I see them . . .' Her words were vengeful but her voice was weak and reedy. She was trying to sound stronger than she felt. Really, she felt utterly desolate inside. She felt betrayed.

On a sudden impulse she turned back into the bar and checked the till. Of course, it had been completely emptied. 'Where are the takings?' she asked Minnie, who followed her with greasy, wet hands dripping at her sides. 'Has Noel been banking up each night and keeping it all straight?'

'I'm afraid I don't know . . .' Minnie said softly. 'I don't get trusted with things like that.'

Cathy stared into the spartan emptiness of the till and felt robbed in every conceivable way. She slammed the drawer shut and stood there trying not to scream. What to do now?

Minnie suddenly had the answer. 'Let's get out of here for a few minutes. You've had a shock, Mrs Sturrock.'

'Yes . . . yes . . . I have . . .' And in that moment she thought about the poor dead cat, Thomas, left forgotten on the carpet of the good front room. Oh, they had some things to answer for, did her husband and daughter. How could they be so cruel and neglectful and stupid?

'Come over to ours. Come and have tea and get your wits back . . .' urged Minnie.

Across the road and down the hill they found Minnie's mother Betty sharing a cuppa by the front wall she shared with Ma Ada of the Farley family. The two older women were sitting on their low wall in their pinnies with their hair up in rollers, sipping on sweet tea and rolling woodbines. It was late afternoon by now and the delicious scent of Wight's Biscuit Factory was wafting up the hill.

The two older women from number fifteen and thirteen Frederick Street respectively eyed Cathy Sturrock carefully as she came hurrying down the street with Minnie Minton by her side. As she got closer, they could see how upset she was and how strenuously she was trying to keep her feelings hidden.

'Aye, aye,' Ma Ada said. 'You'll be home then.'

'I'm just now arrived,' Cathy said, coming to a halt on the pavement before the two matriarchs. 'What the bloody hell has been happening round at my place? What's the old divil been playing at? And why didn't any of you lot stop the bloody bastard? You're supposed to be my friends!'

Betty Minton gasped at her words. 'Eeeh, pet! There's nay need to gan attacking us two, y'knaa! We're your bloody friends, we are! We're not the ones who made a muck of your pub! We've not been near the place since you've been away.'

'She's right,' added Ma Ada, in a gentler, more conciliatory tone. 'There was nothing we could do to stop your Noel doing what he wanted. You know what he's like.'

'I wasn't happy with our Minnie working over there, with all those rough types . . .' Betty frowned.

'At least if I was there I could try to keep things as they should be,' said Minnie hopelessly.

'They've ruined everything,' Cathy said. 'I've never seen the place in such a state. And the house, too! They've turned it into a . . . a midden. They've lived like pigs, the pair of them.' Then she let out an involuntary sob. 'They even let one of the cats die and it's lain there dead maybe the whole time and the pair of lazy swine never even noticed . . .'

Cathy's shoulders were shaking and fat tears were suddenly rolling down her face. Betty, Minnie and Ada all stared at her in shock. When was the last time they had seen the landlady of the Robin Hood crying like this? And out in the street, to boot.

Ma Ada hopped down off the low wall and bustled over to her. She put her arms around her old friend. 'Hie now, hinny. You come inside our place and have a cuppa with me. I'm not having you like this.'

Cathy felt weak and she was trembling in the shorter woman's ham hock arms. The pair of them were more or less the same age but there was something infinitely maternal about Ada Farley. She exuded a wonderful motherliness which was what Cathy needed just then. She submitted to her embrace and nodded. Yes, yes, she'd drink tea in Ma Ada's parlour for a half hour with her. They would talk and between them they would start to tackle this problem. Just as they had with so many other shared problems in the past.

Chapter Forty-Seven

Even though it was still the summer, Ma Ada was wearing three cardigans and two pairs of tights. 'I think it's this house. It's always facing the shadows and I can never get warm.'

She bustled around her tidy back parlour, shooing cats out of the way and readying the vast brown tea pot and the best cups. Then she guided Cathy gently into a straight-backed chair at her table.

'I'm sorry . . .' Cathy smiled sadly, trying to regain control over her feelings.

'You've no need to apologise to me, pet,' Ma Ada told her beadily. 'You've done plenty for me in the past, and that's a fact.'

She stumped off and returned minutes later from the scullery with a tray of piping hot tea and some broken biscuits. They came from her usual supply of factory seconds.

'You'll be wrung out and tired after all your travelling,' Ma Ada told her, sitting heavily in her own favourite armchair. 'You're bound to be emotional.'

'Eeeh, if you'd seen the mess they've made of the house,' Cathy said, shaking her head.

'I can't believe they let your cat die,' Ma Ada said woefully. 'That's really bloody awful. My heart gans out to you, pet. Now, drink your tea.'

The Farley house was oddly quiet in the daytime. Usually it would be ringing with the boisterous clamour of Ma Ada's four sons.

'Remember when you were the one helping *me* out in my hour of need, pet?' Ma Ada asked her. Her eyes were glimmering as she asked. 'It were a few years ago, and it was when my fella was getting out of his mind on the drink every night. He was beating my lad, Bob, here in this room. Remember?'

Cathy nodded grimly. 'Was that when Bob hit his head on the fire surround?'

'It was, yes. That poor bairn. That was where all his troubles started, you know. Before his father hit him like that, and sent him flying into the fireplace, he was never slow before. Not our Bob. As a babby he was bright as a button. But then he saw his dad hitting his mam, didn't he? And he came racing to my rescue. He got in the middle of us and his dad sent him flying . . .' Ma Ada took out her handkerchief and dabbed at her eyes. 'Ah, my poor Bob. He's a sweet-hearted lad, but that knock on the head did him no good.' Her eyes flicked up at Cathy. 'It was lucky our front door was open and you heard all the palaver from the street. You came running, didn't you, hinny? You didn't think twice about it. Never even considered your own safety. You came running in to help me and Bob.'

Cathy shuddered. 'I thought the pair of you were being murdered . . .'

'I was screaming fit to burst, you're right. Trying to get someone's attention. It really seemed like my fella was going to do us in. But you sent him off, Cathy! You sent that bugger off with a flea in his ear. You kicked his bum for him, all the way down Frederick Street!'

Cathy smiled weakly at this. 'Well, not quite, but I remember getting him out of the way so you could see to little Bob's injuries.'

Ma Ada took a long sip of hot tea and smacked her lips. 'See? We look after each other. We help each other out when we need to. It's just what we do round here in the Sixteen Streets.'

Cathy drank her own tea and nibbled absent-mindedly on a misshapen custard cream. She longed to say to the woman: if we look out for each other, how come you never did anything to protect my pub while I was away? Why didn't you do something to stop Noel?

'You'll soon get things back to normal,' Ma Ada reassured her. 'You're a good worker. You always were. And now you've got that young lass to help you.'

'Her!' Cathy said. 'I think she's as responsible as Noel is for all the mess. She's done it on purpose. She wants to make me suffer, I'm sure of it.' Cathy scoffed down another biscuit, suddenly realising how hungry she was after all her travelling. Had she eaten anything at all since re-entering the country?

'Nay lass, can that be right? Yon Junie is your family, in't she? Your niece?'

'She's my daughter,' Cathy told her friend miserably. 'And she hates my guts, I just know it.'

'Your daughter!' cried Ma Ada, though the wily woman had already figured out most of the truth for herself. 'You don't say?'

'I had to leave her behind in the north when she was just a few months old. I was . . . tricked.'

'Tricked . . . !' Ma Ada poured them both another cup of tea, avid for the details of the story straight from the source. She and her friend Winnie had speculated over these very matters for some time.

'Aye, my aunt tricked me and stole my daughter from me. She brought her up poisoning her young mind against me. Saying I didn't care and I didn't love her. She brought Junie up to be pampered and primped and spoiled. I hate to say it, Ada, but my daughter isn't as sweet-natured as she might appear. And she loathes me, I know she does.'

'Ah, that can't be true, hinny,' Ma Ada refused to believe any of it. 'A child knows instinctively that its mother loves it regardless of who or what it is or how it behaves. She knows you love her and, believe me, she returns that love. That's how this world works.'

Bitterly Cathy shook her head. 'Perhaps your world, where you rule the roost and everyone loves you, Ada. But not everyone is as lucky as you. My Junie resents me because she grew up being fed lies about me. Now . . . now that she's here, she's teamed up with that husband of mine. With Noel! The two of them are ranged against me and they both resent me as much as each other. They'd do anything to torture the life out of me.' Cathy felt herself about to submit to her tears once more and she struggled to control herself.

'I can't imagine loathing anyone,' Ma Ada said. Even her husband, even when he was at his worst . . . he still wasn't someone she hated. She feared him and sometimes she wanted him out, but she didn't want to see him suffer unduly. He was her man, in the sight of god, and that was just how it was. In sickness and in health, and even if he was a right bugger – he was still her man.

'I don't know what I'm going to do about them,' said Cathy unhappily. 'What do you do when your loved ones hate you?'

'I'm sure I don't know, hinny,' said Ma Ada. Above all, the slightly older woman was pragmatic. 'First things first. We have to get started on your home and make it somewhere you can return to. We have to get that poor cat of yours buried first. You can't have that lying about in the place.'

'Oh, Thomas . . .' sighed Cathy. 'And there was no sign of the other cats, either, as if they'd all upped and left ship because the place was so terrible.'

'They'll come back,' said Ma Ada. She reached for her shawl and pulled it on. 'Now, I'll come back with you over to your house for moral support. I can help you face all of this so you'll not be on your own.'

Cathy smiled her thanks at her.

A thought struck Ada. 'Hey, do you want me to get my oldest lads to rough your husband up? Nothing nasty, just teach him a lesson?'

As they bustled out into the hall, Cathy found she was even considering it. Was Ma Ada serious? Would the Farley boys – strong, strapping, young lads they were – really consent to putting the fear of god into her shiftless, conniving Noel? Oh, it would be worth it just to scare him a little . . . but no. It wasn't the way. She had known families before who'd settle scores in such a way and she knew it wasn't right. 'I'll fettle him myself,' she decided.

Then, full of hot tea and broken biscuits, the two women were back on the dusty cobbles of Frederick Street.

They were just in time to see Minnie in the middle of the street, talking to a proud, defiant Junie. The girl's hair was shining golden in the late afternoon sun. She was beautifully dressed and carrying bags in both hands from the nicest shops in town. Junie had been on a shopping spree and she was looking very pleased with herself.

'*Junie . . . !*' her mother cried, her voice coming out as loud and raucous as that of a fish wife on the quay. Cathy couldn't help herself. The sight of her daughter triggered her and sent her barrelling across the street, even as Ma Ada tried to advise caution. Cathy wouldn't listen, however, and was over there in a flash. 'I want a word with you, young lady!'

Junie's mouth dropped open and she stared at Cathy stomping towards her. Then, as the surprise faded, a strange kind of relish settled over her features. 'Oh, you're back from your holidays, are you, *Aunty* Catherine?' she smirked.

Cathy couldn't help herself. She drew back her arm and slapped the girl's face with the flat of her hand.

Chapter Forty-Eight

Everyone seemed to be frozen for a few seconds as Junie fell backwards onto the pavement under the force of the blow. Her mother had slapped her quite hard, but it wasn't hard enough to knock the girl to the floor. The shock of it was what sent Junie reeling, her arms windmilling and scattering her fancy shopping bags as she took her tumble.

Minnie and Ma Ada stood either side like startled fish with their mouths hanging open. It wasn't until Junie was flat on the ground that anyone else could move. She was silent with fury as they leapt into action.

'Eeeh, Mrs Sturrock . . . !' was all Minnie managed to say.

Cathy was silent, her hand still raised in the air and smarting from the blow she had so unthinkingly administered. Her eyes were wide as she looked down at her daughter. Junie stared back at her from the ground, her own eyes round and full of horror.

'Oh . . . ! What have I done?' Cathy whispered at last.

Suddenly the air was filled with raucous shouts and cries. It was like the feeding frenzy of gulls that covered Marsden Rock each morning; there was such a noisy flap and palaver. People were coming out of their front doors and hanging out of their top windows to see what the carry on was about. Any hint of a scrap in the road and the denizens of the Sixteen Streets loved to come out and watch. Word went round that this was an extra-special one today. The biggest shock was that it was all down to the Queen of the Sixteen Streets herself! How on earth had she lowered herself to such an awful scene of familial violence, where everyone could watch?

'Junie . . . Junie . . . I'm so sorry . . .' Cathy was stammering, looking helpless and stricken, reaching out to her daughter. The hands that had attacked the girl were now stretching out to help her up.

Junie took full advantage of the scene. Her eyes flicked round, and she realised that quite a sizable crowd was gathering around them. 'Get away from me, you harpie!' she cried. Then she appealed to the onlookers. 'Get her away from me! Did you see what she did? Do you see how she treats me? My own kin . . . !'

'Junie, no lass, hush . . . !' Cathy begged her. 'Let's go home . . .'

Junie's eyes hardened. She was determined to milk every moment. Already a red welt was showing on her cheek and she touched it with her shaking hand. 'Is it bleeding?'

Ada Farley nudged Cathy in the side brusquely. 'You'd best get her inside before she starts a riot. They'll be wanting to lynch you by the time she's finished.' Ma Ada wasn't taken in for a second by the girl's opportunist exaggerations. She had that girl's number and she wasn't impressed by her one bit. 'Here, I'll help you pick her up.'

'Get away from me!' Junie shrieked, lashing out as the older woman came nearer with her pan shovel hands.

'Nay, hush your trap, lass!' Ma Ada growled. 'I'm trying to help you get back to your feet.'

With furious dignity, Junie told her: 'I can get up by myself, thank you. I don't need any help from the likes of you. Or *her*.'

Then Junie stood up very carefully, balancing herself precariously like a newborn foal testing out its legs. Her beautiful outfit was creased and there was a tear in her skirt. Some of the onlookers noticed this and her dishevelment touched their hearts as they watched her try to regain her dignity. There was even a scattering of applause as Junie stood up straight and faced them all. She took a deep breath and told her public: 'I'm all right. I'm . . . a-all right.'

Minnie was at her elbow, having gathered up the scattered shopping bags. She was ready to catch her friend should she become dizzy or incapacitated suddenly.

'Oh my god,' moaned Ada Farley. 'Such playacting!'

'I'll help you home,' Minnie told Junie. 'Here, walk with me . . .'

Junie gave a theatrical sob. 'What, back to *her* house? The woman who beat me? I've nowhere else to go! Just back to the home of the woman who beats me like a dog . . .'

Limping slightly, Junie allowed herself to be guided by Minnie back to number twenty-one. As they passed the mortified Cathy, Junie winked at her, very discreetly, so that no one else could see. The girl was wearing a malicious smirk that she then covered up with her hand, pretending to sob.

The crowd turned on Cathy then. There were cries of 'boo!' and 'shame!'

Ma Ada shouted at them all. 'Ah, hadaway, the lot of yous! You all know nowt! I'll have you know yon lass is a little bitch! She deserved a feckin' smack!'

No one in the crowd, as it began to disperse, looked very convinced by this.

Ma Ada returned to number twenty-one with Cathy and spent some minutes staring at all the mess and decay. 'Well, it seems to me that this is more than neglect and dirtiness,' she said.

'This is purporseful, wilful destruction. Those buggers have set about ruining your home while you've been away.'

Cathy didn't say anything. Her eyes were full of misery. 'Can you smell the dead cat? God, that's horrible. Where can we bury the poor mite?'

Upstairs, Junie had taken to her bed and Minnie was up there, helping her and petting her.

'We'll take him to the waste ground and dig a little hole,' Ma Ada suggested. 'Do you have something to wrap him in?'

Cathy went off to fetch an old tea towel, trying not to notice the chaotic mess around her. What a disaster everything was. What a horrible homecoming this was turning out to be.

Together with Ma Ada, she rolled the stiff little form of the cat into a shroud of frayed tea towels. 'Poor little soul,' Ada Farley muttered. 'He didn't ask for any of this. He only wanted to be looked after . . .'

'Don't rub it in,' Cathy snapped. 'I feel guilty enough!'

'It's not your fault,' Ada said. 'You have every right to go away for a few weeks. You've never stopped working since the first time you stepped foot in this house, all those years ago.'

But Cathy was all remorse, hugging the bundle of Thomas's cold body to her chest. 'I should never have gone. It all went wrong in Naples, too. And I've made the situation with June here ten times worse as well.'

Ma Ada pursed her lips. 'That's a little madam upstairs. I know she's your kin, but I think she's a bloody demon. She'll wrap you round her little finger if you don't watch out for yourself.'

But it was already too late on that score. In her own mind, Cathy was pledging to do everything she could to make it all up to Junie. She would beg and plead and prostrate herself before her daughter. She would try to do better. She was determined to be a better mother to the girl.

'What sort of a mammy hits her child in the street?' she moaned.

'I did, I'm afraid!' Ada offered. 'I have to admit that I belted all four of mine in front of anyone who'd watch. And really, I have to ask myself: has it done any of them any harm? No! That Junie of yours has grown up wrong, Cathy. It could be that she needs a bit of firmness. A few more slaps might well be in order! That's what I think, if you ask me.'

But Cathy wasn't asking Ma Ada. 'Let's get this cat buried,' she said. 'Let's go and get it done before it gets dark, and before anything else horrible happens today . . .'

As if on cue, there was a rattle and a bang at the front door. Cathy knew at once what it signified. Her husband Noel had chosen that exact moment to return home, and he was steaming drunk.

'So!' he glared through red, watery eyes at Cathy. 'You're back after all, are you? Forgive me if I don't put the bloody flags out! What have you got there?' He greedily eyed what she was holding. 'Is it a present? Is it something you've brought for me . . . ?'

Chapter Forty-Nine

It was much later that evening that Cathy and Noel managed to have a decent conversation. After she had disposed of poor Thomas's body on the waste ground with the help of her neighbour, and after she had swept through her scullery with the bleach and the vim. Making the place decent enough to drink a cup of tea in took a couple of hours work. A more thorough clean would have to follow the next day. Noel didn't have anything at all to say about the death of Thomas. It really meant very little to him.

She popped over to the shrouded Robin Hood and put a handwritten sign on the saloon door: 'Temporarily closed due to unforeseen circumstances.'

'What does all those long words mean?' asked one of her regulars on the doorstep.

'It means you'll have to go down The Grapes tonight, Harry.' She frowned at the old man.

'Is it true that you beat your young lass in the street today, with a crowd watching?' the old man asked her keenly, as he turned to shamble away.

'Why, no!' She flushed red.

'If you ask me, that lass was far too saucy-mouthed standing behind that bar. You'd do well to put your house back in order, missus.'

Cathy dismissed the old soak like the queen she was, and hurried home. By now, after her travels, the shock of arrival and all the unexpected cleaning work, she felt dead on her feet. The day had been much more arduous than she had ever expected, both emotionally and physically. Fancy having to dig a shallow grave for one of her beloved cats! The sorrow was weighing heavily on her as she stepped back inside her home.

At least it smelled less foisty and nasty now. She had opened all the windows so that the fresh air could come streaming through the rooms. She would soon have the whole place shipshape again. Cathy couldn't think straight until she was sitting in a tidy house. It was just the way she was, and it was probably down to her entering service at Marwood Hall at such an early age. She had been trained to deal with mess like this. The urge to put everything right was in her very bones.

'Ah, there you are, lass,' said Noel, hunched over beef tea in the parlour. He looked more sober now. His eyes were a mite less rheumy. His hands trembled slightly as he dunked a biscuit in his Bovril and sucked it greedily like a baby with a rusk. Cathy felt herself recoiling in disgust from her man.

'Is there enough hot water for tea?' she asked him, and soon they were sitting across from each other at the table.

'I'll help you clean out the pub tomorrow,' he told her. 'I'll be up and ready first thing. We'll do it together, hinny, and we'll get it back on track.'

She was surprised by his offer. 'Good,' she said. 'I'll need all the help I can get.'

'It . . . it just got away from me,' he said, in a weak voice. 'Everything. I couldn't cope. I s-see now, Cathy . . . I see now how much I've come to rely on you, pet. I've leaned on you for so many years. You're my rock. And when you were gone . . . it all fell to pieces.'

She frowned, feeling her heart twinge at the pitiful voice he was putting on. Was he speaking the truth? With Noel you could never be too sure. He was slippery. Was he just putting on an act to get round her sympathies again? Was he reeling her in?

'I've always had you here to rule over everything, Cathy. Since before my mammy died. You've always been here to make everything right. You going away was like the rug being pulled from under me feet. And when it seemed like you were never coming back . . .' He shook his head and she was astonished to see fat, salty tears welling up in his brilliant blue eyes.

'Of course I was coming back!' she scoffed gently. 'What made you think I'd never come back?'

'Junie,' he said simply. 'That's what she kept going on about. She kept saying that we'd both been abandoned by you. That you'd ran out on the pair of us and we'd never see you again. She wouldn't shut up about it. Like torture it was! I'd cry out, "Stop it, Junie! You're doing my bloody head in, lass!" But she'd just laugh.' He coughed and sobbed and hiccupped all at the same time, then he swigged his beefy tea. 'She's cruel, Cathy. I don't mind saying. That lass has a cruel streak as wide as Tynemouth.'

All she could do was nod in agreement because she knew it was the truth. 'But she's been badly treated. It's not her fault . . .'

Noel pulled a sour face. 'You're a more godly woman than I am, preaching such forgiveness. Look at the mess she's made everywhere. She's laid waste to our lives. It's all down to her, y'knaa. All this chaos and mess . . . I'd say, "We have to put it right, Junie. We have to make things right again, in time for your mammy coming home." Then she would just laugh and everything would get worse. She's been bleeding me dry . . .'

'What do you mean?' Cathy frowned.

'The takings!' he spat. 'I take it you've looked in the till and found it empty?'

'Aye, I did,' she said.

'I've been trying to put all the cash away each day. Sometimes, though, the girl was in there before I could stop her. Or she'd wheedle her way around me. After more money and then more. Saying she deserved it. Saying she'd worked hard and been a good girl. Telling me she'd been neglected all her life. Before I knew it, she'd softened my heart – my stupid, rotten, hopeless old heart – and then she'd be waltzing off with fistfuls of cash. Eeeh, if you could see all the fancy stuff she's bought for herself in the town, Cathy. It's been like a fashion parade round here.'

Cathy hardly knew what to say. In her mind's eye she could see Junie this afternoon, parading up the hill swinging fancy paper bags from shops in town that Cathy would never dare shop in herself. So her daughter had been making off with their profits! She had been spending like there was no tomorrow. That room of hers upstairs would no doubt be full to overflowing with the spoils of her shopping sprees. The very thought made Cathy feel bilious.

But it was true that the bairn had been deprived all her life, hadn't she? She'd been deprived of love and affection. A mother's love had been denied to her and deep in her soul she felt betrayed by Cathy. Cathy could see this now.

'I've brought this on all by myself,' Cathy told Noel. 'Whatever that girl has done is all my own fault.'

'Nay, lass,' Noel worrited. 'That's not true. She has to bear responsibility for the way she carries on. She's been bloody awful, Cathy. You should have seen her down the pub each night. Some nights it was free drinks for all! It was rougher than I've ever seen it. The people that she drew there . . . I've never seen the like! Why, it were like the very dregs of town!

It was like she'd put a dreadful spell on the place . . . she'd put a special marking on the door and it drew evil spirits! It dragged in the worst element from the houses right by the docks. And she revelled in it all, Cathy. The brawls and the bother. All the things that she knew would appal you if you knew they were going on . . .'

Cathy listened quietly as Noel filled her in on the kinds of things that had been happening while she was away.

Then she said, 'But you're a man. You're her adopted daddy, remember?' Cathy could hardly keep the bitterness out of her voice. 'Couldn't you have said or done something to stop her? Couldn't you have controlled her?'

He snorted with laughter. 'Cathy . . . I'm frightened of her.'

Chapter Fifty

Tonio Franchino thought: we're getting back to normal, aren't we? We're getting back on track.

He was making lunch for his wife, carefully, lovingly, just as he had these past several days since her return home. She was gathering her energy back after all her travels and Tonio was only too glad to spoil her. He was making her cheese on toast and it was only a little bit burned at the edges.

Maybe she was quiet and subdued. Maybe she wasn't exactly like her usual self. But people often felt flat and depressed after their holidays, didn't they? Surely they were even more likely to be affected by a trip to their home city after so long? I must be careful and kind to her, Tonio thought. I must wait for her to return to me in her mind and her heart, as well as her body.

At least their reunion hadn't been like the Sturrocks of Frederick Street. Through various gossipy channels and mutual friends, Tonio had heard a little about what had happened when Cathy Sturrock had arrived home. All the mess and the turmoil and the upset. That young lass who'd moved in with them had them both over a barrel, Tonio thought. Everything he had heard about the Sturrocks sounded like a nightmare. Well, perhaps they deserved it. Perhaps it was just what they had coming to them. He wouldn't mind hearing more about old Noel Sturrock stewing in misery.

Nonna was in the kitchen, fussing about him. 'You give her burned toast?' she asked, her voice caustic. 'You think she'll like that?'

'It's just a little round the edges . . .'

'Pah.'

Tonio grumbled, but he knew the old Nonna was right. He jumped then as one of her old claws clutched at the front of his shirt and drew his face down level with hers. 'I can read your face, Tonio Franchino. And you look like a man who's hiding something. You have a bad secret.'

'What . . . ? Why, no . . .'

Nonna snapped her twiggy fingers in his face. 'What kind of a family and a home is this? When everyone in it is keeping their own secrets? You all have them clutched to your heart. Is no good.' She released him them and shuffled away on her stick, muttering to herself.

'What do you mean, everyone has their secrets?' he called after her, but she was gone. She ambled out of the back door to inspect her garden vegetables.

Who else has a secret, Tonio wondered. And how does the old woman know about it? His heart went cold at the thought that Sofia had told her mother something terrible and wounding. Something, perhaps, that would blow this whole family apart. Tonio had suspected as much and was braced for disaster.

Meanwhile, he was struggling to keep his own disaster secret.

Upstairs, Sofia was feeling wretched. She stood braced in the doorway of the bathroom and her guts were churning like the twin tub. Her mouth was filled with the acrid taste of her own vomit. She rinsed it quickly and cursed herself for a fool. She should have expected this. Hadn't it been the same when she was expecting Bella and Marco, all those years ago? Why, those times almost seemed like another life now. But here she was again, throwing up all morning and feeling like hell. Ready to put herself through the whole thing again.

She'd have to tell Tonio. He wasn't dim. Surely he would guess for himself soon enough?

Sofia struggled back to her room, feeling dizzy and unhappy. She sat at her dressing table and took stock of her haggard looks. She looked so wan and washed out. The beneficial effects of the southern sun had vanished in a mere matter of days, leaving her looking sallow. It was almost as if her Neopolitan sojourn hadn't really happened.

What was she doing, mooching about in the house this late in the day? It was almost lunchtime. It was time she got some work done. Surely one of the reasons she had been so low since returning was because she'd sat around doing nothing and feeling sorry for herself?

My god, now I'm sounding like my mother. I don't even need her standing here and berating me. I can do it just as well for myself. Her glance turned to the window and the garden below, where she could make out the diminutive, black-clad figure of her mother with her basket and her knife. She was hacking at the roots and stems of the vegetables she had tortured into life. 'I take out all my aggression and temper on them, when I go harvesting,' she had said recently, making the whole family laugh.

Nonna knew about Sofia's secret. She kept telling her, 'You must let Tonio know. The longer you keep it quiet, the more he will think there is something iffy about it.'

'Iffy?' Sofia asked, startled that her mother would even know such a colloquial English term.

Nonna's expression had darkened. 'What if you left it so late he thought there was something you wanted to hide? What if it started to look like the child was really Mario's?'

Sofia gasped at this. Her mother was absolutely right, and it was a terrible thought. Really, she had no idea why she was wavering like this. She wanted to be sure. She wanted to know that Tonio was ready to hear news like this. She wanted the moment to be a happy one.

But her suspicious, moody old mother had made a very good point. Sofia didn't want any confusion, did she? She didn't want Tonio to doubt her fidelity?

Suddenly he was with her, smiling hopefully as he brought her a tray of coffee and burned toast. She hoped there wasn't still a lingering whiff of vomit on the landing. That might spoil her moment.

'I brought you this.'

'Tonio, you don't have to make me lunch every day. I'm not an invalid.'

'You're still recovering from all your travels,' he said, setting down the tray on her sewing box. 'And I want to look after you, anyway. I missed you. A man is allowed to miss his own wife, isn't he?'

She started combing out her raven hair. Yes, today she would dress herself up. She'd get herself out of this funk. She'd get back to normal today and dress nicely for him.

'And I did miss you, you know,' he told her earnestly, stepping closer and trying to hold her gaze. 'We have never been apart for so long in all our lives together.'

'I know,' she said. 'Now I feel like I should never have gone. It was a mistake.'

'Oh?' He didn't push. He had learned over the years that it was best to let his wife unburden herself of her thoughts at her own pace. But he couldn't help asking, 'Was it Mario and his family? Were they not nice to you? Did they not look after you properly?'

'No . . . they . . . he . . . was very good. He was a proper gentleman.'

'I see. I'm glad about that.'

'You must never doubt it.'

He nodded, picking up a triangle of toast and munching on it himself. 'I trust you, Sofia. I would never have let you go if I didn't trust you.'

She bridled slightly at that but didn't say anything. Trust, he said! He was the one talking about trusting her when he'd been skulking about looking so shifty for days. 'Mark my words,' Nonna had muttered. 'He has some awful secret. I've tried to wheedle it out of him, but that man is tighter than a clam. He is ashamed, though, Sofia. Do not trust him!'

Sofia and Tonio stood staring at each other in the bedroom of their dream house and they both felt the weight of all that was unsaid between them.

Sofia couldn't stand the silence any longer. 'I'm going to have a baby,' she told him. 'That's what I've been waiting to tell you, until I was absolutely sure. Now I am. We're going to have another child, Tonio.'

She watched his reaction very keenly. It wasn't disappointing to her. His whole face lit up like someone had flipped a switch. She had never seen anyone so animated by delight before. He staggered on the spot and laughed like a maniac. Then he was grabbing her up in his arms and crushing her to his chest. 'Oh, my love . . . my love . . . I didn't know what you were about to tell me. I've been so scared about what it might be. But this! This is wonderful! Wonderful! I can't wait to tell everyone! Why, we'll shout it from the rooftops, won't we? We have to let everyone know at once!'

Chapter Fifty-One

Tonio was determined that the whole Franchino clan should go out that night to celebrate. He proposed an Italian restaurant at the Marine Park end of Ocean Road, but Sofia pooh-poohed the idea. She didn't want a big fuss. 'Besides . . . the expense! It's not necessary.'

Tonio shrugged. 'But I want us to have an evening we will remember. To mark the day you told me you'll make me a father again.' He was gleaming with pride when he said this. She hadn't seen him so happy in years, she realised.

Bella took the news calmly, blinking and staring at her mother and her father as they explained about the new addition to their household. The girl looked as if she could barely believe that her geriatric parents ever managed to have sex with each other still. 'It's wonderful news, Mama,' she murmured in Sofia's ear as she hugged her close. 'I can't believe it.'

Nonna snarled at them all, 'One less secret I have to keep! I am glad it is out in open now.'

It was decided that they would keep the ice cream parlour closed for the rest of the day and have a special family celebration on the premises just for themselves. They would toast the baby with best Franchino coffee and ice cream. Sofia hardly had the heart to point out that closing the café for the evening would actually cost them more than a slap-up meal at a restaurant, but she bit her tongue. Tonio was in an ebullient mood and she didn't want to spoil it.

'Dress up in your finest!' he told the women of his family. 'Hey, this child will be a boy. Somehow I just know it. And then little Marco and I wouldn't be so bloody outnumbered anymore, eh?'

Bella kissed her father on his forehead and found he was trembling. 'You will always be my precious child,' he told her. 'Whatever happens.'

The Franchino's had picked the most gorgeous, balmy evening to sally forth into town for their small celebration. People noticed them as they sat up straight on the trolley bus that ran along the coastal tracks. They were dressed up more than most people – Sofia in a bright dress she had treated herself to on holiday. It was peach and lemon coloured, topped off with a shawl that Mario had given her. Tonio was in his favourite suit, with caramel and vanilla-coloured stripes. Marco was in a tiny blazer and shorts. They all sat up straight on the bus and they each seemed to be quivering with a special kind of energy. Excitement and happiness seemed to radiate from them in waves. Even the old woman was cracking a smile that evening, though she still wore her usual widow's weeds.

They strolled in an unhurried fashion up Ocean Road, appreciating the warmth of the breeze and the gentle sunshine. When they came to Franchino's, Tonio unlocked the doors with a happily proprietorial air. He was like the king of the castle, pushing open the heavy chrome doors and ushering his ladies inside.

Soon they were sitting at the best table in the house. The radio was tuned to Tonio's favourite jazz station and he was bringing them hot, strong coffee topped off with dollops of cream. Then came the ice cream. He had created a new batch of his speciality: fior di latte. Bella was never sure afterwards whether it was her imagination, or whether the ice cream they ate that night was the sweetest, most delicious that her father ever made. Little Marco almost fainted with pleasure as he tucked in.

Tonio picked up his glass cup and toasted each of the ladies present, very gallantly. Then he bade them raise their own coffee cups to toast the anticipated new arrival. 'I believe he will be here before the year is out,' Tonio beamed. 'Why, he might even be a Christmas baby.'

The old Nonna was muttering under her breath, 'That's if my daughter has done her sums correctly.' She refused to repeat her comments when asked, shovelling her mouth full with ice cream.

Duke Ellington was playing on the large radio speakers Tonio had installed above his counter. He turned up the volume and got them all up dancing. He took Sofia in his arms and led her around the gaps between the tables in stately, too careful fashion, as if he thought she might break at any moment. Bella held her grandmother's hands and led her in a curious sideways-stepping dance. The jaunty music got under their skin and they joined hands, the whole lot of them, dancing together in a circle in the middle of their café. In some ways it was absurd, Sofia thought, but it was also a very beautiful moment. A wordless kind of bonding between the members of the Franchino family, after weeks and weeks during which it had felt that their precious unit had been developing various hairline fractures.

They danced and laughed and turned in a gentle circle.

This went on until Tonio became aware that someone was rapping on the glass doors. It was an irate and insistent sound. Someone clearly wanted to be noticed.

The dancing stopped as Tonio relinquished his wife and daughter's hands and turned to see who it was, wanting to get in.

'We are closed this evening!' he called to the interloper. 'Is a private family party!'

But the person outside wouldn't be deterred. Tonio turned the radio down and hurried over to send the person away.

As soon as he saw who it was, he realised that he couldn't do any such thing.

'Noel Sturrock,' he murmured in a hollow tone. All at once Tonio felt his goodwill and optimism drain away. He went cold as he took the door off the latch. It felt rather like he was giving admittance to a kind of nightmare creature. A monster or a vampire. Or something much closer to what Noel Sturrock actually was: a vengeful hobgoblin, determined to extract his own dues from the man he had bested in a game of cards.

Oh yes. Because all at once reality came crashing down on the bald, pink sweating pate of Tonio Franchino. It hadn't been a dream or a nightmare, that last night he had spent deep in gambling madness at the Robin Hood. He had sat till late by the smouldering cinders of the fire with Noel and his rough mates.

This was back before Sofia had returned from holiday. Tonio had thought nothing of staying out most of the night indulging his basest whims. Noel had been only too happy to let him stay for a game and another game and another game after that. Sometimes they stayed doling out the cards and sitting hunched over them until the sunlight came pouring into the harbour, touching the rooftops of all the houses of the Sixteen Streets one after the next, finally lighting up the frosted panes of the public house. Noel had kept him there, staring at his cards, chancing his arm, for as long as he liked.

Even though it was some weeks later and now Sofia was back and had told him her wonderful news, even though everything for the Franchino family was looking so wonderful and rosy all of a sudden, everything that had happened during those late nights with the cards was still quite, quite true.

In the end Tonio had lost.

He stared at the gurning, hated visage of Noel Sturrock and he blanched. 'You,' he said. 'It's not a good time. You are interrupting a private affair. Is a family celebration.'

Noel sneered up at him and barged his way past Tonio, his thickly deformed shoulders hunched up like a pugilist. Suddenly he was inside the ice cream parlour and the three women were staring at him. 'Good evening, ladies,' he snickered at them.

Sofia stepped forward. 'What is it, Noel? What do you want?' A sudden thought came out of nowhere to her. 'It's not Cathy, is it? Cathy's all right?'

He tossed his head and his greasy strings of hair flapped free of his skull. 'Her? She's fine. Why, I'd say she was better than fine.'

'Oh . . . good,' Sofia said, puzzled. 'But why are you here, Noel?'

'I saw the place was lit up and you were enjoying yourselves,' he smiled. 'I was passing this way and I thought: well, maybe I'll put my head round the door. See what's what.'

Tonio was very pale still. He tried to urge Noel back out of the main doors. 'Look, we can talk about this another time. Not tonight. Not right now. Is not the time.'

Noel shook his head firmly. 'I think it's very much the right time, Tonio old chum. It's time for you to tell your family.'

All eyes were on the Franchino patriarch.

'Tell us what, Tonio?' Sofia asked gently, but firmly. 'What's Noel talking about?'

All at once it was as if Tonio had been robbed of his voice. He was like a character in a fairy tale whose voice is stolen by an evil witch, or a vile hobgoblin. Tonio felt like all his remaining strength was draining out of his limbs. He sensed

Bella coming up to support him with her own strength and he realised he needed it, just to keep on standing there under the gloating eyes of Noel Sturrock.

Suddenly his wife could see it all. 'It's the gambling, isn't it?' She turned on the landlord of the Robin Hood. 'What have you done, Noel?'

He laughed raucously at that. 'What have *I* done? Are you kidding, lass? It's what he's done. Your precious fella there. He didn't give a fig about you lot, not when he was playing cards with me. All he could think about was the game. The game that goes on and on and never, ever ends. The fool's game.'

A shiver went right through Sofia's whole body. This was just like being visited by the devil. Her friend Cathy had called her husband such several times over the years and Sofia had always thought she was exaggerating and making him seem much worse than he was for effect. But tonight, Sofia was seeing close at hand what Noel was like when he was in this mood, and when he was holding all the winning cards. He had clearly come to take his portion of the winnings. He had come to claim his prize.

'What is it you want?' Sofia asked him curtly. 'Tell us and go. Leave us alone. We don't have to put up with you here.'

Oh, this made him laugh a lot. He started dancing about on the gleaming tiles. The old Nonna was clutching onto her ebony cane, as if biding her time for the right moment to crack him a deadly blow on the skull.

Tonio looked utterly defeated. Sofia had never seen her husband like this before. His shoulders were slumped, and his whole frame seemed to have shrunk. He looked helpless as Noel produced a single scrap of paper from inside his ragged jacket. It was stained and crumpled and the handwriting was almost illegible.

'What does it say?' Sofia asked, dreading the answer.

'He signed it,' Noel said. 'He signed it right there, look. And with that he agreed what the stake was. It's there in black and white and it's legal. It's all completely binding. And he lost, didn't he?' Noel hooted with laughter. 'Of course he lost, the bloody fool!'

'What did he lose?' Sofia ground out between her gritted teeth. 'Just tell us, you horrible man!'

Noel couldn't care less what she thought of him. She could call him all the names in the world. This was his greatest strength and he knew it. He had never cared what anyone ever thought of him. He had been abject, ugly, deformed, ridiculed, hated for all of his life. But he was a winner. He had always been a winner. Noel Sturrock had always ended up with all the winnings, whatever the game he was playing.

'What did he lose?' Sofia repeated angrily.

'This place,' he said simply, lifting up his claw-like hands and sketching out arabesques in the air. 'He gambled Franchino's itself. Can you believe it? When it came down to it, he put your family business in the pot with all the rest. He must have been feeling lucky . . . or desperate. And he lost! He lost the whole bloody lot. And now it's mine. Every bit of it is *mine*.' Noel took malicious note of the shocked expressions on the faces of the three Franchino women. 'Oh, didn't he mention it to you yet? Didn't he? Oh *dear*.'

Chapter Fifty-Two

It took several days for the impact of Noel's nasty revelation to fan out from that scene at Franchino's. Ripples were soon to be felt everywhere amongst their friends and relations. The Franchino family themselves returned home, much less content than they had set out that evening, and a serious rift was immediately apparent between Tonio and Sofia.

'You gambled away our livelihood?' she asked him on the tram home.

'Yes,' he said, hardly able to look her in the face.

'And our home?' she demanded. 'What about our home?'

'Is safe,' he tried to assure her. 'Believe me, it's safe. It never got as bad as that. I . . . stopped myself.'

Sofia laughed bitterly and couldn't bring herself to ask any more of him.

The old Nonna sat glaring at her son-in-law. She was seething with all kinds of unaired thoughts, which anyone merely glancing at her face could have guessed at. Later that evening she distilled them all into a single sentence for her daughter: 'I always told you that man was bad news for us.'

Sofia couldn't face arguing with her mother at that point and merely waved her away.

'What?' Nonna gasped. 'Now you won't listen to me? You should have listened to me more years ago, lady.'

Rifts were opening up everywhere, even between mother and daughter. 'I don't want to discuss it now,' Sofia told Bella on the landing late that night. Their house settled down to sleep later than usual and it really felt like a house at war.

Bella retreated to her room and sat up till very late, trying to come to terms with what they had learned. Her father had staked everything he had ever worked for on a game of cards with Sturrock. He had been so drunk and miserable and lonely and desperate he had placed everything in jeopardy. Bella loved her father and thought that she knew him well. She believed that he would never do such a thing capriciously or for no reason. She tried to imagine the sequence of crushing blows and defeats that had led him to gamble with more and more valuable stakes. He wouldn't have done this if he didn't have to.

She knew he must have been scared and hopeless and she couldn't imagine what it must have felt like to ultimately lose. Her poor father. He must have been so scared and felt so alone. And all this time he had been waiting for the news to break. It must have been like a cataclysmic storm hanging over his head.

Tonight's visit to the ice cream parlour, and their celebratory fior di latte, was coming to seem like the last moments in paradise for her family. It had been a valedictorian party, as they bid farewell to Franchino's as they knew it.

The Italian girl sat up till almost dawn at her window overlooking the sea. This view! This wonderful room in their sumptuous house! How did she have any right to it now? What right did any of them have to live here? It would all go, wouldn't it? The last vestiges of their good fortune, as all their money disappeared. Now Noel Sturrock would end up with everything and they would be turfed out. Why, they'd be lucky if they ended up living anywhere as decent as even the Sixteen Streets.

Mama always said we were maybe rash and foolish for taking on the expense of this big house, and she was right. It was Pa who kept up his enthusiasm for living here. He said we could afford it. Even in these difficult times, when everyone was scrimping for a living. It was all upwards and onwards for the Franchino clan!

But Papa was an addict. That was all there was to it. He couldn't help himself sitting at that table and offering up everything he valued to sheer chance. Did that mean he couldn't be blamed?

Maybe not. But his self-control had been sorely tested by Mama's absence. In her heart Bella knew the truth of that. Tonio had been mortally worried and upset that she had returned to Naples for keeps with cousin Mario. He had been far more distressed by it than he would ever let on. Bella realised: that was how much he really loved Mama. He had been prepared to quietly let her go in order to explore her own future as well as her past. Even if it had left him here, prey to all of his tempting demons.

Bella knew that, in her own furious turmoil, her mama would realise this eventually. She would know that she had played her part in this disaster, too.

It wasn't until the following evening that Bella left her quiet house (no one had really emerged to confront each other and discuss their predicament. Her father was lying low). The day was beautifully sunny and she knew that the young people of the town would be congregating in their usual spot by Marsden Rock.

It was after work for most of the youngsters and they were happy to laze on the sand, taking advantage of every drop of sunshine that came their way. It was an unusually long and warm summer that year, and everyone was quite familiar with the damp autumn months just around the corner, when the freezing winds would start stealing across the North Sea, little by little freezing the coast and sealing them into a wintry trap that they wouldn't emerge from until next April. Who could blame them for playing here between the long shadows of the cliffs and rocks in the golden sunlight while it lasted?

Bella knew she would find Junie Sturrock here with the Farley boys and all the rest of the gang. As she hurried down the cliff steps, she felt her scalp giving a twinge of remembered pain, reminding her of the last time she had confronted young Junie down here, when the two of them had fought with everyone watching. That time, June had been the one with the grievance. She'd accused Bella's mother of bewitching her own mother away. Such nonsense! The girl was clearly crazy. She was selfish and crazy, the same as her adopted dad.

There Junie was, dancing around on the sand by the campfire. She was in a baby blue swimming costume that looked like it was expensive, to Bella's expert eye. As Bella approached, she saw that Junie was demonstrating some sort of dance she must have seen at the pictures, with all the boys standing around her, slaveringly attentive to her every move. There was no doubt about it, Junie was sexy. She seemed to know just how to draw everyone's hungry attention to herself.

Minnie stood to one side, watching on with the others, looking both miserable and proud at the same time. Wherever Junie was, you were more or less sure to find Minnie Minton, Bella thought. That poor girl! She deserved better than this sinuously nasty snake of a girl.

'You!' Bella shouted at her, surprising herself. Her pace had quickened as she reached the beach. Her pumps were flying through the sand and her skirt flared around her. She couldn't help herself running towards the dancing girl. 'You, Junie Sturrock!'

Above the noise of the radio, everyone suddenly heard her shouting and they all turned to see the usually composed and sweet-natured Bella thundering towards them. Robbed of their attention, June stopped dancing and put her hands on her hips. She derisively tossed her headful of golden curls. 'Ha! Look who it is! The Ice Cream Queen of all South Shields!'

Bella suddenly saw red. She felt that jagged rip of her scalp again, from the last time they'd fought when Junie had yanked out that hank of hair. She thought about the crumpled, defeated look of her father and the blazing fury of her mama and she knew that it was all down to this snide bitch and her kin.

'You can tell your father to bugger off!' Bella shouted, thrusting her fist into Junie's face. 'You tell him he doesn't get a penny out of us! He's getting nowt!'

There was a flicker of surprise on the younger girl's face. 'What are you talking about now, you silly cow?'

'I tell you, Junie Sturrock. You better warn your horrible old father. He's picked the wrong family to mess with here. If he tries to take Franchino's off us – he's dead! I swear it! And so are you!'

There was an audible gasp from everyone watching this little scene on the beach. Everyone knew that you were best off not messing with Italians. Even Junie looked disconcerted.

'I don't know what you think he's done, but it's got nothing to do with me,' Junie spat at her enemy.

Bella was flushed with anger. 'I will break your legs and your arms and I will put your pretty little face into our coffee grinder,' she told Junie. 'So just you and your father think on.' Then Bella turned on her heel and marched away, across the burning sand.

Chapter Fifty-Three

It was one of her few evenings off work, but Minnie forsook her time at the beach to follow Junie all the way home. Her friend would never have shown her feelings in public, but Minnie knew she was upset and rattled. She threw on her coat and tottered up the cliff and back into town muttering to herself as Minnie tried to keep up with her.

'What was the daft mare rabbiting on about?' Junie frowned. 'These Italians are crazy. Her mother's crackers, too, according to the bits and pieces I've heard from Cathy.'

Minnie didn't think either Bella or Sofia were at all crackers. To her they were glamorous goddesses, and both had always been more than friendly to Minnie. There was clearly, however, something dramatic going on, involving both the Sturrocks and the Franchinos, and Minnie was avid to find out what it was. Also, she was very keen to look after Junie.

Her feelings for the Northumbrian girl hadn't abated one jot. Even though she knew that she was, in many ways, an absolute nightmare, Minnie couldn't help herself. Junie was obnoxious and spoiled and this was plain for even the most infatuated to see. But it seemed that Minnie was in the grip of a fatal fascination and she clung to the girl's side as much as she possibly could. Even when Junie made no attempt to hide her irritation with her constant shadow.

Soon they were back on Frederick Street, where Cathy and Noel were beginning a quiet-ish night at the Robin Hood. The whole pub had – through dint of hard work on Cathy's part – been restored to its usual orderly state. In fact, she had overcompensated and now the place was gleaming like a new pin. Even the brass fittings and the horse brasses hanging on the walls had been polished brightly.

'I thought you girls were on the beach this evening.' Cathy greeted them warmly. 'Junie, you're not properly dressed for going about the streets. Is that your macintosh over your swimsuit?'

Junie scowled. 'I had to get back in a rush.'

'There was a fight!' Minnie burst out excitedly. 'You'll never guess. Bella Franchino attacked Junie! She just about strangled her, right there in front of everybody!'

Cathy gasped and came running out from behind the bar. The couple of old drinkers showed mild interest as the landlady examined her fuming daughter. 'What's this? You're joking, surely, aren't you, pet? Bella Franchino would never hurt anyone . . .'

At this point Junie started milking it. She deliberately made herself sound weak and defenceless. 'I didn't know what she was doing. She came charging over . . . she was grabbing me before I even knew what she was on about . . .'

'Are you all right, Junie?' Cathy cossetted her. She was very careful and solicitous around her daughter. She was still trying to make up for attacking the girl in public herself.

'It's all to do with Mr Sturrock and something he's done,' Minnie said, feeling important. 'That's all I could make out from what Bella was ranting about.'

'Noel . . . ?' Cathy frowned. She should have known it would be down to him. Just then he was through the back, messing about with the barrels, doing whatever thing it was that he did for hours back there. Tippling and supping, probably, and dodging work. 'Noel! Are you there?'

He emerged moments later, cobwebbed and bleary-eyed from tasting and checking on the quality of the beers. When he saw the girls, a crafty look came over his face. 'Oh yes, what's this?'

'They've had a row,' Cathy told him. 'Bella Franchino picked a fight with our Junie.'

'Oh?' smirked Noel. 'Is that a fact?'

'She was more upset than I've ever seen her,' Minnie told them. 'Eeeh, you should have heard her! She was stottin' mad.'

Noel idly poured himself a pint of ale. 'Aye, well. I just had to tell those Franchinos what was what, didn't I? Last night. As they all sat round there, looking so smug with their fancy ice cream and their coffee. I had to tell them what's gonna happen. And none of them were very happy about it all. That's as likely as what yon Bella was skriking about. That'll be what it was.'

Cathy was losing her patience now. 'You're talking in riddles! What did you tell them? How did you annoy them?'

Noel looked like the cat who'd got the cream at last. He smiled preeningly and announced: 'I had to inform them that I am now the proud owner of the Franchino ice cream empire. Me, Noel Sturrock!'

'What . . . ?' cried Cathy. 'How can you be?'

'You know what he's like, that old Tonio. He's a divil with the cards. He's hopeless. And when you and that Sofia were off gallivanting, why he came here, didn't he? He couldn't keep away from the card games I ran. And I thought: whey, I'll teach you a lesson, you bloody Franchino lot. It really was like taking ice cream off a babby. And I won it fair and square, Cathy.'

His wife's eyes were out on stalks. 'H-he gambled his whole business?'

'Aye, lass! And it's ours now! It's ours to do with what we will!' The old crookback laughed raucously at this, like he'd never heard anything so funny in all his life.

Junie had stopped sobbing and acting quite so wretched by now. She was listening in astonishment, and starting to look just as pleased as Noel was.

Minutes later, Cathy was dashing out of the pub.

'Where the hell are you going? You've got to serve behind the bar!' Noel thundered after her.

Her face was red. 'Bugger that! And bugger you, you cruel, insensitive old sod.' All Cathy knew was that she had to get to her friend. She had to get to Sofia's side and reassure her. She had to tell her: this has nothing to do with me. I don't want to take your business off you! What must she be feeling like? What state must all the Franchino's be in? Noel had robbed them all blind!

'I'm not serving at this bar by mesel'!' Noel cried, and she realised that he was three sheets to the wind.

'You've got Junie and Minnie here with you. They'll help!'

And then Cathy was gone, bolting over the cobbled road to number twenty-one. She already had her purse and her shawl. She just needed to change out of her work shoes and then she could make a dash for the tram that would take her to the Franchino house. Oh, why did they have to move so far away? It was so much easier when they just lived in the next street! Cathy shook her head, worrying on their behalf. Why, that fancy, expensive house would be like an albatross around their necks now, if they really had lost their business.

But Tonio couldn't really have lost it, could he? Surely something as stupid as a drunken, late night game of cards couldn't count . . . *officially*, could it? Would what Noel was asserting stand up in a court of law?

Cathy realised she didn't understand how any of these things worked. All she really understood was that her wicked and underhand husband had done something dreadful. He had taken advantage of a poor man's fatal weakness. He had exploited him when he was down and lonely, and now people who Cathy cared about were suffering as a result.

Oh, sometimes she hated her Noel's guts, and she cursed that old mother of his who had wheedled, cajoled and finally bribed her to put up with him.

Cathy thundered up the stairs of her house and onto the landing. She hared into her bedroom and she had only one thought in her mind.

Helping Sofia. She had to do what she could for her friend Sofia.

As Noel had explained how he was going to relieve the Franchinos of their livelihoods, a sudden thought had struck Cathy. There was something practical she could do to help them. Maybe Sofia would think it a bad idea. Maybe she would be horrified at the thought. But if she needed money, then it might be the only thing for it.

The ring. Mario's mother's glittering heirloom.

Cathy was looking after it for Sofia. It was in her safekeeping.

It would be a horrible betrayal of Mario to sell it . . . but perhaps it could be a kind of insurance.

Cathy had decided that she needed to pick it up and take it straight to Sofia in her hour of need. She had to let her friend know that she was on her side and not that devil Noel's. She had to prove she was thinking of ways to help the Franchino family.

To this end, Cathy hastened into her unlocked bedroom and flew to her dresser. She ransacked each and every tiny wooden drawer, opening them all in a panicky flurry, though she remembered very well which one she had hidden the precious ring inside.

The dreadful realisation settled over her even as she went checking all the drawers and hidden nooks for a second time.

But there was no mistaking the plain fact.

The ring was gone.

Chapter Fifty-Four

Minnie liked above all to be needed. With Cathy haring off that night, it was a case of all hands to the beer pumps and she was only too glad to step behind the bar beside Junie.

Mr Sturrock was getting increasingly drunk, propping up the end of the bar sinking pints and following them up with shots of whisky. He was bragging like a man who'd won the pools.

'It'll be a little goldmine, you'll see,' he was telling Junie. 'Much better than this place has ever been. I'll make a real go of it. It'll be much better than it's been up till now.'

Junie laughed at him. 'What do you know about running an ice cream parlour? How could you know better than them Eyeties?'

'Ha!' he grunted. 'There's my genius, you see. Because what I'll do is, I'll hire them! The whole bloody family will be glad for work, won't they? And I'll hire them back at slave wages to do the jobs they're already doing. They'll keep the place going, but all the profits will be mine. See, that's how ownership works, dunnit?'

Junie shook her head in mock admiration. Maybe he had good business sense after all. 'It'll be good to see them suffer, that lot,' she smiled. 'They think such a lot of themselves. Especially that awful snotty Bella.'

As she worked at the bar, Minnie was eavesdropping and had to admit to herself she didn't like the way the two of them were talking. To her they sounded as cruel as each other.

Now Noel Sturrock was smoothing out a piece of crumpled paper on the bar and gazing at it reverently. 'See? He's signed it there. This is all above board and legal.'

Junie read over the scribbled document, her eyebrows raised in amazement. 'This is it? Because of this little scrap of paper, a man can lose his whole livelihood?'

'He signed it, look!' Noel grinned. 'The bloody fool. He put his name down here and then we played the game again and he lost . . .'

Junie frowned, unsure if this would ever get through the courts. 'Hadn't you better look after it, then?' she said. 'If everything depends on that paper?'

'I just wanted to show you, Junie,' Sturrock said, his words slurring slightly. 'This is all for you, you know. You're our future, me and Cathy's future. I've told you before, haven't I? You're like the lovely daughter I never had.'

'Aye, you did,' Junie said, smiling at him. Only Minnie could see the tightness in that smile. Junie was repressing her disgust at the gurning old man. She did it quite successfully, even bending to kiss him on his whiskery cheek. Minnie could tell, though. She could see a mile off that Junie was holding her breath and crossing her fingers all the while she sucked up to Noel. Once again Junie was thinking only of herself.

None of that altered Minnie's feelings about her. To Minnie, Junie was an angel who had been set down upon a corrupted and benighted world. She just did what she had to do in order to survive, and Minnie would follow her anywhere as she pursued her own path.

'What do you think, Minnie? Would you like to work in an ice cream parlour with me, eh?' June laughed. 'We could have glamorous outfits made, with little hats and pinnies. It would be nicer for you than working in Swetty Betty's!'

Minnie was shocked. 'But I'll always have to work at the chip shop. It's me mam's shop. I have to help her. It's loyalty, you see.'

Junie let out a peal of tinkling laughter. 'Loyalty, she says! That's why you'll never get anywhere in this life, Minnie Minton. You're too stupidly loyal. If you carry on like that, the people you're loyal to will only drag you down.'

Minnie felt stung by that. Sometimes the things Junie said made her feel horrible. 'My mam says that loyalty is all that matters. Doing the right thing for the people you love.'

Junie tossed her golden curls and went off to serve her next customer. 'Your mother is a sweaty fool.'

I can't say anything about it, Cathy thought. I can't tell her now. Not right now. It would break her heart right now. I don't want to add to all her troubles. Poor Sofia's got enough on her plate . . .

Cathy was sitting alone, almost the only passenger on the trolley bus on the coastal road. It clanked noisily on the tracks, the wires overhead sparking in the darkness. She could still hear the roar of the ocean as the tram lurched along. The tide was in and darkness had fallen. As she stepped off at Seahouses, there was a faint mist that chilled her and filled her with gloom.

'Cathy!' Sofia looked surprised to see her when she answered the door of her grand house.

'I had to come as soon as I knew about it all,' her friend said.

Sofia took her into her arms and cuddled her on the doorstep. 'I know it had nothing to do with you,' she told her, drawing her indoors.

Everyone had gone to bed. Nonna had tottered up to her room over thirty hours ago and she was just going to die, she had announced. Bella was reserved after some sort of fracas on the beach that she wouldn't talk about, even with her mother, and Tonio was subdued and exhausted. It was as if, with the airing of his shameful secret, all the life had gone out of him.

'So, as ever, it's left to me to hold the fort,' Sofia shrugged, making tea for her friend in the kitchen.

Cathy sat at the breakfast bar she had so admired when the Franchinos had first moved in. How many months ago was that now? They had been so proud of their success and their wealthy trappings. Cathy had never begrudged them an ounce of that pride, but Noel had. She remembered him being here with her, examining their friends' new home. How surly and envious he had looked! When he clapped eyes on their sea view from their picture window, the old hunchback looked as if he could have spat!

'I'm only grateful,' said Sofia, 'that my foolish husband didn't gamble away our house as well. I could imagine that happening too. We could all have been out on our ears.'

Cathy could imagine it as well, and the relish Noel would have taken in such a scene. 'Thank heaven for small mercies. But you've lost enough as it is, Sofia . . .'

'I know,' she said, and poured milk into their teacups with a sigh. 'We've lost everything we worked all these years to build up. He threw it all away in one night. All those years of scrimping and saving . . .'

'You'll get it back,' Cathy promised her. 'I'll see to that. I don't know how. But I'll think of something.'

Sofia looked at her in surprise. 'You will?'

'Of course! It's not fair, Sofia. My bloody husband can't just swoop down and take away everything you've built up since you've lived in South Shields. He has absolutely no right to it. No matter how hopeless your Tonio is at cards – my fella has bugger all right to thieve off him!'

Sofia sobbed with relief. 'I'm so glad you're on my side.'

'Of course I am! We're best friends, aren't we?'

'Yes, yes . . . I should have known that I can always rely on you, Cathy.'

Cathy was frowning hard. 'Now we just have to work out what the best thing is. What's the best way of getting Noel to back down?'

Sofia sagged again. 'I don't think he'll ever back down.'

Cathy pursed her lips. 'Then we have to think of something else. Some other way.' In her mind she had started to think terrible things. Cathy was starting to have thoughts that appalled her.

Chapter Fifty-Five

It was the following afternoon and Minnie called round at number twenty-one to see her friend. There had been something shrill and hard about her manner last night that had disturbed Minnie. Junie had been lashing out and acting quite nasty at times. She seemed like she was happy to see the Franchino family suffering as much as they were at the hands of her conniving uncle. She was contemptuous and dismissive of everyone, including Minnie's mother.

Minnie was alone in that she could actually see the good in Junie. She knew that when the girl said harsh things, it was all a put-on. It was just her trying to seem brave and hard. Deep down, she was nothing of the sort. There was a tender streak in her. Minnie was sure of it. Junie was wounded, Minnie knew.

The next morning, she took tea to Junie in bed and found her friend in a reflective mood. She started talking, all by herself, about Cathy and her early memories of her. Memories from a time when the young Junie had no inkling that Cathy was her true mother.

'She doesn't think I remember, but I do. I was only a very little girl, but everything from that time has stayed with me. I do remember her coming to visit the cottage. I can still see her now, standing at the door and my aunty letting her in. My aunt really didn't want her there. She wanted her to stay away. I didn't really understand what was going on. I just knew that this young woman coming to see me would look upset and sometimes she would be crying. She would hug me and cry and rock me in her lap and then I would get upset too, even though I didn't know what any of it was about . . .'

Junie and Minnie were quiet together in Junie's rather messy bedroom in the half-gloom of the afternoon, with the heavy curtains drawn on the grey daylight. Minnie was sitting very quietly on the chair by the dressing table, listening attentively to her friend. She was amazed because she had never heard Junie come out with such personal business before. There was a soft and rather raw quality to her friend's voice as she spoke. For once it was as if she was truly making herself vulnerable. She was giving herself away to Minnie and the younger girl found herself thrilled beyond measure.

Junie lay back on her pillows with her eyes closed and her petite figure seemed swamped by the vast antique bed and the beautiful satin coverlet. She seemed dwarfed in that room of ornate Victorian furniture.

'It must have been upsetting for you,' Minnie ventured, in her most sensitive tone, 'to have this woman visiting. Someone you hardly knew . . .'

'I didn't understand anything,' Junie sighed. 'And my aunty didn't ever really explain anything. She never said, why, this is your real mother come to see you. She still loves you. She never told me that. What was more, she forbade Cathy from saying anything of the sort to me, also. She supervised all our visits and Cathy lived under the threat that she could be sent away at any time and never allowed back to visit me. My Aunt Liz held all the cards, and she knew it.'

Minnie was quiet then, thinking about what a rough deal Cathy had been given. Perhaps she didn't deserve all the trouble

Junie had brought to her after all. Minnie hesitated and then asked, 'Do you believe Cathy now, then? That she had no choice but to leave you behind? Are you seeing it all more from her side now?'

Junie blushed angrily and opened her eyes to glare at her friend. She admitted, 'I don't know anymore, Minnie. I don't think I know anything anymore. I came here, to the Sixteen Streets, so sure of myself. I knew I was right. I knew that I had been wronged and I came here to get my dues. I would get my so-called mother to admit that she loved me and that she missed me . . . and what happened? Why, Cathy went and said all those things almost immediately. She tried to explain everything to me, but I was so cruel and callous because I was furious. I didn't know what to do, when love was just offered to me freely like that . . . it made me feel so confused and horrible.'

Minnie gulped, amazed by Junie's words. Yes, yes, of course she would find it hard simply to accept love. She had been brought up to cast it away, to reject it.

Junie went on, 'Seeing Cathy as she is now, so upset by what we did to the house and the pub while she was away . . .' She shook her head, shuddering. 'Me and Noel . . . we just let the whole lot go to hell. Oh, we sneered . . . she would tidy it all when she got back. She could bloody well put it all to rights . . . but it's her little kingdom and we turned it into a flamin' midden. We even killed the cat with our neglect. I could see her heart break in two . . . I felt bad about it, Minnie. I felt rotten.'

The younger girl sat smiling uncertainly. She gave her blouse a surreptitious sniff as she mulled over Junie's words. Oh god, I reek of fish and chips, don't I? My friend is opening her heart to me and I smell like a fish supper. Minnie felt hopeless; how could she ever offer comfort and affection when she always smelled of chips?

'I-it's not too late, surely, to put things right? To make everything OK with your mother?' Minnie smiled and inched closer on her chair. 'You just have to go to her and talk to her like you talk to me. Explain everything to her, like you have done with me. Cathy will understand everything. She's so clever and strong. She will be wise about it, like she is about everything. She'll see that you've been made like this. She'll see that it's all down to the woman who brought you up.'

Junie looked tearful. 'Maybe. But maybe I've gone too far already. I've been torturing her, Minnie. I was doing it on purpose. I found that I knew exactly how to hurt her feelings and I just kept turning the screws. Winding her up by favouring Noel! That horrible beast of a man. I was calling him "Daddy" just to make her suffer! That was awful of me, wasn't it?'

Minnie had to admit, 'Yes, it was cruel. But you were confused. You can be excused, surely, for being so mixed up and upset . . .' Minnie suddenly remembered Noel jeering at her for being too loyal. If you're loyal to people, they will drag you down with them. That's what he said. What an awful view of people that man had!

Junie let her sighs calm down. Her feeling of hopelessness subsided. She glanced at her best friend, Minnie. 'And you. I haven't always been as nice to you as I might have been, I've been quite sharp, haven't I? I've snapped at you and called you awful things. And all you ever wanted was to be my friend, didn't you? That's all you set your big, soft heart on, Minnie Minton. You knew I was worth being friends with, and you persevered.'

'I did,' said Minnie proudly. She wasn't used to praise and she lapped this up. Yes, I'm loyal. Yes, I see through the dross to the real person inside. I'm clever and shrewd and kind: that's who I am. And I am loyal to a fault. Even if I do smell like a fish supper in yesterday's blouse.

'So, I'm sorry if I've mistreated you, Minnie,' Junie sighed. 'I should be nicer to someone who thinks a lot of me like you do.' She patted the counterpane by her side. 'Come and be over here with me. Cuddle in, Minnie. Come and sit with me.'

'Really?'

'Yes, of course. Sit with me.'

Very carefully, very quietly, Minnie got up and scooted over to the bed to sit beside her friend. She was terrified in case Junie could hear the pounding of her heart inside her chest. She tried to make herself keep calm.

'Are you all right?' Junie asked as Minnie sat stiffly beside her. 'Lie down next to me. You're so comforting and soft. Here, let me cuddle you. You're a good friend, Minnie. You've been so good to me from the start . . .'

Chapter Fifty-Six

It was a stupid, ridiculous plan. Cathy knew it even as she set off to make her clandestine visit that day.

Ten, twelve years ago, she had done everything she could to extricate herself and her pub from the clutches of the mad Johnson clan. That old witch at the head of their family – Gracie Johnson – had been demanding twenty per cent of the takings, in exchange for leaving it in peace! They brought hooky goods and Noel was forced to buy them at inflated prices. The evil old woman would send round her awful boys to put the menaces on him.

And Cathy had fallen in love with Matty, the most handsome of those boys. Oh, now that was a story and a half!

She travelled across town, almost all the way to Jarrow and Boldon Colliery, back to the home of the mad Johnson clan. It was foolish and dangerous, but it was a plan, of sorts.

She knew just how to put the fear of god into Noel Sturrock, and that's what she intended to do.

The streets were narrow and darker here. Palls of dreadful, ominous smoke hung over the rooftops, spoiling the summer skies. It was quite different to the airy heights of Cathy's end of the Sixteen Streets. No fresh sea air had ever penetrated this warren of dingy alleyways. You couldn't even hear the seagulls crying this far upriver.

Cathy shuddered at the thought of confronting old Gracie Johnson again. There was no love lost between the two of them. Years ago, when their paths had crossed, the old matriarch had been at the height of her powers, like an awful spider at the heart of her web. Cathy had found her frightening, and only her fierce attraction to Matty, Ma Johnson's son, and her love for her hapless and doomed friend Ellie had made her brave enough to beard that wicked old bitch in her den. At one point Cathy had found herself so enraged she had almost strangled the life out of Gracie Johnson with her bare hands. Matty and Sofia had only just prevented her from committing murder on Tudor Avenue.

Cathy knew that she had been lucky to escape unscathed from all her tumultuous encounters with the Johnsons. Relatively unscathed, that is. The family of ruffians had left her and hers mostly alone for quite some years since then.

Now here Cathy was, about to stir up the hornets' nest once more.

Rumour had it that the Johnsons were a depleted force, anyway. Their influence wasn't what it was. They had lost some of their boys, who'd moved away to other towns. Some had even gone to America. They weren't the frightening presence they had once been on the streets of Shields. At least, that was what all the talk said.

Here was the door. An unassuming painted door, cracked and blistered, on a run-down terrace. Hardly the home of criminals who were doing well. They hadn't moved an inch in all the years since Cathy was last here. They had stagnated.

She recognised the big brute who answered the door to her as Jan, whose thick red hair had receded alarmingly. She remembered his huge pan shovel hands and his neanderthal features. Jan had always looked like he could fettle you with a single blow, without even trying. And yet now there was something so gentle in his manner. He looked like it would pain him terribly to have to deal you the death blow. Like all his brothers, he assiduously followed the orders of his malicious old mother. By the looks of things, he was the last one left here at home with her.

To Cathy's astonishment the giant brute recognised her. 'Long time no see, hinny!' he beamed as he stepped aside to let her into the Johnson manor. 'Eeeh, it must be years!'

She smiled at him. Something about this daft, gentle giant touched her heart – even though he could be terrifying in the right circumstances. 'I've come to see your mam, Jan. Is she all right? Is she at home to visitors?'

His dull expression brightened. 'Why aye, lass. She's allus home these days, y'knaa. She's got her little bed made up in the front room and she barely gets out of it. I dee everythin' for her now. All the others have buggered off.'

Maybe this wasn't as daft an idea as Cathy had thought. 'Look, Jan. I know that me and your lot haven't always seen eye to eye . . .'

He laughed at that. 'Ah, it's all water under the bridge, Cathy lass. I allus had a soft spot for ye. All the Johnson lads did. Especially wor Matty, eh?'

She winced at the mention of the lad she had stupidly fallen for. 'Is he still in Newcastle? Is he doing all right?'

'Very well! He's in Manchester now. He sends back money regularly. Good money, too. But he works so hard. We never see him. We don't see many folk at all.'

There came a screeching cry from the front room. 'What's that flamin' draught coming in, you bugger? Who are you talking to on the doorstep?'

Jan laughed at his mother's querulous tones. 'Ha'way through and see the old dame. Say your piece. Will you be wanting a cup of tea and some seed cake?'

Cathy's eyes widened at the prospect of being offered tea and homemade cake at the Mad Johnson house. She'd have expected broken ribs and a black eye first, but here was Jan, scurrying off to the kitchen, once he'd got her settled beside the bed of his queen.

'Hey, Mam. You remember Cathy, don't you?' he asked gently, and the sweetness and solicitude in his voice touched Cathy's heart.

'Mrs Johnson?' Cathy asked, sitting down on a stuffed pouffe beside the bed.

The springs rumbled and the old woman turned over to face her guest. She looked eager, her eyes avid to take in Cathy's features. A waft of stale air and body odour washed over Cathy as the bedclothes shifted. The old woman looked like she had aged fifty years in the time since Cathy had been here last. She looked like an elderly baby in her frilled nightie and her lacy cap. Everything was spotlessly clean and ironed, though, Cathy couldn't help but notice.

'Eeeh, it's been some years, Cathy,' the old woman chuckled. She sounded much less harsh and wicked than Cathy remembered. Perhaps she had mellowed with age? Maybe she was more helpless now. There was something even wary in the way she eyed her visitor. 'That was all a long time ago, eh? We were just lasses then! Back when you tried to throttle me, eh? Do you remember? You almost strangled the bloody life out o' me!' The old woman laughed until she started coughing. 'Help me sit up straighter, will you? And then tell me what you want. I bet this isn't a social call. You wouldn't come here unless you needed something from me.'

Yes, she was right, the old besom. Cathy felt almost guilty for not sparing the old woman a single thought over the years. 'I thought you hated me.'

'Ha!' Ma Johnson rolled her cloudy eyes. 'I don't even know what hate is anymore. As you get older, the things that used to make you furious, or greedy, or desperate . . . whey, they all seem to lose their sting somehow. Their importance fades and it's hard to get quite so het up anymore. I used to be all for my family, didn't I? I'd do anything for my lot. But they get up and go and they leave you. Most of them do. They all walk out on you in the end. They're buggers, the lot of them.'

Jan brought their tea and the cake he told them he had baked his very self that weekend gone. He was extremely proud of it and watched as Cathy took a careful bite. She made sure to look appreciative, even though it was rather dry.

'Look, I need your help,' she said at last. 'And Jan's. It's Jan's help I really need.'

The old woman's lips curled with pleasure. 'Oh, you do, do you? And why's that? What do you need help with? I thought Cathy Sturrock was a dab hand at getting all her own way, all by herself?'

Cathy smiled at the barb. There was an acid-tinged touch of respect in Ma Johnson's voice. 'You remember who I married?'

'That dreadful old hunchback, yes. Folk round here could hardly believe it. All my boys were heartbroken.'

Cathy couldn't even think about that now. She didn't dare let herself think about her lost love, Matty. 'Well, I married him. And it's been hard. We've had our ups and downs. But now . . . now I need some help. You see, I want to put the fear of god into him . . .'

Chapter Fifty-Seven

Bella felt that she had to support her papa more than she did her mam. This was because she knew that Sofia was strong as an ox, really, both physically and in her heart. Tonio was far more fragile and liable to break. Right now, he was under a lot of pressure. He knew that it was he who was to blame for the current crop of misfortune the Franchino clan was facing. Lately he was needing to be man of the house, with a new baby on the way, but he felt old and defeated, and he had whistled away their fortune to an evil hobgoblin.

Bella was damned if she was going to let Noel Sturrock waltz away with everything her family had worked for.

She dressed herself up in her neatest practical working clothes and tied her hair up under a hairnet. Then she sallied forth into the crisp morning – the first day that really felt like autumn was approaching – and marched into Franchino's with a determined stride.

Her father was cleaning his beloved coffee machine and he looked up in surprise at her. 'I told you I'd be OK watching over the fort by myself today . . .'

She unbuttoned her coat briskly. 'I know you did, Papa. But I wanted to be here with you. I don't want you facing that man by yourself.'

Her father coloured slightly at the allusion to Sturrock, and also the implication that he couldn't be trusted to look after affairs by himself. 'I can face up to him.'

'You need support,' Bella said steadfastly. 'You need to be firm with that horrible little man.'

Tonio looked almost cross with her. 'I will deal with things in my own way.'

She shook her head. 'I'm a grown woman now, Papa. I can help you. I want to help.'

He could see that there was no use arguing with her. It wasn't that Bella was mule-headed, he just knew that she had a temperament very like his own mother's. She would see things through, come what may. She wouldn't give in to defeat, like he was prone to. 'Very well,' he sighed. 'You may serve customers when Mr Sturrock pays his call, and I will talk with him.'

Bella felt a flash of fury at the deferential way her father mentioned Mr Sturrock. Her anger only increased when the old crookback arrived in person some thirty minutes after his appointed time. There was only a scattering of coffee drinkers in the ice cream parlour at that time and the atmosphere shifted when Sturrock crept inside. The convivial warmth of Franchino's seemed to change in an instant, as the opened door let in a breath of autumnal air with dread leaves blowing onto the tiles. With a gruesome, conniving grin, Noel Sturrock made his entrance. He glanced around the gleaming parlour like a Roman emperor examining some new exotic province his legionnaires had conquered.

'Good morning,' he nodded to Bella at the counter, and she scowled openly at him. She was damned if she was going to be polite to the man. He stood there in what looked like a cloak of some kind and a flat cap that sat absurdly on his lank and greasy hair. And that twisted, malformed back of his looked worse than ever. It was as if, as he grew older, his character grew more twisted and his body was matching it as the years rolled by. Oh, but these were cruel thoughts, Bella told herself. Unworthy of her to think so uncharitably of even the man who'd set out to ruin her family. The man must be in pain with his physical ailments. Perhaps it was chronic pain that had cankered his nature?

Papa appeared and asked Bella to make Noel's coffee just how he wanted it. 'So much choice!' the horrible man said, with a breathy laugh as he read the hand-painted menu above the counter. 'What would you recommend, my dear?'

She shrugged. 'I don't know what you like.'

'Neither do I, really, but I will learn. Now that I'm here and Franchino's is mine, maybe I'll try every kind of coffee, one after the next. And you, my dear, can make them for me. Maybe you'll stay here and work as my favourite coffee girl?'

Bella glared at him. 'I'll make you an espresso,' she said. It was quickest to do, and quickest to drink. Perhaps she could get him to expedite his visit.

'Make him your best espresso,' her father told her. 'You do them so well.' He told Noel, as he guided him to the most secluded table in the room: 'I have taught my daughter everything I know.'

'Then perhaps I will keep her on, working here,' she heard Noel muttering. 'Does she deserve to keep her place here? Perhaps she does . . .'

Moments later the coffee was ready and Bella delivered two espressos to their booth. The men were already deep into their conversation. They were clearly talking business. The old crook was hunched forward, spittle flying out of his thin lips as he lectured Tonio about what was to be. Bella's heart hurt to see her father looking so compliant, merely nodding as Noel raspingly told him what was what.

'Here's your coffee,' said Bella, setting down her tray, somehow managing to convey an air of defiance as she served them.

Noel's hand reached out to pat her own and she froze. It made her skin crawl to have his tough, yellowed flesh come into contact with hers. 'Let's see what the girl thinks about my idea, eh?' he cried. 'What do you think of this, Bella lass?'

She eyed him suspiciously. 'About what?'

He grinned at her, revealing truly horrid tobacco-coloured teeth. 'What do you think of when I say the work "kiosk"?'

She blinked. She didn't have a clue what he was on about.

'Ah, you're as dopey as your dad here!' cackled the old man. 'Kiosks, eh? Lovely little Franchino kiosks, up and down the seafront. Picture them on summer days, with queues leading from their windows all the way down the beach. Dozens – even hundreds – of customers queueing up for your ice cream and coffee! Just think of the profits, lass!'

Bella and her father looked at each other.

'And vans!' Noel enthused. 'What about ice cream vans patrolling all the streets in town? Taking your wares straight to the customers? Imagine that! Driving all over South Shields! Up and down the Sixteen Streets! You'd have all the lazy buggers dashing out of their houses to part with a few coins. Whey, we'd make a bloody fortune! With just a bit of investment and planning . . .'

Bella stared at the awful man. He had a real point. It was tough to admit it, but he really had some good ideas. Her dad once had talked about expanding the business. A few years ago, when money had been less tight, he had floated the idea of maybe one day letting the Franchino empire grow. There had been mention of a second ice cream parlour, perhaps in Sunderland.

Now, all this talk of kiosks and ice cream vans was heady stuff.

To herself, Bella thought these sounded like wonderful ideas, though she tried to resist admitting it out loud.

Chapter Fifty-Eight

It was in the early evening that June saw Cathy again, before they both set off over the road to open the bar of the Robin Hood.

Cathy seemed distracted. She'd been somewhere in the afternoon and she was late coming back. It was clear to June that she was up to something and her head was buzzing with half-made plans. June felt unsettled by Cathy's mood. For once her supposed mother's attention wasn't trained on her.

'Is something the matter?' she asked Cathy as she watched her tie up her hair, standing in front of the parlour mirror.

Cathy was amazed by her daughter's query. 'It's not like you to show any concern!'

This stung June. She wasn't used to being rebuked round here. What she was used to was acting just as badly as she felt like, and always getting away with it. She stood there, staring dumbly at Cathy. 'I just thought . . . you seemed . . . well, sort of strange, that's all.'

Cathy pursed her lips. 'I'm worried sick about the Franchino family, of course. And what's going to happen to them now that they've lost their business.'

June pulled a sour face. It was of no interest to her what became of an uppity foreign family she hardly even knew. 'I thought . . . maybe it was something to do with me?'

'With you?' Cathy gave a harsh laugh and turned to face her daughter. Her heart softened at the sight of Junie dolled up in one of her fancy outfits she'd bought for becoming a barmaid and being on show every night. She looked really lovely. Her features were so much finer and her skin clearer than Cathy's had ever been at the same age. She supposed that was her father's side coming out in her. Why, he had been a fine-looking lad, with such lovely fine skin and hair just the same colour as June's. Cathy shook her head to clear it of such soft, sentimental thoughts. 'Something to do with you, Junie?' she laughed. 'My god lass, for someone who grew up in the middle of nowhere, you really do believe that the whole world revolves around you, don't you?'

'I-I . . .' Junie stammered.

'Well, let me tell you, lady. It doesn't. It bloody well doesn't, y'knaa.'

Junie stared, shocked, at her mother's angry face. Twisting up like that as she spat out her words, Cathy looked almost ugly. 'But I never said that I thought it did . . .'

'No! But it's what you do! It's how you behave! You're spoiled, Junie. You're a spoiled little madam and you've done nowt but cause bother since you got here. God forgive me, but sometimes I wish you'd never come.'

'What . . . ?' Junie couldn't believe it. She'd thought that, just recently, she'd had her mother eating out of her hand. She thought that everything was on the up. 'What's the matter with you?' she frowned in disgust. 'Have you been drinking while you were out, Mother? Is that what you've been doing this afternoon?'

Cathy felt like giving her daughter another slap across the face, but she resisted. 'No, of course I haven't. But I've been trying to sort things out. And I've had some time on my own, enough time to have a little think. Now I can see clearly what you're about, Junie Carmichael, and I think some of the scales have fallen from my eyes when it comes to you.'

Junie took a deep, shuddering, teary breath. '*Mammy* . . .'

'Mammy, she says! Now she calls me Mammy!' Cathy cried bitterly. 'You'd say absolutely anything just to get your own way, wouldn't you?'

There was a terrible tension between the two women. Junie was left with nothing to say. She had just played her trump card.

Cathy's face was dark with anger. 'You don't think of me as your mammy. You never did, and you never will. You don't have any true feelings, do you? You just wind people around your little finger. You like to make them dance to your bidding.'

'No, no . . . that's not really me . . .' Junie sobbed, her shoulders slumped inside her bonny green blouse. 'It really isn't . . .'

But Cathy had made herself hard and resistant to tears. She had a direct question to ask. 'Where is it, then?'

Junie blinked in confusion. 'What? Where's what?'

'You know what I mean. You've been in my room and you robbed it. My own daughter! I'm ashamed of you. Creeping around in the house we told you to treat as your own. And you go nicking precious things. You're a disgrace.'

'Mother, I . . .' Junie looked pained. 'I really don't know what you mean.'

Through gritted teeth Cathy spelled it out to her. 'It was an antique wedding ring. In my dresser drawer. It's not even mine. I'm looking after it for Sofia. It belongs to Sofia.'

'A ring?' Junie said, playing for time. For now she knew exactly what Cathy was talking about and her heart was pounding like merry hell.

'Yes, a ring. A ring that's probably worth more than this whole bloody house and the Robin Hood put together.'

'Then what were you doing hiding it away in a drawer? It should have been somewhere for safe-keeping.'

Cathy said sadly, 'This house *was* safe, until you moved into it. You took it, didn't you, Junie? You went through all my things and you found Sofia's ring. I bet you could hardly believe your luck, could you?'

Now her daughter was hanging her head in defeat. 'Yes, all right.' She gave herself up quickly. There was no point in denying it further. 'Yes, I went through your room. I was looking for . . . I don't know. Anything. I was trying to find out about you . . . about your life . . . I was trying to get *closer* to you . . . my mother.'

Cathy felt these words like a knife twisting in her guts. 'Don't give me that. How could you be so cruel? Still wriggling out of it. You were thieving, plain and simple!'

'I promise, I wasn't. But then . . . *he* caught me, didn't he? Your Noel. He was suddenly standing in the doorway and he barked out with laughter. He thought I was thieving, too.'

'The pair of you . . .' Cathy gasped. 'What did I ever do to deserve you two?'

'He took the ring from me,' said Junie. 'Oh, he was delighted. He couldn't believe his luck. He grabbed it off me and said I was a clever little girl. Then he danced about on the landing. He said that all the prizes were going to be his. He said after a lifetime of nothing good and settling for second best, at last everything was going his way.'

Hearing this made Cathy's blood boil. Second best! Is that what *she* was? Second best!

She grasped Junie by the upper arms and was surprised at how flimsy and light her daughter felt. She was indeed like a little doll. Cathy shook her hard until her pearly teeth rattled. 'You – are – going – to – get – that – ring – *back*,' she told her. 'And I don't care what you have to do to take it back off him. Just you get it back to me – or you are *out* of here, lady. And I'll never – I mean never – want to see you again.'

Then she let go of Junie and swept out of the parlour, up the hall and out of the house. Her daughter was left standing in the unlit room, feeling the force of her fury. She was in no doubt that her mother meant every word she said.

I've underestimated her, June thought. My mammy's tougher and harder than I ever knew. She's tougher than me and Aunty Liz and everyone I know all put together. She looked at her arms where Cathy had gripped her and knew she was going to have dark bruises there.

What to do now? How to tackle Noel? How the devil was she going to get this ring back?

Chapter Fifty-Nine

Sofia arrived for her early evening stint serving coffee at Franchino's to find her husband and daughter still in conference with Noel Sturrock.

Sofia was in no mood for putting up with the old man who had ruined them. She was late and mithered and when she swept in through the glass doors, she was cross to see that their customers were being neglected. A queue was biding its time none too patiently at the counter. She dashed round, tying on a pinny: 'Yes, yes, what will you have . . . ?'

When he noticed her, clattering away with crockery and the gigantic brass till, her husband hurried over. He seemed to be in a trance. 'Have you been drinking?' she frowned. 'Why are you sat with that old monster?' A dreadful thought occurred to her. 'My god, you aren't playing cards with him again?'

Tonio shook his head and smiled worriedly. 'Of course not. What do you take me for?'

She decided not to answer that. Instead, she whittled down her queue of querulous old folk, all avid for frothy Italian coffee. When she'd settled them all she turned to see Tonio popping two crispy wafers onto a bowlful of delicate ice cream. 'My special. It's his third helping.' He raised his eyebrows and looked proud of himself as he poured lashings of raspberry sauce onto the dessert.

Sofia gasped. 'You're feeding that old creep? It's his *third* lot?'

Noel looked very serious and intent. 'It is indeed.'

'But why? Why should he have the special treatment?'

Noel tried to pacify her. 'You'll see. You must come and sit with us for a moment. Listen to him. What he has to say is very interesting.'

She couldn't help but be sceptical. 'Oh, really? Him?'

Tonio nodded. 'Now, I must take him this before it melts . . .' And off he went bearing the frosted glass bowl on a tray. It pained Sofia to see her husband acting like a supplicant to the man who had ruined all their lives.

Soon she drifted over, trying to keep the distaste off her face as she bade him good evening.

'Oh, Mam . . . !' Bella smiled up at her. 'You ought to listen to Mr Sturrock's ideas! They're out of this world. I can't believe we haven't already done all of these things . . .'

The old monster turned his gurning smile on her and his bright eyes were the same blue as the china cups and saucers. He reached greedily for the ice cream Tonio had brought him and started gobbling it up at once with the tiny spoon. 'This is so deliciously more-ish,' he sighed. 'I knew it was good, but I never knew your ice cream was *this* good.'

'This is the special recipe from the Grapelli family in Naples,' Tonio told him, with a quick glance at Sofia. 'It's pretty special, huh? Every batch has to be hand-made on the premises. It's a long, complicated process . . .'

Noel paused and wiped his mouth on the back off his dirty sleeve. 'Yes, well, that's as maybe, and this is very nice. But in business you can't afford to be quite so fancy. You'll have to find a way of making more of this and faster and cheaper, if you're to keep up with the demand.'

'What demand?' Sofia frowned at him. 'We do all right for ourselves here, just the way we are . . .'

'Mama, you have to listen to him,' Bella implored her. 'He's talking about the future. He's talking about kiosks and ice cream vans and . . .'

Sofia hated the sound of all of it, and the sudden light in her daughter's eyes. 'He is stealing from us, Bella. Don't listen to a word this man says. His ideas are only for his own greedy benefit, no one else's.'

Noel laughed as he spooned up the rest of the specially-crafted ice cream. It gurgled in his throat as he chuckled. 'Hey you, lady! You were glad of my money and my attention and my ideas when you needed a job at the Robin Hood. Perhaps you'll have to suck up to me again, eh? You'll need to stay on my good side.'

Sofia wanted to grab him by the scruff of the neck and chuck him out of her ice cream parlour. She couldn't abide the sight of him nowadays. With a great effort of will she managed to get herself under control. 'You think I worked in your pub because of you? Or because I needed to? Ha!' She shook her head firmly. 'We were doing fine here. This place is a little goldmine. I only had to work at yours to help out your Cathy, who was in dire need of human company and sympathy. She was so miserably sick of living and working with you! I was there all that time as her friend. Her only real friend.'

Noel sneered. 'You women are all the same. You all stick together and you all hate men. You're all bitches.'

She tossed her head. 'Some of us have good reason to hate men.' She felt like kicking him up the arse, she really did. She couldn't conceal her disgust for him as he smacked his thin lips, finishing up his third bowl of fior di latte. 'Well, it's been most charming, seeing you all,' he snickered, sliding out of the booth. 'Thank you for your wonderful hospitality.' Suddenly he had hold of Bella's small hand and was bending to kiss it smearily. The very sight sickened Sofia.

'Get out! Get out of here at once, you hobgoblin!'

He straightened up as much as he could and tipped his hat at Tonio. 'You'll all see me soon enough. I'll be here quite regularly, learning everything I need to know about my new business. Now, Tonio, remember everything I've said today. Remember all my brilliant ideas! You're going to help me. We're going to turn Franchino's into an amazingly lucrative franchise!'

And with that, he went capering out of the glass doors and onto Ocean Road.

Sofia sat down heavily at the table and put her hands to her face. Her daughter and her husband stayed with her for a moment as she regained her strength. 'I hate him,' she said at last. 'How can the pair of you bear to sit here with him? Listening to his chatter and his plans? He's stealing from us! He's getting away with blue murder!'

Her husband was wearing a strange, inscrutable expression.

'What choice do we have, Mama?' Bella said. 'He's got that piece of paper. Papa signed away everything to him . . . we must listen to him. And his ideas . . . you know, I actually think they're really good.'

'I'd rather take this spoon and pop out both my eyes than look at him and listen to his plans,' Sofia growled, reaching for the spoon in Noel's dish. Before she could take it, Tonio whisked it away. He moved with jerky alacrity. 'I'll take this away,' he said, and got up to dash to the kitchen.

Sofia followed him, frowning. 'And what are you doing? Feeding him the best ice cream in the house? Three dishes? What is he, visiting royalty?'

'No, no,' Tonio said. 'But we have to keep him sweet, don't we?'

She grumbled, 'It'll take more than fior di latte to make Noel Sturrock sweet.'

They left Bella to take charge of the counter, whipping up drinks for their steady flow of patrons. Meanwhile Tonio ushered his wife into the small kitchen, where they could talk more freely.

'What is it?' she asked, feeling despair in her heart as she leaned on the counter.

'This,' he said. 'This is what I've been feeding him. He's been spooning it up quite eagerly. I've been lacing our delicious ice cream with *this*.'

Tonio opened the small cupboard under the sink. Sofia crouched to see what he was silently gesturing at. But she already knew what it was before she read the front of the box.

She felt a sharp twinge in her chest and she reeled as if she was about to pass out. 'A-are you serious, Tonio . . . ?'

'Yes,' he said grimly.

'But . . . you can't . . . we can't . . . *can we*?'

'To defend what is ours?' He narrowed his eyes at her. 'Yes, we can.'

She stared at the opened box. She saw a slogan in thick black letters: 'the fine art of rodent control'.

She stared at her husband in shock. This was something she would never have expected of him. It was something that made her see him in a different light. It was almost as if she had come home to a man who had changed. A man who was prepared to kill to protect what was his.

The box was full of rat poison.

Chapter Sixty

'What have you got to be so happy about?'

Minnie's mother was in a terrible mood. They had been let down by their supplier and the fish bar was running low on almost everything. The potatoes had more eyes than potato and she'd cut her finger nastily with her peeling knife. 'Swetty' Betty's mood was only exacerbated by her daft daughter's dreaming and mooning about.

'It doesn't matter, Mother. I'm just happy, that's all.'

'Happy! You don't know the meaning of the word.'

Oh, but I do. Minnie smiled craftily to herself. I really do. I know things you'll never know, Mother. Things I'll not be telling you in a hurry.

She offered to nip out to the fishmonger's to buy in supplies. Even at his inflated prices they'd still make a decent profit. She just had to run along to the corner. She could be back in a jiffy.

'Using your initiative, eh?' her mother smiled, fiddling in her purse. 'Maybe you're not as daft as you look, Minnie Minton.'

The girl took the notes her mother gave her and a scribbled list of what they needed. Then she quickly hared off through the Sixteen Streets in the last of the day's glorious sunlight. Ah, but the season was surely changing. There was a crispness in the air. There were curling dead leaves in the gutters, blown down the hill from the cemetery trees.

Summer was fading at last, the best summer of Minnie's life. It was the summer she had actually worn a bathing suit in public and scampered about in the frothing foam at the shore. She had played on the beach with other lads and lasses her age. She had felt – really felt, for the first time since she was a little kid – properly carefree.

And . . . she had fallen in love.

She made no bones about it. She had stopped lying to herself about it. Inside the wonderful privacy of her own heart and mind she could be honest with herself at last. Minnie Minton was in love. It felt exciting and frightening and strange all at once. It felt like six o'clock on Christmas morning when you were the first one awake and you didn't quite know what the day might bring. It was the moment when all hopes and dreams were still possible.

It was Junie who had brought all of these feelings to her.

For weeks Minnie had put her head down and blushed and felt the shame welling up in her heart like the drains on a stormy day. She felt the darkness of her desire pushing against her chest from the inside, desperate to let itself be known. When she was in the presence of her beloved, she had hated herself for being so quiet and demure and for putting up with mere crumbs of affection.

In Minnie's eyes, Junie could never do wrong and a small, rational part of herself knew that this wasn't right. She could see that Junie was . . . well, not nasty, really. But she was misguided sometimes and furious. Her anguish came out in ways that could be hurtful to others. Only Minnie knew that there was more to Junie than this. There was a sweetness to her nature, underneath all that bridling resentment.

The late summer sunlight felt golden and wonderful on her face as she emerged from the shady warren of the Sixteen

Streets. She hardly realised it but she was grinning as she lolloped along. In her enthusiasm, her feet were carrying her faster and faster. She was virtually skipping along the pavement in a way she hadn't since she was a bairn of ten years old. A couple of old biddies, standing at their front walls watching the world go by as they smoked a tab end, tutted when they saw her. Look at that daft lass, skipping about.

Even if Minnie had heard them, she wouldn't have cared.

Now she felt impervious. Now she felt buoyed up and invincible. She had never felt so happy in her life.

Junie . . . why, she could hardly say the words inside her own head. She had to slow down to hear them echo inside her mind. *Junie – felt – the – same.*

Now she knew. She knew the truth. It was impossible but it was true.

Her hand clenched hard on the rolled notes and the list of fish fillets. She flew along the streets like her feet were hardly touching the floor.

It had been just the other afternoon. That wonderful afternoon when she had visited her beloved and sat by her bed. The sun was slanting in through the antique lace of the nets at the window. Beautiful filigree patterns on Junie's pillows and her soft, wonderful face in repose. She had been saying all those heartbreaking things. She had made Minnie's heart hurt when she described being a kid on that farm with her awful manipulative aunt. It felt like Junie had been deliberately robbed of love and affection. Her life had been spoiled at such a young age by adults who knew no better.

Then Junie had asked Minnie to come and lie down beside her. She wanted her comfort. She wanted to have her large arms around her.

Hardly able to breathe, Minnie had simply done as she was bid. She lay down on the smooth counterpane face to face with her lovely friend and listened to the springs rumble and clink. Junie budged up and pressed herself into Minnie's comforting warmth.

'You're my only friend,' Junie told her. 'The only true friend I've ever had.'

How Minnie's heart had glowed when she heard that! It was like a coal in the darkness of the grate, burning bright orange and red, warming her from tip to toe.

And then . . . then Junie had pressed her face into Minnie's and kissed her. Smack. Right on the lips.

It was everything Minnie had ever dreamed about. In the heat of her most private, fevered imaginings, in the darkest, latest part of every night. She had wondered what it would be like to kiss her dearest friend. Now here they were. Kissing not like sisters or cousins or even best friends. It wasn't a peck. Junie held her face there, right close to Minnie's. Her lips stayed pressed against Minnie's own. The length of their bodies was pressed against each other's too and for one dizzying moment it was as if they had fused and become one single being. A complete and contented being at last.

Junie's mouth moved like she was trying to say something. Minnie almost pulled away to ask, 'What?' But then she thought: no. Don't move. And she lay there quite still, as Junie kissed her and kissed her and wouldn't stop.

It seemed to go on forever. Minnie would have been delighted for it to do just that. But after some moments, Junie had stopped and turned round and pressed her face into a cooler part of the pillow. Minnie was left with a racing mind and lips that felt swollen and bruised. 'Junie?' she asked.

All her friend would say was, 'Lie with me here for a while. I feel so tired. I can relax with you here, Minnie. It's only with you that I can feel relaxed.'

So they lay there for a while that afternoon, until the time came they had to get moving and get on with everyday things again.

Minnie knew that she would never forget that oasis in time for as long as she lived.

She still felt the wonderful warmth of it, and the delicious prickle of pins and needles in her left arm as she held her position to let Junie doze in peace. It was the best hour of Minnie's life so far.

Her mind was still full of it as she rounded the corner of Ocean Road, coming within sight of the fishmonger's.

'Mr Sturrock . . . !' she gasped.

It was Junie's stepfather (was that the right word?) and he was leaning against a lamp post, looking terrible. Was he drunk in the daytime? Was hc poorly? Hc had slobber down his chin, and he was hanging onto the iron post. As she got closer, Minnie saw that he had been sick on the pavement. There was a watery pool of gruel at his feet. It was yellowish and white and she felt herself go queasy at the sight of it. She hurried up to him, nonetheless. 'Are you all right?'

He blinked at her. 'What?'

'You don't look very well, Mr Sturrock. It's me, Minnie. I work in your pub. Can't you even recognise me?'

He blinked those bright blue eyes at her and something seemed to click. He returned to his senses. 'Of course I recognise you,' he growled, and spat phlegmily into the road. He groaned. 'I'm all right. Get away from me. I don't need you.'

She stepped back as he let go of the lamp post. His strength seemed to return to his limbs and he scowled at her. 'There's nothing wrong with me. I don't need you interfering. And we don't need you coming round our house anymore. You're not to come round ever again.'

Minnie jolted like she'd been slapped. 'What?'

'Junie doesn't want you as a friend. I know she doesn't.'

Minnie's eyes widened and she could feel them prickle with tears. It was ridiculous! As if this man could say anything at all to ruin her mood. What did he know about anything? 'You can't stop us being friends. Junie can choose her own friends.'

His shaggy eyebrows knitted together. 'She doesn't want a friend like you. I know what you're about. I know what you're trying to get her to do. I've met women like you before. All the strumpets and women of ill repute I've met over the years – many of them were like you. You come to a bad end, wrong' uns of your kind. You're wrong in the head, you are. She's innocent, our Junie. She doesn't realise what you're about.'

Minnie felt herself go hot and pink. 'No . . . no . . . ! You mustn't say that . . . !' It was as if this nasty man was looking straight into her soul. He was seeing things she had barely made plain to herself, let alone anyone else. And he was making them into something horrible.

'You are unnatural,' he told her, and belched. 'So you just leave our Junie alone. She doesn't want you pawing at her and hanging around her skirts. You're disgraceful, you are. Stay away!'

Then he was off, tottering drunkenly up the lane towards the Sixteen Streets.

Minnie was left clutching her mother's money and her hastily-scribbled list. She felt like the ground had opened up beneath her and was giving her a glimpse of the hell to come.

Chapter Sixty-One

June heard the front door clattering and knew that Noel was home. He was lumbering about in the hallway, even more clumsily than ever. There was a furious squeal from one of the cats as he kicked it out of the way.

She waited for him in the parlour, gathering her wits and her strength of mind. She had to tackle him. For a while she had been content to side with the repulsive old monster. It had been funny to drive her so-called mother demented with the sight of them being so lovey-dovey with each other. Oh, the way Cathy had bridled and steamed each time Junie called Noel 'Daddy'! It had been worth all the effort. She had hung about his neck even though he revolted her completely.

Now though, Junie had to get on Cathy's good side. There was something she had to do, or else the game was all over. Cathy was perilously close to chucking her out – and disowning her yet again! June was in no doubt that Cathy would do as she threatened. That hardness in her face and her voice before she left for the pub tonight . . . it had put a chill into her daughter's heart.

Now here came Noel, looking the worse for wear.

'Have you been drinking that awful Italian brandy with the Franchinos?' she asked him. 'You look hammered.'

Stumbling, he tottered into the room and leaned against a chair. 'What? No. I've taken no drink today . . .' There was something strange about his manner. Something Junie couldn't put her finger on. No matter. There was something she needed from him and she wasn't going to be distracted.

'You need to give me that ring,' she told him.

He blinked at her. He was playing for time, clearly. 'What ring?'

'You know exactly what ring. I was in her room, remember? Cathy's. You caught me going through her things. You caught me red-handed.' The girl seemed almost proud of her misdemeanour. She seemed to be smiling purringly at the very thought of it.

'Oh yes,' Noel said thickly. For a second she thought he was going to spit or vomit on the carpet. He struggled to overcome a surge of nausea. 'I remember that. You looked so flamin' guilty.'

'I found the ring first,' Junie snapped. 'You shouldn't have taken it off me. Finders keepers.'

'You're nothing but a little thief,' he accused her. 'You came here pretending you wanted a family and that you wanted your mammy back. But you only ever came here to see what you could get. You wanted to bleed her dry.'

She shrugged. 'I never knew she had anything. How could I have known what she had? I certainly didn't know she had treasure stashed away in her dresser drawer.' Junie's eyes were lit with avarice. 'Do you know what she told me? That ring is worth more than this house and the Robin Hood put together, probably.'

'Is it now?' Noel smiled. 'And you want it, do you? You want to take it from me?'

'Yes,' she said, standing up and towering over him as he crouched against the wooden chair. His guts were churning and spasming inside of him. He fought to keep from gasping, from crying out. 'You should give it to me.'

He looked at her and, smiling, turned back into the hall and led the way upstairs.

What? Junie thought to herself. He's just giving in without a fight? This greedy, foul old man? Surely she'd have to twist his arm or threaten him somehow? But no . . . look at the way he was leading her up the top stairs to the very top landing. Why, he was leading her into his room in the attic. He was showing her into his holy of holies!

He's going to give it to me, Junie thought. Why, he must think something of me after all! Or maybe he's just frightened of me? Maybe I *do* have the gift of wrapping everyone around my little finger?

She was thrilled with herself and what she felt was her power.

Noel produced an old iron key from his waistcoat pocket and unlocked his attic den. 'Not even Cathy gets in here. No one gets in here but me,' he said. 'So it's a little bit dusty and messy.'

'I don't care about that,' Junie told him. 'Just so long as you give me the ring.'

'Oh, aye,' he smiled. 'I'll do that. I'll give you the ring.'

He put his rounded, deformed shoulder to the heavy door and thrust it open. Pearly moonlight from the attic window was flooding down on the ramshackle bric-a-brac of Sturrock's secret life.

'My god . . .' Junie whispered. 'You weren't joking when you said it was messy. What is all this stuff?'

There were heaps of papers and letters. There were paintings and photographs in antique frames. There were cases and trunks of old clothes and sundry belongings, all crammed hugger mugger into the deepest recesses of the attic. 'My collection,' he said. 'Everything that ever went missing in the Sixteen Streets. Every lost love letter or last will and testament or precious misplaced thing. They've all ended up here.'

'You're the biggest thief round here . . .' Junie said, wonderment in her face. 'What do you want with all this stuff?'

'I own everyone's secrets,' he told her. 'Birth certificates. Confessions. Medals. Jewels. All sorts of precious things.'

'I see.' The mention of precious things had put the ring back to the forefront of her mind. She could picture the glittering stones right now. She had held it only briefly in her fingers but it was the most gorgeous and expensive thing she had ever seen. It was her passport to the life that she felt she deserved. 'Are you going to give me it, then?' she said.

Noel Sturrock beamed at her. When he showed his horrid, manky teeth she almost gasped. They were usually yellow, but today they seemed pinkish. Was it the evening light with the sun coming through the clouds of smoke from the Biscuit Factory? Was that what was making the colours strange? But no, as she looked more closely, she saw that his gums were bleeding and his teeth were streaked with pinkish red.

'Here, here . . .' he was saying, oblivious to what she'd noticed. 'Here it is.' And then, after fiddling around in the drawer of a rather beautiful antique desk, he produced that ring box with the worn velvet nap. Just how old was it, and how many brides had it belonged to? Junie couldn't care less, really. All that mattered was that it was about to be hers.

Very carefully, almost reverentially, Noel eased open the lid of the box. The beautiful ring lay exposed. It was like a whole night sky of stars crushed together into one tiny constellation. Junie held her breath and inched forward. Was he just going to let her take it from him? As easily as that? All at once she knew one thing for certain: if he wasn't, she was prepared to fight him for it.

But what was happening now? He was muttering and gasping and doing something peculiar. Still holding the ring aloft he was making some big effort to do something untoward.

Oh god. She couldn't quite take it in. Please, no . . . tell me he can't be doing what I think he is . . .

He was kneeling down before her. She looked down at the flaking scurf of his scalp.

'Junie,' he said, licking his bloody teeth and coughing down a wad of foaming phlegm. 'I love you, hinny, and I know you think a lot of me. Now, you know that you call me Daddy and I was very touched by that. But we aren't really blood, are we? So there's really nothing against it. It's not illegal or incest or anything. But it's love, isn't it? It really is love, I think.'

Junie's face had drained of all colour. Her mouth hung open as she stared down at him. 'I . . . I . . . Noel, I . . .'

'Do me the honour, Junie hinny . . .' he gasped, and now his breath was ragged and his chest heaving as he knelt there before her. 'Please do me the honour of being my wife? Just as soon as I get your flamin' mother out of the way. Junie, please? Please won't you take this ring . . . ?'

She hesitated and then she took it from him.

He looked delighted. He smiled the most guileless and happy smile of his entire life. 'So you will? You'll say yes to me? Is that true, our Junie . . . ?'

Chapter Sixty-Two

'I just wanted to frighten him! I never asked you to kill the fecker . . . !'

Cathy's words rang out in horror. She was standing in the shadowy, damp, beery-smelling stockroom of the Robin Hood and staring at her best friend, Sofia. She could hardly believe how queerly calm her friend was being, after what she had just told her. 'It was Tonio,' Sofia said. 'This whole business with Noel has driven him pazzo, I think. He's gone crazy.'

'B-but . . . Noel!' Cathy burst out. 'Where is he? Is he lying somewhere? Is he a-already . . . dead?' Her mind was racing frantically. They were all discussing the murder of her husband as if it was the most normal thing in the world, as if they had been driven to it by his greed and awfulness. Mild, bumbling Tonio – a murderer!

'Tonio says it wasn't so much poison,' Sofia explained. 'He lost his nerve while he was putting it into the ice cream. He put a little in each dish Noel ate this afternoon. He just wanted to make him ill, make him suffer, to teach him a lesson, maybe . . .'

'But that's crazy.' Cathy shook her head. 'He'll just have made everything worse!'

'Tonio never thinks things through,' sighed his beautiful wife. 'Look at how he had us run away to England all those years ago. Just to avoid poor Mario!'

Mention of the Neopolitan cousin reminded Cathy of the third person in the storeroom with them. The huge man – Jan Johnson – was standing in the corner and looking at them both in dumbfounded horror. He was dressed as a stage villain. Presumably his mother had helped him get all done up for his role tonight and he wore a flamboyant fedora atop his dark navy, chalk-stripe suit. He looked every inch the violent thug but his eyes were wide at all this talk of poisoning. 'You women don't mess around, do you?' he gasped. 'You really are vicious!'

Cathy cursed herself for letting one of the Johnson clan hear her business. Why, if Noel really did succumb to poisoning, then word of who was responsible might get all round town. She instructed Jan very clearly: 'Forget everything you hear tonight. All you have to do, Jan, is play the part I've asked you to. When Noel comes over here for a drink at his usual time of half past eight, you're to confront him, saying you are Sofia's *other* cousin from Naples and you've heard what he's done, cheating her family out of her business.'

'Yes, I understand all of that,' Jan said, adjusting his fedora in a flyblown mirror, rather pleased with his newly-dandified appearance. 'I'm to put the fear of god into the nasty crookback, right? I can do that, nae bother, lass.'

'That's if he survives the poisoning,' Sofia put in – a mite too glibly for Cathy's liking.

'This is life and death this,' Cathy told her friend. 'Don't you care?'

Sofia's eyes flashed. 'About Noel? No, I don't. He's a nasty piece of work and he always has been. You know that better than anyone. I've never told you how many times he's tried it on with me, while I've been working here. I never told you half of it. But his would be no loss to you nor anyone, Cathy.'

The landlady of the Robin Hood felt hot tears of frustration welling up in her eyes. 'No one has the right to decide who can be offed and who would be missed and who wouldn't. Yes, he's awful . . . but he has his good sides, too. I threw my lot in with Noel years ago and there's been good things come out of it. It hasn't all been bad.'

'If you say so,' Sofia muttered, and turned to lead the way back to the saloon bar, where the rest of her family were waiting for her.

Cathy was left staring after her: like that, she had dismissed Cathy's whole married life. It must be nice, to have such a happy marriage as Sofia had. It must be lovely to live in such a warm devoted family. For a second Cathy felt like calling her back and telling her, 'Listen, lady . . . you're far too pleased with yourself. How dare you look down upon my choices? And who's to say yours are so perfect anyway, when you went running off to Naples and yes! Only I know how close you came to making a new life with Mario!'

But Cathy didn't call her back, or say any of those things. Tonight wasn't the place or the time for a row with her best friend. However, a wedge had been driven between the two of them tonight and Cathy never quite felt the same about Sofia again.

'Shall I wait here, then?' Jan interrupted her train of thought.

'Yes, till I call you through, when Noel comes in for his pint.'

'If he's still alive, after his poisoning . . .'

Cathy shuddered. 'You heard what she said. Tonio never gave him enough to bump him off. That Tonio can never do anything properly . . .'

Cathy left Jan Johnson in hiding, supping a pint of beer she'd poured him for while he waited. Then she returned to the lively saloon bar, where Aunty Martha was playing her favourite songs again. What seemed like the entire population of Frederick Street and several of the streets beyond were gathered together that night, as if they knew that something momentous was about to happen. Perhaps word had got round, somehow? Perhaps they were all waiting to see Noel Sturrock get the fear of god put into him by a fake gangster? Maybe they all couldn't wait to see him get his comeuppance?

Ada Farley was at the bar, sipping a pint of dark stout. 'All reet there, are ye, Cathy?'

Cathy nodded, with a tight smile. She felt nervous and strange. She felt as if she was coming to a big turning point in her life. A shiver went through her, like a cold autumnal wind had snuck in from the North Sea and wafted into the open door of her merry pub. She knew that feeling. Things were about to change in her life.

For several minutes, Noel had been beseeching Junie. His face was twisted with emotion. It was running with sweat and he had turned bright red.

'Shut up about this now, you're not well,' she told him.

He shrugged. 'It was just something I ate. I feel a bit sickly, that's all. But this is more important. You have to say yes to me.'

Her mind and her heart were racing. 'I can't possibly marry you. Why . . . have you somehow forgotten? You're married to my mam!'

He scowled. 'Why, that's been nothing like a proper marriage for years. She don't care about me. All she ever wanted was this house and the pub. She's never been near my bed for ten years or more! And she wonders why my eye strays . . . !'

Junie felt ill at the thought of his bed and his lascivious eye. It was a disgusting thought. She could feel his burning eyes crawling all over her right at this moment. 'It's wrong! You've been thinking about me like this the whole time while getting me to call you *daddy*!'

He laughed at her plaintive misgivings. 'Ah, hadaway pet. You were part of the game, too. We were both dead set upon driving our Cathy crackers. You'll laugh like a drain – same as I will – when I chuck her out of here. When I tell her I want her out of my life and I want a divorce. Ha! And just wait until I tell her that I'll be taking you to be my wife!' He cackled with glee, bringing up more creamy phlegm, which he spat heedlessly onto the hall carpet. 'Come on, Junie . . . say *yes*!'

She had turned away from his attic and its horde of stolen secrets. She tottered down the attic stairs and along the top landing. She couldn't believe she was living through this scene. She wanted to scream for help. This was like her worst nightmare coming true.

Ah, but you brought all of this on yourself, a small, rational part of her mind was telling her. This is where nasty thoughts of revenge and interference bring you. Now you're alone with this terrible man and it's all your own fault, Junie Carmichael.

He was trying to seize her wrists. 'Get off me!' she burst out.

'No, no . . . look at this . . .' he gasped. From his jacket pocket he had produced a tatty bit of paper. He flapped it in her face, trying to gain her attention. 'Look! Read it!'

'What is it?' She feared some grisly declaration of love.

'It's our future. It's our riches,' he grinned up at her.

'What?' She looked at the scrawl on the grubby sheet but could hardly make it out.

'It's the paper Tonio Franchino signed when he played poker with me,' Noel smiled. 'Look at it! That's his whole fortune, there!'

Junie held the flimsy sheet in her hand and shook it. 'Do you think this will really stand up in court? Do you? You're even more crazy than you look!' She whirled away towards the staircase, letting the paper flutter to the ground in her wake. 'You've got nothing to offer me, Noel Sturrock! Bugger all! You're unnatural and creepy and wicked! Why, you've got nothing to offer anyone! Why would anyone ever look twice at you?'

Behind her he went scrabbling for the precious piece of paper. He clutched at it, gasping: 'That ring! The ring is worth having, isn't it?'

Junie had already put it on. She examined it in the murky amber light of the stairway and still it glittered fantastically. 'Oh yes, of course. This is worth having, you're so right. But not if it comes with *you* attached. With your horrible old claws attached.'

'Give it back to me,' he said, his eyes turning frantic. He made a grasp at the ring, his hands lashing out violently.

Junie laughed. '*No!* It's mine now! It's on my finger! You can't have it back, you old devil. I don't want you – god, who would, except my ridiculous mother? You can go to hell for all I care! But I'm going to keep this beautiful ring! It's an heirloom, I hear?'

All at once Noel let out the most startling roar of anguish. In that scream was bound up all the frustrations of a lifetime. He was the boy who'd been mercilessly bullied by his peers for his looks and who felt that their normal lives had always been denied to him. He was the man who skulked about in the shadows, prey to his own appetites and foibles. The man who had sought solace in hoarding money and secrets and stolen things. He was a man riven with anguish and frustration and despair. Unloved, deeply unloved. He had felt not one single drop of human affection ever since his old mother had died. His soul ached for some kind of sign; some indication that he wasn't the most despicable man in the town.

'You're not having it back!' Junie jeered at him as he lunged again. 'You can go to bloody hell, Noel Sturrock!'

His efforts to best her were almost comically feeble. She was a strong girl, in the prime of life. He shambled and stumbled at the top of the stairs. Then, as she stepped adroitly aside to dodge him, he swung round dangerously. His body weight was oddly balanced on account of his deformity. He lost his footing and fell, very quickly, head over heels down the steep staircase.

Junie had barely a split second to realise what had happened. She heard his screeching cry and the abrupt way it came to an end. She saw his flailing limbs. She heard a sickening crunch as he hit step after step and then the worst noise of all as his head cracked against the wall at the bottom.

He lay spraddled and awkward at the foot of the stairs. His head was bent round strangely, as if he was trying to peer back up the stairs at her. He was extremely still.

Junie fought to get her breathing under control. Then she checked that she still had the ring on her finger and she picked up the scrap of paper Noel had dropped before he fell.

Then she went downstairs – very carefully – and stepped over his body.

She headed for the door in a blind panic. She couldn't even bring herself to check if he was dead.

Chapter Sixty-Three

It was almost dark by the time Junie ran out into the street. Frederick Street was deserted and her footsteps scraped on the cobbles. Her neat, new shoes shone as her feet carried her lightly away from the slammed front door of number twenty-one. Her outfit was immaculate as ever, but there was something harried and peculiar about her.

She fought to calm herself down. She stood in the middle of the road and tried to get a grip on her panic. When she put her hands to her face she found it burning hot. The ring scraped her cheek and she suddenly thought: I'm not supposed to have this. Hide it. Hide it quickly away! It went into her deepest pocket, along with the note from the poker game.

Then, all at once, she was no longer alone.

'Junie! Junie, love . . . are you all right?'

It was that lummox Minnie Minton, and she was lumbering up the steep road towards her. She's all I need, Junie thought with a groan. Next thing, Minnie was all over her, suffocating her with panicky love and affection. Those ham-hock arms were around her and she was petting Junie like she would a china doll. 'Are you all right, hinny? Are you OK? You look like you've had a shock, you do . . .'

'No, no, I'm fine,' Junie said, trying not to sound too terse and irritated.

Minnie hugged her close. The two of them stood in the middle of the road and Minnie started rocking her friend gently. 'I've got you. I've got you now. I will look after you, Junie.'

Junie felt like elbowing her and casting her off. What kind of rubbish was she saying to her now in that daft, singsong voice? Did June really look as if she needed looking after? She could see to herself, thanks very much! And now Junie thought with a sick feeling about how she'd gone along with that kiss. What had she been thinking of? Was it only: what can I make of this? Or had she, even for a second, felt like she needed to return some love and affection to someone? Had there been a moment of strange, unlikely tenderness there?

But no, that was revolting. It was disgusting. She didn't need anyone, let alone this lass. Junie had always been on her own, hadn't she? She had no need for the likes of this . . . this fat girl from the fish shop!

'Have you seen Mr Sturrock?' Minnie asked her.

'What?' Junie looked immediately guilty. 'Why do you ask?'

'It's just . . . I saw him in the street just before and he looked worse for wear. He was being sick on the pavement! And he was saying such cruel things to me . . .'

Junie extricated herself from Minnie's cloying hug. 'Well, I've not seen him. I don't know where he is. Come on. Let's go to the pub. It sounds like there's a whole crowd in there tonight. I could do with a drink, I could . . .'

Biting her lip, fretting for her friend, Minnie followed her all the way to the Robin Hood. She was desperate to ask her: 'It's all true, isn't it, Junie? When you kissed me, when we lay on your bed the other day. We were in each other's arms. We were just like a lad and a lass would be. I know it truly happened. I know what we both did and what we both must have felt. But is it all real, Junie? Tell me . . . is it real?'

But Junie was hurrying ahead of her up the hill to the boisterous noise and light of the pub at the top of Frederick Street. It was as if she was trying to shake Minnie off.

The gloom was almost complete in the downstairs hall of the Sturrock house. Only a glimmer of dusky light came in through the transom window above the front door.

Noel took a great gulp of air and opened his eyes very slowly. They were gummed together. Something sticky. And his neck felt very peculiar. There was a grinding noise, like bone on bone coming from somewhere inside of him. He felt sick with shock. He remembered falling, reeling through the air. He remembered being out of control.

And the girl's voice ringing in his ears. He remembered that, too. She had told him – in her sweet, beloved voice – that he belonged in hell.

She had taken the ring. She had taken everything.

Noel groaned and everything felt strange and somehow wrong. Even his voice sounded wrong. It sounded strangulated and trapped in his throat. Down here with his nose pressed to the hall carpet he could smell a lifetime of dust and dirt from everyone's shoes. The dust from the cobbled streets outside. The cat pee and the crushed beetles and the spilled milky tea. It was a terribly vivid smell: the reek of home.

'Eeeh, lad,' said a voice in his ear. 'Eeh, our Noel. What are we going to do with you, hinny?'

He blinked his smarting eyes. When he tried to sit up on the carpet he was like a crab upside down, washed up on the beach. His old claws flailed and nipped at the murky air, but with a cry of pain he managed to sit upright. He managed to see who it was addressing him in such warm, familiar terms.

Such a loving voice. There was something in that voice that made him choke up and sob.

'Our Noel,' she said.

He rubbed his eyes and felt them burning with unshed tears. With tears that had waited so long to come out. '*M-mam . . . ?*' he gasped.

For there she was. Standing once more in the hallway of number twenty-one Frederick Street. She was in her best pinny and housecoat and her oldest, most comfortable slippers. Theresa Sturrock had come home again. In her arms she was cradling the cat – Noel had forgotten its name – the one who had died while Cathy was on holiday. It arched its back happily in her arms and seemed to be purring with glee. 'Mam, it can't be you. I don't believe in things like this . . .'

She laughed at him. 'What you believe in is neither here nor there, Noel Sturrock! Why, you've never believed in much besides yourself and everything you want. It's all want want want with you.' She petted the cat gently and shook her head at her son. The coloured light from the architrave lit her gold and green and red, like she was a figure in stained glass, down the hill at St Jude's. Noel still didn't believe in what he was seeing. 'I've hit my head. I've gone delirious . . .' he said.

His mother smiled at him fondly. 'You were such a sweet bairn. At first you were, you know. You smiled at everyone. You were trusting and kind. And aye, well . . . I suppose if the world isn't kind back to you, you soon learn your lesson. You learn not to trust. You learn to be more canny and smart . . . and eventually cruel.'

He was gripping hold of the banister now, grimacing as he exerted every bit of his strength. Everything felt strange and uncoordinated. He had to put his whole concentration into pulling himself upright. He could barely take on board what his mother was saying.

'You – can't – be – telling – me - anything – anyway . . .' he panted. 'You – can't – even – be – here – Mother . . . you're – long – gone . . . ! Daen't ye even know that?'

There! He was up on his feet again! Wobbly. Strange and wobbly, like a newborn foal. But he was back on his feet.

His mother was smiling at him sadly. 'Ahh, Noel. You're a big disappointment to me. I'm so disappointed in you, my lad.'

The tears were starting to come. He shook his head savagely. He was damned if he was going to cry now. He was seeing things! He was being taunted by a dream! 'Why should I care about anyone else being disappointed?' he snarled. 'You're gone! You left me! You left me alone in this . . . *horrible world* . . . !' His own candour shocked him. It shocked him to the core to realise this was how he really felt. Yes, he had lived all these years and now he knew for sure: the world as he knew it was a horrible place.

'I wish I'd never been born,' he told his mother.

She looked shattered by that. 'That's the worst thing you could say to your mother. It's the worst thing any mother could hear,' she sighed. 'You make me wish I'd never come back.'

'You *haven't* come back!' he growled. 'You're just . . . you're just . . .'

She smiled at him. 'I left Cathy with you. She's been a good wife to you, I know. She's put up with more than anyone else would. You should have made it up with her. Before it was too late.'

He grunted. 'Aye. Mebbe I will. Mebbe I've no choice to make peace with my wife.' He headed for the door, lumbering heavily on his shaky legs.

His mam frowned as he fiddled with the sneck. 'And where do you think you're going now, lad?'

'I'm going to my pub. If you don't mind, Mother? I'm going over there and I'm having a drink. And I might just make it up with my wife. Is that all right with you?' He pulled open the front door and was about to stride out into the evening.

'Oh, Noel. You can't. It's too late.'

He glared back at her. 'What do you mean?'

She sniffed and rubbed her nose on the furry back of the cat in her arms. 'Don't you see? You're dead, son. You're already dead. It's much too late to say or do anything now. You've had your life, son. It's over, now.'

He simply stared at her, uncomprehending. Theresa Sturrock smiled gently and waited for him to cotton on.

'It's time you came with me, lad. You're back with your mammy, now.'

Chapter Sixty-Four

He was dead and no one was ever going to miss him, but Noel Sturrock went to the pub anyway. It was his pub and he could drink there any time he felt like it, thank you very much!

He stomped up the cobbled road and took in huge lungfuls of the evening breezes. He could smell the usual fishy fug of the harbour and the lingering sweetness of the Biscuit Factory. There! If he was dead like his mother claimed, surely he'd not be able to smell things like that, would he?

But he pushed her words out of his mind. He'd hit his head when he fell down the stairs. He was knocked senseless by a nasty fall.

Why, that little bitch June had left him lying there on the carpet! She'd have stepped over him to leave him on the floor! He'd give her a bloody thrashing when he saw her. To think he'd offered her everything! Just as he once had Cathy, too.

He patted his pockets. Where was the ring? And the other thing? There was some vital piece of paper, wasn't there? Shouldn't it be rustling in his pocket? But the details were eluding him. He was forgetting things. Perhaps it was the bump on the head. Why, a pint of best ale would do him good. It would revive him. Bring him back to himself.

He stood before the golden lights coming through the frosted windows of his pub and felt more at home than ever before in his life. There came from within the muffled hullabaloo of Aunty Martha playing that thundering old upright piano. My god, he thought, there she was, playing Cushie Butterfield yet again! Her voice was a warbling shriek, leading the singalong drinkers through verse after verse and back to the familiar chorus. It was the noise and rowdy, endless palaver of home.

Noel pushed through the saloon doors and felt immediately warmed by the fire in the grate and the crush of all these familiar bodies. There were the older Farley boys, drinking with their ma. Singing along with Martha. And old Winnie, bending someone's ear and telling them all about their future.

None of them looked his way.

Noel sneered at them and made through the crowd towards the bar. He saw the Italians sitting at a table by themselves. The bonny young lass, Bella, was sipping her drink. Sofia looked proud and hawkish. Silly uppity cow, thought Noel. And Tonio! What did he look like? He looked fearful and haunted. He was sweating as he sat there, talking with his mother-in-law. Noel crept closer, unnoticed by any of them. He could hear the old Nonna lecturing Tonio: 'You fool. You should have tipped the whole box into his dish! Why, when I use it on rats I spread it all over the place. It takes guts and determination to kill a rat stone dead!'

Tonio looked as if he was about to weep. 'I didn't want to kill him. Oh, pray god I haven't killed him . . .'

The Nonna tossed her head. 'I hope that he's lying stone dead somewhere. He won't be missed.'

Noel turned away, upset despite himself. What did he care what the likes of that lot thought of him? Horrible, foreign lot. Then he came to a table where Minnie was sitting chatting away to Junie. She was pulling on her arm and bending her ear. Even from this distance Noel could see that Junie had no patience with the girl. That lumpy, moon-faced lass, filled to the brim with unnatural appetites! Why, everyone thought she was so lovely and innocent. But he knew. He knew her sort. Noel looked forward with great glee to spreading around all the filthy truth about Minnie Minton!

He stared at Junie. She was white-faced with shock. She was drinking the best brandy. She had clammed up and wouldn't say a word. She wasn't telling anyone – even Minnie – about Noel's fall down the stairs and how she had simply left him there.

Noel stood right in front of her, but she didn't give any indication that she could see him.

What was wrong with people tonight?

The whole world, it seemed, had gone mad.

Where's my wife? he wondered. Yes, it was about time he made things up with her. He needed some peace at home at last.

Here she was at the bar, where she had presided for so many years now. Queen Catherine of Frederick Street. At home, here at the heart of the Sixteen Streets. In many ways – he could see it now – his wife was herself the very heart of the Sixteen Streets. She was here at the centre of it all every night and all life hereabouts beat to the pulse of her own loving vitality.

Yes, he could indeed see it all now, as he watched her working at the bar. She was a wonderful woman. Ah, he had known it all along. But it was just too much effort for him to try to be a good enough man.

What was she doing now? She was talking to a huge bloke who emerged from the stockroom. Who was this in that great big hat? He looked like a gangster.

'No, he's not here yet,' Cathy murmured to the man. 'I don't know where he is. Yes, you might as well come out front. Come and sit with everyone else, Jan. It doesn't matter now. It was probably a silly ruse anyway . . .'

The large man looked relieved. As the evening had gone on, he'd become less and less fond of the idea of putting the menaces on someone just for a joke. It reminded him of older days in his family, when he had been forced to do such things for real. 'Can I just sit with everyone else and have a drink in the saloon?' he asked brightening up. 'You don't want me to scare him no more?'

Cathy nodded. 'That's right. He's late coming over, anyway. Just sit down and have a drink, Jan. Life's too short for making more bother, isn't it?'

Jan beamed at her and took his pint to a clear space by the piano.

Cathy was left to look around at the pub then, and she was trying to quell the stirring of unease in the pit of her stomach. Tonio claimed that he hadn't put that much poison into the ice cream after all, but what did he know? What if Noel was lying in the street somewhere, sick and in need of help?

She thought she would know if Noel needed her. Over the years they had fought like mad, but the bond between them was somehow strong. She thought she knew what he was planning and what he was thinking. She thought she could sense him when he was close.

But not tonight.

Tonight Cathy had no inkling that her husband was standing close beside her. He was peering into her face. He was battered, broken, poisoned, robbed, furious and bitter. But when he looked into the face of his wife he wanted nothing more than to kiss her.

One last time.

Cathy felt a tickling on her lips and on her cheek. She thought she heard a sound. A word or two, whispered in her ear.

She shook her head. She was tired and her mind was playing tricks.

'Ha'way, everyone!' she cried out loud to the whole bar. 'Let's all have a round of drinks on the house, shall we? I'm feelin' generous the neet, an' I don't know why!'

There was a great cry of approval from her regulars.

They started to cram around the small bar, keen to get a free drink, and Cathy had to call on Sofia and Junie to help her serve them all.

No one turned to see one lone, somewhat broken figure turn to leave the pub.

He slipped out of the saloon doors without a sound. They swung closed behind him.

Outside there were barges hooting mournfully down in the harbour. The stars were out over Tynemouth and the sky was beautifully clear.

His mam was there waiting for him. She looked tiny and insubstantial, standing out in the street in her pinny and her slippers. 'Come on, kidda,' she smiled at him. 'Ha'way with me. All is forgiven. Leave them all to it, now. All of their everyday dramas and palavers and carrying on. It's time that *we* were gannin' home.'

Acknowledgements

Thanks to Jeremy, my family and friends, agent Piers, editor Rhea, Snigdha and everyone at Orion.

Credits

Elsie Mason and Orion Fiction would like to thank everyone at Orion who worked on the publication of *The Forgotten Daughter* in the UK.

Editorial
Rhea Kurien
Snigdha Koirala

Copyeditor
Alice Fewery

Proofreader
Linda Joyce

Audio
Paul Stark
Louise Richardson

Contracts
Dan Herron
Ellie Bowker
Oliver Chacón

Design
Jet Purdie

Editorial Management
Charlie Panayiotou
Jane Hughes
Bartley Shaw

Finance
Jasdip Nandra
Sue Baker
Nick Gibson

Production
Ruth Sharvell
Francesca Sironi

Sales
Catherine Worsley
Esther Waters
Victoria Laws
Rachael Hum
Frances Doyle
Georgina Cutler

Operations
Jo Jacobs

Also by Elsie Mason

The Runaway Girl,
the first in the Sixteen Streets series

1918. Fleeing from her past, Cathy Carmichael is new to the Sixteen Streets. She has nothing to her name, no plan and nowhere to go.
Cathy thinks she's struck gold when she runs into Mrs Sturrocks, an elderly lady who offers her a room at her boarding house. Her son, Noel, might be strange and sulky, but he gives her a job at the Robin Hood pub and before long, Cathy is thriving as the new barmaid.

The Sixteen Streets was only meant to be a temporary stop for Cathy. . . but could it become home instead?

The Biscuit Factory Girls

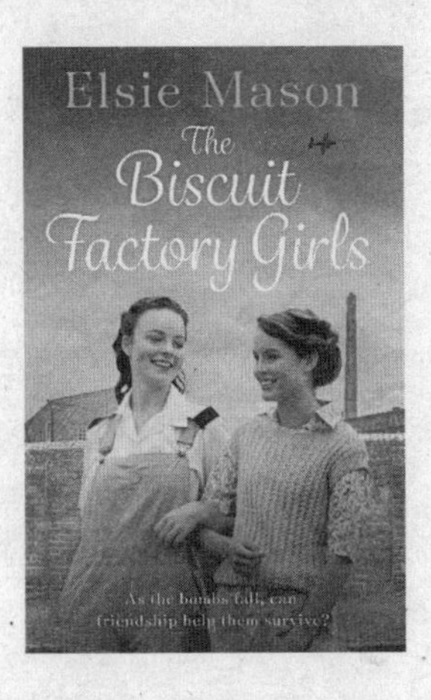

Can Irene find a new home by the docks?

Newly married to dashing RAF officer, Tom, Irene Farley leaves behind her safe countryside life to move in with his family by the docks in South Shields. Little prepares her for the devastation the Jerry bombers have wreaked on the Sixteen Streets or that they would be living under her mother-in-law's roof, alongside Tom's three brothers and two wives!

Irene's only escape is her job at the local Wright's Biscuit factory packing up a little taste of home for the brave boys fighting for King and country across the channel. As the threat of war creeps ever closer to the Sixteen Streets, the biscuit factory girls bond together, because no one can get through this war alone . . .

The Biscuit Factory Girls at War

Home is where the heart is . . .

Beryl was the first Farley clan bride, finding a home in the arms of loving, attentive, elder son Tony. Yet even now, wrapped in Tony's embrace, Beryl has never quite been able to forget the past she ran away from, nor the shocking family secret she tried to bury.

With Tony away fighting the Jerries alongside his brothers, it's up to Beryl and her sisters-in-law to keep the family afloat. Hard, gruelling work doesn't faze her, but the sudden arrival of a devastating letter does. . .

Will Beryl be able to hold her family together and face up to her past? Or will the war take away the one thing she holds most dear – the one person she never thought she deserved?

A Wedding for the Biscuit Factory Girls

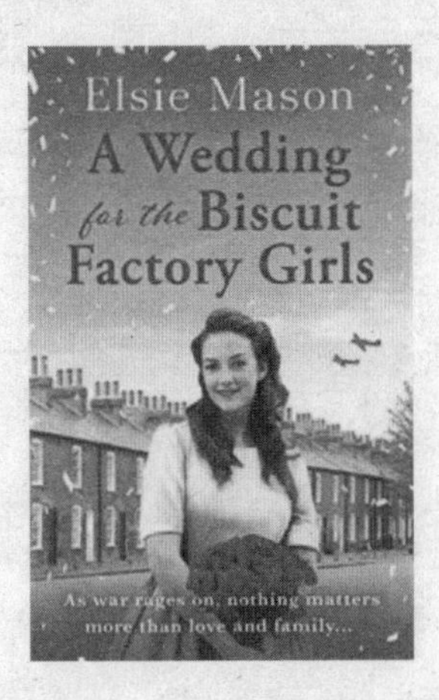

The third novel in the heart-warming and heart-wrenching WW2 saga series set in South Shields

Her wedding day should have been the happiest day of Mavis Kendricks' life. Marrying handsome Sam, the youngest of the Farley boys, means joining the Farley clan, and there's nothing Mavis has ever wanted more than a family of her own. But the appearance of an unexpected guest ruins everything . . . and brings back painful memories Mavis would rather forget.

It's not long before the war-torn streets of South Shields are buzzing with rumours. One of the biscuit factory girls, funny little Mavis has always been a bit of a mystery. As far as anyone can remember, Mavis and her twin Arthur have been orphans. So who was the grand old lady at the wedding? How do the twins own their own house? And just what is Mavis hiding? On the Sixteen Streets, nothing stays a secret for long . . .